ODIUM IV

The Dead Saga

By *USA Today* & bestselling British Horror Writer
Claire C. Riley

Love for Odium The Dead Saga Series.

"*Odium The Dead Saga* is an emotional ride, super funny, and full of heartache and death. But it's one unforgettable series. Claire always delivers an unexpected ride that will have you laughing so hard one minute and crying your eyeballs the next. Lovers of suspense, post-apocalypse and The Walking Dead will really enjoy this series."

Loyda - Crazies R' Us Book Blog
https://craziesrusbookblog.wordpress.com/

"*The Odium series* is must read for any zombie fan. Claire C. Riley takes readers on an emotional rollercoaster of terror and tension. I devoured each page, dreading what would happen next but desperate to know. Between the masterfully crafted endings and relatable characters, I can't stop coming back for more!"

R. L. Blalock author of the Death & Decay series
@RocBlalockauthor
www.rlblalock.com

"In a world gone mad, with enemies both alive and dead, Claire C. Riley takes her readers on one hell of a heart-pounding journey alongside a very relatable heroine. Filled with nail-biting twists and turns, *Odium* isn't a story you'll soon forget."

Madeline Sheehan
***USA Today* Best Selling Author of The Holy Trinity Series & the**
The Undeniable Series
www.madelinesheehan.com

"*Odium The Dead Saga* is a well-balanced horror tale filled with vivid imagery, engaging characters, and heart-racing action. This series quickly made my favorite zombie reads of all time!"

Odium IV The Dead Saga
Copyright © 2016

Written by Claire C. Riley
Edited by Amy Jackson
Cover Design by Eli Constant of Wilde Book Designs

Claire C. Riley is represented by Michelle Johnson of Inklings Literary Agency. Please contact her in regards to foreign rights or film rights.
www.inklingsliterary.com

Thank you for respecting the hard work of the author. She thinks that you are totally badass for purchasing this from a reputable place and not stealing it!
You're 100% awesome.

Odium IV
The Dead Saga

The dead aren't the only thing to fear…

A kid, an old lady, and a heartbroken man…What could possibly go wrong?

Mikey is holding true to his promise to Nina, and is doing everything he can to keep the group alive. But when something attacks the threesome in the middle of the night, things begin to take a turn for the worse.

Luckily a new group, the NEOs, is on hand to ease Mikey's burden and help fight alongside him. But first he must prove his worth to the leader, Aiken, and the people that follow him. Within this new group, Mikey begins to find a form of peace that he didn't think was possible after losing Nina, and he discovers his place within this new world. A place where killing isn't for fun, and is only ever committed as a last resort.

His heart is still aching, but at the end of the world there's no time to stop and mourn, and as he searches out a circus freak show and the horrors begin to stack up around him, Nina slips far from his mind.

It's probably best, because there are many more terrors in store for him. Because within the folds of a small town, inside an old candy store, he meets a woman named Clare, her two dogs, and something that he never saw coming.

ODIUM IV

The Dead Saga

By *USA Today* & bestselling British Horror Writer
Claire C. Riley

Dedication:

To my fellow zompoc lovers.
I salute you.

Chapter One

Mikey

The truck rumbles along with as much gusto as it did previously, yet now it feels empty. Everything feels empty. Nina went back inside. She left me with Adam and Joan, knowing I wouldn't be able to leave them. She wanted her vengeance no matter what the cost to herself or anyone else.

I hate her.

My shoulders shake as I try to contain my sadness, as I try to ignore the ache of despair that bubbles away in my stomach. Adam cried himself to sleep at some point in the last hour, and Joan is still staring numbly out the window like she has been for several hours. It's the quietest she's been since I met her, and I wonder how much of her so-called craziness is actually real. Because the look on her face makes it clear that she fully understands the importance of what just happened.

We won't get much farther before the gas runs out. We'll need to stop soon, find somewhere safe to spend the night. But nowhere is safe. I can't run away from my past anymore. It's all caught up with me, and now I've lost everything and everyone. How many more times can I do this? Run from it and them? Hide and hope that I can escape the memories of friends and family that have died because of my selfishness and stupidity? I slow the truck, wanting to turn around—and not for the first time—but then I think of Adam and Joan, and how they rely on me now, how Nina has put their safety in my hands.

I hate her.

Rubbing away the tears that have trailed down my dirty cheeks, I grit my teeth. My anger will be my fuel—my anger at her and at them, but mostly at myself. I look in my rearview mirror, seeing the setting sun behind me, slipping below the tree line and buildings that we're passing, and I panic again.

We'll need to stop. They need to eat, and I'm pretty sure one or both of them has pissed themselves. I can't care for them; I can barely care for myself. Damn her! My hands grip the steering wheel tighter, my calloused knuckles going white.

I hate her.

All she had wanted was to help people. Even in her bitchiest moments, that was all she had wanted. She covered her kindness with attitude, but she wanted the world back to how it was, when we helped one another, when we cared, and felt, and loved, and we survived as a human race and not as selfish individuals.

I have never regretted anything in life—not until this moment. Even my fucked-up past I haven't regretted, because to regret it was to change it, and if I changed one damn thing I might never have met her. And to never have met her would have been my biggest regret yet.

I love her.

And now she's gone. She went back to do what I had been running from—what I had been hiding from. She went back to end this fight. And it cost her everything, it cost me everything. She was brave and beautiful, and I lost her.

What the hell am I going to do now?

Chapter Two

"Wake up," I whisper into the back of the dark truck.

Adam is still fast asleep, and Joan joined him around thirty minutes ago. Their soft snores had echoed throughout the truck, almost lulling me to my own sleep, but every time I had started to drift off, Nina's face had appeared and I had jumped awake, full of anger and sadness all over again. I envied them fiercely, and their ability to slip away into their dreams—away from this day and all the nightmares that came with it.

Neither of them has stirred, so I repeat myself, a little louder this time, and then I wait again. I check my gun, though I know it's loaded since this is the third time I've checked it. It's a worthless piece of crap, but it still works, thank God. I pull out my knife and hold it up to the waning moonlight, watching as the light glints off the tip, and then I put it back away. The knife is just like the gun—a piece of crap—but I've fought with worse and I'm still here, so I guess I'm still a winner. What a joke.

"Joan, wake up," I whisper once more, irritation finally getting to me.

The truck has finally run out of gas, but thankfully it's stopped only half a mile from what looks like a large farmhouse or possibly a barn. I say "possibly" because the sun has set, leaving the road, and everywhere else you look, pitch black. The world is just a murky dark shape amongst more darkness. It's stupid to get out and travel on foot, but staying in the truck right now seems just as dangerous. It's happened before, where I've slept the night inside a vehicle that's run out of fuel, only to wake the

3

next morning surrounded by the living dead. Both times that happened, I had a partner at my side that could help me to fight our way out. But with Joan and Adam in tow I don't have that same luxury. So on foot to the farmhouse it is.

At least if we get stuck in there we have more escape routes. I hope.

Or maybe I'm acting irrationally. Maybe I'm the one that needs to get out and walk—to try and somehow walk out the frustration and sadness that I have inside me. In which case, we should probably stay where we are. Yet I still find myself checking my weapons and readying us to leave the safety of the truck and head out on foot.

I hear movement from the back of the truck and realize that one (if not both) of my companions is finally waking. I wait a beat for whoever it is to come closer, the whites of their eyes two bright spots in the darkness.

"Where are we?" Adam speaks, sadness and sleep still tinging his young voice.

"Not entirely sure, kid. Is Joan awake yet?"

He shrugs, I think, and then blinks, but has the decency to stifle a yawn. "Why'd we stop? Won't they catch us?"

I swallow down the hard lump in my throat at the mention of people catching us. People that were chasing us, chasing me. People that we have left behind. Friends, family…Nina. My voice gets lost when I open my mouth to speak, the words abandoning me in favor of the oppressive sadness that's crushing me from the inside out.

I can't get the words out.

I can't breathe.

I feel trapped and suffocating under guilt, sadness, and anger. *She gave me no choice*, I want to scream. *She gave me no choice in any of this!* I'm angry and sad and full of so much emotional baggage that I can't think straight.

I need to be strong for Joan and Adam, but I find myself weak and broken. A shell of a man. Maybe not even a man at all.

She gave me no choice in this, I tell myself again and again, hoping that my anger at her and the situation will fuel me onwards and stop me from being so blind to the dangers around us.

"I'll go wake her up," Adam says quietly before vanishing back into the blackness. I think he senses my despair. It would be hard not to. It feels like a real and whole thing—something you could pick up and put in a backpack. An angry, faceless monster full of rage and sadness.

I turn to face the windshield again, looking out onto the night beyond and wishing I didn't have this hollow feeling in my gut. Nina would hate me for acting like this. She'd want me to carry on, to get a grip and deal with the situation. She'd probably insult me with that sharp tongue of hers while she tried to motivate me too.

The thought makes me smile for the first time in several hours. Not a full smile, but a small tug at the corner of my mouth as I hear her voice ring out in my head.

Stop acting like a little bitch, Mikey, and get these people to safety!

"Are we safe yet?" Joan's croaky voice says from behind me.

I turn in my seat once more. I want to say yes—to tell the old broad that everything is going to be okay, that I've rescued them

5

both and gotten them to safety, and now I'm going back for Nina and our friends. Or at least to get my revenge for her and them. For us. But I know it isn't possible.

We aren't safe. And if these last few years have been anything to go by, we will never be safe again. Not just from the monsters, but from the people that remain. Because the men and women that have survived this long, they're just as bad as the monsters that roam the earth.

"We ran out of gas," I reply instead. "I think there's a house a half a mile or so due north. We need to hole up there for the night and assess things in the morning when I can see more than a couple of feet in front of my face."

I wonder whether Joan will argue with me and tell me my plan is stupid—perhaps even refuse to get out of the damn truck. The woman is a little bonkers, after all. And I'm not exactly coming across as Mr. Reliable right now either. But she doesn't argue, and I'm grateful, though she'll never know it.

"Okay, come on then, Advil," she says, reaching for Adam.

Adam blinks at her, his face smooth of expression even though I know he's confused at what she just called him. But he doesn't say anything. Instead he takes her hand in his.

I open my door, letting in the damp night air, and I listen for any sound of deaders. Moments go by before I jump down from the truck and look back inside, watching as Adam and Joan climb over the headrests and over my seat before climbing out too.

Joan carries a large piece of wood in her bony hands; it looks pretty dangerous too. Large nails and jagged bits of wood stick out of it from where it was ripped away from the side of something. Color me impressed.

6

"Stay close behind, no talking, as quiet as you can," I whisper to them both.

"You're talking now," Joan whispers back in confusion. "Or do you mean no talking from this moment on?"

I huff out my annoyance. "From now on."

"So you mean from now?" she questions, her voice so close to my face that I can smell the stench of her decaying teeth. Yet the night is so dark that I can barely make out her expression to see if she's being serious or just being an asshole.

"What?" I snap.

"Silence from now?"

"Yes," I reply and turn away. I turn back and add on, my tone angry because this is ridiculous: "From now. Like right this second, no talking." I point at them both—not that they can see it, but taut tension is in my arms and shoulders and it's difficult to ignore.

"Okay," she replies. "No need to get all bent out of shape. You hear that, Advil? No talking."

I scowl and turn away from her, and together we began walking toward the dark shape of the house in the distance. Or at least what I hope is a house. Without streetlights the air is thick and black like tar. It's suffocating in its closeness, and as we are swallowed up into it, it becomes darker still.

We stay in the middle of the road, avoiding the thickened bushes and trees at the roadside which grab at the dark, clinging to it like a lifeline.

Each step we take echoes around us.

Each breath sounds too loud.

7

Even my heartbeat can be heard above the crickets in the night.

Zombies—or deaders—don't bother me. Not anymore. I've killed more than my fair share of them. What bothers me is the being alone in the dark with them. How can I defend myself, never mind a kid and an old lady like this? It's stupid, and with each step we all take, the night seems to swallow us up more and more, drenching us in its darkness, drowning us in the blackness of it all.

Even the moon has hidden itself behind dark clouds that are ready to burst their banks. I shake my head and grip my gun tighter.

Adam coughs, a small splutter that he tries to stifle with his hand or sweater—or perhaps it was Joan. But he coughs and the sound is almost immediately stifled. It doesn't matter, though, because beyond the raging beat of my heart and the quickening breath at my neck from Joan and the tip-tap of Adam's small footsteps on the asphalt—beyond that is a sound I dread more than anything.

The sound of growls.

I've only encountered this once before, and even then, with another fighter by my side, we barely made it out alive. My stomach clenches tightly and I unbuckle the knife from its sheath as I grit my teeth and prepare myself to fight.

Another growl sounds out, closer this time, and I suck in a sharp breath and glance over my shoulder, meeting Joan's gaze.

"Was that me?" she asks. "I guess I am getting hungry."

"We're going to need to run soon." I say the words as quietly and as calmly as possible, ignoring her comment. Yet my voice still sounds too loud. "Like run really, really fast. You hear me?"

Joan doesn't speak this time, but even in the dark with only the whites of her eyes to light up her face, I can sense that she understands that something is about to go down.

"Keep ahold of the kid, and keep going straight. No matter what," I say with dread sinking in my gut as the growls grow louder and more obnoxious. "You don't stop for me."

The obviousness of the growls against the quiet night is too much for Adam and I hear him give a soft whimper of a cry. The farmhouse is rising out of the night like a phoenix rising from the ashes. Yet it doesn't matter because I know in my gut that we won't make it that far.

At least not all of us.

Was this what it was like for her? I wonder. *Are these the dark thoughts that she had when she was making the decision to sacrifice herself for me and Adam? Did she feel strong yet sad, broken and yet ready to die?*

The bushes at the side of the road light up with the glow of wild dogs' eyes, and I feel my heart pause as it waits in fearful anticipation for what's going to happen next.

"Mikey?" Joan says my name, her tremoring voice close to my ear.

But I don't answer her, I'm too busy counting how many sets of eyes there are. How many starving wild dogs there are waiting to tear into us…

…their teeth sharp and deadly.

…their hunger ravenous.

…their desperation and desire to live at any cost palpable.

I have never wished for deaders to appear in all my damned life—but I do now. Because at least then we'd have a fighting chance. The deaders would go for the dogs and us. The dogs would have someone other than us fighting against them. It'd be almost fair if deaders turned up.

But of course they don't. Of course it's just me, a kid, and an old lady fighting against these wild dogs. Of fucking course it is! Ain't it always that way? The odds forever stacked against us.

We're still walking, our footsteps quickening with each step we take. Our silence is pointless now, yet we're still trying to be quiet. Silence and calmness would be the best advice all round right now, but my muscles are tense and my body is ready for battle. We're not silent and I'm certainly not calm.

The house is almost upon us, but it's even farther than I realized. The dogs growl again, a chorus of angry snarls echoing back and forth as if signaling to each other that we are getting away.

I open my mouth to speak, my words getting stuck in my throat and making me almost choke on them. Because it's now or never, I realize as I finally stop counting the yellow eyes. When the number is higher than the fingers on my two hands, and it all seems too damn impossible.

"Now," I whisper to Joan. "Run!"

And at that we all begin to run. Silence be damned as we run hell for leather, and the barking and growling grow as the beasts dive from their hideouts and begin to chase us through the night.

The farmhouse is too far away, but there's a chance Joan and the kid can make it if they have a distraction. Yet something deep down tells me we aren't going to make it. Deep down, I know that. War needs its casualties, and we will be them. We can't outrun dogs—that's insane—and I can't fight them all off on my

10

own. Yet still we run, hoping that these wild dogs will be too weak from starvation to keep up with us. Hoping that deaders will appear from somewhere and begin tearing chunks out of the dogs instead of the dogs tearing chunks out of us.

Hoping and hoping and hoping…and that's all it ever is. That's all we can ever hope for now—hope. We hope for hope. Because each day is harder than the last. Each day more hopeless. Yet we have to have hope, because without hope we'd all just stop and succumb to death. Let the virus take us. Let the deaders take us. Let the Forgotten take us!

No! Nina calls in my ears. *Run.*

And so we run. Our shoes slapping against the asphalt. Our breaths coming short and sharp. No words spoken because there's nothing more to say. We all want to live. Despite it all, the human spirit isn't ready to give up on this shit life just yet. It wants to live.

We run, and we run, and we run. Our chests burning and needing air. Our legs aching from exhaustion. Running and running for all eternity. The growls of the dogs getting closer with every futile step we take, until Adam cries out and I immediately swing back around to help him without a second thought.

A dog has caught up and dived onto his back, dragging him to the ground. I can just make out that his backpack is the only thing stopping its teeth from making contact with his skin at the moment. Because in its ravenous attempt to eat him—to get at the fresh meat it knows is somewhere underneath his clothing—it's going for Adam's back instead of his legs.

I aim my gun, firing at what I hope is the animal's head, and feel satisfied as I hear a yelp of pain from it. It jumps back from

Adam, only to stand its ground and snarl at me until it's joined by several more dogs.

"Shit," I breathe out, seeing more dogs than I know I can fight.

Joan is motionless behind me, her piece of wood held high as we both stand ready to defend Adam until the death. He climbs up to his knees and then his feet, whimpering and coming to stand between us. He has a small knife in his hands, and I know he hasn't survived this long without using it.

"You ready?" I ask her and she nods. And I have to give it to the old broad—she's a brawler just like me.

"Can we get some whisky after this?" Joan replies shakily, her voice laced with what I hope to be sarcasm, or at least optimism. Though with Joan you never knew. "Christ, I'll even take some hooch if I have to."

I almost laugh. Almost.

Then I raise my arm and aim at a yellow pair of eyes as a dog bounds toward me. I squeeze off a round and the dog cries out, and then the rest of the dogs surge forward, jumping into the air as they fly toward us, their bodies arcing through the night sky almost serenely.

I don't think, I react. Shots are fired, hitting their targets but never stopping the relentless onslaught of dogs. A pair of teeth sink themselves into my ankle, sharp canines cutting their way through my flesh until they hit bone. I cry out and aim my gun downwards, shooting the thing in the head and thanking my lucky fucking stars that I don't shoot myself in the damned foot!

"Mikey!" Joan's voice cries out from somewhere in the darkness, her voice muffled.

My gun is empty and I swing the hard barrel of it against the skull of another dog that charges at me. Its full weight crashes into me and sends me to the ground with a grunt of pain. We barrel over and over, my hands gripping it by the neck and holding its snapping jaws away from my face.

I grunt again as another set of canines sinks its way into my injured ankle, the blood drawing the dogs to me like I'm fresh meat. Shit, I *am* fresh meat. In fact I'm fresher than beef at a butcher's counter, because I'm still alive and kicking!

My muscles tremble as I hold the dog at bay, its frothy spittle trailing from its jaws and landing on my face in heated, sloppy pools. Its breath is hot on my cheeks as I turn my face away, not wanting to see my own death reflected back in its eyes as it sinks its teeth into my face.

I kick out with my feet as the grip of the dog that's currently gnawing on my ankle like I'm a T-bone steak loosens. And then I kick and I kick and I kick, ignoring the pain that blisters its way up my shins and calves, and the burning ache in my arms and shoulders. And instead I relish in the yelps from the dogs around me as I do what little I can to put off the inevitable.

Somewhere I know Joan is fighting her own battle, and God only knows where Adam is. I hope at least the little kid made it out of here alive. Otherwise Nina will hunt my soul down to the end of time.

Sweat pours down my face, trickling into my eyes and making them sting like it's acid and not sweat, and the entire time I hear Nina's voice in my head, screaming at me to get up, to fight back…to protect Adam and Joan at all costs. And God do I want to scream back at her, because I'm doing everything I can. But that woman, even dead, is fucking relentless in her bitching!

Chapter Three

My body is being tugged all over the damn place as more jaws find their way to me, and teeth sink into my flesh. My arms grow weaker and my breath burns in my throat, but I'm still trying my damndest to get them off of me. And then, like a call from a guardian angel, a gunshot rings out from somewhere and a couple of the dogs loosen their grip.

From somewhere, the sound of a vehicle coming closer gives me a surge of strength. There's a dog almost straddling my entire body, its face inches from my face. I let my fingers dig into its neck, pressing harder and harder, digging through sweaty fur until I can feel its windpipe. I squeeze with everything I have, once again ignoring the teeth at my legs and feet, and the snarling at my face.

The dog's eyes bug out but its jaws are still relentless, its starvation driving it onward no matter what. It continues to snap at me obstinately, right until I crush its windpipe and I feel its heavy yet bony weight go limp in my arms. It falls on top of me, knocking the wind out of my lungs.

Another gunshot shot rings out from somewhere and the tugging at my ankle stops, and I push with every ounce of strength I have to get the dead dog off of me. I'm gasping for breath and panting against the pain as I climb up to my knees.

Lights abruptly flood the road, bright and illuminating, alighting the horrors we've just fought through, and I watch as bony, vicious dogs scatter away in every direction.

I try to stand, but cry out in pain and almost fall onto my face when I put weight on my injured ankle.

"Mikey?" Joan calls to me fearfully.

"I'm okay, I'm okay," I gasp out, happy to hear her voice. "You good?"

I squint against the lights, lifting a hand to shield my eyes.

What fresh new horror is this? I wonder morbidly.

Dead dogs litter the blacktop, and blood is sprayed everywhere, pooling. Unfortunately I can't feel any satisfaction at the sight of the dead dogs and puddles of blood, as most of the blood seems to be coming from me right now.

Joan rushes toward me, her ratty hair wild around her face. "I'm okay, I think," she says and looks down at the blood pumping from the bites I've received. "Better than you anyway," she adds on.

I grumble and let her help me up to my feet, leaning on her harder than I want to. I look to Joan's side, noticing that she's alone, and then I frantically scan the area, still coming up short of the little kid that I was tasked with protecting.

"Adam?" I yell, dread sinking like a lead weight in my gut.

"Where is he?" she asks, her voice trembling.

I shake my head. "I don't know, I don't know," I say as I frantically scan the area. "Adam?" I call for him, praying he's not dead. I have a vague recollection of him leaving my side, his small feet pounding the ground as he ran away from the carnage. But I hadn't been able to stop him, since I was being chewed alive.

15

The sound of a door opening has me tensing even further, and both Joan and I bring our gazes forward as the sounds of people getting out of a truck echo toward us. Shadows move across the too-bright headlights, stopping us from seeing who or what has just saved our sorry asses. And despite the fact that they just saved us, I'm still incredibly wary and ready to fight my way out of this situation if I have to.

The footsteps grow louder as whoever it is comes closer, until they're standing directly in front of us. The brightness of the lights is no longer important as two other people move to stand in front of the headlights and blot their glare.

I blink and look up into the face of a man a good six inches taller than me, at least. And I'm a tall man. He's broad too, looking like one of those freaks that used to work out on the beach, advertising the fact that they could lift five hundred pounds if they wanted to. (I may be exaggerating there.) In his mouth is a thin slip of wood that used to resemble a matchstick, and he smiles as he moves the pick from one side of his mouth to the other using only his tongue. In his hand is a weapon of sorts…I'm not sure if he's a friend or foe yet, but by the looks of his weapon of choice, I'm hoping for friend. He has a tall-handled scythe in his hands, like he's the grim reaper, and by the dried blood on it I can see that he's not afraid to use it either.

"Name's Aiken, and it looked like you could do with some assistance." He smiles again.

Joan lets go of my arm and I almost fall over. She holds out her hand as if she's meeting royalty of some sort. "Good day, sir, how wonderful to meet you," she says with a weirdly distinct British accent that seems to have come from nowhere.

"We had a little kid with us," I say, ignoring Joan's weirdness. "I need to find him, he's out here, somewhere." I turn around, looking across the bloody blacktop warily, and wonder if Adam's small body is buried beneath one of the furry hounds. It seems so unfair—cruel, if you will. He survived for so long on his own, and then we came along and rescued him, only to deliver him to his death regardless. I try to walk and almost collapse in agony when I put weight on my chewed-up ankle.

Aiken sticks his fingers in his mouth and whistles. "Boys," he calls out, summoning a group of around five people without looking away from me.

A mixture of both men and women, all of them heavily armed with guns and knives, comes forward.

"Sir?" one of them asks, paying me no mind.

Aiken finally looks away from me. "Ricky, help these people search for their friend."

"Yes, sir," Ricky replies before looking at me. He's a shorter man than me, and in theory it feels like I could easily take him if I needed to. But he isn't alone; he has a whole crew surrounding him, including Aiken, which means that Joan and I have no chance if these people decide to take us out.

"Let's get on with this," Ricky says matter-of-factly. His gaze falls to my ankle and he gestures to two people just behind him, one of them carrying a small box. "Bandage this up for now," he says, and then glances back at me. "We'll need to fix this properly back at Haven. I reckon you'll be needing some serious stitches on this. Not to mention a shot."

I nod, wincing as a man—or rather a barely-man—drops to his knees and starts pulling my torn and bloody cargo pants away from my busted-up leg. He swiftly wraps a bandage around the entire bloody mess, and he doesn't even look at me when he pulls the bandage tightly around it all. I wince in pain again.

Thankfully it's enough to stop the bleeding, or at least slow the blood loss.

When it's done, he stands up and nods at me. "Good to go," he says and walks away.

I turn on my heel and join the other people searching for Adam, moving the dogs' bodies out of the way so I can see underneath them. Four dead dogs lay covered in their own blood, their matted fur dirty and crusted. One of them is still alive, though barely. Its eyes stare up at me, the bright fire inside them dimming as I watch. A soft growl erupts from between its lips, which slowly turns into a whine of pain. I kneel down, pressing my hand to its neck to hold its head to the ground, and then I stab my knife through the side of its skull, feeling satisfaction as its taut muscles go slack beneath my palm.

I check everywhere, not finding Adam—whole or in pieces— but I feel only a little better for that fact. The others call to each other, yelling codes at regular intervals. I shout for Adam, my voice echoing out through the night air, moving with the breeze as it pushes between the overgrown fields. But no matter how loud I call, he doesn't come and he doesn't reply.

Panic is building in my guts, worry threading through my veins. He can't survive out here on his own. There are too many uncertainties, too many threats. I shout for him again, my voice being thrown back to me as a gust of wind blows.

"Adam!" My throat is dry and tight. I'm guessing this is how a parent would feel if their child were missing. The unwavering dread running through you. Wanting to find something, anything to explain what happened to them. But also not wanting to find anything at all. Because if you don't find them then you can still have some hope, right?

There's that word again: *hope*.

From somewhere behind me I hear Joan join in the shouting, the screeching tone of her voice grating on my nerves more and more. I head to the edge of the road and look across the dark, overgrown fields, knowing there's a strong possibility that Adam, in his panic, might have run off into them to hide. I feel sick at the thought.

The fields are thick and dark like black tar; who knows what's hiding in them? I consider going into them to find him, but know that my going is just as dangerous. Anything could be in there, and with the night as black and dark as it is, I'd have no chance of protecting myself. At least Adam is smaller; he has a better chance at hiding.

"Come on, kid. Let me know where you are," I mutter.

A soft breeze moves through the overgrowth, rustling the leaves and the shadows, and I squeeze my hands into fists, feeling anxiety running through them as if it were something real and solid. Something I could hold in the palm of my hand. Something I could destroy.

"Not a lot out here but wild dogs and ruins," Aiken says, coming to stand next to me, his matchstick still between his lips. "And the zeds, of course. Can't ever forget about them."

I don't reply but I turn to him, still trying to assess who this man was and what his worth is. I have met many men since this all began, but only a handful have been worth a damn, and even those broke down when push came to shove. Even me.

Aiken is holding the scythe loosely in his hand. It hangs by his side, but I know he's not relaxed with it. He'll use it on me if he has to, no doubt. Because that's how people work now, and I'm not stupid enough to believe this man is any different from all the rest.

His eyes narrow, but his lazy smile stays firmly in place like he doesn't have a care in the world. "My boys haven't found anything. I got them to check the house down there, but that place is locked up tighter than a bank vault, so I can't see how he'd be in there."

"Thanks," I say, shaking my head at the irony of his statement. Bank vaults are nothing to me. I always found a way into them; perhaps Adam had found a way into the house. I look across at the dark shadow of the building.

"So the way I see it is your friend either ran off to die, or ran off to hide," he nods his head in the direction of the field, "but I'm not sending my people into that to find him. Not tonight, at least. But we can come back tomorrow and look, if you want."

My gaze moves back to his face, my eyebrows pulling in tightly. "I can't leave him here to die. I made a promise," I reply with a heavy breath. My jaw twitches as I grind my teeth together.

"Promises aren't worth shit these days," Aiken replies drolly.

"You're telling me," I say, looking away from him and back toward the field. "But this one is."

Silence eclipses between us for a moment or two until he breaks it. "I can see that. However, that being what it is, we're heading back on home. You can come with us, or you can stay here. The choice is yours."

"I can't just leave him out here!" I yell. The bottle of anger and grief I've been holding in for the past couple of hours is ready to tip over.

"If you want him to live, you will," he retorts. "Your blood will be attracting all the wrong sorts of attention right now—zeds, dogs. You're not doing him any favors by staying out here. If you want my advice, the best thing you can do is come back with us, get yourself cleaned up, and we can bring you back tomorrow to search."

I drag a hand through my hair, my guilt already betraying me. "I…"

I know he's right, and though I don't want to leave, I have to. We've been looking for almost an hour with no luck, my leg is killing, and the bandage is almost soaked through with blood again. I have to leave him here and hope that he's hiding somewhere safe. Nina would have hated me for going, but she couldn't possibly hate me more than I hate myself already.

Joan comes over to me, her eyes wide with concern. "He's a crafty little thing," she says, her gaze moving out of the field. "He'll be hiding somewhere safe."

"Do you really believe that?" I ask, not wanting this decision to be solely mine.

Joan turns and looks at me. "He survived this long without anyone else's help, didn't he? So yes, I think he can survive a night out here. We can't just sit and wait for him to show up, now, can we?"

I nod and she pats my shoulder before walking away. I look back at Aiken. "I guess I owe you," I finally say.

His smile widens, and he flicks the matchstick to the other side of his mouth. "I guess you do."

Silence falls between us, and despite the throbbing in my ankle and foot, and the anxiety coursing through me, I square my shoulders and raise my chin. Aiken chuckles, reaching out and patting me on the shoulder like Joan just did.

"Come on," he says, turning away from me and walking back toward the truck. "The zeds and the dogs will be sniffing us out before long, especially with the way your leg is. If your friend is alive, he'll likely stay that way if we're not here to draw attention to him."

I turn, my gaze following him. "I don't like owing people," I say seriously.

Aiken stops walking but doesn't turn around. "Good thing I don't like people owing me either," he says, and continues to walk away. "We'll be back tomorrow for you, kid. Stay safe."

I watch him get to the truck and climb back in, and then I notice that everyone is loading up inside too, including Joan. The road floods with light again as people move away from the lights, and in the shadows I see the glowing eyes of the dogs from earlier. I glance back toward the overgrown field, feeling like a bastard for leaving, but not having any other choice. I can't stay here, and I can't go into that field looking for Adam—especially not in the state I'm in; the bandages have already begun to turn red as my blood soaks through.

"Adam!" I call one last time, hoping beyond hope that he'll come out of hiding. Silence echoes back at me and I look away from the fields with a heavy sigh. "Hunker down, kid, I'll be back for you tomorrow," I mumble and head toward the truck.

With every step, I feel the burden of heavy guilt stretching across my shoulders and growing stronger with every beat of my heart. Nina wouldn't have left…would she? But I'll bleed to death if I don't get my leg sewn up, and by the sound of the howls in the distance, the dogs are already sniffing me out as an easy meal.

22

I step to the side of the truck, where two of Aiken's people are waiting for me to get in. Their gazes watch me carefully, their guns staying trained at the ground, but I notice that their fingers never leave the triggers.

No, Nina wouldn't leave, but I realize now that this probably isn't really a choice at all; Aiken would make Joan and I leave and go back to their camp whether we wanted to or not.

I grab the side of the door and climb into the truck, a new sense of unease growing in me. Inside, more men and more guns sit waiting for me, and I find a seat and sit down in it.

Perhaps I am the fool after all, I think, *and Adam is the one who's safe.*

Chapter Four

"I'm just so excited to meet some more strapping young men like yourselves," Joan giggles. "It's not often that a woman like myself gets so many strong men coming to her aid."

I shake my head as I listen to the crazy bat jabber on with herself. Joan is verging on at least seventy. And that's being kind. These men are young enough to be her sons, maybe even her grandsons, and you can see the shock on their faces at her incessant flirting with them.

The truck rumbles along loudly, the smell of too many people crammed into too small a space almost palpable in the air. Sweat and dirt and the stench of blood fill my nostrils. It's dark in the truck, but I can still see enough to get a rough approximation of how many people are here, and the odds are not in our favor.

"So where are you from?" Aiken calls from the front of the truck. "I know it ain't from around here."

"Yeah?" I say, my tone laced with wariness.

"Yeah. You're a virgin to these roads—otherwise you would have known to stay in your truck. No one gets out of their vehicle without adequate backup around these parts. Rabid dogs, zeds, and God knows what else rule these parts." Aiken laughs darkly.

"Not to mention you guys, huh?" I reply with dry sarcasm.

Aiken laughs again and his crew joins in with him. "Yeah, not to mention that."

"And here I was thinking that you were all good boys," Joan chimes in. "Didn't realize you were as bad as the people we were running from."

A loud slap sings out, and I look sharply across to where Joan is sitting, my fists already clenched and ready to take down whoever just hit the old broad. But my assumptions are way off base—or at least it seems that way. By the look on the man next to her, who's gingerly rubbing his jawline, I'm wrong.

"Fiends! All of you. Only after one thing," Joan curses.

The man looks shocked and shakes his head as one of the others laughs at him.

"Someone chasing you two down?" Aiken says, ignoring Joan.

I notice that all humor has gone from his voice now.

I think over whether to be totally honest with him or not, but decide on keeping my mouth shut for the time being. What he doesn't know can't hurt us. But what he does know could kill us.

"It's like that, huh?" he says in return for my silence.

"Yeah, it's like that," I reply.

I hear him chuckle again, but he doesn't say anything else, and the rest of the journey is done in silence. Who knows where they are taking us, or how far from Adam we will end up. I have to hope, though, that since he hinted at sending people out searching for Adam when it was daylight that he will hold true to that. Well, as long as neither Joan nor I piss him off too much.

My thoughts stray to Adam, out there on his own, and I find myself not knowing what I wish for him. He's just a little boy, yet he's been through more than any grown man should ever have to go through. Is it really fair for him to have to live in this

25

world anymore? Wouldn't it be better for him if I wished him dead? Release him from this world so he can finally go wherever it is we go after death takes us? Or is that my own guilt talking because I've left him out there to survive all on his own?

My chin falls to my chest as I lower my head, aching remorse running through me.

The truck finally pulls up to a large set of wrought iron gates covered with sheets of metal to keep out probing hands and eyes. And deaders, of course. I crane my neck to look out one of the small windows of the truck, expecting that at any moment someone will stop me, but no one does. Dark shadows in the shapes of people with guns move along the top wall. Two men swing open the large gates, both armed to the teeth and gesturing for the truck to move inside.

"Home sweet home," Aiken says from the front seat.

"You the only one who can talk around here?" I snap, stress making me short-tempered. The sight of so many guns is making me anxious. That and the fact that the throbbing in my leg is getting difficult to ignore.

"Mikey, don't go being rude to these fine men," Joan tuts. "Apart from this one, of course," she says, glaring at the man she slapped earlier, though there's a definite glint in her eye when she looks at him.

Aiken turns in his seat to look at me. "Nah, my people can talk— they just choose not to talk to people they don't know," he says. "They don't like to get to know people unless they know they're going to be sticking around, if you get what I'm saying."

"I don't," I say.

"Until they know the color of their blood, my friend," Aiken says calmly.

I don't bother to reply, but continue to stare out the window, noticing the shadowed structures dotted about the area. The walls are high, but not so high that they can't be infiltrated, I decide. Which means one of two things: either people don't know about this place, or they're so afraid of it that they stay away.

For some reason option one worries me as much as option two.

Aiken is talking quietly to the driver and the other man up front, but I can't make out what they're saying as Joan leans forward in her seat and begins to speak.

"Mikey?" her voice whispers to me. "We're going to find the little one tomorrow, aren't we? Advil needs us. He's just a little boy, all alone in the big wide world."

I swallow, not wanting to worry her any more than she already is. "Yeah, we're going to find him tomorrow. Don't you worry about that."

None of the other people in the truck say anything to disagree with me, though I'm not stupid enough to take that as a good sign. In fact, the opposite. But there's no time to ask questions, or try to reassure Joan anymore, as the truck comes to a stop and the doors are flung open.

Aiken stands in the doorway, with two other men by his side. "Sorry about this, friend."

I grit my teeth. "We're not friends," I reply, my adrenalin spiking.

"That's what I thought," he says, and gestures with a nod of his head to the men beside him.

27

Both men reach in and I'm simultaneously dragged and pushed out of the truck and a bag is immediately shoved over my head. And then we're walking. Or rather I'm dragged as I turn my body into a leaden weight, trying to pull from their grip. The ground is hard and compact, the occasional crunch of gravel underfoot and the cussing of Joan to keep me company in the dark.

The screech of a metal door opening and then closing has me on high alert, and then I'm being forced to sit down in a chair while my hands are cuffed behind my back. Honest to God metal handcuffs! The kind that my wrists used to be so familiar with, all those many moons ago. It's both a blessing and a curse, I decide.

A rope is tied around my waist to keep me strapped to the chair. Nina's sarcastic voice is ringing loud and clear in my head.

Stranger danger, Mikey! Stranger danger. Get your sorry ass out of here!

And then there's nothing.

Just the sound of retreating footsteps and the door closing behind them as they leave.

"What, no parting words of wisdom?" I yell into the dark, the soft cloth of the material sticking to my sweaty face, and not even Joan's talk to keep me company. Either she's dead or they took her somewhere else, I decide.

I listen intently, willing my raging heart to quiet the hell down, but to no avail. It's hard not to panic when you're tied to a chair with a bag over your head! The worst possible scenarios are flung to the forefront of my mind—deaders released into the room to eat me alive being the main culprit.

But after what seems an eternity, there's still nothing but silence.

Not even outside noises can be heard, no matter how hard I strain my ears.

And then the paranoia kicks in—the thought that perhaps I'm not alone after all, but that there are others here. Men, women, who the fuck knows. But they're all sitting around watching me, and waiting to see how long it'll take before I freak out. Before I move and try to escape. Or before I call for help. And what then? What happens to me then? And not just me, but Joan. Where have they taken her, and what will happen to Adam if they kill me here tonight?

"Damn you, Nina," I mutter, hating her once again for the fact that she's thrust the responsibility of other people's lives on me.

I grit my teeth and will myself to calm down, to think through everything I have heard and seen thus far.

Aiken and his crew rescued us out on the road. There's no doubt about that. I was about to become a prime rib for those wild dogs, and I have no doubt in my mind that Joan would have been the accompanying rack of ribs.

So that makes Aiken a good guy. Doesn't it? Surely he wouldn't put his life and his men's lives at risk for nothing. He has to be getting more out of this than just tying me to a chair and feeding me to the deaders.

I swallow and take a slow, steady breath, the black material of the bag on my head making me feel claustrophobic as it presses against my mouth. I listen harder as my heartbeat begins to level out. No more a rampaging train, but the steady *thump thump thump* I'm used to.

But beyond the blackness there's still nothing but silence.

My eyes strain to distinguish something beyond the material, but there's nothing but blackness, so I do what any man would do when he got sick and tired of being tied to a chair with a bag over his head…

I dislocate my right thumb.

Pain spasms through my hand and tears well in my eyes. Damn, I'd forgotten how much it hurts to do that. I hiss and grit my teeth as I take a couple of slow breaths while I wait for the pain to subside. Once it slows to a dull ache, I wriggle my hand free of the cuffs. And once one hand is free, I drag the bag off my head and stare around the room, eyeing up left and right quickly in case anyone is standing around watching my little contortionist act. However I'm only disappointed by yet more blackness in every direction.

It looks like I'm in a warehouse of some sort, with a high roof that has several huge holes in it, letting in a cool night breeze. *I guess I'm a lucky boy that it's not raining,* I think with a frown. I squint into the darkness around me, trying to remember which direction the footsteps had retreated in, but I can't work it out. The warehouse is vast with large ceilings, meaning sounds echo, throwing me off the direction they could have gone.

Happy that I'm alone, I grit my teeth and push my thumb back into place, almost gagging on the pain. I wait several moments to let the nausea subside. Bile has built in the back of my throat as yet again pain throbs through my hand in waves. There was a time, once, when I had popped my thumbs out like this quite frequently—to the point where the pain had even stopped bothering me. It was part and parcel with the territory. Breaking and entering, thievery, robbery, whatever you wanted to call it. I hadn't been a good guy, though I had tried for a while, and while I was learning my trade I had escaped more than my fair share of handcuffs.

With the pain at the point of being a low throb now, I begin moving the rope from around my waist to bring it to my front so I can try and untie it. It only takes a couple of minutes of fumbling in the dark to get the knot untied and then I stand up and take a step away from the chair, readying to make my escape from this place.

And then I stop moving, my left foot hovering in the air mid-step. I stare into the darkness around me with a frown. The more I stare, the more I frown. Because deep down I know this isn't right—it can't be.

It's too easy.

The ache in my thumb continues to jar me back to the here and now every time I try to think what the hell they could be playing at. The thing that gives it away the most is that I haven't heard a peep from Joan. Not a single cuss or grumble. Which means she's either dead or she isn't here at all. And if she's not here, then why am I?

Why would they separate us only to kill us?

My mind grabs hold of the reason and holds on tight: Joan isn't a threat—but I am.

My left foot settles on the ground to join my right, and I close my eyes and listen once again for any noises around me, but still don't hear anything. My choices are simple: I either make a run for it and leave Joan here, or I sit my ass back down, tie myself back up, put my cuffs back on, and wait to see what happens.

I know for a fact what Nina would do. Damn it and damn her.

I look up at the sliver of moon through the hole in the roof, and then I sit back down in my chair. My ass hasn't even hit the seat when footsteps come forward from the darkness.

"Good choice, my friend. I knew we were going to get along," Aiken says.

I stay silent, watching as lamps are lit around the room.

"I said to my men, 'he's all right, he's one of us,' and it would seem I was right, wouldn't you say?"

I can see him now, much better than I had at the side of the road.

"I know, I'm a pretty boy, ain't I?" he chuckles, running his hand along the long red scar that's etched into the side of his face.

"What the fuck is this?" I reply, forcing myself to look away from the scar.

"This," Aiken says, with his arms wide open, "this was a test. I wanted to check out your loyalty. Because loyalty is what I'm all about." He smiles, ignoring my frown. "What you said at the side of the road about promises meaning something, well that's the sort of philosophy we tend to live by around here. But not many others in this world do anymore. What I just saw in you—sitting yourself back down and not abandoning your friends—well, that showed me exactly the color that runs through your veins. And it ain't yellow."

A meat hook from an slaughterhouse hangs on a metal chain from one of the crossbeams of the warehouse, and Aiken grabs hold of it with both hands, letting his weight rest as he leans. He flicks the matchstick from left to right with his tongue, watching me carefully for several moments as he assess both me and the situation.

32

"There are a lot of people here, and we can't just go letting anyone in." Aiken cocks his head to one side. "I mean, have you met some of the people that survived?" He whistles. "They are not good people."

"Boss?"

Close to my right-hand side, a voice from behind has me automatically tensing, but I control myself enough not to show it.

Aiken's gaze shifts from me to the person behind me before coming back to me again. His smile grows, and he lets go of the meat hook and stands up straight again. "Come and meet my men, get something to eat, and let's fix up that leg of yours before you pass out. I'd like to hear your story."

"And what if I say no?" I say, slowly standing up. I wait to see if someone—one of his men, crew, whatever he wants to call them—will grab me and slam me back down in my seat, but no one does.

Aiken laughs. "Well, then you can be on your way. But I wouldn't suggest you do that tonight—not with your leg all banged up like it is." Aiken laughs darkly. "So much blood will have all the monsters in these parts making you their Sunday lunch, and if you're going to find that kid of yours, dying isn't a good way of going about it." And then the squeak of the door sounds as he leaves the warehouse.

I turn to look behind me, putting a face to the voice. Three people are standing there, each of them looking threatening, yet none of them move toward me. They don't look happy about me being here, but if Aiken's their boss then they're his underlings, and what good little underlings they're being right now.

"Is that his thing?" I ask the biggest underling. "Walking away dramatically?" I move my gaze across to the other two. "I reckon he watched too many cowboy movies as a kid and he's trying to reenact the dramatic walk off into the sunset. What do you think?" I smirk.

"I think you should take the boss up on his offer," the smallest of the three replies.

"Yeah?"

"Yeah," he says.

"And why's that?" My tone's full of attitude, but I thank God that no one can see the raging in my blood, or the pounding in my ears as worry strokes up my sides.

"Because the boss normally knows what's best for everyone," the biggest underling says, making no big show of his statement, which only irritates me more.

None of this makes any sense. Why rescue me and Joan, convince me to leave Adam behind, and then lock me in a warehouse and see if I would try to escape, only to then patch me up, feed me, and send me on my way the next day? No, none of this makes any sense at all.

This still feels like one big test. And with Joan and Adam's lives on the line, I'm not about to mess it up. I make up my mind and decide to play it cool. To play a part in all of this until I decide what the best thing to do is. Because he's right in that I couldn't leave right now—not in this sort of mess with my leg busted up the way it is. I wouldn't make it a mile down the road before I got eaten by something. And I can't let that happen, because I have a promise to keep.

"So, what's for dinner?" I ask, my cocky smirk still in place—mainly because I can tell it irritates the shit out of Aiken's men. "Please tell me it's steak, because I've been hankering for a steak for a good few years now."

Chapter Five

Dinner looks good. Real good.

And for a brief few moments I forget how I got here, and instead I stare down at my full plate in ravenous hunger. I haven't eaten or drunk anything in almost two days, and up until now I haven't really thought about it. Hunger is a way of life these days. It's sort of part and parcel with the damn zombie apocalypse. You begin to forget what the empty, hollow ache in your gut or the shakiness of your hands means. But now that food is in front of me, I take note of how my vision is swaying from both hunger and thirst.

Thank God my plate's full. And full of things I haven't eaten in far too long. Things I thought I'd never see again.

Tomatoes and carrots, mushrooms and onions, all cooked together with some honest-to-God meat. I have no clue what type of meat it is; I only know that my mouth salivates at the sight of it. I'm about to dive in with both hands when a new underling hands me some silverware—a knife and fork—and even a little white paper napkin, which makes me want to bark out a laugh.

I'm hallucinating.

I have to be.

But it's the best hallucination I've had since…well, since forever.

I pick up my fork, the metal object feeling foreign in my clumsy, uncivilized grasp. It's equally heavy and light, all at the same time. I stare at my hand for a moment, feeling a frown cross my features as I stare at the metal implement, and I try to think back to the last time I held a fork. I think for minute upon minute, letting my mind go further and further backwards through history, but the only thing that comes to me is the day my world fall apart. I squeeze my eyes shut to try to think harder, because that couldn't be it…could it? It couldn't have been that long.

"Alfie here's our medic. He's going to patch up your leg before you eat, if that's okay." Aiken says, disturbing my inner turmoil.

I open my eyes, ignoring my own distress, and I force myself to smile once again. It's just a fork. A stupid damn fork. Yet in the grand scheme of things, it means everything right now. The fork is civilization. It's life. It's real. And it's here in my hand.

A man so young he's almost a kid is standing in front of me— the same young kid from the roadside. He's wearing a black vest and jeans, and I notice that his arms are covered in small scars all the way down. Teeth marks, I realize as I stare.

"You mind?" he says, pointing to my leg and ignoring my stare.

I shake my head no and he gets down on his knees and opens up his bag.

He begins pulling out all sorts of things, and then he drags on a pair of gloves and unwraps the bandage from my leg. I have to look away because it looks like a dog chewed on my leg…Yeah, yeah, a dog did chew on my leg. That's my point exactly, and no one wants to see that crap.

"Where's Joan?" I ask. I don't feel good. In fact, I feel damn shitty. I feel exhausted from fighting, and from the lack of eating and drinking, but mostly I feel like I've gone ten rounds with my emotions. From sadness and anger to suspicion and guilt. I'm not sure how much more I can take. The bottle has started to tip over and everything is ready to spill out.

"She's getting treated by our other medic. She took a couple of bites as well—nothing as serious as yours, though. Then she asked for a bath and an apple pie." Aiken shrugs and laughs. It's a deep, booming laugh that bounces off the walls and soaks into your skin. "She's a crazy one for sure."

I wince as I look back down at my throbbing leg. The blood had started to congeal, but the wound has opened back up with the bandage moved out of the way. He sprays something on it and begins to clean the wound, but I refuse to pay too much attention to what's happening. The pain is enough of a notification on that front.

"Yeah, she is," I reply.

I look around the room, taking in everyone and everything. Several more minions are peppered around the room, all looking unimpressed that I'm here. I give one of them a little wave and a flash of teeth. His angry gaze darts to Aiken, who chuckles and waves off his minion's glare.

"This is Ricky. He's not too happy about letting more people join us. Can't say I blame him. Most people aren't the good sort, if you know what I mean," Aiken says. "I should tell you more about us. Seems only fair. We've seen the color of your blood, so maybe you should know ours, right?"

I shrug, feeling the pinch of a needle in my skin, but I still refuse to look down. "I won't be sticking around, so it's up to you," I say.

Aiken smiles. "Well, we're the New Earth Order. NEO for short. We're a community of people who are sick of all the killing."

"As in NEO from *The Matrix*?" I joke, ignoring the "no killing" remark because that's just another absurdity all on its own.

"I hadn't thought of that. You're a funny guy." He laughs again.

"So I'm told," I bite out, finally giving in to the temptation and glancing down at my leg—and wishing almost instantly that I hadn't. It's not pretty. Not at all. "You sure you're qualified to do this, kid?"

Alfie looks up at me, catching me in his blue-eyed stare. "Not really." He grins. "Whatcha' gonna' do though, right?" He shrugs and gets back to work.

I can't argue with that point. "So, you're named after a long-dead movie character and your group doesn't kill?" I say, holding Aiken's stare. "I think I can see the color of your blood just fine."

He smiles, a slow smile that creeps up his face as if he knows something that I don't. "Never said we didn't kill, only that we don't like to. We do what we've gotta' do to protect our own," Aiken says. "I'm sure you can understand that, my friend."

He picks up his silverware and starts to eat, gesturing with a nod of his head that I should do the same. I look down at my plate, my stomach rumbling loudly just as Alfie finishes up his job on my leg.

"Not going to be entering any beauty pageants with legs like this," he jokes, "but the stitches will hold." He packs all his things up in his doctor's bag and stands back up. "Someone will drop off some antibiotics and pain relief later on for you."

"Okay," I reply with a frown. He seems like a good kid—the sort that was once a boy like Adam. The thought makes my stomach clench in guilt and anger. How could I have left him there? All alone? I squeeze my eyes closed, feeling disgusted with myself.

"You had no choice," Aiken says, as if reading my mind.

I open my eyes and avoid his stare, instead choosing to look down at my plate and stab a tomato with my fork. Now that the immediate danger is over, I've made eating my next priority, and my stomach is thankful as it grunts in pain and hunger. A little juice squirts out of the side of the tomato, and a small laugh abruptly leaves me. Aiken's sitting at the other end of the long table we're at, and though he's eating his own food, I can feel his gaze shifting to me every once in a while.

"Never really liked vegetables before all of this," I say in an attempt to break the awkward silence in the room. My voice carries down to him, and when I look up, he's placed his own fork down and is staring at me. He smiles and nods his head slowly.

"Can't say I did either," he replies. "Apart from tomatoes. My ma used to make the best tomato pasta sauce. Made the entire thing from scratch as well. None of this premade jar stuff. All homegrown vegetables from our backyard." He falls back into silence, probably thinking about the pasta sauce his ma used to make.

I can't say I blame him. I can't even think about my mom's apple pie without my eyes welling up. What I would do for one last slice of that pie. My mom was a terrible cook when it came to anything else.

I push the memories to one side and move on, like I always do when I think of my past life—my old family and friends, or anything to do with that part of history. Because that is what it is: history. A past life.

I have to live in the here and now if I'm going to survive.

"Well, I hate to break it to you, buddy, but tomatoes aren't really a vegetable. They're a fruit." I finally raise my fork and push the tomato into my mouth almost nonchalantly, as if this isn't the first fresh-grown piece of food I've eaten in years. The truth is, I have now been a part of several new colonies that have begun to grow their own food. It isn't an uncommon thing, really. What is uncommon is that it's a tomato, and tomatoes are my favorite. Now if someone could mush one of these bad boys up and make it into some ketchup, I'd be running on gold.

The flavor is amazing, and I would like several minutes in silence just to let my taste buds jack themselves off, but Aiken breaks my intimate moment.

"Yes, they are," he says, sounding pissed off at me—which is surprising, really, since I haven't once seen him angry since we met a couple of hours ago. Actually, that's not really that long, so forget I said that. I also decide then and there that some of Nina's talent for making friends must have rubbed off on me. "Tomatoes are a vegetable," he says indignantly.

I shake my head and stab at another tomato while my teeth continue to work at the one still in my mouth. "Nope. Tomatoes are a fruit. I can promise you that. How's the woman that I came in with," I ask, referring to Joan since I hadn't seen her since I was blindfolded and tied to a chair.

The second tomato tastes just as good as the first, and the urge to groan in satisfaction is growing stronger. My head is all over the place—one minute up, the next minute down. My usual selfish nature is at war with the side that Nina has brought out in me—the compassionate side. Or perhaps it's just exhaustion catching up to me and fucking with my brain.

41

I glance up as Aiken puts down his fork. The noisy clatter of it against the porcelain dish seems to make everyone in the room look uneasy.

"The old lady you came in with is fine," he says gruffly. "But I'm telling you, tomatoes are a vegetable." Aiken looks over at one of his underlings. "Shane, I'm right, right?"

The underling named Shane looks unsure. He glances across the room at someone else, his cheeks flaming a little red because he clearly doesn't know the answer. His breathing hitches and he shuffles from foot to foot and continues to look around.

"I could go ask Phil. He might know, boss," Shane says with a small shrug, his face still looking flushed with embarrassment that he doesn't know the answer.

And I can't help it: I laugh.

All eyes in the room immediately move to me, but I don't even care that there are six heavily armed men and women staring at me and wondering why I'm laughing my ass off at them and their boss. If anything, I laugh even harder.

"Is this some kind of joke? Are you punking me right now? Is Ashton Kutcher going to come through that door with a camera? Because honest to God, of all the things that have happened to me in the last couple of years, it really wouldn't be the weirdest," I say between laughs. I stab my fork into another tomato and it explodes, and the sight of the juice and seeds sprayed across my plate of food like bloodied brains is more than I can take and I laugh even harder. "And just so you know, I'd punch that dick Ashton in the throat if he did walk in here because he's annoying as fuck and Demi Moore was way too damned hot for him if you ask me, and so is Mila Kunis. I seriously don't understand how he keeps getting such hot women in his bed. I mean, he's not even funny!"

The room, barring my laughter, is still silent—almost deafeningly so—and I feel rage begin to bubble inside of me. I'm laughing my ass off right now because we're discussing whether a tomato is a fruit or a vegetable and the world is infested with zombies. I just lost the woman I love because of my own stupid mistakes, and I'm still alive. Adam is out there somewhere, maybe alive but probably dead, and I'll be dropping my pants later to get a rabies shot. How is any of this even possible? How do I continue to escape death at every turn and yet everyone else, people I care about, die every other day?

Everyone is still staring at me like I'm a dumbass, and all it does is make me angrier. Where once I was full of grief and sadness, now I'm filled with rage. I need to get the hell out of here. The walls are closing in, exhaustion and frustration ready to topple my feeble walls. I don't belong here; I should be on my own, away from anyone that can get hurt in the aftershocks of the walking bomb that I am.

"Ashton's a dick," Aiken begins, "but you need to take it easy. You're making my men nervous. And I don't like it when they get nervous. So eat your food and calm down."

My stomach growls louder, eager for more food, and I laugh again, not feeling the humor but laughing all the same. Shane laughs with me, and I glare at him to shut him the hell up. This isn't funny. None of this is funny. Yet that's all I am to these people—that's all I ever am. A clown. A joke. A Goddamned fucking laugh-a-minute Larry. That's all I was to Nina too. Probably why she ran back inside—so she could get away from me and my patheticness. Well fuck her.

And just like that my jar topples over and everything comes spilling out.

I drop my stupid damn fork to my plate and I start scooping the food up and shoveling it into my mouth like an animal. Because that's what I am. That's how I've been made. That's how I live now. I don't need Joan or Adam, I don't need Aiken and his damned silverware, and I certainly don't need Nina and all her emo bullshit. So I'm glad she's dead and gone. And I'm glad Adam's probably dead too, because there's no place in this world for someone innocent like him. And I'm glad Aiken brought me here because now I can leave Joan's wrinkly old ass behind and go back to my roots. Back to it being just me looking after me. None of this Kumbaya bullshit I've been doing for the past year.

I don't need anyone.

"I said, calm down," Aiken says. "We need each other, but right now you're not making yourself very likeable to my people."

But I don't listen. Instead I shovel more food in, and then the food is gone, and I'm swallowing down the last tomato and throwing my glass of water to the back of my throat and letting it dribble down my chin. I shove my chair back angrily, letting it scrape along the floor.

"I don't need anyone!" I yell and push my plate across the table, knocking over the salt and pepper shakers as I do, and I do a double take.

"Salt and pepper." I laugh louder. "You have salt and fucking pepper!" I grab the salt and tip some into my hand and I throw it into my mouth. It's disgusting and foul and makes my tongue want to shrivel up like a slug, but it's also great, because it makes me feel sick and brings me back down to earth with a heady dose of realization.

"I'm out of here," I say, my laughter dying away from my lips and turning my words to throaty whispers. "I'm sorry, but I need to leave. Now. Tonight." I turn away from the table and walk toward the door.

No one stops me. In fact, one of Aiken's underlings even opens the door for me.

And then I'm out, and it's me giving the dramatic last words as I turn tail and leave.

Me who watched too many cowboy films as a kid.

Me who dreamed of being the Lone Ranger.

"*Adios amigos*," I say, flipping them all the finger as I walk out of the room.

Chapter Six

The door slams shut behind me and I keep on walking, focusing only on the heavy stomp of my boots on the musty hallway carpet. The anger is there, burning below the surface like lava, and I can't seem to shake it; I can't make it disappear, no matter how much I try to make it go. I can't swallow it down anymore and pretend that everything is going to be okay.

Because it *is* there.

It's real and haunting and painful as hell.

And it's not going to be okay.

My anger is begging to be felt, to be heard, no matter how much I want to pretend. I'm on a one-way train to doing something stupid and irrational, and I'll probably get myself killed. Or worse, I'll get Joan killed. And then what? Then what will I do? I'll be responsible for another death. Another person I've gotten killed. The list is endless. A damned ocean of souls all snuffed out because of me, because of who I am.

My steps slow as I near the end of the hallway, as the door leading to the outside gets closer and closer and my chance of leaving here unscathed goes amiss.

"Goddamn it," I mutter under my breath.

I slow my steps, and by the time I'm standing in front of the door with my hand resting on the door handle, I've stopped. My body and mind frozen in blind panic. I'm panting—not from exertion but from the fear and anxiety of not knowing what to do. I simply have no idea what the hell to do anymore.

I've wanted to ditch everyone and everything for so long, to go Lone Ranger-style. And this is it—my chance to finally be alone. But I realize now that it's not what I want anymore. I want her—Nina. I want Adam and Joan, and Nova and Susan and Jessica, and even Michael. I want all of those sorry sons of bitches, but they're all gone. Dead. And now it's just me.

The anger drives up my arms, and I curl my hands into fists and squeeze my eyes closed. But then all I see is her beautiful face. I lash out, my fist connecting with the wall in front of me, but there's no pain as I pound it again and again, letting my skin split and the blood draw. I just feel empty, angry, and fucking lonely.

I punch the wall one last time, just for good measure, and I feel something crack in my hand. But fuck it, I don't even care. I stare down at my hand, watching the blood trickle over my knuckles, but all I'm seeing is white. White-hot anger.

"You're filled with a lot of rage," a woman says from next to me, and I open my eyes and glare at her.

"Kinda need to be alone right now," I reply curtly. I look behind her, expecting to see a group of men coming toward me, but it's just me, my broken knuckles, and this woman. She's attractive and curvy in all the right places, and her dress skims the tops of her thighs, but it's her boots that draw my attention. She may be feminine up top, but on her feet are a pair of big black boots that remind me of Nina's. My heart pangs for her at the sight of this woman's boots.

"I haven't seen you around here," she says, leaning back against the wall as if we're old friends from high school.

I don't reply, mainly because her voice is only just audible through the rage still burning through me.

"These are good people. If you can believe that." She laughs.

"That's funny to you?" I ask through gritted teeth.

"Yeah, it is. I didn't think there were any good people left until I came here." She looks around us, her gaze appreciative.

There's something about this woman that manages to calm me down, and I feel myself taking a step back from the ledge of insanity.

"What's going through that head of yours?" she asks.

I close my eyes and take a deep breath, feeling sick from the swelling anger inside me. "Nothing."

"Gotta' be something or you wouldn't have stormed off like your grandma just died."

I shake my head and open my eyes. "You saw that?" I ask in surprise because I hadn't seen her in the room.

She laughs again, throwing her head back as if it's the funniest shit she's ever heard. "Couldn't really miss it, since you nearly busted in my face with the door when you stormed through it."

My gaze skips over to the door I had stormed through and then I look back to her apologetically. "I didn't see you."

"I figured." She laughs again. "Want to know what I see when I look at you?"

"Not really."

She laughs and carries on like I didn't just tell her no. "I see pain. It's burning, bright and deep inside of you. It's like a beacon calling to Him."

"Who are you talking about?" I snarl out, my jaw twitching as I try to hold back the vicious tsunami of words that's bubbling up my throat.

She points to the ceiling and I stupidly look up, expecting to see someone there. But of course there's no one. It's just a dank ceiling in need of a fresh coat of paint that it'll never get. "I'm talking about the big guy."

"As in God?" I say in confusion. I stare at her, confounded, for several beats of my furious heart. "Are you kidding me right now?"

"No, I'm not," she replies, casually pushing off from the wall.

I'm speechless, and I'm grateful when Aiken comes out of the room at the end of the hallway. He smiles when he sees me and this God-loving woman talking. When he reaches our side he smiles even wider.

"I see you met Kelli. She's one of our best shooters. Came here a couple of months ago after stumbling upon us. We fixed her up and she's been with us ever since." Aiken pulls a small tin from his pocket and takes out a cigarette before lighting it.

"You saved my life," Kelli replies, looking up at him.

"And you've saved plenty of others since you arrived," he returns. "Everything go okay today?"

She nods. "As good as ever can be expected. I'm heading to bed. G'night, boss." She turns and starts to walk away before glancing back at me. "See you around."

"You still leavin'?" Aiken takes another drag of his cigarette.

"Yeah, I think so," I say, looking back at him. I feel calmer now, like I'm fully in control of myself again. Maybe that's what I needed—to let go, to explode and hit something. Because I can think clearer again now, and I'm ready to do what needs to be done.

"Why?"

"Because I don't belong here," I say, and though I feel frustrated, there's no anger in my tone. I turn away from him and place my hand back on the door handle, yet I still don't go, even though everything is telling me to.

"So tell me, where do you belong?" Aiken asks. And in fairness to him, he doesn't sound like he's trying to be an asshole. It seems like a genuine question. But the truth of the matter is, I don't have an answer for him. I don't know where I belong anymore. I don't know who the hell I even am anymore.

Thief. Criminal. Friend. Foe. Somewhere between leaving the Forgotten and meeting Nina I've lost the Mikey I once was, and now I'm just a hollow shell. An empty sack of no-good air.

"Nowhere," I finally reply. "I don't belong nowhere."

My grammar is shit, but the sentiment is still the same. I don't belong anywhere. Or at least it feels that way. I don't know if that will change in the future, but right now it's how I feel.

I finally push at the door and head outside, but Aiken's voice stops me in my tracks.

"We sure could use a man like you around here. None of us really belong anymore, my friend. We just try to make it work the best we can."

The air's cool on my heated face and I tilt my chin to look up at the sky, hoping to see some stars, or a sliver of moon—just something to make me feel anything more than empty. But the sky is dark. Not just dark, but barren and stripped back of everything. Devoid of life and light.

"We've all been where you are. We've all felt that lonely ache in our stomachs. That ball of anger. And that tidal wave of grief. We've all lost someone, everyone, and everything. It's the way of the world now. What I'm trying to say is that you don't have to go it alone. We support each other here. No matter what." Aiken hasn't moved, yet his voice is louder. Perhaps it's his words trying to get through to me, trying to worm their way into my head.

I turn back around. "It's the 'no matter what' that worries me," I say with a heavy heart. "There's been too much of that for too long, way too long, and I just can't justify it anymore. I can't put anyone else through my crap. And honestly, I don't want to go through anyone else's."

He frowns and drops his cigarette to the ground before stomping on it. His fingers reach into his top pocket and he pulls out his matchstick and places it between his teeth again. I have a feeling it's all to buy himself some precious seconds of thought.

"You were right," he eventually says.

I cock my head to one side in confusion and he smiles, the glint of white teeth shining in the dark.

"A tomato is a fruit."

Despite myself, I grin. "Told you."

Aiken laughs darkly—or maybe it's just his normal laugh and it's the mood that is dark. I'm not sure anymore.

"I'd really like you to stay. Stumbling across you and your friends on the road was fate. I believe in fate, even though I know I shouldn't. I can't touch it. I can't own it. I can't make it mine.

And yet I still believe in it. Meeting you was fate—though whether it was your fate or mine, I'm still not sure. I'm not even certain if it was a good thing or a bad thing. All that being what it is, I'd still like you to stay."

"You don't even know me," I reply, still feeling frustrated. Wanting to stay, and yet go. Like every other emotion inside of me, my desire for freedom is just as messed up as everything else.

"I told you. I tested your worth, the color of your blood, and what I saw is what I need. You could have left, but you thought of the old broad and that kid of yours that you lost, and you sat your ass back down. That takes guts. Despite the guns and all the other bullshit that you see when you look around at us, we're peaceful people. We don't want no trouble," he shrugs and smirks, "but we'll give it if it means we survive." By the looks of his face and his build, I have no doubt about that.

Behind him, the sound of footsteps echo and he breaks my stare to turn and look. Three of his men are on their way toward us, each with their weapons at the ready and all of them looking stressed.

"Trouble at the front gate?" Aiken asks.

"Yeah, boss. Bunch of zeds. Aimee's on night watch with Vicki. They need help up there," Ricky says. His eyes glance at me briefly before disregarding me altogether.

"You feel like giving us a hand," Aiken asks me, his eyes narrowing fractionally, "while you decide what you're doing?"

I glance at Ricky but he doesn't return my stare. If anything he looks vexed that I've even been asked to stay. Which of course only makes me want to help.

"Sure thing. We can call it a thank you for fixing up my leg," I say. "I won't owe you then," I add on, and Aiken nods.

"And saving your asses back out there on the road," Ricky replies. "Don't forget that."

My jaw ticks in irritation. "You didn't save all of us."

Ricky turns his body toward me. "Should learn to take better care of your kids then."

I step forward instinctually, but Aiken puts a hand on my chest. "Easy there." He looks at Ricky with a hard scowl. "I was just telling Mikey what a strong and helpful community we are at Haven and how every NEO member looks out for one another. If he's to join our community, perhaps you'd better be showing him some of that NEO hospitality." He sounds pissed, and Ricky swallows nervously.

"Sorry, boss." He looks at me, his expression a little less aggressive. "We could use the help, if you're willing."

"Sure," I reply, trying to tone down my own anger out of respect for Aiken. But I can already tell that Ricky and I are not going to be best buds.

"And Joan?" I ask Aiken.

He smiles. "She's already sleeping, my friend."

Ricky and the two men behind him begin to walk away, gesturing for me to follow. I glance at Aiken one last time before turning to follow them all. I'm not sure why I'm helping them, after all my internal ramblings about going out on my own and being selfish about survival. But here I am, heading over to kill some zeds for the sake of a safe place to sleep and a thank you for fixing up my leg.

Damn it, I'm getting as confusing as Nina.

Chapter Seven

As we get closer to the main gate, the sound of deaders can be heard on the other side. The loud, guttural growling and moaning they make gets louder with each heavy footstep I take. The steps to get up to the perimeter come into view and I jog past Ricky and the others and began to climb. I'm not sure why it's important to me that I get there before them. Maybe because I feel the need to prove myself. Maybe because I have the urge to kill some deaders and rid myself of some more of this rage.

Or maybe it's because I know it'll piss Ricky off that I get there before him. Yeah, I'm almost certain it's the last option.

I realize, as my head pops up to floor level, that these two people up here have no idea who I am. And I of course realize this almost too late as a boot comes toward my face. I manage to duck out of the away before I get a throat full of my own teeth.

"I come in peace!" I yell.

"There isn't any peace anymore," a female voice replies.

"That doesn't sound very New Earth Orderly," I call back. "Look, my name's Mikey, I've come to help—Aiken sent me." I take a chance and lift my head again, letting my gaze travel up to her.

"He hasn't mentioned anything to me," another woman says from farther back. "Last I saw was you being dragged in kicking and screaming."

I snort out a laugh. "I was not screaming." But I grin despite myself and know that I already like her.

"Vicki, just give him a damn weapon," Ricky says impatiently from below me.

Vicki steps back, and I climb the rest of the way up, eventually coming to stand beside her. She looks me over once to assess me, and finally happy, she hands me a rifle and a seven-inch knife from a basket.

"Over here," she says with a jerk of her head, her gaze only once drifting back to Ricky.

I follow her to the edge of the platform and look down to the other side. A large group of deaders are below, all looking up at us with a hungry glint in their eyes. Arms reaching, foul smell emanating, you know how they are. It's hard to distinguish how many are there, but if I had to take a rough guess, I'd say less than a hundred and more than one.

What? I said it was a rough guess.

"Where did they come from? We haven't seen a cluster like this for weeks," Ricky says as he moves to stand next to me. The other two guys are already moving their way farther along the perimeter, and a couple of the deaders that were watching have followed them along, looking up hopefully.

"I think they came out of the lake. I was doing a perimeter check with Kelli earlier today and it looked like there'd been a disturbance at the water's edge. I'm thinking something big got taken down," a Milana Vayntrub lookalike interrupts while looking through her scope, one eye squinting against it.

56

She's younger than Vicki, with pale-as-snow skin and long dark hair tied back at the nape of her neck. She's beautiful, but of course she's not Nina.

"Well shit, that's not good," Ricky says.

"Death never is," she retorts, still without looking away. "I think we can handle going hand to hand rather than waste the ammo." She finally pulls her eye away from the eyepiece and looks at me. A small frown puckers between her eyebrows. "I'm Aimee by the way."

"Mikey," I reply. "I'll come down with you."

Aimee laughs. "I'm not going down there. I'm a sharpshooter. I'll pick off any zeds that get too close and keep an eye on any more coming." Her gaze shifts to one of the other men. "Phil and Ricky normally go out. I'm sure they'd be happy for the help."

"Whatever works best," I reply.

Ricky, Phil, and I head back down the ladder and over to where the main gate is. Alfie and a huge beast of a dog, which looks like a German shepherd, are waiting for us. He nods a brief hello and begins to pull on a large chain. The main gate begins to open and all three of us and the dog slip outside, and then the gate closes behind us immediately.

Phil reaches down and pats the dog on the head as we begin to follow the stench and the growls. It lifts its nose to the air and nuzzles the palm of his hand, and I'd think it was a touching scene, but instead I'm left wondering how the hell I got myself into this mess as we come face to face with the deaders we were just watching.

Up close they're worse than expected. Their waterlogged bodies are bloated, and the stink from them is unbelievable. I'm only glad that it's dark and I can't see them too good in this lighting.

I grip the handle of my knife as the deaders begin to catch wind of us and turn in our direction. They stumble forward, the sound of their hungry growls getting louder and more eager the closer they get. I dance around the first one and come up on its back before it can turn, and then I slam my knife through its skull before it can turn to grab me.

It drops to the ground with my blade still in its head, and I fall to my knees to pull it back out, almost getting taken out by a deader that collapses on top of me. I grunt and throw the body off before scrambling over and straddling it so I can get close enough to thrust my knife through the side of its head.

Its body goes slack about the same time that its stomach decides enough is enough and splits wide open. Water and putrefied organs gush out all around me and I gag at the smell, which brings tears to my eyes. The entire mess begins to soak into my cargo pants and I stand back up quickly, panting at the exertion and grossness of it all, and knowing that I'll need some bleach to scrub this smell off my skin.

Ricky is fighting with a deader, but he seems to be handling it so I head over to help Phil, who has three of our dead enemies on him. I grab one of them by the scruff of the neck and drag it away from him. I swing its body around until it loses its balance and falls over, face first into the dirt. And then I put one foot on its back, reach down, and use my knife to snuff out its non-life.

Phil takes care of the other two with ease using a long piece of wood with a sharp blade on the end. One quick swipe and he takes them both out, and I almost applaud him, it's that cool a move. The German shepherd is by his side also, charging at the deaders' ankles or gnawing at them to make them fall over so that he, or I guess she, can ultimately tear the deaders' heads off with her teeth.

We take care of the others quickly, with Aimee and Vicki only having to fire off one round apiece. We all stand back, exhausted from the quick yet violent fight. My leg is throbbing again, and the German shepherd comes over and sniffs at my bandage. I'm seconds away from kicking it, because I'm having brutal flashbacks to the wild dogs in the road that caused this mess, when Phil comes over.

He kneels down and takes the dog's head in his hands, and begins to scratch behind the ears.

"Hello, girl. You did a great job, well done." He nuzzles against her, and I look to Ricky for a reaction.

He actually smiles and turns to walk away. "Come on, let's get back inside."

Phil stands up and looks at me. "This is Fluffy." He smiles. "She's had my back since day one." He looks back down at her. "Haven't you, girl? Yeah you have."

"She's yours?" I ask, making small conversation as we make our way back to the gate.

"Nah, not really," he says.

"Free spirit, huh?" I joke.

"Actually yeah, you could say that. I'm not normally a dog person, but Fluffy here saved me right at the start of all this, and we've been inseparable ever since." Phil walks through the open gate, Fluffy on his heels, and I follow in last.

"Damn!" Alfie says as I pass him. "That's bad."

59

"Thanks for that, Captain Obvious," I snap. I'm desperate to get out of these clothes now. The feeling of sloppy insides is sticking to my skin as it dries.

"Phil, the new guy is yours," Ricky calls as I pass him. He smirks and I want to punch him in the face and then ask questions later. But I don't. I try to play nice with the stupid ass instead. If not for my sake, then for Adam and Joan's.

"Sure thing," Phil says with a small laugh and then begins to walk away. "New guy, follow me."

"The name's Mikey," I say, catching up with him and throwing Ricky a scowl as I pass. "Where are we going?" I ask in irritation.

Not that I really care. I'm personally just glad for anywhere to stay right now. I'm exhausted, anxious, and in pain. I need some pain relief and some sleep, in that order. Then I can wake up early and set about trying to find Adam. Kid's gotta' be hiding somewhere close to the dog attack. I refuse to believe that he's dead. I don't think I could handle it if he was. That and Nina would haunt my ass if he was, and a ghostly ass-kicking from her is not what I want for the last days on this earth.

"Most people share when they first arrive. It's just until you get settled and you know your place." He smiles again, and I decide that I really like him. He seems like a good guy, and there aren't enough of them in the world anymore. He stops and pushes his glasses up his nose. A smirk sits on his face as he taps the side of his nose. "Also, no sense of smell."

"And don't we all know it," Aimee says as she sidles up to him and presses a kiss to his cheek. "I'll see you tomorrow, okay?"

Phil brushes some loose hair back from her face. "You know it."

60

She strokes the top of Fluffy's head before walking away, heading back up to the perimeter, and Phil watches her every step with a smile. He notices my stare and raises a hand to pat me on the back and then thinks better of it.

"Come on, dude, let's get you cleaned up." He turns and keeps on walking and I follow him, feeling self-conscious as we pass people and they grimace.

I get to see more of Haven, and the more of it I see, the more I wish Nina were here to see it with me. It's like a real street. A home away from home. With houses and stores and things that make me pine to go back in time, if only for one more day. It all seems so normal. I reckon this is the sort of street she would have lived on before the world went to shit. I can almost see her now, climbing into her car and heading to work. I'd lean in her window and kiss her on the mouth and tell her not to work too hard. And she'd laugh and probably call me something insulting. I smile and swallow the lump in my throat.

Phil's house is a large white-clad two-story job, with shutters on the windows and a swing on the porch. He climbs the three steps and stops at the top before turning to me, his expression full of concern. Fluffy sits by his feet and watches me carefully.

"Do you smoke?" he asks.

"No," I reply.

"Good stuff," he says with relief. "I'm a big smoker, and it's the one thing I prefer not to share if I can help it. I'll share my space, my booze, even my weed—because what fun is getting stoned on your own, right?" He laughs. "But not my cigarettes. I can tell me and you are going to get along great. Come on in, meet the family."

He opens the front door and I follow him in.

61

"Family?" I ask, smelling something strange as I shut the door behind me. Not so much strange but it definitely smells bad, yet I can't put my finger on what it is.

Phil laughs and turns a light on. I glance up at it with a frown. "Solar panels," he says by way of explanation.

"You have a family? Aimee?" I ask.

"Nah, she's a good girl, but we're nothing serious yet. I mean the kids—come and meet my kids." He laughs and continues moving through the house, checking every once in a while that I'm still following him.

"You have kids?" I ask, feeling unnerved as the smell gets stronger the deeper into the house we get. The man doesn't seem old enough to have kids—certainly not ones that can be left alone while he goes on guard duty.

I stand back warily as he opens a door to one of the back rooms, flicking the light on as he goes in. I stand in the doorway with my heart hammering in my chest. I can't see much in the room except what looks like wooden crates, but the smell is strong. And bad, if I'm honest. A few seconds later and Phil comes back to the doorway. His hair is tied back away from his face now, and in his arms is an animal. At first I think it's a puppy or a kitten, but then I notice the distinct stripe down its back.

"Is that a skunk?" I ask, taking a step backwards.

Phil smiles widely. "Sure is. This is Lavender."

The skunk—sorry, *Lavender*—sticks her head up and looks at me with her small, beady eyes.

"Sure, you have a pet skunk, that's okay, I guess," I say with a grimace, keeping an eye on her ass to make sure that tail of hers doesn't lift.

Phil chuckles. "It's okay, she's as soft as anything. She won't spray you unless she feels threatened. Skunks make great pets, honest. She's only a baby and she's as sweet as anything. I rescued her from certain death a couple of weeks ago. Come and meet the rest of the gang." He steps back into the room, and I once again wonder if Ashton is going to jump out at me any moment now. I can only be glad that I'm not currently holding onto that skunk in case she might squirt in fright.

"The rest?" I say, following him in and wishing I hadn't. "Are you insane?" I ask, momentarily stunned as I look around at the crates and tanks of animals and insects.

I've never been a big animal fan, but I've had girlfriends who were. That was always in the zone of puppies and kittens, maybe even a guinea pig. Hell, one ex even kept a horse, and I was cool with that. Insects, however, are my nemesis I guess you could say. And as Phil reaches into a glass tank and gently coaxes a tarantula into the palm of his hand, I'm reminded why.

"This," he says coming toward me slowly with another of his trademarks smiles, "is Miss Foxxxy Love. Easy on the eye and heavy on the X's."

Chapter Eight

"You keep that thing away from me," I whisper-shout, backing up another step.

"It's okay, dude, she won't hurt. She's a beautiful pussycat, honest!" Phil says seriously.

I take another step back. "That thing might be able to *eat* a damn pussycat, but she definitely isn't one." I stumble over my own feet and almost land on my ass. "Seriously, don't bring that near me."

I like to think I'm a brave man. I mean, I've come up against a lot of things in my life—everything from the police to gangsters to henchmen to zombies. I'm actually quite partial to a little danger now and then, and never shy away from a fight. But spiders…those things make me break out in hives. And that big—supposedly beautiful—beast in the palm of Phil's hand is making every part of me itch.

"Okay, okay, I'll put her away. Don't freak out." He laughs and walks back toward her tank and places her carefully back inside it. "Everything's okay, darlin'. I hope you've had a good day. I've missed you."

He puts the cover on top of the tank as he speaks to it—sorry *her*—like he expects her to answer him at any moment. Perhaps even tell him about the various other bugs she's captured and tortured throughout the day. Maybe she painted her toenails and soaked in the tub. Wait, do spiders even have toenails? I'm 99% certain they don't, yet I still shudder at the possibility. I've seen a lot of messed-up shit since the end of the world, and if there's one thing I've learned it's that you can never take things for granted—not anymore.

"I'm taking it this is why you and Aimee aren't a serious thing then," I say, feeling better now that the giant man-eating spider is away.

He looks over at me and grins while he moves from animal to animal, talking to each one of them and checking their food and water.

"Yeah, sort of, but she'll come around. She just needs to realize that these will always be my first loves. I mean, I care about Aimee—she's beautiful and she's really fun to be around—but I'd pick these guys over her or anyone else." He stares hard at a long tank with a snake in it. "Well, maybe not. But these guys are my family, and whoever stays here needs to accept them as that."

He stands up and looks across to me, and I realize that he's waiting for me to reply. The animals behind him seem restless, and that in turn makes me even more uncomfortable.

"Do you ever let them out?" I ask, swallowing down the hard lump in my throat.

He pushes his glasses up his nose and looks confused, so I continue.

"You know, to like run around or climb the walls or…" …*wrap themselves around my throat in the night and squeeze the life out of me,* I think.

Phil laughs again and comes toward me. He slaps me on the back. "Don't let your mind run away with you, dude." He guides me from the room and shuts the door behind us. "You need to shower and change clothes. I might not have a sense of smell, but these guys sure do, and they are not happy about it right now."

I'm so glad to be out of that room that it takes me a moment to realize he's telling me that I stink. But I don't have time to be offended as he guides me toward a small room at the top of the stairs.

"Shower runs a little cold at times, towels are under the sink, and the body wash is on the shelf." He turns to walk back down the stairs before stopping and looking back at me. "Oh, and don't use my loofah."

And by his serious expression I can tell that he's not messing around.

"All right," I say.

"You're sticking around for a while, right?" he asks, his expression still serious.

I shrug. "We'll see what happens. I need to find someone."

"The kid," he says.

"Yeah." I frown. "How'd you know?"

Phil smiles. "Word travels fast in Haven. If you're sticking around, that means you're a NEO, and that means you've got every resource available to you."

"That's good to know," I say. And it is. It's really good to know. The more I learn about this place, the more it seems too good to be true. But right now, I'm fresh out of other options. My leg is throbbing painfully, and I still need to get a shot for the dog bite.

Phil turns and makes his way back down the stairs and goes into the small room. I look around, feeling weirded out by the normality of everything, until I catch sight of my reflection—

which is anything but normal. I stare at my reflection in the mirror and another shudder runs through me as I see how filthy I am. It's not the sort of thing that you normally give a shit about. Surviving day to day, hour to hour, you don't have time to think about how bad you might smell, or how sweat-soaked your body might be. It's only times like this, when you get to hit the pause button on this messed-up life and you come face to face with yourself. It's then that you see, then that you know, how much this world is killing you.

I might be a living, breathing man, but I'm dying from the inside out regardless. And with Nina gone, I'm not sure if there's anything left to make me want to keep on going. I'm not talking about putting a bullet in my own head or some crazy shit like that, but I have to admit to myself, if only myself, that the thought of this all being over sounds like heaven right now. And maybe I'm jealous of Nina and the fact that she's finally out of all this. Probably laughing it up in heaven and drinking margaritas on the beach.

I strip and turn the shower on before climbing in. Phil isn't the cleanliest of guys when it comes to housekeeping, but then what guy ever really is? But he obviously takes his self-hygiene seriously, by the amount of products on the shelf. There's everything from a bar of soap to squirty body wash, and even a bottle of bubble bath. Not to mention the loofah, of course. He may not have a sense of smell, but at least he makes an effort for the sake of everyone else.

The bathroom is small, and the bulb isn't too bright, meaning that there are shadows cast on the walls that make me nervous. I stand under the water and let it run over my body, and I try to enjoy it while I can, but my gaze keeps straying to the shower curtain around the tub and the thought that anything could be on the other side of it. Eventually I can't take it anymore and I pull the curtain back, forgoing any privacy. Because old habits die hard, and danger is only ever one step away from safety.

After my shower I climb out and dry myself before staring down at my putrid clothes with rotten guts all over them. The thought of putting them back on makes me feel sick. A sharp knock on the door makes me jump, and I keep the towel wrapped around my waist as I pull the door open a crack and look out.

Phil is there, laden down with a fresh set of brightly colored clothing for me. "Thought you could use these," he says with a smile. "And this." He hands me two bottles—one looks like antibiotics and the other pain relief, which is good because my leg is really beginning to hurt now.

"You have no idea," I reply and gratefully take them.

"Alfie swung by and said I needed to take you over to him tomorrow so you can get that shot." Phil leaves and shuts the door behind him, and I open the bottles and throw some of the pills to the back of my throat. I probably should have checked the labels first, or at least tried to be a little more cautious, but I'm just so relieved to be clean and have some pain relief.

Once dressed I take another look at myself in the mirror and contemplate shaving off my stubbly beard and maybe even shaving my head again, since the hair is now just about long enough to be tied back. I run my hands through the hair on my head, eventually deciding I can't be bothered, and instead I snag one of the hair bands from the bathroom cabinet and tie my hair back. I run a hand over my jaw and decide I can sort that out tomorrow too, if at all.

I look strange, not like myself at all. Maybe that's not such a bad thing and that's why I decide to leave it all on. The idea of being someone else makes me feel better. I never liked the man I was before. I had done wrong and done good, yet it all accounted for nothing as I had lost everything and everyone anyway.

Even my eyes seem different, almost like my soul has been sucked out of them, and now the eyes that stare back at me are cold and dead.

I leave the bathroom with my own clothes balled into as small a package as I can get them. They need to be tossed. No, they need to be burned, for everyone's sake. My eyes are watering just holding them, and I'm a little shocked that I actually wore them without noticing the smell so much. Fluffy is sitting outside the bathroom door and she follows me down the stairs, never taking her eyes off me the whole time. I like that she's wary of me—it means she can be trusted. Because you should never trust someone you don't know. Shit, maybe you should never trust someone you *do* know.

Phil comes out of the animal room with a long snake draped over his shoulders, its hissing head balanced in his hand. "Hey, dude. Feel better?" he asks cheerily.

"Much," I say, eyeing up the snake. "Do those things bite?"

"Of course. Mostly they just swallow their prey whole, though," he replies without skipping a beat. "I mean snakes in general bite when they feel threatened, but not Zazz here. She's used to being held by me, so she's friendly. And she's already been fed." He winks at me and I grimace.

"Zazz?" I question.

"Yeah, Zazz Blammyatazz," he chuckles. "Zazz for short."

"You name all of your animals?"

"Yeah, dude, they're my family, they've gotta'' have names. There's Clipper, Vlad the Nibbler, Lavender, Zazz, Miss Foxxxy

Love, and tons more." He laughs again. "Come on, let me show you your room and you can get some sleep. Aiken wants to see you first thing tomorrow. He likes you." Phil wanders into the other room, and I think about going in after him but change my mind. Thankfully, a minute or so later he comes back out. "You planning on sticking around then, dude?"

I frown, because as much as I want to go all Lone Ranger-style, I know I won't. Being on my own has its benefits, but it also has its drawbacks. And as much as I hate to admit it, I'm a people person now. Besides, until we find Adam, I can't go anywhere.

"I guess so, if I have any value to the group." I shrug.

"Everyone has value. It's whether you choose to use it wisely or not." Phil's expression grows serious for a fleeting moment—so fleeting that I wonder if I imagined it. Then he claps his hands and shows me to my room.

Later that night, as I lie on my bed, I think about this place and of course I think about Nina. Would she want me to stay? Or would she want me to head to the cabin on the island, like we talked about? I have no idea anymore, but I know that whatever happens, until I find Adam I won't be going anywhere.

Chapter Nine

I wake to the sound of snoring, and it's not my own, and I jump up, my hand reaching out for a gun, a knife, anything to defend myself with. Instead it lands on a furry head and I jump upright in bed.

Fluffy's snoring ceases and her eyes open, and then we're staring at one another wondering what the hell is going on. Eventually she closes her eyes again, deciding I'm not currently a threat, or that sleep is more important right now. As her snoring starts up again, she lets rip with a horrendous smell that is worse than what washed off me last night, and I'm almost surprised that she didn't cock her leg up.

"Oh God," I say and I dive out of bed.

The German shepherd is lying on her back, her front paws curled upwards and her tongue lolling out of her mouth as if we just reenacted a love scene from a porno and she's all worn out from her hard stint of submission. Her head pops up and her eyes follow me as I walk the room to the door, her nose twitching like I made that damn horrendous smell. Moments later she follows me out of the room, stopping halfway down the stairs to stretch.

I head for the kitchen, where mercifully, I can smell coffee. And sure enough, there's a coffee pot brewing. I grab a mug and pour myself some, giving myself a moment to relish in the taste of the hot caffeine as it slides down my grateful throat. The morning sun is pouring in through the kitchen window and I head over to it and look out, seeing people milling around on the street with seemingly nothing to do but go about their everyday lives like this isn't the end of the world.

I open the back door and look out, seeing Phil sitting on the back step drinking a coffee and smoking a cigarette. He looks up as I approach, and he yawns and smiles. In the cold light of day I can see that he's older than I first thought, perhaps mid-thirties, where last night I had thought he was in his twenties given his taste in Hawaiian shirts and long hair.

He pushes his glasses up his nose and offers me a smile. "Morning, dude."

"Morning. I um, I got a coffee, hope that's okay."

He nods. "Of course, *me casa es su casa*, dude." Fluffy sits herself down next to Phil and he strokes the top of her head. "Morning, girl."

"She umm, she slept in my bed," I say, feeling like an animal pervert even though nothing happened between me and Fluffy.

Phil shakes his head and finishes off his cigarette before stubbing it out by his foot. He stands back up. "Nah, you slept in her bed. Come on," he says with a laugh. He goes inside, coming out moments later with a large machete and a handgun, and he attaches both of them to his belt.

He hands me a hatchet and a gun also, and I stare at him wide-eyed for a moment, surprised that I'm allowed a weapon inside the town at all. In fact, as I look around I can see that everyone is carrying a weapon of some sort—even the teenagers have something strapped to their hips or backs. Longswords, small machetes, even an axe or two, and almost everyone seems to have a gun.

"What?" Phil asks.

I look at him, my wide-eyed stare turning into a frown.

"You're wondering why we let everyone walk around with weapons on show?"

"Well yeah. I guess it just seems like everyone here is relaxed and at ease. I didn't expect them all to be armed to the teeth." I watch a man and a teenage boy walk past. The man's arm is across the shoulder of the teenage boy in a fatherly gesture, and the kid is looking up at the man with respect. It makes my heart ache.

"This is Haven—homes for everyone and protection for all. We're all NEO and we all protect each other, no matter what. We have nothing to fear from anyone inside these walls. It's outside of them that's the danger." Phil pats Fluffy on the head and then heads down the steps.

All three of us—Fluffy, Phil, and I—walk through Haven, and I try to take in as much of it as I can. The walls surrounding this place are high, but not overbearingly so. They obviously have their shit together, I decide. I just hope they really are the good guys, because so far it would seem that I have a habit of picking the wrong team.

"Aiken trusts us all to look out for one another. If there is an issue, he has ways to deal with it. But we're all here for the same thing," Phil says. "And that's reason enough to keep the peace."

"And what's that?" I ask. "The reason you're all here."

"To live," he replies with genuine confusion at my question.

We pass Kelli and she waves at me, though she doesn't look like she did last night with her dress and boots. Today she's wearing army camo pants and a white tank with a gun holster hanging at her hip. She keeps on walking to wherever she's going and I turn back to Phil.

73

"Kelli's a good girl, you'll like her," he says with a grin.

"It's not like that," I reply, immediately shooting down his thought, and he nods and looks away.

Phil takes the three steps up to one of the larger houses and knocks at the door. The house isn't like the rest. It's all brown brick and wood instead of the white of the other buildings, and I can't decide whether this is purposeful or if it just wasn't finished before the apocalypse. Walking around, I can see that not everything here is finished, though for every half-built dwelling there are three or four people working on it.

A mean looking dude opens the door and we're ushered inside and directed through to the living room. The walls have been painted, but barring a lick of paint, there's nothing else on them—no photos or artwork, not even a map, it's oddly disconcerting compared to the rest of the room. The room is part homely, part work/office space, and part, 'I've been too busy surviving the apocalypse to give it my own personal stamp.' I like it though. It makes Aiken seem like even more of the real deal. Like he's not just putting on a leader front for the sake of the easy life and the finer things. He doesn't seem to care about how things look for himself, and by the way people are walking around with weapons, he clearly trusts his people to not go on a killing rampage.

Aiken is standing by the window, talking to one of the women I met last night. Vicki, I think her name is. His expression is serious, verging on almost angry. When he sees me, he stops talking and sends her away, but I make a mental note to try and find her and talk to her later. I want to know what that conversation was all about.

"Mikey, my boy, how'd you sleep?" Aiken comes toward me and holds his hand out. "Phil here looking after you, I hope?"

I shake his hand and nod. "Yeah, barring the giant snakes and spiders, and Fluffy's noxious farts, we're getting along pretty well, thanks."

Aiken and Phil laugh, and as if on cue, Fluffy lets rip with another fart.

"She always does that after a fight," Phil clarifies, as if the death smell emanating from her ass needs explaining. "I think it's the zeds—they don't agree with her guts. I'm going to take her for a quick walk, let her clear out the old pipes."

Phil nods to Aiken and leaves with Fluffy at his heels. Aiken directs us both to his sofa and I sit opposite him, feeling anxious and apprehensive.

"So look, I'm not going to beat around the bush—we'd like you to stay, Mikey. There's not many good people out there, at least not ones that can fight like you can. What can I say to convince you?" Aiken holds his hands out, palms up.

I know that this is my cue to milk this place for everything it has, get myself a decent home, some great weapons, a vehicle, and probably a ton of whisky and coffee, and then get the fuck out of here. But the truth is, I don't want to be that person anymore. I like that Aiken sees me as one of the good guys. I don't think I've ever really been one of those, and I can't deny the warm fuzzies it gives me. So yes, I want to stay, but I also don't want to not tell the truth and bring trouble to this group, so I decide to come clean and let Aiken in on my past.

"I'd love to stay."

"Well that's great!" He claps his hands together and smiles, the red scar on his cheek rising.

"But I should warn you," I say, hating to spoil the warm welcome. "I'm being hunted. At least I *was* being hunted before." All being well, Nina took out Fallon and the rest are history, but you never know with those guys. And Fallon had lived through a lot worse than a gunshot wound. "They may have even given up hunting me now…now that they've taken everything from me," I say, taking a deep breath. "Either way, I wanted to be upfront and let you know the truth before you make your decision."

My stomach is in knots as I speak. I want to stay, to do Nina proud and help protect people like she always did. I don't want to run anymore, hiding from my dirty secrets and even dirtier past, but I come with a lot of baggage, and it may be too heavy for others to carry. I can understand that. Some days I find it too heavy to carry that burden also.

"These people," Aiken begins, his face a mask of concern.

"The Forgotten," I say, knowing that to give up the name of the group will be the real clincher. If Aiken has heard of them I've probably just fucked myself, and if he hasn't, well, he probably should if I'm going to stay.

I notice the subtle change in his posture, but his expression doesn't give anything away.

"They've killed to get to you?" he asks, leaning forward, his frown deepening.

"Yeah."

"So, I'm going to take it that you're a valuable asset to them."

"That's not a question," I reply, trying to keep my calm, but I'm already disliking the direction of his questions.

Aiken laughs dryly. "No, sir, it's not. But I should know exactly who you are and why they're killing people to get to you if I'm going to let you stay. You've told me half of the story—now I'm asking for the rest."

I think over his request for a moment, but it doesn't take long for me to agree that he should know the full story. So I tell it to him, and I don't leave anything out. I tell him how I came to be a part of the Forgotten, who they are, and why they are like they are. And I tell him why I left. The death count is high, and the bodies are racked up, but through it all Aiken doesn't flinch or show any emotion. And then I get to the part about Nina, and how she was the craziest woman I have ever met, and how she sacrificed herself for me and Adam and Joan, and how I let her.

With each word I speak, I feel worse and worse, my decision to leave her behind to save Joan and Adam, like she had asked, feeling like the wrong one.

"So, if she killed him, then maybe it's over now, maybe it's not. And if he killed her, he could still be looking for me." I shake my head, letting my guilty gaze slip from Aiken's and slide to the floor like a puddle. "But either way, I can't go back and find out, just in case. Because if I do and they get me, she'll never forgive me, and it will all have been for nothing. Do you get that, man? Do you understand? So either way, I've lost her no matter what." I think over those words, and how hard they still are to digest.

In a world like this, you get attached to people quickly. It can't be helped, it's just nature, because you never know when people will be snatched away from you. You never know when it's all going to be over. So you love hard, fight hard, give everything, because it's the only way to live anymore. We, as humanity, have no future. It's the little minutes, the seconds between waking and sleeping—those are the ones that matter the most. The ones we pray for and hope for. We all want more of those quiet moments where life seems worth a damn again. But there's never enough of them to go around.

"Unless," Aiken begins, and I look up, my gaze connecting with his. "Unless she killed him and lived and then came to find you."

I've actually had that same thought too, and it's one of the only real reasons that going to the island where her parents-in-law lived could still be a viable option. Because I'm pretty sure that's where she would head too. But if I went there and she didn't come, then I'd know for certain.

"There's always that, I guess," I mumble, my thoughts still lost as I think about the Forgotten and their way of life.

To think I had once been with them and had that same mentality makes me feel sick. But there's no denying some of the things I've done. They're the things that keep me awake at night when all I want to do is sleep. Especially since Nina had told me what life was really like on the inside of those walled cities—the murder and rape, the starvation. Fallon and his families have a better chance of survival on the outside, but there's never going to be a way to get him to see that.

Aiken stands up and walks toward the window. His expression is serious and he's clearly trying to decide if I'm worth the risk or not. I sit in silence, waiting for the axe to descend, and knowing that no matter what happens—if he sends me and Joan away or not—I'm glad that I've told him the truth. I've already met some good people here, people that don't deserve to die because of my mistakes. I've done that to too many people already, and I won't let it happen again.

Aiken finally turns around to face me, and I stand up, ready to hear my sentence.

"Well Mikey, I'm not going to lie, that's a fucked-up story for sure. But," he walks toward me, "I can see that you're a good person still. You haven't let this stuff blacken your soul."

"I've done some bad things, Aiken," I reply almost immediately, my chin lifted.

He laughs lightly. "We all have, my friend. None of us is blame free. But it's how you act now that matters to me, and from what I've seen you're worth the risk."

I stare at him in confusion, because I honestly expected him to kick me out—probably let Joan stay, but I was definitely out of here. And my heart had ached at the thought of Adam. What would I do? How could I find him on my own? But here Aiken is, taking a chance on me, even after I told him the truth about the shit that comes part and parcel with me.

I remember having a similar conversation with JD a long while back—though he hadn't known the entire truth, of course. Only bits of it. But, like Aiken, he'd taken me on board and let me stay with his group. It hadn't ended well for him, and I can't help but worry that it won't end well for Aiken either.

"At some point we're probably going to have to face these Forgotten people, but I'm not too concerned by that," Aiken says with a wave of his hand. "We have a good, strong team here. *Everyone* can fight to some degree or another, and *everyone* will. Because that's what we do here. We stand together, as one force, and we will not be stopped by the evil of this world."

He holds out his hand and I look down at it and then back up to him as I shake it, hard, feeling eternally grateful for this chance.

"I meant what I said to you, Mikey. We'll do anything to protect each other here. We train each other in whatever skills we have, and we share our rations and knowledge. It's the only way to make this work. You have a lot of knowledge which I think you could impart on our group…our family, and in turn, we have a lot we can share with you. We are the New Earth Order, and we will bring order to this new earth."

I nod and smile, uncertain as to what to say to that. The sentiment is great, but it's also worrying. Have I just jumped from one insane group to another? God, I hope not.

"Now, about your friend out there—Adam, was it?"

"Yeah."

"Little kid, right?"

"Yes, sir." I nod.

Aiken rubs a hand over his jaw. "Well, we'll need to arrange a search party for him. And quickly. I'll ask O'Donnell to go along—she's a great tracker and hunter, and a prepper through and through, and so is Ricky, my number one."

I swallow. "Aiken, if I may, I have a feeling Ricky doesn't like me too much." I sound like a kid in school—*Ricky won't be my friend*—but still, I feel the obvious need for it to be stated, regardless of how it makes me sound. "Not that I give a shit," I add on. "But do you really think he's the best one to come along with us?"

Okay, so maybe I do care how it makes me sound.

Aiken laughs. "He doesn't like much of anyone these days—at least not until they've proved themselves—but he'll have your back regardless."

"Because that's how things are done around here," I state. It isn't a question, and if I'm being honest, that unwavering loyalty can be seen as a bad thing as much a good. I saw what it could do when I was a part of the Forgotten.

"Pretty much."

"So the sheep follow blindly?" I ask, deciding that maybe it's time for me to see the color of his blood, since he'd seen mine and then gone on to root through the skeletons in my closet.

His smirk grows wider. "The sheep are led to where the food, warm beds, and safety are at, because they want to sleep soundly at night knowing that they're not going to be chewed up out there." He jerks his thumb toward the window. "Plus, I've heard the shepherd is a handsome fucker."

I burst out laughing, unable to contain my surprise. Aiken laughs too and then pats me on the back.

"Look, we don't go around killing strangers, but we only take in those that we think will be good for the group—people that can give as well as take. You must know that. We do things as a team, a group…a family, if that suits. We protect each other at all costs. We don't murder and maim on a whim, we don't execute people because they have what we want or they look at us the wrong way. We give a shit about our people." He shrugs. "About all people, but not everyone has something to offer, and we don't take in leeches. Is that what you want to hear?"

"Pretty much, yeah." I nod.

"We're trying to build something good here, a society of like-minded people who want to save this country, each other—hell, maybe even the world. You don't have to stay, you can go, but like I said last night, we could use someone like you here. We can never have enough fighters with a conscience."

81

I open my mouth to speak, but voices can be heard coming in from the front door, and I recognize one voice in particular right away: Joan's.

She comes into the room, followed by a woman and teenager. Joan is the only one smiling.

"Aiken, I'm done. I can't spend another goddamned minute with her!" the woman says, ignoring the scowl from Joan.

"I was only singing in the shower!" Joan says, placing her hands on her hips.

"You sang—"

"Ninety-nine bottles of beer on the wall?" I interrupt.

Chapter Ten

The other woman stops talking and stares at me. "Yeah, actually."

I laugh. "I told you to stay out of trouble, Crazy Pants."

"I was only singing!"

"It was annoying!" the teenager says, on her face a look of fearless defiance that only a teenager could have. "Really fucking annoying!"

"Language, Moo!" the other woman snaps.

Joan steps forward and jabs a bony finger toward the woman and Moo. "Poppycock! My fella used to love my singing. It's you and all of your teenage gangster rap. A cuss word in every sentence and grabbing your crotches like you're trying to hold your pants up! Your music insults the blacks, the whites, and calls all women bitches! Now that's annoying, young lady!" Joan glares at Moo.

"I wasn't even playing any music, you crazy old bat. It was five a.m.!" Moo yells loud enough to make my ears ring. A teenager's fury knows no bounds.

"What? So now you're the timekeeper?" Joan replies indignantly.

I try not to laugh, but it's hard not to because for once I'm not stuck in the middle of Joan's craziness and I can appreciate the humor in it.

"All right, all right," Aiken says, his voice commanding everyone's silence and respect in equal measures. "Joan, is it? No more singing unless you're on your own, you got that? That's an order."

Joan nods and sticks her tongue out at the teenage girl as if she's won the argument.

"SJ, meet our new recruit Mikey," Aiken says, introducing me.

SJ reaches over to shake my hand. Her grip is firm, though her hands are soft. "Pleased to meet you. This is my daughter Moo."

I nod at both of them, happy to see a gun at both of their hips. Nothing pleases me more than seeing that. It means that there's enough trust between everyone to deem it acceptable. It means that no one walks around unarmed. And it means that Aiken wasn't bullshitting me when he said that everyone here pitches in when it comes to jobs and fighting.

"Is she a friend of yours?" SJ says, jabbing a thumb in Joan's direction.

I glance at Joan, who's currently picking her nose and wiping it down her shirt, and I hesitate, wanting to say no, but in the realm of being truthful about everything I can't deny Joan completely.

"Yeah, sort of," I relent. "I've been entrusted to keep her alive."

"Well, she has no skills, she's batshit crazy, and she's annoying as fuck. She can't stay," SJ says to me before turning her gaze to Aiken. "Please say she can't stay!"

Aiken rubs a hand over his jaw, his gaze slipping from SJ to Joan before coming back around to me. "Unless she's got a skill, she can't stay, Mikey." He shrugs, and I know he's serious. Especially after the speech he just gave me about what this new society is all about.

I look toward Joan, who at least has the decency to look worried.

"Joan?" I plead. Because I'm hoping she's going to pull something out of the bag, because I don't want to leave her, but I can't let her go out there alone either. And of course, the bigger issue is, I need the NEOs help me find Adam.

Joan puts her hands on her hips and blows some loose hair out of her face like she's flustered and frustrated with all of us. And perhaps she is. Perhaps in her world, we're the ones inconveniencing her.

"Well, I'll tell you, I'm offended. No, more than that, scratch that off completely, wipe the sides and dust the shelves, vacuum the floor and maybe even mop up too. Because *that's* how hurt I am that you all think I have no skills." Joan feigns tears, but none of us are convinced.

She blows at the hair in her face again, going a little cross-eyed as she does.

Aiken looks to me and purses his lips, and I notice SJ and Moo are both smiling, happy in the thought that they've gotten rid of their new annoying-as-hell neighbor.

Ricky comes in from the hallway and looks at Joan. I wonder how long he's been standing there listening in on everyone's conversation. "We'll take you somewhere safe, ma'am," he says to Joan. "Give you some food and a pistol. You'll be okay." He smiles as if dropping this crazy bitch off in the middle of a zombie-riddled world with a picnic and a handgun isn't the worst thing he's ever done in his life.

Joan reaches back and slaps him across the face as hard as she can, and I'm already guessing the handprint is going to stay there for at least the next hour or two. The poor guy looks stunned into submission and I have to hold back the laugh I want to release.

"I'll have you know that I have many skills, young man. Many!" she snaps, and then glares over at Aiken. "I can cook, I can sew, I can knit, and I can bake. I can make clothes, blankets, hats, scarves, coats, gloves, teddy bears, curtains, practically anything with wool. And did I mention that I can sew?" She looks furiously around at everyone. "And, did I mention that I can knit?" She folds her arms in front of her chest and raises a gray, bushy eyebrow at Ricky, who's itching to pull out his gun on her, by his angry expression when he looks Aiken's way. "And bake!"

Joan gaze snakes Ricky up and down. "And you, sir, you need some new shirts, I bet—not to mention that I bet your socks haven't been darned in many months."

Silence falls around the room as everyone takes in Joan's furious glare at Ricky, and then Aiken suddenly throws his head back and barks out a laugh. When he manages to compose himself, he claps his hands and looks over at Ricky. "Well, it's settled then. She stays." He glances at me. "And Mikey stays. So, welcome to Haven, friends, and welcome to the New Earth Order!"

SJ and Moo glare at Aiken and storm out of the room. "She's not staying with us!" SJ calls back as she leaves Aiken's house. I glance at Aiken but he's just grinning.

"She's a feisty one," he says. "But she'll come around."

"I need to go search for Adam today. He won't survive out there without us," I say, suddenly feeling sick at the thought that we left him out there all alone. At the time it seemed like we didn't have a choice. I was injured, bleeding to death, deaders were on the way—not to mention the wild dogs, which are still out there somewhere. But when you strip it all back, the truth is, we left a little boy out in the middle of nowhere with danger all around him. And whereas last night I wasn't so sure what Nina would have done in that situation, now it's all too clear to me: she would never have left him.

Aiken nods, his expression serious. "Like I said, O'Donnell and Ricky will go with you." He glances over as Phil comes back in. "Phil? You happy to help out on an S&R?"

Phil comes farther into the room. "Of course, anything for this dude. Me and Fluffy would be happy to help."

"Well, it's decided then. Grab some gear and get going. This is a rescue mission, and time is of the essence, people."

"Can I come?" Joan asks, and from her grave expression she's being serious, but there isn't a chance in hell that I'm bringing her with me.

I shake my head. "No, I need you to stay here."

Joan practically snarls at me, baring her teeth like a vicious dog. The image sends a shiver down my spine and a throb through my bite mark.

"I want to help," Joan says, her wrinkled mouth pursed in frustration.

Everyone takes that moment to leave the room, realizing the tension of the situation, and I try to choose my words carefully so as not to rile her up any more. The truth is, if she wants to come I can't stop her. But she would only end up causing me more grief out there on the road.

"I need to do this on my own. I need eyes here, making sure this place is safe enough to bring the boy back to," I say calmly, hoping to get through to her.

"I can help though," she says, grabbing the knitting needles from the long, deep pockets of her floral skirt and thrusting them forward like she's spearing a fish. "I know I'm not always...with it." She looks into my face, the gray of her eyes holding me steady. "But I can fight, and I'll fight for that little boy."

And by God, I believe her. She isn't the weak and feeble old lady that she lets people think. She's a survivor, and you can't train for that sort of thing. You either have it or you don't.

I place a hand on her shoulder. "I know, Joan, I know you will. But I made a promise to keep you and Adam safe, and so far I'm not doing too good a job. Taking you back out there, back into that hell beyond these walls, that's not a good way to keep you alive. At least if I know that you're here, keeping your eyes and ears to the ground for me, I'll be able to concentrate on finding Adam and bringing him back alive."

I realize that I'm being genuine in everything I say to her, and I'm not certain who's more surprised by that fact—me or Joan. I guess the old broad has grown on me.

"I'll hold down the fort here then," she says, clearly unhappy still, but relenting anyway. "Make sure it's safe to bring the little one back to. That sound good?"

I smile and nod. "That sounds perfect, Joan."

She smiles at me, a giant-assed beaming smile that ignites a spark in her eyes. "You called me by my name."

"You're one of the team now," I say with a smile. "Now let me go find the kid."

She reaches out and puts a hand on my shoulder. "All right, Mikey. I've got your back. I'll keep this place safer than a wax model in a candle factory."

She turns on her heel and walks away, and I stare after her, fucking clueless as to what she means. Seconds later, Phil and

Ricky come back into the room. Phil is grinning, and Ricky has his stony-faced expression still on, but I know that both of them have been listening in on the conversation I just had. I feel a pang of unease that they heard me say I didn't entirely trust this group yet, but if either of them thinks anything about it, neither of them say anything.

We head out and load up a truck with supplies. Mainly weapons—guns and knives, of which the NEOs thankfully seem to have an abundance. Phil has a long goodbye with Aimee until Fluffy begins to bark to get his attention. They kiss one last time and then Alfie is pulling back the gate and letting us out of Haven. I watch through the back window of the truck with unease until the gate is closed and Haven is out of sight.

Phil and O'Donnell talk nonstop about mundane shit, and I join in every once in a while. Ricky is driving and is silent the entire time. I'm not sure whether it's me or if he's just not a chatty guy, but I try to appear nonchalant about his silence and listen to what Phil and O'Donnell are saying. Mostly, though, I watch the world pass me by and I silently pray to God that Adam is okay.

The journey seems much longer as we head back to the spot in the road where we were ambushed by the killer hounds, and we all get out of the vehicle. I know it's this exact spot, not just by the farmhouse that we stop outside of, but because of the deaders on their knees chewing on the parts of dead dog that we left in the road the previous night.

"That's gross," O'Donnell says, jumping down the last step, her gaze directed toward the three deaders on their hands and knees. She's wearing figure-hugging shorts that make it hard for me and Ricky to take our eyes off of her ass. She sees us looking and grins before shaking her head. "It would be great if either of you could help out instead of gawping at me."

I look away first, with thoughts of Nina in my head. I move past O'Donnell and head toward the deaders on their knees. She was completely accurate though: it really is gross.

One of them is licking at the ground where I almost bled out, and I decide that that particular deader is mine. If it really wants to taste me that much, then it can fight me for the fucking privilege.

I step up to it as Ricky and O'Donnell make easy business of the other two. It doesn't seem to notice me for a moment, but then like a sixth sense its head turns as it lifts its face to the air and begins to sniff me out. It eventually glances back over its rotten shoulder and our gazes collide. The deader is young—just a kid, really—and part of me expects it to be Adam.

I can't say that part of me doesn't want that to be the case. At least then the guilt that's been eating away at me would be over with. I could get on with the damage control instead of feeling like a piece of shit for leaving him out here all night. I guess that makes me a coward. I want to hurry up and find his dead body because I know he's already gone, yet until I find him I can never rest easy again. It's a shitty thing to think, but the thoughts are still there no matter how shitty I feel about them.

Besides, this world is no place for a child. What chance does he have when all anyone can offer him is relative safety behind some walls until he's old enough to have to be useful to someone?

Old enough to fight, old enough to die, is all I can think.

But of course it isn't Adam. It's just some other poor dead kid that was unlucky enough to get killed at some point, only to wake and find himself with an unquenchable thirst for human blood and meat. Probably killed by his own parents, who had loved him dearly right up until the point that the hunger that drove them onwards was more important than the person they had created and brought into this world.

I don't use the gun at my hip, instead favoring the freshly sharpened hatchet that Phil gave me. I raise it up as the deader kid stands and groans, its gray rotten hands reaching for me like I'm an ice-cream cone. I slice right across the top of its head, through the center of its forehead so that I chop its brain in half, and it dies instantly. The machete sticks halfway through, which is annoying, but at least I've killed it.

I kick the kid in the chest, but the hatchet is lodged in its skull tight so I have to kick several times while simultaneously holding onto the handle of the hatchet before finally dislodging it from its skull. It falls backwards like a sack of rotten meat, its blank-eyed stare looking out across the blacktop as if hoping someone is coming to give it a ride to wherever it needs to go. But its journey is finally over and no one is coming to save it. Him.

Unlike Adam. I will find him and save him. I have to, I think grimly.

"Thought that was gonna' be a keeper," Phil laughs. Fluffy is standing by his side and she gives a small woof of agreement.

I wipe off my blade on the back of the deader, no time for sentiments. "A keeper?" I raise an eyebrow.

O'Donnell comes over to stand with us, a smile on her face. She's an attractive woman—long, dark wavy hair and a full hourglass figure. She reminds me a little of Nina, barring the biting attitude and roll of the eyes.

"He's talking about Moo, SJ's daughter. She likes to keep the heads as trophies." O'Donnell laughs but I can see she doesn't really think it's funny.

91

"Seriously?" I say, trying to hide the disgust from my voice. Because in truth, I can't help thinking that if my kid wanted to keep the heads of deaders as trophies, I'd be booking her in for therapy ASAP, because that's disturbing.

"Yeah, sick little fuck." Phil laughs with genuine amusement, not seeming too concerned at all.

"Let's go check out the farmhouse," Ricky says, avoiding the conversation altogether. He's an all business/no pleasure kind of guy for sure.

"Sure," I agree. I look toward the edge of the field, to the overgrown crops and weeds that are waving in the breeze like a welcome kite. "We should probably check in there at some point too," I say.

Phil's face falls for the first time since I met him. "That's going to be fun," he says sarcastically. "I always wanted to trample through an overgrown field and get lost and possibly eaten by either zeds or wild dogs because I get caught on fucking brambles!" He laughs, but this time it's humorless.

"None of this is ideal, big guy," Ricky says. "Come on, lock and load."

We head up the path to the farmhouse, eyeing up every bush and tree for wild dogs and deaders, but thankfully everything seems pretty quiet. The farmhouse's windows are all boarded up on both the top and bottom floors, and the front door seems to be barred from the inside, because when we push on it there's no give whatsoever. I'd think that there was someone still alive inside apart from the fact that everything is so quiet and seems so undisturbed. I mean, really, how long could someone hole up for? A month? Two? It's been years since the shit hit the fan; surely no one could have lain low for that amount of time.

I examine the nails holding the wood against the windows, seeing how rusty they are and deciding my theory is pretty unflawed.

We make our way around the side of the house and into the backyard, glancing in the distance to a large barn. It's much too far away to be a part of the house, but also close enough that it must have belonged to the same people that had owned the house. It's at the end of a large field that was used for crops at some stage. By the looks of the overgrown field next to it, one had been plowed before the outbreak, and the other hadn't. We try the back door of the house, finding it boarded up from the outside, and then I look at Ricky, who shrugs.

"No welcome party?" he says. "Guess they'd prefer to be alone."

"Or they locked themselves up for everyone's safety?" I guess.

He shrugs again. "Either way, I bet there's food in there." He looks up at the windows, digging his fingertips into the edges to see how easily they'll come off. "Probably gonna' need tools for this," he mumbles to himself.

"Agreed," I say, using the edge of my hatchet to pull up the corner of one of the boards. "This should do it," I say, grunting with effort as I rip the first board free.

He nods and takes the board from me, and then I set to work on the next one, ripping up each board until the doorway is free.

"The kid's not in there," O'Donnell states from behind me.

"You never know," I say.

"It's pretty obvious, Mikey. No one has been in this place for a very long time," O'Donnell sounds apologetic when she says it, which makes it hard to be mad at her. Yet I still am. All I want to do is find him—no matter what state he may be in.

93

"He's a clever little thing, survived out here for years on his own. He could have found a way in that we can't see." I look over my shoulder at her. "But I get that it's unlikely."

She nods, her lips pursing in regret. "Well, who knows what else could be inside, right?"

And it's true: you never know what you're going to find, and any time an opportunity comes up to search somewhere new, you should take it. There's no way Adam could have gotten inside this building, but with it having been boarded up for so long, there's bound to be some un-raided spoils for sure. And going back laden with weapons and food would definitely be a good welcome message to send.

"You ready?" I ask Ricky.

"I was born ready," he snarks back as he tries the handle, finding it stiff but thankfully not locked.

O'Donnell laughs a short, sharp laugh that makes Ricky glare at her. "'I was born ready,'" she mocks. "Could you sound like any more of a doofus?"

"Now now, you know how it is with Ricky," Phil says, a slow grin spreading across his face. "He's been waiting for this moment his entire life. He was *booorn* ready."

O'Donnell and Phil begin to laugh even harder, and I try my damndest not to join in, deciding I really need to get Ricky on my side somehow, and laughing in his face probably isn't the best way of doing that.

"Laugh it up, assholes," he snaps and pushes the door open.

The door creaks as it swings open, the light filtering inside an old kitchen. Dust motes float in the air, and a dusty scent floats out to us. We all wait, listening for the noise of deaders coming

94

from somewhere within the building, but when nothing comes out, Ricky shoots me a quick glance and steps inside.

I hold my hatchet tight and go in after him, sensing O'Donnell, Phil, and Fluffy behind me.

Chapter Eleven

I t's dark inside, the air stale and unused. O'Donnell and Phil head over to the kitchen cupboards, opening them and checking out the food stores. I'm happy to see that the cupboards seem to be relatively full.

Phil opens a top corner cupboard and several packets fall out, giving loud, sloppy sounds as they hit the work surface.

"Ughh," he calls out as he steps backwards, bumping into the counter behind him and knocking over a mug rack.

I reach for it in an attempt to stop it from falling over, but either I'm too slow or it's too fast, and it crashes to the floor, each of those carefully hung mugs smashing loudly.

"Shit, sorry," Phil whispers, turning to look at us. He shakes his hands out, and whatever leaked out of those packets drips from his fingers.

Fluffy whines and steps away from him, giving a small sneeze as she does.

"Asshole," O'Donnell says without malice. "What is that?"

"No fucking clue," Phil replies, pulling open some drawers which protest and screech. He looks up at us sharply. "Sorry," he apologizes, pulling out a dishtowel and wiping his hands with it.

"That's okay," O'Donnell says. "It's not like we were aiming for the element of surprise or anything. I mean, I'm sure there's nothing that would want to eat us in here anyway, right?" She smirks and steps away from Phil, falling in behind me where I notice that Fluffy has also taken residence.

"Traitor," Phil shout-whispers to the dog, but she only whines in response and stays behind me.

I laugh and Ricky grumbles something, and we continue through the house.

The downstairs is empty of anything useful, barring the food in the kitchen, so we head to the hallway, ready to check out the upstairs and hopefully find something of more use than a couple of cans of food and some boxes of indigestible slop.

Ricky stands at the bottom of the stairs, a pistol in hand. The hallway is dark, since all of the windows are boarded up and the light from the back door can't filter this far into the house, but my eyes have adjusted to the darkness enough for me to see my companions, at least.

Ricky takes the first step on the stairs, his weight leaning down on the unused steps and making another loud creak as if we're in a haunted house movie and he's the dumb blonde.

"Keep the noise down, will you?" I joke.

He turns his head to glare at me over the top of his shoulder, but my gaze skips his and instead looks up to the top of the stairs to see a deader take a step down.

It misses the step completely and comes tumbling down the steps in a jumble of limbs and growls, landing against Ricky, who in turn collapses backwards onto me. Fluffy is directly behind me, but she darts out of the way with a bark and yelp and Ricky, the deader, and I collapse in a heap together.

My hatchet has flown off somewhere into the darkness and I try to shove Ricky off of me so I can get out from under him and grab a weapon, but the deader has clambered on top of him and is currently trying to chew his face off.

"Get it off me!" he screams as another growl sounds out from the top of the stairs, followed by the *thud thud thud* of its body falling down them.

"Fuck!" I yell, trying to drag myself out from under them as deader drool lands on my face.

Fluffy bites into the side of the deader, her loud growls and snarls echoing through the darkness. The other deader lands at my feet, and it instinctively grabs for them. Of course it grabs at my injured ankle and digs its fingers into the already-damaged flesh there, and I cry out in pain and try to kick it off.

The deader on top of Ricky is suddenly dragged off of him and Ricky quickly rolls over, allowing me to kick my leg out with more force and send my booted foot into the face of the second deader. Its head snaps backwards, allowing me precious seconds to roll over and drag myself up to my knees. I grab for the pistol at my waist and aim it at the deader's skull as it lurches forward again, and this time its head snaps back, followed by its withered body.

I gasp for breath as I watch O'Donnell use my hatchet to smash into the other deader's skull. It turns into a dead weight in Phil's hands and he lets go of it.

Ricky is bent over at the waist trying to get air into his lungs, while I touch around my ankle, feeling blood trickling out from beneath the bandage.

Phil whoops loudly. "That was intense! Anyone else up there?" he calls up the stairs, banging the side of his hand against the wooden spindles. A sound comes from above, and Phil takes off up the stairs in search of whatever it is.

"You two all right?" O'Donnell asks as she starts to follow Phil.

"Fine, fine," Ricky replies, actually not sounding fine at all. He pats over his body, checking for any bites before standing upright and looking relieved. "Yeah, fine." He reaches out and helps me back up to my feet. "You good?" he asks.

I put a little weight on my injured leg, testing out its strength, but it doesn't hurt any more than it did this morning. My figuring is that some of the stitches have been ripped free. I can live with that for the moment.

"More or less," I reply.

Ricky takes off up the stairs after O'Donnell and Phil and I follow suit, pausing to give a brief look at the two deaders we just killed. They don't look like they belong around here, with their tattered business suits and what were once white shirts and blouses, and I wonder how the hell they got caught locked up in this place at all.

Upstairs Phil is pushing against one of the bedroom doors, but he isn't having much luck.

"Just leave it, man," Ricky says. "If they can't get out, that's all that matters."

Phil turns around. "No, it's not. We need to take them all out to secure the house."

Ricky and O'Donnell share a look, but neither of them says anything.

"Is it locked from the inside? Barred maybe?" I ask.

"No, I think it's just the weight of them all pushing against the door. They can hear us—can't you, you dirty rotters?" Phil bangs a fist against the door and laughs, and the groaning from inside increases. "They want their lunch. Hungry bastards," he says with a laugh again.

Fluffy whines at his feet, her nose pressed against the bottom of the door.

"So, where did the other two come from?" I ask, leaning down to tighten the bandage around my bleeding leg. "Have you checked the other rooms out?"

I don't want any more deader surprises is what I'm really thinking. That's what I've always hated the most—being caught unaware. I was never a guy that loved Halloween and all those types of creepy things. I'd once had a girl who loved all things horror. I made it through two weekends of horror movies before I had to call it quits on the relationship. It was falling asleep in the middle of *Nightmare on Elm Street* and waking up with her wearing a stripy red-and-green sweater that did it for me. She was dragging her nails down my chest and telling me to wake up because she had a treat for me. I still shudder at the memory.

"Yeah, nothing in the others," Phil says, banging against the door again. Fluffy jumps up and puts her paws against the door and begins barking at it.

"So stand back and let's bust it in," Ricky says.

Phil taps on the door with his machete. "See you in a minute, boys." He grins like he can't wait for the slaughter. It's the first thing I've seen in this man that I haven't liked. He lives for this gore, this horror, and I bet that in his old life he would have gotten along really well with my ex-girl.

"Don't be sexist," O'Donnell says as Phil stands by her side.

I'm still standing on the second-to-last step from the top, since the hallway is small.

"Sexist?" Phil asks.

"Yeah, there may be girls in there too."

"Okay." Phil steps forward and taps his axe on the door again. "See you in a minute, boys and girls." He stands back at O'Donnell's side and looks at her. "Better?"

"Much," she says. "On three. One…"

"Two," Phil says.

"Three," Ricky finishes off as they all charge at the door.

The sound of their three bodies hitting the wooden door and bouncing back off it reverberates through the house and they all groan out in pain. I take the final step up the stairs.

"Looks like it is barred from the inside after all." I smirk. I turn around and go into one of the other rooms to check for supplies, since Phil's first look around was only a brief one.

It seems to be a spare bedroom, with minimal furniture, and it only takes a quick glance around to see that there's nothing of value here. The window is boarded up like all the rest, but there's a gap in between the boards and blood smeared over them like something tried to eat its way out of the room.

I leave the room and almost walk straight into O'Donnell.

"Anything?" she asks, standing close to me—definitely closer than necessary, and I take a step away, trying to make it seem like a casual move.

I shrug. "Nah, nothing barring a failed escape out the window." I go into the second room with O'Donnell at my heels. Ricky is still helping Phil try to get into the room full of deaders, though it seems like a pointless exercise.

This had been a kid's room at one point, with books and toys on the shelves and a small chest of drawers stacked with diapers. My stomach twists because if there's one thing I can't stand the thought of—other than Halloween, of course—it's zombie kids. That ex-girlfriend of mine had been reading a book while we were dating called *Z-Children*, or something like that, and she'd insisted on reading it aloud to me at night before we went to sleep, stating that I'd like it if I just listened. Well, I didn't like it, not even a little bit. It was creepy as fuck and I'd had nightmares for weeks afterwards about zombie kids attacking me while I slept. Seriously, a grown man having nightmares because of a damn book! I hope to never meet the author in question because I can only imagine that their mind is as fucked up as this world.

We move around the room, a shitty sliver of light sliding in through the cracks in the wood panels across the windows. I kick a couple of toys around, my feet nudging old trucks and dolls. I kick a toy baby buggy out of the way and it falls over, tipping onto its side, and for some reason I lean over and pick it up, setting it upright again.

Still crouched down, my hand still resting on the handle of the toy buggy, my gaze lands on one of the baby dolls—only, I realize in horror, it isn't a baby doll at all. It's a real baby. It's long dead, and thankfully—or not—it had never awoken as a deader. There's a small piece of satisfaction in that.

"O'Donnell." I say her name, my voice quiet in the dark.

I hear her coming over, I even hear her gasp, and then she reaches down and picks up its small body from the floor before laying it back in its crib. She pulls the pink blanket over its tiny face and looks back at me.

I'm staring, confused as to why it never reanimated. I mean I'm glad, of course I am, but mercy isn't something that lives at the end of the world, and the fact that it died and didn't come back is a merciful thing indeed.

"Someone went in through the side of its head," she says as she leaves the room, her eyes downcast.

I follow her out of the room, clicking the door closed behind us and saying a silent prayer to whoever did the right thing for this child, no matter how hard it was.

Chapter Twelve

We scour the house from top to bottom and find nothing barring a couple of cans of food and some dried pasta. Phil gives up on getting at the deaders in the locked room, and I'm glad. I honestly don't see what the point is, since they're doing no harm. But then I wonder if that's what's worrying him at all. Perhaps it's just that he doesn't want them suffering any longer. I know I want someone to do that for me if it comes to it. I can't imagine having to live forever as one of these things. That hunger, that pain, that aggression. It's hard not to wonder if they realize what's happening to themselves, or if they have no knowledge whatsoever.

It's an easy thing to hate them, and of course we all do. But there has to be that small part of you buried deep inside that feels at least an ounce of sympathy. How can you not? They sure as hell don't want to feel how they do.

We leave the house feeling dirty and sweaty, and not just because the temperature has risen and the dust inside was everywhere. No, it's more than that. It's the sort of dirty that doesn't wash off.

"We should check the barn," I say, not wanting to but knowing we have to. I'm beginning to lose hope in finding Adam alive. I had honestly pinned all my hopes on finding an easier way into that house and finding Adam inside, hiding and safe. With every passing minute it seems that his chances of being alive are shortening.

I turn to look at the barn, seeing that it's almost as big as the farmhouse itself, though it isn't boarded up like the house was.

We all head over, our weapons at the ready—swords, machetes, axes, and guns. We're armed to the teeth, yet I still don't feel safe. Then again, in this world I never do. This is more, though. The feeling of being watched is making my skin crawl, but no matter where I look there is no one in sight.

O'Donnell sees my gaze shifting around us, and her stare follows my own to a set of three trees at the side of the barn.

"You got something, Mikey?" she asks.

I shake my head no, but my gaze stays on those trees regardless. I can't see anything—not a flicker of clothing or the blink of an eye—yet I can't tear my gaze away. It's like my instincts are warning me of something.

"Mikey?" O'Donnell says my name, slowly and quietly.

"Nah, nothing, just paranoid," I finally reply, looking away from the trees.

"From my experience, paranoia tends to come from past experience of a situation," she says matter-of-factly.

I look back the way we came from, half expecting to see the boards gone from the upstairs windows and someone's face to be at one of them. But when I look, there's no one there.

Fluffy whines as we walk, and I notice that her leg is bleeding.

"Stop," I say crouching down to look at her injured leg. "Looks like we're twins today, girl," As I squat down I hear the loud crack of a gun going off shortly before something whizzes over my head. "What the hell was that?" I yell.

We all dive down to the ground and quickly make our way over to a broken-down tractor to hide behind as more bullets zoom past our heads.

"Did you see who it was?" O'Donnell yells, sticking her head out from around the tractor only to snap it back when a bullet bounces off the corner with a loud *ping*.

"No," I yell back, pulling out my pistol. "I just, I had a feeling. Like someone was watching us. I thought I was just being paranoid."

Ricky looks at me, his eyebrows furrowing together. "Dude, paranoia is normally an experience of a—"

"I know!" I snap, cutting him off. "She already said."

"We need to work out where they're shooting from, how many of them there are," Phil says, peering around the corner carefully. "And what the hell they want!"

"I think they want us dead," I bite out sarcastically, ignoring everyone's glares of irritation.

Another bullet bounces off the metal, followed seconds later by one after another after another, the noise so loud it has us all crouching as low to the ground as we can get and covering our ears.

"Fuckkkk!" Ricky yells as a window in the tractor is blown out and the ground is peppered with glass—and so are we. We all cover our heads and wait for the glass to stop falling.

I look over at Phil and Fluffy. Her leg is still bleeding and she's panting heavily. Phil sees my gaze and strokes her head and she nuzzles against his hand, licking across her leg to get rid of some of the blood. She farts, and I thank God that we're outside and not trapped inside the deader house behind us, fumbling around in the dark while being simultaneously gassed to death.

Ricky spits on the ground to get rid of the fart taste from his mouth and then he crawls under the tractor to get a better look out front.

"Anything?" I call to him.

"It's coming from the barn," he says. "Can't see how many, but there's definitely more than one shooter."

"Why are they shooting at us?" O'Donnell asks, her voice sounding obviously stressed.

I watch as she puts away her pistol and swings the rifle from around from her back. She adjusts the scope on the end as she looks through it, her mouth set in a grim determined line.

"How the fuck should I know? They aren't waving a welcome flag with a list of demands!" Ricky snaps back to her.

"Get out of there," O'Donnell says. She grabs hold of Ricky's leg and starts trying to drag him out.

Ricky scoots backwards. "Alright, woman!" he yells at her, but she ignores him and takes his place under the tractor. More shots are fired, and the ground to the side of the tractor is once again peppered with bullets.

"Goddamn idiots! Wasting ammo like that!" Ricky says, covering his head.

I watch Phil tear off a thin strip of material from his Hawaiian shirt and wrap it around Fluffy's leg. He glances across at my leg, which is still bleeding out, and tears off another strip before handing it to me.

"Thanks," I say, putting my pistol down next to me and using the colorful material to wrap around my leg.

Fluffy whines and Phil pats her head again. I look behind us, seeing shapes moving in the distance. It takes me a moment to work out what they are. And not for the first time in twenty-four hours, I wish that they were the shapes of deaders in the distance. But no, the wild dogs are back, and bounding across the field right toward us.

"We've got company," I say, my voice sounding grim even to my own ears. "And I'm not talking about the good kind. I'm talking about the mother-in-law-from-hell kind of company."

Phil and Ricky follow my gaze, both of them cussing at the same time. For the second time in twenty-four hours, I'm coming face to face with our newest foe. And this one isn't slow like the deaders, or emotional like the Forgotten. These are feral dogs, and they are quick and savage, with sharp teeth and a desire to survive that goes way beyond a chemical spark in their dead brains. They are animals, and as animals they have no rules.

The ground erupts around us again as Ricky tries to look around the tractor to see what's going on at the barn and O'Donnell calls out to stay still. Actually, her exact words are, "stay the fuck where you are before I crawl out from under here and kick your asses!"

The dogs stop running when the second round of gunshots sounds out, their heads low, their ears flat against their heads, and their tails tucked between their legs as they watch us. Fluffy stands up, though her injured leg is lifted in the air. She bares her teeth and snarls, froth foaming at the corner of her mouth as she watches the dogs coming slowly toward us.

I look at where I am, trapped between some insane shooters and a pack of wild dogs, with no escape in sight, and wonder how this moment could get any worse. As if answering my unspoken question, a growl to the left has us all looking, and we watch as

108

three deaders shamble around the side of some abandoned equipment. These are definitely the original homeowners, I decide. All three of them are wearing dungarees, the clothing of a red necks.

O'Donnell lets out a round and I hear a short, sharp cry of pain coming from the barn. More gunshots sound out, but this time they're coming from O'Donnell and not just the barn.

"That's two," she calls back to us. "How are we looking, Mikey?" she asks.

Phil, Ricky, and I look at each other, our gazes straying to the wild dogs circling closer and then to the deaders shambling toward us.

"Uh, not good," I reply.

"Not good? How so?" she asks, firing off another round. "Gotcha, you little fucker," she yells happily. "Come on, boys, what's going on back there?"

"There are a bunch of dogs headed toward us, and they don't look like the friendly kind," I say. "Plus there's deaders."

O'Donnell scoots back from under the tractor with me and Ricky dragging her out the last couple of inches. She sits up and wipes the sweat from her brow.

"What did you say?" she snaps.

"Dogs, deaders, shooters—pretty lousy fucking odds if you ask me," I say, jerking a thumb in one direction and my head in another.

"Aaah, crap," she replies. "We need to get moving."

"Which way, smartass?" Ricky asks without an ounce of sarcasm in his voice.

I eye the hand grenade on O'Donnell's belt. "I'm seriously doubting that Adam is in the barn, and if he is," I shake my head and swallow, "I don't think it ended well for him. But I don't think he would have been dumb enough to go anywhere near them. The kid knows how to survive, trust me on that one. So I think we need to hightail it back to the truck and get our asses out of here."

"So, what are you thinking, dude?" Phil asks, pushing his glasses farther up his nose. His bright Hawaiian shirt seems so out of place right now that it makes me want to laugh.

Fluffy's ears are flat to her head as her snarls get louder, and Phil removes his hand from her head in case she gets lost in the moment and bites him.

"That." I nod toward the grenade. "That's what I'm thinking. Drop and run," I say.

"That's for emergencies only, Mikey," Ricky says matter-of-factly.

"Dude, this is an emergency!" Phil and I say at the same time.

"Jinx," Phil says with a laugh. I smirk but don't say anything.

The deaders have stopped walking, and are looking around trying to find their source of food. Their noses lift to the air as they catch scent of the blood both Fluffy and I are losing, but thankfully they mistake it for the live feral dogs and then begin shambling toward them instead.

The dogs are barking and growling as the deaders get closer to them. And I'm surprised that the dogs know the difference between deader and human. *Then again,* I think, *it's only the difference between good meat and bad, and I should probably be at least a little glad that I'm classed as the good kind.*

"That was lucky," O'Donnell says looking surprised. She turns away from the dogs-and-deaders situation. "Okay, can you run?" she asks me.

I nod yes and she looks over at Phil. "And her?"

"She'll be fine," he says. He strokes Fluffy's head gently. "You're going to be okay," he whispers to her. Her ears are still back but she's turned the snarling down to almost silent.

"Who's chucking it?" I ask. "Because whoever chucks it needs to be able to run fast to avoid the deaders."

"I was a high school volleyball champion. Trust me when I say a little Zed action is nothing to worry about," O'Donnell says.

Her gaze is back on the deaders-and-wild-dog dance-off happening and I half expect 'It's Like That' by Run DMC to begin playing over some imaginary speakers.

I get a firm grip on my pistol, my machete in the other hand, and I crouch down, ready to run. From our position, we can see our truck farther down the road, but there's no way we can make it with all of those dogs hot on our tail. We have to shake some of them off. Not to mention that all this noise is bound to bring more deaders to our position.

O'Donnell stretches out her shoulder, circling it twice until she hears a satisfying click of bone. Then she pulls the grenade from her belt.

"All right, on three," she says.

"Three didn't work out too well for you guys last time," I say, referring to inside the house only ten minutes before.

Ricky glares at me, Phil finds the energy to smirk, and even Fluffy cocks her head in my direction as if to say *dude, now's really not the time for your smart-assed remarks.*

"All right, on two then, funny guy," she says with a soft shake of her head.

"Sounds good." I smirk.

"One," she says, "two!"

And then we all run. The dogs being circled by the deaders catch sight of us, one of them breaking from the pack to chase us. O'Donnell pulls the pin on the hand grenade and throws it at the circle of dogs and deaders, and it explodes as it bounces across the ground in front of them.

The force of the blast almost makes me lose balance, my feet coming out from underneath me until I manage to gain my footing again and continue to run. We run as fast as we can, a lone wild dog still giving chase, the others writhing on the ground as the deaders clamber to get at them. A grenade is nothing to these deaders and their ability to withstand almost anything other than a short, sharp blast of anything to the head. Unfortunately a grenade at their feet only slows their forward momentum, I realize grimly as they begin crawling toward us on their stomachs.

We're closing in on the truck, my leg throbbing, the blood now freely flowing from it, and my chest is burning as I struggle to catch my breath. I really need to work on my cardio, I decide.

Ricky gets to the truck first and he throws the door open before diving inside. I'm second, and I grab the handle at the back and pull it open so I can get inside. The dog that's chasing us is gaining on Fluffy, and Phil is calling her to hurry up even as her steps slow down.

O'Donnell climbs in next to Ricky, automatically grabbing her rifle and looking through the scope.

"I can't get a clean shot," she says as she gasps for air.

"Come on, Fluffy!" Phil is calling, his steps slower than they should be so he can run alongside his dog.

Her tongue is lolling out of her mouth as she runs, her injured leg lifted and only going down every third step. I'm not sure what makes her stop and finally turn to face the dog. Maybe she knows it's futile to continue running, and that this dog is leaner than her and uninjured. Maybe she just simply knows that it was only a matter of time before it caught up to her and she wants to go down fighting. I watch her eyes glance at Phil the second she makes the decision to stop.

And even though she's only a dog, and I've only known her for two days, I still call out for her to keep on running. But it's too late as she turns and faces the other dog, bares her teeth, and lets out the most bloodthirsty snarl that she can muster.

Chapter Thirteen

There's something to be said for loyal animals and their ability to love and fight to the very end. Phil stumbles in his steps but then keeps on running, his feet pulling him forward toward the truck even after he's left his heart behind with Fluffy. I see his expression, and know that I had a similar look on my face when I had to leave Nina behind.

Phil makes it to the truck and climbs inside. O'Donnell stands upright, using the top of the door as a rest for her rifle. She watches down the sight as the two dogs square up to each other, teeth bared, ears back, their snarls and growls heard across the field.

"I can't get a shot," O'Donnell calls, sounding distressed. "She's in the way!"

"Take a shot, O'Donnell," Phil yells at her. "Kill that thing before it kills my girl!" His words break on his sentence.

"We need to go," Ricky yells at them both. "She's just a fucking dog, our lives are more important."

"Don't ever say that to me again," Phil says to Ricky through gritted teeth.

I hold my breath as the two dogs dive at one another, their teeth clashing as they each go for the side of the neck, both missing and rolling onto their sides before immediately getting back up. The other dog dives at Fluffy again, its teeth finding purchase in the soft fur on her stomach and she screeches out, her pained cry echoing loudly.

"No, Fluffy!" Phil calls out. He tries to get out of the truck but I grab ahold of him to keep him back. "Get off me!"

"No can do, man," I reply regretfully.

He shrugs under my grip, but his movements are slow and full of reluctance.

In the distance, I watch another two dogs moving away from the carnage of the grenade and slowly starting to make their way over to Fluffy. They're slow—injured, no doubt—but between the three of them the slim chance Fluffy has is obliterated to nothing.

"O'Donnell, will you take a fucking shot!" Phil roars when the first dog dives at Fluffy again, its teeth sinking into her once more as another pained cry leaves her.

"I can't!" she cries back. "I'll hit her."

O'Donnell looks at Phil, her eyes full of desperation. Phil squeezes his eyes closed and when he opens them, he looks determined. "Do it," he says, his voice full of regret. "Don't let her be torn apart by them, please," he says, tears escaping his eyes. "We'll take out every last one of the bastards afterwards."

She nods and looks back through her scope.

I know that he's right, and if Fluffy had a choice she wouldn't want the agony and pain, but I can't let O'Donnell do it. I just can't. I honestly believe we can still help her, maybe even save her, I decide. Maybe I'm growing soft, because to risk my life for a damn dog is ridiculous, but I've already made my decision when I push past Phil and jump out of the truck. My feet hit the dirt heavily and I jog, feeling protected from behind by O'Donnell, as I move forwards. The wild dogs' eyes flit to me briefly, giving Fluffy a second or two to dive at the other dog and take a chunk out of its leg.

The dog howls in pain, and the two dogs making their way over to us speed up, ready to help their comrade no matter what.

I move closer still, my pistol aimed and ready. All I need is to get a single shot on this dog. I'm ten feet away, and I crouch down to one knee, my aim following the other dog. Fluffy must sense me behind her, and she moves in front of me as if trying to protect me. But it's the opposite of what I need her to do.

I wait, letting the two dogs growl and snap at each other for a couple more seconds, and when the wild dog launches itself at Fluffy I stand up and shoot downwards at it, gaining the upper hand because of my height.

It cries out and Fluffy launches herself at it, her teeth sinking into its neck where she bites down and then shakes her head to tear the hole wider.

"Fluffy!" I call, and she stops what she's doing and hobbles over to me, her energy failing her as she reaches me and collapses in a heap. I holster my pistol and reach down to pick her up, letting O'Donnell pick off the other two dogs as they bound toward us.

I jog to the truck as quickly as I can and hand Fluffy over to Phil. He lays her across the backseat and then I climb in myself, slamming the door shut behind me. Ricky starts the truck, the roar of the engine sounding quiet against the rushing of the blood in my ears.

"We're heading back to Haven," he says, as if there's any other plan right now.

Phil is hunched over Fluffy, the rest of his shirt pressed against her side to stem the blood. I'm at the back end of her and I stroke

116

her side as Phil speaks to her and she whines in pain. My leg is bleeding profusely again now, and I stop petting Fluffy long enough to take off my shirt and wrap it around my leg to stem the blood loss.

He glances at me. "Thank you, dude, thank you." Tears are in his eyes when he speaks.

"It's the NEO way right? Never leave a man behind." My gaze slides from Phil to Fluffy. "Or a girl," I say, giving her a soft pat.

I'm not sure if I got to her in time, but at least I tried. If this is the NEO way then I hope I have just proved myself. But there's one thing that bothers me, and that's Ricky. He didn't move to help any of us get out of that mess, and I have a sinking feeling about the guy and that he quite possibly would have left us all behind if he thought he could have gotten away with it.

I hope I'm wrong and it's just my paranoia. But as both Ricky and O'Donnell had said, paranoia is usually remembering a past experience. And I have plenty of those.

*

Ricky drives us straight to Haven, honking his horn once as we get close so that the gate is sliding open as we arrive and we can pull straight through it.

He slams on the brakes and I open my door, grabbing the back end of Fluffy as Phil grabs the front end.

"This way," Phil says, directing me toward the center of town and to a small store with a large front window and a big-ass crack down the center of it. "Doctor's office," he says.

"Veterinary too?" I ask.

"Whatever she can learn from a book," O'Donnell says, walking with us. "I'm going to let Aiken know what happened. Ricky's already on his way over, but I need to be there too," she says. She pats Fluffy's side gently. "You've got this, girl."

And then she breaks off into a run and I'm left wondering why the hell she feels the need to be there while Ricky lets Aiken know what just went down. Joan is walking across the street, and her eyes widen when she sees me. She runs over, looking relieved that it isn't Adam that I'm carrying.

"Mikey? The boy?" she asks, her words tremoring.

"Not now, Joan, I'll come find you later," I reply, walking away from her.

She looks hurt by my easy dismissal of her, but there isn't the time now to explain everything.

The door to the doctor's opens as we get closer and a young dark-haired woman comes out, her face immediately filled with concern. She holds the door open as we go inside and then she directs us to a back room and to a long table covered in Saran Wrap.

"On here, quick quick," she says.

We lay Fluffy on the bed and I take a step back to let the woman do her thing.

"Okay, grab that tray and bring it over here." She lifts the Hawaiian shirt off of the wound in Fluffy's side. "Damn, girl, did you fight with a werewolf?"

A noise comes from a door on the other side of the room, and I glance at the woman and Phil but neither of them has heard it, and since they're both engrossed in trying to save Fluffy's life I decide to take matters into my own hands and deal with the situation.

I pull out my pistol and take a step toward the door, my nerves twitching and raring to go, but I take it slow and steady because I don't want to shock Fluffy and risk the dog's life. The last thing anyone needs right now is me charging full pelt at the door with the deader behind it and scaring the shit out of everyone. Phil and the woman are still frantically working on Fluffy. There's blood bubbling out of the wound on Fluffy's side when the doctor lifts the shirt, and she presses it back down and orders Phil to grab her some gauze and a needle from the tray.

I take slow, cautious steps toward the door, listening to the soft scratching and noises coming from within. A slight growl followed by the telltale noise of sniffing. Typical deader behavior. But how the fuck did one get in here? Is this more than a makeshift hospital and a veterinary clinic? Is this woman performing tests on the deaders to work them out? It wouldn't surprise me, and it wouldn't be the first time I've stumbled into something like that. I guess I just thought better of the NEOs.

I reach the other side of the room, my gun raised to shoulder height, and I lean to one side of the door, my hand reaching for the doorknob.

"Achillies will kick your ass if you try to hurt him," the woman says. "Not to mention what I'll do to you."

I look up, my heart in my throat and my eyes wide. "Achillies?" I ask, my voice sounding steadier than I feel.

"My dog," she says, her tone serious, but there's a slight smile on her lips. "You can go ahead and let him in. He'll want to see his girl here."

119

I nod several times, my mind still processing the information. "Her dog," I mumble, grateful that I was wrong and the NEOs are turning out to be everything they say they are.

I turn the doorknob but the door is snatched out from under my grip, slamming open and banging against the wall as it swings wide and a large eighty-pound dog charges through the room and jumps up at the table where Fluffy is lying. His large paws land heavily on the edge of the table near her head, and his tongue laps out and he begins to lick at Fluffy's face. Both of the dogs are whining and licking at each other, and it's sort of beautiful if I'm being honest—that even dogs can still find love in this world.

"All right, boy, come on, give her some space," the woman says, but Achillies doesn't quit. The concern he has for his partner is evident in the frantic whining and licking of her.

"Is she going to be okay, Stormy?" Phil asks, his palm gently rubbing over the top of Fluffy's head.

Stormy peers down at the bite mark, her face pinching in concern. "I don't know, not yet. It's pretty deep and it's torn a lot of muscle and tissue. If I can get the bleeding to stop and…" Her words trail off and she looks up into Phil's face. "I'll do everything I can, but you need to prepare for the worst, just in case."

Phil nods but doesn't say anything, but by the glint in his eye I don't think he can right now without crying.

"I'm going to get some fresh air," I say, genuinely needing some space to get my mind around what just happened.

I walk across the room, passing Stormy, Phil and the two dogs. I pat Fluffy's hind legs as I walk by. "You got this, girl," I say, mimicking O'Donnell.

Phil's hand reaches out and grabs my arm. "Hey, thank you," he says and lets me go. He looks broken. Not just in his torn clothes, and the blood smeared across his arms, but it's in his eyes. Like a light has gone off at the thought of losing Fluffy.

I nod and head outside, shutting the door behind me. Outside O'Donnell is pacing in front of the store, looking a mixture of concerned and furious.

"Whatsup?" I ask.

"Nothing. I mean nothing but the bullshit of someone almost killing us all, being attacked by zeds and rabid dogs, and then the bullshit of politics," she snaps. "Come on, let's walk." She tugs my arm and we begin to walk.

"What was going on with Ricky and you?" I ask, glancing at her.

She shakes her head. "It's just his way. He can be a big fucking drama queen when he wants to be. I wanted to be there while he told Aiken what happened so he didn't blow that shit up out of proportion."

"Out of proportion?" I ask, feeling confused. "How could he blow up what just happened? You said it yourself, we were almost killed."

O'Donnell pulls me to a stop, her gaze flitting around us, scanning the area for anyone listening in. "You wanna' find that kid of yours, right?"

I nod and she continues.

"Then we need to play down what just happened, or Aiken will send us to that barn guns blazing, bombs going off, and we'll probably never find him."

"He'd do that?"

She nods. "We've done it before. He doesn't take chances with assholes. Not anymore. None of us do." Her gaze stays on mine, our eyes connecting. The intensity coming from her suddenly makes me feel uncomfortable, like I'm betraying Nina somehow, and I look away. "He took the time today to talk to the rest of Haven about you."

"About me?" I frown.

"Yeah, he told them about your…umm, about the haze of shit that seems to be following you around. The Forgotten." She swallows and I can see that she's uncomfortable with even talking about them, which means she's worried about them, and she should be. "Everyone here thinks that you're worth the risk, Mikey. Don't let us down."

"I don't know what to say," I reply. And I don't. I'm shocked. These people are either stupid or they see something in me that I don't. I look over at Phil's house and watch Ricky heading up the steps to the front door. He doesn't see me because he's so focused on where he's going. "And are you willing to take such a big chance, a risk?" I ask.

O'Donnell's hand reaches out and touches my arm, and I look back to her. "I am for you," she says, and everything about her tone makes me know why.

There's something to be said for desire. It's something that you can see, and hear and feel. When someone desires you, it's not arrogance that lets you recognize it, it's just something that's easily recognized.

"Look, you should know—" I begin hesitantly, because this is not a conversation that I want to be having, now or ever. I can't avoid her gaze, no matter how much I want to, and I witness the flash of hurt in her eyes before I even finish what I'm saying.

Because just like desire, regret is easily recognized to. And she can hear the regret coming from me already.

"Hey, Mikey!" Ricky calls as he comes towards us, his eyes narrowing in on O'Donnell's hand on my arm.

O'Donnell lets go of my arm and we look away from each other and turn to look at Ricky.

"Fluffy?" he asks as he falls in beside us.

I shrug. "No clue yet, the doc—Stormy is it?—she's working on her. Says it doesn't look too good, though."

"That's a shit deal," he says. "But look, I think we're going to have to rethink looking for your friend. The shit that just went down," he shakes his head, "it's not good, my friend."

"What did Aiken say?" O'Donnell snaps, all softness gone from her.

A breeze hits me and I turn to look behind, half-expecting to see something coming toward us, but there's nothing there.

"He's thinking it over," Ricky growls out. "No thanks to you." His gaze moves between O'Donnell and me, as if it's finally just hit him why she played down what just happened. "Don't put everyone at risk, all of NEO, just for your selfishness, O'Donnell. He's not going to be sticking around." Ricky flashes me a dark look and storms away, leaving me and O'Donnell to watch after him awkwardly.

She finally turns back to me. "Ignore him. He's had a shit time."

"We all have."

"That's true," she returns. "Come on, let's get Alfie to stitch you back up before you bleed to death. Stormy's been training him up for a couple of months now and he's pretty good." She starts to walk away and I follow her.

"Yeah, he was the one that did these stitches to start with. Can't say he did too good a job, if I'm being honest."

She laughs. "Can't really blame him for them tearing open, Mikey. I think you need to blame the zed that tore you back open." She smirks over her shoulder.

"All right, I'll give you that," I return.

She smiles again. "I bet you'd give me just about anything I want."

I stare after her as she walks on ahead, my heart aching and my stomach clenching. I'm not sure how to take this woman, or her feelings toward me, but I know that I need to let her know how things are before it gets too serious. Right now, I'm not looking for anyone but Adam. Certainly not another woman.

In fact, I can't see myself wanting anyone ever again—not after losing Nina. I don't want to go through that sort of loss again. I'm boxing off my heart and putting it away for good. It's out of commission; and at the end of the world, when all anyone wants is to connect with another person… all I want to do is disconnect from them all.

Chapter Fourteen

"Wow, you really messed this up, didn't you?" Alfie says as I step out of my khakis and let them fall at my feet.

"Technically a deader messed this up, not me," I reply.

"Hmmm. Well I hope that you put that…what did you call it?"

"A deader."

He smiles. "We call them zeds. I like deader though. It's more literal, I guess."

"No," I say. "'Evil fucking deaders' would be more literal, but it's also a bit of a mouthful to say in a hurry."

Alfie laughs. "True enough."

I sit down in the chair and he sprays the open wound with some solution and wipes it all over carefully. I grit my teeth against the burn of pain that sings through my leg. Once cleaned, it isn't as bad as I first thought. I've lost maybe two stitches, but the rough pull from the deader tore the flesh and made the cut wider.

"Can't go in through the original stitches," Alfie mutters to himself as he pokes around my leg, testing the flesh by separating the two flaps of skin. He rummages through his med kit and comes out with a little tube. "I'm going to put fresh stitches in and then glue it all. I'm warning you, it's going to hurt, though."

"I'm a big boy," I snark, my gaze moving to O'Donnell leaning against the wall and watching us. Her lips quirk at my words. "I can take it," I clarify.

"You've been taking your antibiotics, right?" Alfie asks, getting everything he needs set out next to him so he can grab it all easily.

"Of course," I reply, pulling my antibiotics out of my pocket and throwing one to the back of my throat.

O'Donnell laughs. "I'll go get us something to eat and check in on Fluffy," she says, her gaze washing over me. "I'll be back soon, don't go anywhere."

"Couldn't even if I wanted to," I joke.

She smiles at me and turns to leave.

"I'll take something to eat too," Alfie says, looking surprised when O'Donnell simply laughs at him and leaves the room. "Or not," he mumbles under his breath. He glances up at me. "Favoritism," he says and looks back down at my leg.

He stitches my leg up and then glues the wound shut, and he was right: it hurts worse than I expected, but I pant through the burning sensation that travels through my leg and he wraps it in a fresh bandage.

He hands me a fresh set of khakis—though I say *fresh* with reluctance. "Best we got," he laughs. "Keep up with the antibiotics. A dog bite is no joking matter."

"I will. It's just been a busy day," I reply, standing and testing my weight on my ankle. It's not too bad, maybe a little more tender than it was before, but I've had worse than this. He was right though—a dog bite isn't something to mess around with. Rabies is a real thing, and rabies leads to death and then to a life of the undead. Definitely not in my life plan.

"No luck finding the kid?" he asks, cleaning up his tools and piling them back into his med kit carefully.

126

I shake my head. "Didn't really get much chance to check things out properly."

"The shooters?" he asks, raising an eyebrow at me.

"Yeah." I think about what O'Donnell said about if Aiken found out how bad it had gotten at the barn, and how he would go in all guns blazing and blow that place to high hell. While I don't see that it would be such a big problem to do so—because hey, they nearly killed us—until I know for certain that Adam isn't in that area, I can't possibly let that barn get blown up.

"It wasn't too bad," I add. "They just caught us by surprise."

"Yeah?"

"Yeah, we were just unlucky. Damn wild dogs caught us again. Between the dogs and the deaders, the shooter was the least of our worries. In fact, I'm not even sure they were shooting at us."

I look away from him. I've never been a good liar.

O'Donnell comes back into the room as I'm buttoning up my khakis. "You ever heard of knocking?" I joke.

She laughs back. "I've heard of it. Can't say I ever did it though." She smirks. "Besides, it's nothing I haven't seen before, Mikey."

An uncomfortableness settles across the room until she breaks it with a sharp laugh.

"Oh come on, stop acting like little boys." She places some crackers, an apple, and a bottle of water on the table next to me. "Eat up, you're going to need your strength." And then she turns and leaves.

Alfie looks at me with a grin. "Lucky guy."

"Lucky?"

"Oh yeah, I'd do anything to get that sort of attention from her," he says, picking up my apple and taking a bite.

"Well, I'm not really interested in anything right now," I reply, feeling uncomfortable having this conversation with someone I don't really know. I'm not a sharing type anyway, and this is definitely delving too deep for my liking.

"I get it. We've all lost someone, we've all had that pain. But sometimes companionship can help heal that pain." He takes another bite of the apple, watching me.

"Maybe I don't want anything healing. Maybe I like the pain," I reply.

Alfie shakes his head and smirks. "A good woman can soothe that pain though. Who wouldn't want that?"

He bites into my apple again, not waiting for me to respond, and leaves the room. I stare after him, wondering how I've gotten myself into this situation in the first place and why I'm discussing anything with him anyway. I have no intention of starting anything with O'Donnell or anyone else, and I'll make that clear to her just as soon as I can.

When I finally leave the room and get back outside, the day has grown even hotter, and within seconds I'm sweating. I make my way back over to where Fluffy is being cared for. Phil comes out as I make it to the doorway. There's blood smeared across the front of the t-shirt he was originally wearing under his Hawaiian shirt. His expression is grim and he lights up a cigarette and sits down on the step with a heavy sigh. His eyes are swollen and red and he puts his head in his hands.

It hits me like a lead balloon and my heart sinks at the thought of Fluffy being dead. Sure, she's just a dog, I get that, and I know that human life is much more important than any animal's. And

I know I didn't know Fluffy long, but it's still painful to think of her being gone. To think that she gave her life for ours—for Phil's.

"She was brave. You can't buy that in this life," I say to Phil, my words sticking in my too dry throat.

He looks up and nods and takes another drag on his cigarette.

"She loved you," I add. "You could tell how much she loved you."

His eyes are still shiny from crying. "You should go see her, dude. You were the one that got her out of there. You risked your life for hers. You saw that she was one of the team, one of the family." He reaches up with his hand and I take it in mine and we shake hands. "Thanks, dude, for being there."

I nod, realizing that I haven't thought about it like that. But I *did* risk my life for hers because I saw her as one of the team. I helped bring her home, even if it was only for her to die. At least she died here, with her family.

And I know that whatever happens next with the NEOs, I secured mine and Joan's place in this community by doing that. I'm glad that it happened, but I can't hide away from the tragedy of the situation.

I push open the door and head into the back. Achillies lies by the table, his head resting on his big front paws. His eyes watch me as I cross the room, and he gives a soft whine in my direction. Stormy is washing her tools at a small white sink, and she looks over at me and offers a sympathetic smile before turning back to the sink.

I nod and go to stand by Fluffy. Her eyes are closed, her mouth open and her tongue lolling out. She's still, yet I still expect and hope that she'll move—but of course she doesn't. When I place my hand on her side, she's still warm, her fur soft under my hand. I swallow before speaking, feeling sad and uncomfortable.

"I'm sorry," I mumble, aware that Stormy and Achillies are in the room listening to my every word. "You were a good dog. You'll be missed." I clear my throat, my gaze shifting down to Achillies, who is still watching me with a sad expression on his face. He whines again. "I didn't know you long, but I'm grateful that I got to meet you, Fluffy. Thanks for being—" I stumble on my words, not sure what to say. "Thanks for being awesome."

Stormy comes to stand by my side, and Achillies sits up. "You should hug her," she says softly. "I bet her spirit would like that." She smiles. "And Achillies, he'd like that too, wouldn't you, boy?"

I look at Achillies again. His ears are pricked up as he listens to us talking. "Oh, yeah, sure," I reply.

"Be careful of her bandages, they're still wet with blood," she says sadly, avoiding my gaze.

I feel like I have no other choice, so I nod and lean over, awkwardly pressing my cheek to the soft fur near Fluffy's back end. I hear the door open and Phil walks back in. He smiles at seeing me hugging Fluffy, and then his smile grows even wider when Fluffy lets out a noxious fart that has me jumping back in surprise and gagging as the stench fills my nostrils. I look at Fluffy's face, watching as her eyes open and she groggily pulls her tongue back into her mouth.

"She's not dead?" I ask, waving a hand in front of my face to get the stench of fart away from me.

"No," Stormy laughs, "as if I'd let Achillies's girl die. She's just recovering." Stormy pats me on the back and Achillies jumps up at the table and begins licking at Fluffy's face again. "She'll be fine after some rest. The bite wasn't too deep when I got down to it."

"But you let me think…" I let my words trail off, knowing that it doesn't really matter. Hell, I probably would have done the same thing.

I can't even pretend to be mad, because I'm just so happy that Fluffy isn't dead. I'm just so damn happy to see Achillies and Fluffy licking at each other, happy that they've both survived another day, together.

I take a step back from the table as Fluffy lets out another fart, my gaze going to Phil. "I thought she was dead," I say to him.

He laughs and pushes his glasses up his nose. "Yeah, I figured that when I walked in and you were hugging her backside." He laughs again. "It's never a good idea to be at her back end, dude." He strokes her fur gently and she quits her kissing of Achillies's snout and looks over at Phil, her long tail making a slow *thump thump* on the table.

"I'm going to get some fresh air," I say, smiling. And for the first time in several days, the smile feels real, not the fake show that you put on for others to make them quit asking questions. I'm genuinely happy for Phil and Achillies and Fluffy.

They've made it through another day, another drama. We don't all get that second chance, and it makes me realize that we should be taking life by both hands and holding it close to us, not pushing everything good away.

Life is for living. And sometimes our life isn't very long, but we have to live it as best we can, while we can.

That's what Nina did. She loved and helped, and gave and survived, until she couldn't. But if I knew anything about Nina it was that she wouldn't regret a single second of what she did. She never did anything by half measures; she was an all-or-nothing girl. That's just how she worked. That was one of the reasons I loved her so much. But it was also one of the reasons she ended up dead.

I'm still not ready to forgive her for sacrificing her life for ours, but I understand it, and I can respect her for it. And I won't let it be for nothing.

I'll find Adam, no matter what the cost, and I'll make her proud. I'll live this life, this second chance that she gave me. I won't let it all go to waste.

I walk out of the doctor's room and back out into the street and keep walking, needing to clear my head. I walk the outskirts of the entire community, getting a real outline of this place in my head. I pass other members of the community, and each one waves a hello and offers me a smile. Each one of them is happy to have me here, happy to have another fighter, another protector. Because that's what this group is. We are all protectors of each other.

And the best part is that this community knows my bullshit and is still ready to stand by my side. They aren't frightened of facing the Forgotten, if that's what it takes, and they will support me no matter what. For the first time in my life I feel fully accepted—not just for the good things, but for my faults also. It's a good feeling. Especially after feeling so many bad things for so long.

"Hey Mikey."

I turn to see O'Donnell standing on the front stoop of her house. She's leaning against the front porch and smiling at me. Her jacket is off and her hair is down. She looks so much like Nina that it takes my breath away.

"What?" I ask as I walk over to her. I climb the three steps so that we are both standing on the porch together, and she smiles again.

O'Donnell takes my hand. "Come on," she says, and begins to pull me inside her house.

She looks back over her shoulder, and I know I should say no, that I should tell her that my heart is broken and I don't think it will ever be fixed enough to allow anyone else into it. That I don't really ever want it to be fixed, because I don't want to ever get over Nina. But that I want to live and make this life mean something. I want to do something good with whatever time I have left here.

And more than anything, I want to hold onto this happy feeling for a little longer. Because after feeling so full of anger and hate and resentment for so long, I had been worried that I would never find my way back out of that blackness.

Yet now here I am, smiling like I don't have a care in the fucking world. I need to go and see Joan, to fill her in on everything that happened today, but I can't bring myself to do it. Not right now. She can wait.

I'd like to say that it's the stress of the past week or the high of my current emotions that makes me follow O'Donnell inside. But it isn't. Or maybe it is and I just don't know it. Either way, I should say something to her and walk away, but I don't. Instead I follow her inside and let the door shut behind me. I glance back behind us as I click the lock on the door, seeing Ricky standing across the road and glaring at us. And then I turn away and let O'Donnell lead me up the stairs to her bedroom.

Chapter Fifteen

I wake to the early evening moonlight on my face. The curtains are still open, the window cracked just enough to let in a cool breeze. I can almost imagine that life is perfect—that this world never crumbled and that death never ventured upon my heart.

O'Donnell murmurs something and presses her body tighter against my side and I flinch, guilt creeping in on me. I blink against the sleep that's trying to pull me back under, and I look down at the mess of dark hair that's fanned out over my arm. My heart stutters in my chest for a split second until I realize that this isn't Nina, and I work to calm myself back down. Betrayal washes over me, and the good feeling I had earlier is gone.

"Did you just see a ghost?" O'Donnell mumbles, her voice thick with sleep. "Your heart is pounding in my ear."

"I need to go," I say, pulling my arm from under her head. I sit on the edge of the bed and try to ignore the hatred I'm feeling for myself for what I just did. It won't do any good, but I can't stop it.

"Don't go, not yet," she says from behind me, her hand snaking around my waist.

"I need to," I reply, my tone as foreboding as my current mood.

She lets go of me, as if touching me burns her fingertips.

The room is fairly dark, but not so much that I can't see the hurt expression on O'Donnell's face when I turn back to look at her.

Her eyes shine in the darkness, and she quickly sits up and pulls the covers tight around her body.

"Fine, go," she says, looking away from me.

I reach down and grab my balled-up T-shirt from the foot of the bed. "Look, I'm sorry, it's not like that," I promise as I pull the T-shirt over my head despite already being far too hot and sweaty as it is.

She lets out a dry laugh. "Sure, whatever."

"Seriously, it's not," I continue.

She looks at me, the hurt still there but anger bubbling below the surface, so I decide to come clean with her, lest I end up getting my ass kicked by her.

"I lost someone recently." I look down at my feet. "Really recently, in fact. Like, just before I came to Haven. I like you, I do," I say, looking back at her and reaching out tentatively. I expect her to slap my hand away, but she doesn't. "I love her. Loved her," I correct firmly. "She gave her life for me, to help me and Joan and Adam."

"The little kid you're trying to find?"

"Yeah." I take a deep breath. "Yeah, him. I didn't mean to lead you on or anything." I stroke my fingers down her arm and she shivers at my touch, her eyes meeting mine. "I really didn't. The pain," I say, clutching a hand to my chest as if I could reach in and grab my own heart and squeeze every inch of love out of it to stop it from hurting me any more. "It hurts so much, O'Donnell. She was everything to me."

"She's gone now," she whispers, her voice soft. "You can't be alone forever, Mikey."

135

I let out a quiet, dry laugh, because as far as I can believe, this will hurt forever. I can't imagine this pain not being here anymore. Every day it becomes more and more embedded in my skin. "Maybe I can, maybe I can't, but it's barely been a week. That's just downright disrespectful to her memory, don't you think?" I bite down on my bottom lip. The more I think about it, the more disgusted I am with myself. "What kind of man does that make me?"

"Then why bother even coming to my room?" O'Donnell takes my hand in hers and I look up at her. "Because you wanted to forget her," she says, answering her own question. "You wanted to move on."

I pull my hand from hers and shake my head, my words coming out forceful. "No. I just wanted to forget it all. Not her, but everything."

The hurt look is back on her face. "I'm sorry, maybe I shouldn't have come on so strong."

"It's not your fault," I say with a shake of my head. "I'm all fucked up inside, and with Adam being out there, somewhere all alone," I shake my head again, the words catching in my throat, "it's fucking me up even more. I promised her I'd look after him, that I'd keep him safe. I've let her down if I don't find him."

We lapse into silence, both of us trying to control our raging emotions.

"So we'll find him, Mikey," she says, giving my hand a soft squeeze. "First thing tomorrow, we'll set back out and we'll find him. Ricky saw something, at the edge of the field."

I look back up at her. "What was it?"

She shrugs. "It was a shoe."

I let her words sink in for a moment, the image of one of Adam's shoes at the edge of that field—a clue as to which way he'd gone staring me right in the face, and me going in the opposite direction.

"Why did no one say anything?" I ask, feeling sick to my stomach.

"He wanted to check out the house and barn, check for supplies, and for the kid, of course." She looks away from me, guilt flushing her features. "I should have said earlier, I'm sorry. I thought we'd go into the field once we'd checked out everywhere else. I didn't see it as a big deal."

But I know she's lying. She knows exactly how big of a deal it is by the fact that she can't hold my stare. But now isn't the time to get angry. It is what it is. We've both done things we aren't proud of in the last twenty-four hours.

I let go of her hand and stand up, reaching down to pick up my socks and boots. "I'll see you in the morning, O'Donnell."

She nods and forces a smile. "Yeah, I'll see you in the morning."

I walk to the bedroom door and open it, and I look back at her as she calls my name.

"Mikey, don't beat yourself up too much, okay?" she says.

I don't reply. Instead I walk out of the room and head down the stairs, listening as she speaks once more.

"A little sin of the flesh isn't hurtful if you intend to follow it through," she calls, grasping at proverbial straws.

I unlock the door and let myself out before clicking the door closed, and then as an afterthought I open it up again and shout up to her, "Lock the door behind me."

137

I shut the door again and jog down the small porch steps. I have no clue what time it is, but I know I'm not tired. I need to walk, to jog, to fucking do something to expel the anxious feeling running through my blood.

I walk around the entirety of Haven three times over before I feel like I can settle, and I head back to Phil's. He's lying across the swing on his porch with one leg dangling, smoking and staring up at the stars. By the smell that's hanging around him, I reckon he's at least five drinks deep and two joints gone. He looks over at me as I climb the steps.

"Hey," I say, sitting down on the steps.

"Hey, dude."

"How's she doing?" I ask, thinking of Fluffy.

He smiles. "She'll be all right. She's a tough thing. Women always are, though, don't you think?"

I think of Nina and nod in agreement. "Yeah."

"I mean, if I was ever in a fight, I'd always want a woman on my team, ya know? They can separate the good from the bad a lot easier than we can." He reaches down and picks up a small bottle of liquid, and takes a swig before handing me the bottle. I take it without hesitation, glad to have the burn of alcohol in my gut.

"Women complicate things," I say, handing him back the bottle.

Phil laughs. "Yeah, they do that."

He drops the end of his joint to the porch and stands on it with the leg that's dangling down, stubbing it out, and then he uses the same leg to swing himself gently. The porch swing squeaks softly on every third swing, piercing the silence of the night like a whistle. Phil's blue Hawaiian shirt is hanging off the bench like his leg, and it swings back and forth. I turn away and from out of the dark I watch Aimee walk across to us. She waves hello as she gets closer, and Phil sits upright, allowing some space for her to sit.

She passes me, giving me a brief smile as she goes to sit by Phil.

"Hey, darlin'." He cups a hand around the back of her head and leans in, kissing her deeply, and I look away, feeling awkward as the kiss extends into something with more intent than a quick kiss on the lips.

"Hey, you," she returns when they finally come up for air.

"Anything happening out there tonight?" Phil asks her, and she shakes her head no and yawns. "It's funny, don't you think, how we ask about each other's days, adjusting from 'how was work' to 'any zeds out there making noise?'"

"Yeah," I answer, agreeing with him. "How did this become the norm?"

Phil shrugs. "It's a fucked-up world, dude. But I think we're doing all right. We're all getting by and making peace with our fellow man."

"You two are going to make me gag," Aimee interrupts. "It's a fucked-up world, let's just get on with it already and not read too much into the situation. Feel like heading over to my place?" she asks Phil.

"Always," he replies, and they stand up together.

I move over so they can both pass me on the steps, and Phil looks back over his shoulder. "What did I tell you about strong women?" He grins. "They'll rule the damn world one day."

"More than likely," I reply.

"Catch you on the flip side, dude. And hey, Mikey, we'll find the kid tomorrow." Phil drapes an arm across the top of Aimee's shoulders and they walk away.

I watch them until even their shadows disappear into the black of the night, and then I put my head into my hands and let my guilt and worry swallow me whole for five full minutes before I pull my shit together.

Adam is out there, somewhere. Probably frightened, possibly dead, or undead. God, I can't handle that—the thought of him walking around as a deader for the rest of his eternal life. That's no way for anyone to live, never mind a damned kid. He doesn't deserve that. No one does, but especially not a kid. But then on the flip side there's the thought that he had already survived this long, and mostly alone. There's a huge chance that he's okay, that he's hunkered down somewhere and getting on with surviving, like he'd been doing well enough until we came along and took him away from his little safe spot in hell.

The fact that we didn't find him today doesn't mean anything either way—not really. I tell myself that lie to help myself breathe a little easier, and then I stand up and go inside the house before heading up to bed. The smell of Phil's critters has soaked into the walls of this house, and I can't blame Aimee for not wanting to live with him, or this smell. Yet I'm definitely getting used to it—well, at least after the initial slap in the face from the smell each time I come home.

Home.

No, not home. This place isn't home. At least not yet. It's a place to put my head down. To close my eyes and hope that tomorrow will be a better day. A safer day. A day without death. A day with food. And safety. And all the other things that come with living. Things we previously took for granted, but now they're our bread and butter, the balm to our broken souls.

God, if I could just go back and live one more week before all this happened...hell, even one more day, I would never fucking let go of it. A day of walking down the street without carrying a gun or a hatchet or a knife. Or turning a tap on and fresh, clean water coming out of it.

A day of climbing into bed and going to sleep, and knowing that tomorrow was just another normal Tuesday, or Wednesday, or whatever fucking day it happened to be, and not a day of fighting for survival and whatever scraps of life we got at the end of it. It's normality that I crave more than anything else. It's living and breathing, not Krispy Kremes and bottled beer—though of course I wouldn't turn those down either.

I climb on top of the bed, the evening too warm for covers, and I put my arms behind my head and stare up at the ceiling, letting my thoughts trail over the past couple of days—all the mistakes and the errors. The things that happened, the people that got hurt. And I decide that, although we were out looking for Adam, someone that I was supposed to be looking after, all these things that happened were not my fault. Not this time. It's this life, I decide. This life that's the problem.

I think about O'Donnell and the guilt creeps back in. I should never have gone upstairs with her; it was a huge mistake. But a mistake that I can't take back now.

I've only been here a couple of days, yet it's already beginning to feel like somewhere I can relax, at least a little. I really hope that O'Donnell and I can remain friends and that I haven't just messed up my chances of staying here. I can't lie—I like it here. The people, their ways, their beliefs. It's what I've been

141

searching for. And they've accepted me, all of my trouble and more. What else can I ask for?

Maybe that's pathetic, but I don't care right now. Sometimes you just want to feel like you belong, like you have somewhere to go when you can't hack the real world anymore. I haven't felt like that in a while. Even up at the treetop houses, I didn't feel like that. There had only been one place I'd felt that kind of contentedness, and that had been when I was with Nina. She'd made me feel like I had roots when I was with her.

I close my eyes. The image of Adam and Nina was hidden behind my lids and my stomach somersaults at the sight of them. I open my eyes and get up, moving to stand beside the window and look outside.

I won't sleep well tonight—that much is certain. It doesn't matter how many pep talks I give myself, there's still a deep-rooted hatred buried deep within me. And until I find Adam, that feeling won't ever ease.

The streets outside are quiet, like everyone is sleeping and no one has a care in the world, but when I shift my gaze to look at the boundaries of the complex, I notice the shadows moving along the top of the perimeter. I'll have my day of keeping guard here soon, and then my self-torturing insomnia will come in handy.

I turn away from the window, my gaze falling to the bushes beside this house, and I see a shadow move—a split second of something. I stare harder, focusing myself on those bushes and what could be within them, but when I can't see anything I wonder if I was just seeing things, my paranoia holding hands with my exhausted body and seeing things that weren't there. It's easy enough to do.

142

I wait several beats, but still don't see anything, so I climb back on top of the bed and close my eyes, forcing away the images of Adam and Nina this time. Sleep deprivation and guilt are making me paranoid, I decide.

Chapter Sixteen

I wake up feeling like shit. I wish I were one of those people that wakes up with a spring in their step and a smile on their face like I've been cast as the lead singer in a musical. But I'm not.

I always wake with a headache from grinding my teeth—a problem I've dealt with since I was a kid. I'm always tired, no matter how much sleep I get, and I always wake up hungry, though I never complain. Even before the apocalypse I didn't complain. Growing up there was never enough food in the house to feed me and my brothers and sisters, and being the eldest I always made sure that they had enough to eat, knowing that I could beg, borrow, and steal to feed myself. My mom worked hard to keep a roof over our heads. There was no point in complaining that I was hungry; she couldn't do any more than she already was. So the empty hole was never filled, and she never knew. It never even crossed my mind to put that burden onto her, even at nine years of age. See? I wasn't always bad.

I stretch my arms up above my head and let out a long yawn, pausing as something brushes against my arm. I crack open an eye and slowly roll my head to look up at where my hands are, my heart stuttering in my chest.

Zazz, or some equally scary big-assed snake, is coiled around the headboard of the bed and looking down at me, its forked tongue slipping in and out of its mouth. I *want* to punch it between its beady little eyes. I *want* to yell and cuss and dive off the bed as quickly as humanly possible. But I don't, because I remember Phil's words from yesterday about keeping calm and not frightening her. So instead of doing any of the things I want to do, I slowly slither my body down the bed and then roll myself to the edge of it and stand up.

Zazz is still watching me, her tongue hissing louder. It seems she doesn't like being in my room any more than I do.

"Easy, girl, it's going to be okay," I mutter quietly, raising an eyebrow when she seems to be calmed by the soothing tone of my voice. "I'm going to go and get Phil. You just wait right here."

I walk slowly to the door, keeping my eyes on her at all times, and then I shut the door behind me, lean back on the wall beside the closed door, and let out a slow breath. I give myself a minute for my heartbeat to return to normal and then I stand upright and go to take a step forward, almost standing on Miss Foxxxy Love as she scurries across the wooden floor in front of me.

"What the actual fuck?" I yell out, not being able to hold it in this time. Foxxxy doesn't waste any time waiting around to see what I'll do, and I'm glad. Instead she runs off into one of the other rooms and I reach over and slam the door shut behind her.

I decide to seize the day and get the fuck out of dodge, taking the stairs two at a time, jumping over a couple of cockroaches that skitter across the wooden floor at the bottom of the stairs, throwing open the front door, and diving outside before any other creepy critter attacks me. I jog down the porch steps and then jog back up them so I can slam the door shut behind me before jogging back down them again.

I'm breathing hard, the air burning in and out of my lungs. I bend over, putting my hands on my knees and sucking in some air as slow as I can, and attempt to calm myself down. But I can't, this is a damned critter attack!

"Morning, dude," Phil calls, crossing the street in front of the house. He takes in my panicked expression as I stand back upright and he runs over to me. "What happened?"

"Bugs," I gasp, still feeling out of breath. "Foxxxy and Zazz woke me up for an early morning ménage á trois!"

"What?" Phil frowns, his eyes going suddenly wide. "Are you serious?" he asks, already walking away from me and heading up to the house.

"Yeah, man, I wouldn't joke about this stuff." I stay at the bottom of the stairs, not wanting to go back inside the house.

Phil turns and comes back down the stairs before grabbing me by the throat, his face looking furious.

I tense, not wanting to kick his ass, but also not afraid to if I have to, because I have no doubt that I could.

"What did you do to my babies?" he yells in my face, his cheeks flushing red in anger.

"I didn't—" I gasp, threading my arms upwards through his and pushing his hands away from me. "I didn't do anything. I woke up and Zazz was curled around the headboard like a damn...well, like a damn snake."

"Their tanks and cages were all shut. They couldn't have just gotten out on their own, Mikey. So how did they get out?" He paces in front of me. "I swear, if they are hurt in any way!" He jabs a finger in my direction.

"I was sleeping, man, and as far as I'm aware I've never sleepwalked, so I haven't got a clue how they got out," I yell back.

Phil's expression changes, a quick flicker of worry washing over his features. "Okay, okay, I believe you." He climbs the porch steps. "Come on."

"Hell no, I'm not going back in there," I reply without hesitation.

Phil turns back to me. "I'm fucking serious, dude, get up here and help me. I left you in my home last night, in charge of my family, and whatever has happened, has happened, but you're helping to put this shit right before one of them gets hurt."

I climb the stairs slowly, the freshly stitched bite on my leg throbbing because of the running I did only minutes before. "Fine, but I'm not touching the snake or the spider," I snap.

"Pussy," he replies and opens the front door. And there's not an ounce of humor in his tone when he says it.

"Fuck off," I respond as we go inside.

One of the huge cockroaches scuttles across the floor in front of us and I immediately dive down on to my knees and reach over to scoop it up. I cringe as it moves in my hands. The feel of its little legs and hard shell moving over the palms of my hands enough to make me gag. Phil slams the door shut behind me as I stand up and I have to force myself not to vomit as the little beast continues to move around in my handmade cage.

"Go put it away. Where was Zazz and Foxxxy?" Phil says, his head craning to see up the stairs at the sound of something moving around.

"My room, near the bed, and Foxxxy ran into the room next door to mine," I reply as I head down the hallway to what I've now

147

renamed "the room of creepy shit." Lids are lifted off pretty much all of the cages and crates, and insects and animals are scattered around the room. I'm happy to see Lavender the skunk is still in her home. After dropping the cockroach into its tank and putting the lid back on top, I go over to Lavender's hutch and close the door. She opens her eyes momentarily, stretches, and rolls onto her back before going to sleep again.

I can hear Phil moving around upstairs, but I decide to leave him to his two best buddies, and instead I focus on catching the easy critters like the cockroaches—which turn out to not be so easy. Those little guys are fast, and it turned out that the first easy catch was just a fluke.

Phil eventually comes down the stairs with Zazz draped over his shoulders, whispering sweet nothings to her, and I'm glad to see that he doesn't seem as angry with me anymore. He moves over to her tank and carefully places her back inside it before closing the lid, and then he turns and surveys the disarray of the room.

"Did you catch Foxxxy?" I ask, knowing I'm not going back upstairs until he has.

"Not yet, but I know where she is." He checks the lids on the other insect homes, making sure they are on securely before turning to me. "Did you see anyone last night?"

I shake my head no, feeling bad for him, and I guess for myself. I couldn't deny that it looked bad, even though it had nothing to do with me. I mean, I turn up and all of a sudden his 'family', as he called them, get the ole' heave ho from their homes and dumped on to the floor. It was shitty timing, but I was the new guy so I would be the one blamed. I knew how this worked.

"Okay, well, I'm going to grab Foxxxy and then I'll be back and I'll do a full headcount of everyone. Don't want anyone to go missing, do we?" He leaves the room, his face etched with worry and concern, and my guilt intensifies.

Lavender has properly woken up now, probably at the sound of Phil's voice, and she's snuffling in one of the corners of her hutch. I go over to say hello, half expecting her to be wagging her tail like a dog, but she only stares at me with little black eyes and then begins to run in circles.

Phil comes back in. "Move the lid, dude," he says, and I stand up and lift the lid of Foxxxy's tank so he can put her carefully inside. He stands back up and puts the lid back in place, and watches her for several seconds in silence.

"Everything okay?" I ask. I mean, it's obvious that everything isn't okay, but he seems more concerned with Foxxxy than he did with Zazz.

"Yeah, I just don't like these guys getting stressed is all. I've built up a lot of trust with them over the years. I'd hate to think all of that would end because of something like this." Phil moves around the room, checking each tank and cage, crate and hutch, and eventually coming to stand back by my side. "They're all here. None of them looking too happy about it though."

"You mean at being locked back up?" I ask.

He shrugs. "Yeah, I guess. I think they enjoyed the freedom, but this is the safest place for them. Come on," he says as he turns and walks out of the room.

I follow him and we go into the kitchen, where he starts making some coffee for us both. I'm glad for it: though the adrenaline is still running riot in me, I know I'll crash soon enough. I pull out my painkillers and antibiotics and throw one of each to the back of my throat.

"I'm really sorry," I say with a frown and a helpless shrug. I hate apologizing for something that isn't my fault, but I have to say something to him.

Phil watches me for several moments, much like he watched Foxxxy; as if he was assessing if I was really okay. Eventually he nods and continues to make the coffee.

"Before all of this apocalypse stuff, I had my own critter business—Safari Phil's Animal Adventures," Phil begins, his gaze going far off. "I used to do animal roadshows, teach kids and adults alike how to care and look after animals and critters. Some of these guys have been with me since way back then. I managed to save a lot of them when I had to abandon my house."

"But not all?" I reply, watching his expression fall.

He shakes his head as the percolator bubbles and steams, and he grabs two mugs and pours us both a black coffee. "No, dude, not all of them." He tucks his hair behind his ears and pushes his glasses up his nose, seeming even sadder. "Some of them I just had to open their tanks and let them go." He goes and stands by the kitchen window and stares out into the backyard. "I still wonder about them now. Did they survive? Did they find a way to carry on?"

I think of the animals Phil has now, and I wonder how he picked which ones to bring with him. He treats them like family, yet if he had to choose which to leave behind, how did he make that choice? The weakest? The oldest? As much as I don't like ninety percent of these bugs and animals, I can't imagine having to pick which ones to save and which to set free in the hopes that they'd make it on their own. Especially since he viewed them as family.

"I honestly don't know what happened last night," I say regretfully. "I didn't even come downstairs after you left. I went straight up to bed." I think about last night and not being able to sleep, and then I remember the shadow I saw outside my window. "I might have seen something," I say, not wanting to get his hopes up. Or would it be down? I'm sure. All I know is that someone sabotaged Phil's animal room. I just don't know why. Was it to hurt me? Or him?

Phil turns away from the window and looks at me. He tucks his long hair behind his ears and pushes his glasses up his nose while he waits for me to continue.

"It was just a shadow really. I'm not even sure if it was real or not." I shrug again, knowing that I probably sound like an idiot.

"A shadow?"

I drag a hand down my face. "I know how that sounds, but I was tired, and annoyed and I couldn't sleep. I looked out of the window and I thought I saw something—or someone, but then it was gone. So I could have seen someone I guess, or it could have been a trick of the light," I sigh heavily, "who the fuck knows?"

Phil frowns as he thinks about it. "Okay, well, it is what it is. At least for now. They're all back and we'll just have to keep a tighter watch over things," he says, chewing on his lower lip. "I'm heading out for a smoke before I go and check in on Fluffy and then I'm heading over to Aiken for today's orders."

Phil unlocks the back door and goes outside and I head upstairs to my room, my skin tingling at the thought of all those bugs running around the house, and wondering what Zazz would have done to me if I hadn't woken up when I did. Did I look like a meal to him? Is that why he was watching over me? Or did he feel safe close to me and he knew that something wasn't right.

Or worse. Did someone purposefully put him there?

I search my room, even checking under the bed, and when I don't find anything there I leave the room and shut my door behind me, making sure to click it closed, and then I head back downstairs.

Phil is back in the kitchen going through the cupboards. When he sees me he throws over an energy bar and I gratefully catch it. We head out, walking across the street toward the center of Haven where Fluffy is recuperating in the doctor's office. I eat my bar as we walk, finishing it in two bites. Stormy is treating Ricky when we arrive, wrapping his arm with a large white bandage. He frowns and looks away as Phil and I walk in.

I think about him last night, watching me go inside with O'Donnell, and I wonder if he's pissed about that. Maybe he has a crush on her or maybe they already had a thing going and he thinks I just moved in on his territory. There's no easy way to bring that up in conversation, so I decide to leave it alone. If he's pissed about something, it's his choice to let me know so we can clear the air. And if not, I'll just keep my head down and hope it all blows over. Besides, I already have to clear the air with O'Donnell at some point today, and things were a little rocky with Phil now, the last thing I wanted to do was add another name to the list of people I had to apologize or clear things up with.

In fact, fuck it, I'm going to bury my head in the sand on this one completely.

"Morning, dude," Phil says to Ricky. "What happened there?" he asks, nodding toward Ricky's arm.

"Nothin'," Ricky snaps back, pulling his arm free from Stormy and sliding off the table. He moves across the room, his shoulder barging with mine as he leaves, but I refuse to rise to the bait.

152

"A 'thank you' would be nice," Stormy calls after him.

"You pissed him off somehow?" Phil asks, turning to look at me. "You know what? Don't tell me. Not my drama." He laughs and looks back at Stormy. "How's my girl doing today?"

She doesn't seem fazed by Ricky's behavior, instead focusing back on Phil with a smile. "She's much better. Come see for yourself."

We follow her through to a back room where Fluffy is lying in a soft bed on the floor, a large bandage wrapped around her middle. Achillies is lying by her side, and he sits up as we walk in, letting us know that he's in charge here.

Phil goes straight over to Fluffy and drops to his knees by her side. He strokes Achillies's head, giving him a quick scratch behind the ears at which Achillies whines happily, one of his hind legs thumping against the floor. "Good boy. How's she doing, eh? Have you been looking after her for me?" He reaches into his pocket and pulls out a clear ziploc bag filled with a pink meat. Both Fluffy's and Achillies's tails thump against the floor as Phil opens up the bag and they catch a whiff of what's inside. "Now I know that Stormy does her best, but I also know that hospital food ain't the best, so I brought you a little something."

He winks and digs a hand into the bag, grabbing hold of something. He pulls his hand out and places it under Fluffy's nose, and she wastes no time in noisily devouring the contents.

"Spam," he says as Stormy tries to interject. "Didn't even lace it with anything." He chuckles and then scoops up some more and drops it at Achillies's feet. "I promise."

I smile and raise an eyebrow at Stormy in question.

153

"Weed," she says. "In case you hadn't noticed, Phil's partial to smoking it, baking with it, and just about anything else you can do with it."

"Oh, I noticed." I smirk.

"How's the leg doing?" she asks me.

I shrug in response. It's hurting but I don't want anyone messing around with it again, so I'm happy enough to leave it be for now.

"You want me to take a look? Alfie is good, but stitches can get tight if you don't account for the swelling." She looks at me with concern.

"Nah, I'm good, thanks," I reply, and she nods okay but I can tell that she would feel better checking them.

Phil stands up. "All right, we better get over to Aiken and find out what's what." He looks down at Fluffy. "You keep getting better, but for now you need to sit this one out."

Fluffy whines and tries to get herself up, but Achillies lies back down next to her again, placing one of his paws over the top of hers. Fluffy looks at him and they share a look. If dogs could talk, it's pretty obvious what they would be saying to one another right now.

"Keep an eye on her, will ya?" Phil says to Stormy. "Come on, Mikey." And then he turns and leaves the room.

I wave bye to the two dogs and then to Stormy, and we leave and head over to Aiken's house. Even from outside I can hear shouting, and Phil and I share a concerned look before jogging up the steps and knocking on the door. A man is stood outside and he opens it for us as we approach, and we head through to the living room where all the shouting is coming from.

Aiken, O'Donnell, and Ricky are sitting on the sofa with a map spread across the table between them, and Ricky and O'Donnell are disagreeing over something while Aiken leans back on the sofa, watching the whole thing with irritation. Everyone looks up and shuts up as Phil and I walk in.

Chapter Seventeen

"'Bout time you two got here," Aiken says, sounding annoyed, though I have a feeling that it's more to do with whatever's been said between O'Donnell and Ricky than Phil and I only just arriving, because even after everything we've done this morning it's still early, from the looks of the sun still so low in the sky.

"Sorry, boss, had to check in on my girl," Phil says, moving to sit next to O'Donnell.

"Aimee?" Aiken asked.

Phil shakes his head. "Nah, Fluffy. She got all bit up yesterday trying to save our sorry asses."

Aiken looks across at me and gestures for me to sit down next to him. "Yeah, I heard. I also heard that Mikey here saved her."

"It wasn't as heroic as it sounds," Ricky grumbles, glaring across the table at me.

Aiken looks back and forth between the two of us, trying to work out exactly what's going on, and I decide to downplay the whole thing because it will only look bad on me if I cause shit between NEO members.

"Yeah, it was no biggie. I'm sure any NEO would have done the same thing. It was just that I got there first. After all, she's a part of this group as much as any of us, right?" I say, letting my sarcasm drench Ricky from head to toe. His exact words yesterday were that Fluffy was just a fucking dog—a sentiment that clearly not everyone had agreed with—and I know that he pissed off both Phil and O'Donnell by saying that. Well, maybe my downplay of the situation isn't very subtle after all.

I point to the map on the table, wanting to change the subject now that I've made my point to Ricky and made him feel uncomfortable. "What's all this?" I ask.

"A map," Ricky replies dryly.

"No shit?" I say sarcastically. I should probably shut my mouth but I can't help but keep opening it to annoy this man.

"This is where we were yesterday," O'Donnell interrupts before Ricky can say anything back to me.

I look across at her, but she won't look at me, instead she points to a circled area on the map.

"This is the barn and the house, and where all the shooting was coming from. I've tried to point out the trajectory so we can get an idea exactly where they were shooting from, and maybe how many of them there were," she says. She points to a large shadowed area. "And this is no-man's land—an area we haven't covered yet. In fact, most of that area to the west we haven't been through yet. We've been working mostly to the east for the past few months, getting that area cleared of zed packs, and scavenging any supplies. We have no idea what's in this area. My best bet is that whoever they were, they were not skilled with guns. Like, at all. But of course that doesn't mean they're not dangerous. They had us pinned down good and proper."

We all fall silent for a moment, five sets of eyes all staring down at the map in front of us and the shadowed no-man's land area. Someone has circled it with a red pen, making that specific area stand out more.

157

"Well that's ominous," I reply. "Should be a fun day out, I guess." Because regardless of everything she just said, and the stern look on Aiken's face, I'm heading back out there today to try and find Adam.

O'Donnell looks up from the map, her gaze moving to Aiken, and I sense the change in atmosphere. Or at least I see the grin on Ricky's face.

"What?" I ask, sitting up and playing dumb. Though I have a feeling that I know what's going to be said next.

Aiken turns to face me, a deep frown etched on his forehead. "You're not going out there—at least not today."

"Like hell I'm not," I reply sharply. "I need to find Adam, now more than ever. With every day that passes—"

"We get it, Mikey, we do," O'Donnell interrupts. "But with your leg all busted up, and with the uncertainty of who these people are, we just can't take the risk of you being out there."

"I'm a big boy, O'Donnell. If I die trying to find him, at least I'll die doing something good." I glare at her, feeling betrayed by her and wondering if she's doing this because of last night. Is it revenge spurring her on to keep me here? I stand up, my body feeling restless.

Aiken stands up, his large frame towering over me. "Sit yourself down, Mikey."

"I'm good standing," I snap back, my hands clenched into fists. Goddamn, this day is going from bad to worse.

"That wasn't a request," Aiken replies, his tone a direct threat. He walks away from the sofas as if his own body is restless. He's a good man; that much I've surmised already, and I trusted his opinion. But if I wanted to leave, I would. No one was going to

158

keep me here and stop me looking for Adam. He was in my care, and I needed to find him asap

Aiken turns to glare at me. "I said sit down."

I sit down. Of course I do—I'm not stupid.

"This isn't about you," O'Donnell says. "It's about us, Haven, the NEOs. It's about keeping us all safe, and until we know how to either take these people out, or if we can trade with them, we can't go back there. You want to find the kid so much that you might get us all killed in the process."

I shake my head. "I'm not some loose cannon, you know. I have survived just as long as you people and I know how to handle myself. Probably better than you can."

Aiken's hard gaze is still on me. "Take the day to let your leg rest. Kelli, O'Donnell, and Ricky are going to scout the area and keep tabs on whatever crew is in that barn. We'll see how things look tomorrow," he says, looking over at us all. "They'll keep watch for the kid."

"Keep watch?" I yell and stand up again. "Keeping watch isn't going to find him and bring him back safely! I can't leave him out there for another day!"

O'Donnell stands up and comes toward me, but I step back out of her reach, bumping into Phil, who has come up behind me.

"He's just a kid!" I yell even louder, looking frantically from Phil to O'Donnell. "We can't just keep leaving him." I glare at Aiken. "You promised me you'd help me find him!" I point my finger at him, feeling furious.

"This isn't about you anymore, Mikey," Aiken replies calmly, despite my shouting. "This is about Haven, about the rest of NEO. This is bigger than you, and the kid."

"Nothing's bigger than finding him!" I argue.

Aiken shakes his head dismissively. "I'm not risking any more NEO's for you or for him. I don't mind sending people out to look for him when I know the risks are the usual; dogs and Zeds, but when I don't know the risks—when the danger is more than that, that I can't do, my friend. I can't risk people's lives for this."

I open my mouth to argue, but Phil moves closer and stops me.

"Dude, I get it…we all get it, but have you stopped to think that maybe he's already—" Phil holds my gaze.

"Of course I have!" I yell, and then quieter: "Of course I have." I shake my head. "No doubt he probably is dead. But I can't just give up on him." I sit back down and put my head in my hands.

"And we're not either." O'Donnell's soft voice reaches across to me. "We'll keep looking while we're checking out this other crew and seeing what they're all about. I promise we will. But you need to rest your leg. At least for a day."

I look down at my leg. It's throbbing like crazy, and deep down I know that they're all right. But that didn't make me feel any better. In fact, it made me feel worse. It felt like I was choosing Haven over Adam. And I had a feeling that Nina would have taken a very different path to this one.

"Okay," I finally say. I look up as Phil pats me on the shoulder.

"Everything will be okay, dude," he says.

It sure as hell doesn't feel like it, but I don't really have much choice by the sounds of it. I have no doubt in my mind that Ricky won't bother looking for Adam, but I know that O'Donnell will do her best. And maybe they're right. Maybe I would be going in there, all guns blazing, and end up getting one or more of us killed. Maybe it'll be best if they scout the area first and I let my leg heal a little.

I move across the room, wanting to get outside. "I need to go find Joan. Where's she staying?"

Aiken smiles for the first time this morning, the long red scar on the side of his face rising like an extra mouth. "She's got a little house all for herself down by the old church. She's settled in real nice."

I nod my thanks. "I need to go and see her; she needs to know what's going on." And suddenly I feel the full weight of guilt at the realization that I haven't really taken the time for her since we got her. I haven't checked she's okay, or given her an update on Adam. In fact, if I'm being honest with myself, if it wasn't for the fact that I wanted out of this room right now, I probably wouldn't be going to see her today either. I look across at O'Donnell. "Stay safe."

She smiles, a small blush rising to her face. "I will. And I'll keep a lookout for Adam for you, I promise."

"Boss? Can I have a quick word?" Phil says.

Aiken nods and jerks his head toward the door, dismissing everyone else. We all leave and I don't wait around to say anything else to O'Donnell or Phil. Everything that needs to be said has been said, I decide. Instead I head over to see Joan, knowing I'm going to catch some shit off her for being so ignorant.

The small church is at the back of Haven, close to the food stores. I guess that means all of our food is holier than thou. Joan is sitting on the porch in a small wooden chair. A long cigarette hangs between her lips and her hands are moving a mile a minute as she knits furiously. Her gaze seems to be far off as she works,

161

the thick wool gliding across the needles with ease. As I get closer, she slows and then stops before setting whatever it is she's making to one side and removing her cigarette. She drops it into an overflowing ashtray at her feet and waits for me to climb the steps.

"Morning," I say, feeling wary of her. She looks pissed off and of course she's as unpredictable as anything, so I have a right to be wary of her.

"Is that all you have to say?" she grumbles, reaching down to pick up her pack of smokes. "You shrug me off yesterday, you say you'll come to see me, you promise to find the kid, and you do none of those things. But all you have to say to me today is 'morning'?" She lights another cigarette and picks her knitting back up, the furious clatter of the needles clashing against one another filling the empty space.

I sit down on the steps in front of her, looking out across her lawn. "I'm sorry," I finally say.

"That's more like it."

I look over my shoulder at her, seeing her for the first time. She's just an old lady. A crazy one, no doubt, but she's worried about Adam just like I am. Perhaps I purposefully avoided her last night because I didn't want to face her. Because she would make me face up to what a failure I am. I failed Nina, and now I'm failing Adam.

"I didn't find him," I admit, looking away when she scowls at me. "We ran into trouble yesterday and had to come back. I'm going back out tomorrow though. I know I'll find him," I say, my words melting away.

Joan tuts at me and continues to scowl. "I guessed that you hadn't found him, and I guessed that you had trouble by the state of you yesterday. Blood all over yourself, dying dog in your arms, sweaty pit stains ruining that Hippy Dippy flowery shirt of yours. None of it went unnoticed, you know. I'm not completely barmy."

I force a smile. "It's a Hawaiian shirt," I say.

"I know what it is! I was one of the most sought-after hula girls back in the day, ya know! People used to come from miles around to see these hips shaking their thing." Joan stands up and drops her knitting onto her chair before beginning to hula in a circle. "See? I've still got it!"

I try not to laugh, because honestly it's the thing I feel least like doing right now, but it's hard not to. She eventually stops hulaing, and sits back down and continues knitting.

"I'm going to tell you something now, Mikey, and it might come as a big surprise to you." She takes a deep breath before continuing. "I'm not as young as I once was, and this old heart of mine, it can't take much more loss. Do you understand me?" Her eyes are glistening and I nod at her. "I need you to do the things that you say you'll do. I need you to find the boy and bring him home. And I need you to come and see me when you say you'll come and see me, do you understand?"

"I do, I'm sorry."

"But Mikey, most of all, I need you not to die, okay?" She leans forward in her chair, her knitting resting on her lap.

I swallow and nod again.

"Can you promise me that? Can you promise an old lady like me that you won't go and get yourself killed and leave me all alone?"

I can't promise her that. Because to promise her that would be a lie. Every time I leave Haven there is a possibility that I will die, that I'll leave her all alone in this world. Hell, every day that any of us wakes up is a damned miracle, because who knows what's going to happen from one day to the next. Yet I still find myself nodding and agreeing not to get myself killed. It's an impossible promise, yet I promise it all the same.

Joan smiles at me and picks her cigarette back up. "All right then, go on, get. I've got work to do." And with that she continues knitting.

I realize as I walk away that she never even asked me what happened yesterday. And I simultaneously realize that someone else must have told her for me. I think of O'Donnell, but I'm not sure that it was her, but then decide that it doesn't really matter. Joan must be making some friends here if she knows what happened. She has people she can talk to. She has purpose. That's what matters. And hell, it's more than I can say that I have right now.

Chapter Eighteen

I stood at the gate and watched the truck with O'Donnell, Kelli, and Ricky in it drive away. O'Donnell made me promise to rest my leg up so I was strong enough to go out with them tomorrow, and I was going to keep that promise. So as soon as they were out of sight I headed on over to see Stormy, who loosened up some of my stitches and gave me some stronger pain meds.

I checked in on Fluffy before I left, noting that she was wearing one of those cones of shame and looking sorry for herself. I patted her on the hind and smiled before I headed over to the guard tower so that I could sit and wait for the truck to return.

O'Donnell had said I had to rest, but I'm not the sort of man to go and climb back into bed and take a nap—plus I didn't trust falling asleep in Phil's house without him there anymore since the great animal escape this morning. So being on guard seemed a half decent compromise.

There are only seats for three people, so Vicki takes this as her chance to go and clean some of the guns they found on their last drive out. It's a job she apparently loves doing. And it leaves me, SJ, and her kid Moo on guard for the day, which is more than enough.

Moo is the oddest kid I have ever met. Dark blond choppy hair, blue-green eyes, and an attitude that's killer. As the day wears on I realize that there's more to her than just her snippy attitude and typical teenage eye rolling. She's funny, and caring, and she loves her mom more than anything in the world.

Before the world went to hell she loved Justin Bieber, and she loses cool points for that, of course. But she also laughs when I say I hope Justin was the first to get eaten, and she doesn't throw a fit over my flippant comment, so she gains some of those cool points back.

The best thing about SJ and Moo, though, is how they bounce off each other so much. They are both competitive, compassionate, and love each other so much that it makes me ache for Nina. Moo hates being up here because of her fear of heights, but she still does it regardless, and I realize that they are rarely without each other. They've lost the rest of their family over the past few years, but it's clear that they have no intention of losing each other. Even if that means practically living in each other's pockets constantly.

I think of Nina and how often we went off to do our own thing and I wish I could take it all back and live like Moo and SJ. Maybe then I wouldn't be in this situation without her.

I look out toward the horizon, thinking I've seen the truck returning, or at least dust billowing which would imply the truck was returning, but after several tense moments I realize it's just a couple of deaders in the distance and I sigh.

"Nothing?" SJ says and I shake my head no. She seems concerned for me, and it just makes me like her all the more. I think Nina would have liked her too. She's a real protective mother-bear figure—soft and cuddly on the outside, but hard on the inside. And I have no doubt that she'll gut anyone who might try to hurt Moo.

"They'll be back soon," I say, sitting back down. My leg is feeling so much better since Stormy loosened the stitches. The stronger pain relief is helping also, no doubt.

"I hate being up here," Moo says for the sixth or seventh time in the past couple of hours. She's sat cross-legged on the floor, sharpening her knife and doesn't bother to look up at either of us as she says it.

"I know," SJ says, her gaze lingering on her daughter. Her face lights up with a smile a moment later. "Hey, Moo, do the thing, the dance. Show Mikey!" SJ laughs.

Moo rolls her eyes dramatically in a gesture that reminds me of Nina, but then she smiles and stands up. "Fine, but just once," she says and then begins doing some weird dance move—if it can be called that.

I frown and raise an eyebrow. "Is she okay?" I ask, only half joking.

SJ laughs harder. "It's dapping. It was all the craze back then."

"Mom! Dabbing—it's dabbing, not dapping!" Moo groans and sits back down before picking up her knife and continuing to sharpen it.

But I'm still stuck on the *Back then* comment referring to pre-apocalypse. I don't think about *back then* very often. Certainly not in the way of what I miss or what's changed. I always figure, what's the point? I mean, everything has changed and I miss everything too. Well, almost everything.

"Hey, Mikey, do you want Moo to teach you how to dab? She taught me, she's a great teacher," SJ says cheerfully as she tries to pull me back out of my funk.

I laugh but decline the offer. My gaze strays to the horizon once more, where a truck is clearly headed our way. Dust is billowing up behind it, creating a cloud of smoke in its wake. I stand up and look through the binoculars, feeling a little hope as our truck comes back into view.

"I'm heading down to the gate. I'll get Vicki to come on up," I say as I climb down the ladder, not waiting for SJ to reply.

Alfie is already rolling the gate open when I get there, and O'Donnell drives the truck through, parking it in its place. She opens the door and climbs out, with Kelli and Ricky doing the same. Kelli pats my arm and offers me a small smile as she walks by.

O'Donnell nods for me to follow her as she and Ricky head toward Aiken's house.

"Well? Anything?" I ask, trying not to sound too frantic.

O'Donnell shakes her head. "Nothing on the kid. It looks like he went into the field for sure."

"Okay, that's progress at least, right?" I ask.

O'Donnell smiles at me. "Yeah, it is. As my mom used to say, no news is good news, right?"

I'm not so sure on that. Right now I'd kill for some news—any news. Dead, alive, I just want to know where he is. But I also know that that possibility of finding out anything substantial is slipping away each and every day. If he's alive, he's safely tucked away somewhere and we might not find him ever again. If he's a deader then he's shambling the hell away from here. And if he's dead—well, that didn't bare thinking about.

We reach Aiken's house and climb the steps, but when I start to go inside, Ricky puts a hand on my chest. "He'll call for you if he wants to see you."

I glare at him and grip his hand as I move it off me. My gaze strays to O'Donnell, but she purses her lips in defeat.

"He'll call you if he wants to see you, Mikey," she says and turns to go inside.

"Fine," I say, wanting to say something else but know I need to keep my calm.

Ricky glances down at my freshly bandaged leg. "I see you've been resting up. That's good." And then he turns and walks into the house, shutting the door behind him.

I sit down on the steps, feeling like a waster, because that's exactly what I've been doing today—resting. It's what I needed, but not what I wanted to do. In fact, I'm beginning to feel like an injured wolf. And injured wolves get taken down by the other dogs in the pack. As voices drift out to me from inside Aiken's house, I swear to myself that I won't be the weaker wolf for long.

The door eventually opens, and O'Donnell and Ricky come back out. Ricky walks away giving me a mock salute and O'Donnell sits down next to me. I stare at her profile for several moments while I wait for her to speak.

"We're going back tomorrow. We only watched them for today," she says.

"And tomorrow?" I ask.

"Tomorrow we need to take them down." Her voice is filled with frustration and dread, as if this isn't what she wants to do at all, but of course it's the NEO way, and Aiken is calling the shots.

I let her words settle before I reply. "Who are they?" I finally ask.

"Honestly, we don't really know yet. But what we do know is that they're dangerous. There's a lot of them, and they have a lot of weapons," she laughs without humor, the same dread in her tone as moments ago. She turns to look at me finally. "They could turn up here at any time, and though we'd win that battle, we'd lose a lot of people in the process. Aiken won't take that risk. He won't risk any of our people."

She stands up and I copy her, and when she walks away, I follow silently. We head over to her house, but when I try to follow her inside she places a hand on my chest like Ricky had done, and stops me.

"I wasn't," I start. "I mean, I didn't think—"

"I know," she replies. "But I don't want the lines getting blurred again. You've made your feelings clear, and I want to respect that."

I run a hand through my hair. "I wasn't following you for that reason," I say with a small laugh.

"I know, but who's to say I didn't want that to be the reason?" She winks and goes inside, shutting the door behind her, and I'm left all alone on her porch, feeling like a kid who just got dumped before prom.

I only followed her because I don't know where else to go. Who else to talk to. Phil is still out with Aimee and some others on a supply run to an old grocery store, and with nothing new to tell Joan, I don't want to go over there.

I circle around Haven three or four times, eventually heading back to Phil's house and sitting on his porch swing while I wait for him to come back. I'm hungry again; my stomach is growling something fierce, but I don't want to take Phil's food without checking with him first. And I don't feel like I've done anything to earn any food from Haven stores. So I sit, and I wait, feeling lonely and confused. And hungry.

*

I wake in the morning, still on the porch swing outside, only now I'm lay down. A steaming cup of coffee is on the floor, and its strong smell is wafting up to me. I know I woke up several times through the night, with images of Adam being torn apart by dogs and deaders, or Nina being blown apart by Fallon. Yet each time I woke, I hadn't been able to find the energy to go inside and go to bed so I'd stayed on the porch swing. Or maybe I was piss-scared of being attacked by Foxxxy and Zazz again.

I sit up and stretch out my back before reaching down and picking up the mug of coffee. I drink it as I walk inside the house and call Phil's name. He pops his head out of his animal room and gives me a smile. In his arms is a light-brown-haired skunk, but I can't remember what her name is.

I follow him inside and see that thankfully I've missed feeding time. At least the day seems to be starting better than yesterday.

"Good sleep?" he asks with a laugh.

"Oh yeah, the best," I grumble, swallowing back the coffee. "Why didn't you wake me?"

"You looked pretty peaceful out there, dude."

"It was dangerous," I reply. "If a deader would have gotten in," I start but then stop talking, because what's the point? What's done is done, and it was my responsibility to keep myself safe, not anyone else's.

Phil is watching me carefully, a small smile on his face. "I'll wake you next time," he says simply.

"Thanks," I reply. He puts the skunk away and then moves to another tank, and I decide I've seen enough for one morning already and I head out of the room. I put my mug in the kitchen and head back outside to the porch, and moments later Phil joins me. He shuts and locks the door behind him.

"No strange visitors last night then?" he asks.

"I'm assuming you mean your creepy-crawlies?"

He laughs. "Yeah, or anyone else."

I frown and stare off into the empty street. "No, nothing and no one." It's still pretty early and people are only just starting to wake up. I can see curtains being drawn back from windows and such but no one seems to be up and ready to roll yet.

We make it over to Aiken's house and Phil knocks on the door once. The door opens and I see it's Kelli this time. She smiles at me and jerks a thumb to the living room.

"He's in there, waiting for you," she says. "Leg feeling better?" she asks as I pass her.

"Yeah, thanks," I reply.

I'm barely limping today and I'm already feeling a lot better. The swelling has started to go down in my leg, and the antibiotics are doing their job. I'm hopeful that I'll be allowed to go with them today, especially if they plan on taking out that crew in the barn—though I can't say I agree with doing that just yet. Sure, they shot at us, but maybe they saw us as the threat. After all, we had been heading toward their home. And what would NEO do if people were heading towards Haven? Would we wait and ask questions later? Or would we shoot what we perceived to be the enemy before it arrived? I had a feeling that I knew the answer to that question already.

Ricky and O'Donnell are already there, and they look up as Phil and I enter.

"You rest up that leg yesterday?" Aiken asks immediately, his matchstick in his mouth again.

I nod. "Yes, all day. But I was on guard duty, keeping watch, so I was at least trying to pull my weight."

Aiken seems pleased by that. "And how's it feeling today?"

"Much better," I answer truthfully. "Still hurts a little, but I'm not limping and the swelling has gone down. Meds are definitely working."

"All right, all right," Aiken says with a smile. "Well then you better pay attention to what's going on if you're heading out with the group."

I sit down, feeling grateful that I can do something more useful today. "O'Donnell said you want to take out the other crew?" I pose it as a question, though I already know the answer of course.

Aiken nods. "Indeed we do. Can't go having a threat like that sitting on our doorstep. I'm not risking my people."

"I agree," Ricky says. "It's not worth the safety of everyone in Haven."

O'Donnell looks uncertain but she nods in agreement regardless when Aiken looks across at her. She leans over the map and points to a small area. "Yesterday, we hid the truck there and went around the back, here." She points to another part. "I think we can do the same thing today by flanking the other side, here." She points to another part of the map. "We can check for the kid that way too."

Aiken doesn't look completely convinced that it's the best idea, and neither am I, but I'm grateful that she's still trying to think of Adam and how to get him home.

"And if this other crew sees you, what then?" Aiken asks, his voice tinged with irritation. "You're cornered."

O'Donnell shakes her head. "Those fields are so overgrown, there's no way they could see us in there. We'll have plenty of cover to take out that crew and we can look for the kid. It makes sense, Aiken," she says, pleading my case for me.

Aiken goes silent while he stares down at the map. His matchstick moves from side to side while he thinks about it, and I do a silent prayer that he agrees to this plan, because there's not a chance in hell I'm not looking for Adam today. And if they think Adam's gone into that field, that's exactly where I'll be going. Even if it kills me doing it.

"All right, all right, let's do it then. But, O'Donnell, your first priority is taking out that crew. Once that's done, you can properly search for the kid without worrying that someone's going to shoot you in the back. Ya hear me?"

O'Donnell nods. "I hear you, boss."

Phil laughs. "We're gonna' need bigger guns." He turns his attention to Aiken. "Can I take the rocket launcher?"

Aiken grins. "That sounds like a damn good idea." He turns to me then, his expression suddenly serious. He frowns as he thinks over what he wants to say, but I can already tell it's not something I'm going to like.

"Just spit it out, Aiken," I eventually say.

"Ricky here thinks your friend is dead," he replies, his head jerking towards Ricky.

174

I watch Aiken, knowing by the twitch in his jaw and the cool stare that he's testing me, and probably Ricky as well, but I can't work out which way around would make me the winner. On one hand being a NEO means sticking together and protecting one another no matter the cost, so we should go after Adam and rescue him, or make sure he's definitely dead. But on the other hand it's a dangerous mission, especially now with the barn full of lunatics shooting at us. Will Aiken want to risk his crew for one kid? For me?

In the end I have to go with my gut. Mainly because if Nina taught me anything it was that sometimes, there was no other real option than to say what's on your mind and be damned with the consequences. Of course, she also taught me that it didn't always work out so well when you did that.

"I think he might be right, though I also think Ricky is a pussy," I say. "But I have to try and find Adam. I owe him that much. So I think we should go and try to find a helpless little kid, clear that barn of whoever is hiding in it, and take all of their supplies. Then we can begin clearing to the west, and take control of it."

I don't even look in Ricky's direction when I talk, though I can bet what his expression is right now.

Aiken smiles again. "You're a cocky son of a bitch, and I like that about you, Mikey," Aiken says, clapping his hands together.

Aiken stands up and moves to the window, the sun warming his back, and he looks over us all. O'Donnell and Ricky stand up, both tense and ready to go, and Phil and I follow suit.

"Let me tell you a little story," Aiken begins, his hard gaze moving over us all. "My daddy used to drive trucks for a living," Aiken eventually says. "He'd be gone for weeks on end. An ice road trucker, they used to call him. One of the best in the

175

business. Nothin' ever stopped him from making his delivery. Not even zeds." He shakes his head and moves the matchstick from one side of his mouth to the other. "He was a stubborn old bastard. By the time he made it back home to us, my mom was a zed." Aiken reaches up and pulls the matchstick free of his mouth, and then he runs his tongue along his teeth, a look of disgust crossing his features. "She'd already killed my sister before I could stop her, but she didn't get me. No, sir."

"Boss?" Ricky says cautiously.

Aiken's gaze slowly moves to him. "My daddy had put others before his own family. His own pride before his wife. His arrogance before his kids." He reaches up and puts the matchstick back. "I killed him in his sleep that first night home. I waited for him to bar the windows better than I had, and then when he was sleeping I slit his throat."

Aiken stops talking and walks toward us, his stare deadly, and I realize it's the only time since my first night here that I've felt truly threatened by Aiken—that I realize how dangerous he really is. His nice guy act is just that: an act. A pretense to keep us all at ease. I had wondered what made everyone jump when he told them too, because the Aiken I had seen was easy going and laid back, but I saw it now. He was a leader, and he was in control even when it seemed like he wasn't.

O'Donnell reaches out and pats Ricky on the shoulder. "Come on, let's get going." She grabs his jacket and begins to walk away, pulling him with her. "We'll be back before nightfall, boss," she says.

"You see that you do," Aiken replies. His gaze meets mine, a small frown between his eyebrows.

176

It's pretty obvious what he was saying to us, and how far he'd be willing to go to enforce it. And it's obvious that though he trusts me, he knows there's some bad blood that he doesn't understand between me and Ricky. I can't help but wonder whose side he'll take, if it comes to that. Ricky hasn't liked me since I first arrived, and he hasn't bothered to give me a reason either. All I know for certain is that if it comes down to it, I'm not a hundred percent certain that he'll have my back—NEO or not.

We head back outside, with Phil and Ricky going over to get the extra weapons and telling me and O'Donnell to make sure the area is clear just outside the gates. Alfie is there once again, a cigarette hanging from between his lips as he chats with Moo. I frown as we get closer. Moo can't be more than thirteen, and Alfie looks much older.

"What are you two up to?" I ask, sounding every bit the father of a teenage girl.

Alfie pulls out his cigarette and looks at me, his eyebrows pulling together in concern. O'Donnell laughs from by my side.

"He's only fourteen," she says. "Give him a break. They're both just kids."

Moo turns to glare at O'Donnell. "I am not a kid." Her cheeks flush red and I feel bad about calling them both out. I didn't realize that Alfie was so young—otherwise I wouldn't have said anything.

"You shouldn't smoke," I say to him, to which he frowns even harder at me. I turn to Moo. "And you are a kid, and you shouldn't be near the gate." I think about Emily-Rose and what happened to her, and my stomach somersaults. Moo reminds me very much of her—young, feisty, and with a no-nonsense

177

attitude. But she was also too trusting, and would no doubt make stupid mistakes, like kids do.

Moo laughs. "I have the best shot in this place." Her hand is on the gun at her hip, her gaze moving from me to O'Donnell. "You don't need to worry about me."

"Almost the best shot, don't get cocky, Moo" O'Donnell says before turning to me. "But she's right. We teach our kids to fight, to shoot a gun, hand to hand combat, survival skills. Every person here can handle themselves." She looks back at Moo. "Especially this one right here." She says it almost proudly, and I'm guessing that she helped teach Moo how to shoot.

"Anything out there?" O'Donnell says to Alfie.

"A couple," he says, stubbing out his cigarette, his brown eyes fixing on me as his shoulders straighten like he's sizing me up. "Nothing I can't handle."

I have to force myself not to sigh in annoyance. Trained kids are great for survival—at least ours. Kids with overinflated egos are not good for their survival.

"Well, Mikey and I are handling these ones, so you keep watch for Phil and Ricky while we clear the path." She turns to the gate, waiting for Alfie to pull it open, and then she looks back over her shoulder, her gaze fixing on Moo. "You can help too." She grins.

"Watch and learn," Moo says to me as the gate begins to open.

I shake my head in annoyance at her arrogance, but can't knock the kid when she quickly takes out a deader with a clean shot right between the eyes. She turns and grins and then pulls out the knife from her sheath and dives in to slash at another deader. She's quick, I'll give her that.

"Are you joining in today, Mikey?" O'Donnell says with a grunt as she fights with a deader. It's mostly bones, with just a layer of paper-thin skin covering it, and it's completely naked, barring one shoe. One shoe. What the fuck is that all about? How do you lose your underwear but keep a shoe?

She grabs at its neck, her fingers wrapping around the entire thing because it's so thin, and she reaches back with her knife and stabs it through the forehead, and then lets it drop to the ground like an empty sack.

Another deader is closing in on us and I jog over to it, noticing that it's another one of the water zombies from a couple of nights ago. I wonder if it has only just managed to drag itself free of the mud surrounding the lake, or if this is another that washed up on the shore since then. It's almost lost an arm in the process of dragging itself free, and now its limp, bony arm is hanging by threads from its shoulder. It's nothing I haven't seen before—in fact it's pretty tame compared to some of the deaders. The grossest thing is the swishing sound it makes with every step, as if it's filled with rank water and God only knows what else. And of course the smell. The smell makes me retch and gag, even being close to it. The deader is soggy and putrid, its skin bubbled in places where it's previously been burnt.

It lurches for me and I dodge out of its way and slash out with my hatchet, hoping to knock it off balance, but for an old deader it's surprisingly able-bodied. It reaches forward with its one good hand, its mouth open wide, its jaws snapping open and closed as it dreams of chewing on my flesh. I slash at the reaching arm, chopping it clean off so that the only thing it can use to grab at me now is its teeth, and I take care of those by smashing my hatchet into its face. It cuts a straight line right through the center of its head, splitting it wide open like a watermelon. Even makes a super-cool popping sound too. I yank

179

on my hatchet, pulling it free and dragging most of the deader's teeth out with it.

"Took you long enough," Moo's voice calls from behind me.

She's leaning against the wall with her arms crossed, that obnoxious look that only teenagers can have smoothed across her face. A swishing sound has me turning back around and I look back down at the deader with a frown. Its stomach is moving—minutely at first, but as I watch, the movements get stronger.

"What the hell is that?" O'Donnell says.

"Ewww," Moo joins in. "Stab it, kill whatever's in there."

I continue to grimace, dark curiosity burning through me, but the smell emanating from this thing is enough to tell me not to carve it open. Curiosity killed the cat, right?

"I don't know," I say.

"I really wanna' see what's inside of it." Moo laughs.

"I kinda do too," O'Donnell says.

I look up at her and she tears her gaze away from the deader. Her eyes connect with mine for a split second before she looks away, her cheeks flushed.

"Yeah, I'm not opening that thing up. The smell is bad enough as it is," I say, turning away.

The growl of an engine has us all turning around as Alfie pulls open the large gate and a truck pulls out with Phil and Ricky inside. As usual, Ricky's stare is fierce and Phil's is casual. Nothing seems to faze that man, I think as I watch him blowing smoke circles out the window.

180

"Hey, dudes." He waves in our direction. "That looks like a keeper, Moo," he says, nodding toward the deader on the ground.

Moo grins. "I thought so, until this clown broke all its teeth!" She glares at me.

I shake my head. "I'm too old for this shit," I mutter, backing away from the still-swishing deader and heading toward the truck.

O'Donnell matches my pace, waving goodbye to Moo, who walks back toward the entrance where Alfie is waiting to close the gate.

O'Donnell and I climb inside the truck, and I take in the ammo on the bed of the truck. My eyes go wide as I carefully root through the small bag of grenades and the larger guns that I can't even put names to. By the looks of it, there are even three homemade bombs, which is a scary prospect, because God knows who made them and how safe they are. O'Donnell watches me carefully as I go through the weapons, avoiding her stare.

"You like what you see?" O'Donnell asks, and I look up at her. I'm not entirely sure that she isn't goading me for the answer she wants to hear—that she wants me to say that I like looking at her. And in truth, I can't say that I don't. She's a beautiful woman: thick dark hair, dark eyes, and beautiful curves. But I also don't want to lead her on again, her own words from the previous night coming to mind.

"Umm, yeah, there's some big guns," I say instead, deciding that this is a neutral enough answer.

She lets out a laugh. "Big guns, huh?"

I frown and then smirk, realizing what I said and the double meaning of it. "Oh yeah," I agree, trying not to laugh. "Real big guns."

Guilt punches me in the stomach. I shouldn't be joking about stuff like this with her. I know exactly what we're both saying, and I'm doing what I just said I wouldn't do. In a past life, I'm sure I was a woman, because I'm beginning to get as confusing as hell.

"I like big guns," O'Donnell says, holding my stare.

I let out a slow breath. "I uhh…"

"I'm joking, asshole," she laughs.

I smirk and drag a hand down my face, giving my beard a quick scratch. I look over at Ricky and Phil but they're deep in conversation.

"Calm down. Look," she begins, reaching up and tightening her hair band nervously, "that was an asshole move the other night, but whatever, what's done is done. Okay? I don't want things weird between us."

Well shit, that makes things easier, I decide, yet the hurt look still on her face makes me realize that she's fronting. But I accept her front because like she said, I'm an asshole, and it's easier.

"Sure, that sounds good," I say, clearing my throat. "I'm sorry though, okay?"

A pained look crosses her face, but she waves me away. "Yeah, okay, like I said, whatever." She looks away and begins going through her bullets, fake counting them.

It isn't okay, not even a little bit, but instead of saying something to make it right I purse my lips and nod before looking out the window and shutting down the conversation completely.

Chapter Nineteen

The drive back out to the old barn is long, perhaps seeming longer because I feel so uncomfortable, but I feel it in my guts that we'll find Adam today. One way or another.

We park farther away from the barn this time, closer to where I parked my truck when we ran out of gas. We pull into the bushes by the side of the road, keeping the truck out of view of anything and anyone, before climbing out. I look around, realizing that my truck isn't here anymore.

"Where did my truck go?"

"Aiken got it towed back to Haven. There's not many decent trucks that still run anymore—can't go wasting the ones we do find," Ricky replies.

I don't know why, but it pisses me off to think that they towed my truck back and didn't tell me. It's mine, and it might not have gas in it, but it still runs…or it will when I get gas. Besides, there are other things inside it that are also mine. And Nina's.

"I should have been told," I snap, surprising Phil and O'Donnell. But not Ricky. He lets a slow smile rise to his face, as if he's been waiting to find that one thing that'll really get to me. "It's my truck," I grind out, not caring that I'm showing my weakness.

Ricky steps forward and tuts. "No, Mikey, it's NEO's truck now. Remember that. Everything you owned previously belongs to NEO—to Aiken. That's how we work, and that's what you agreed to."

I open my mouth to speak, but then close it, knowing that he's right. This is what I signed up for. The spoils get shared, and everything is split equally. I don't own anything at all. Not until I earn it.

"I still should have been told," I say, the words coming slowly as I try to contain my anger.

Ricky goes to speak but Phil interrupts. "Yeah, dude, you're right, you should have been. But it's done now, no biggie, right? I'll take you to the truck when we get back, okay?"

I swallow down my anger and nod. "Fine."

I refuse to look at Ricky, knowing that with the way I'm feeling right now, if I do and he has that same smug look on his face, I'll smash him in those pretty-boy teeth of his and get myself kicked out of this damned group.

"Mikey," O'Donnell calls from the edge of the field. She's kneeling down and I walk over to kneel by her side. In her hand is a kid's sneaker. "Is this his?" she asks.

I take the sneaker from her, noting the blood splatter across the laces, and I turn it over in my hand and squeeze my eyes closed while I try to remember what he was wearing on his feet. But I have no idea. I don't think I ever looked at his feet.

"I don't know," I say and shake my head. I hold onto the shoe for a moment before dropping it to the ground. "I just don't know." I feel a pain in my chest, a tightening at the thought that when we were attacked, he was so frightened that he lost a shoe as he ran away. I squeeze my jaw closed tight and turn away from the field as I try to obliterate the image of his wide-eyed stare from my mind.

"It probably is his," Ricky says matter-of-factly. "I mean, it's not like little kids go around losing shoes all the time, ya know? Should we go in there and try and find him first, before we take out the barn?" He points to the overgrown field. "Or should we head straight over to the barn and shoot the hell out of whoever is in there? I know what Aiken wants us to do first."

I know he's goading me; setting me up for a fall, but I also don't care right now. We had agreed to take out the barn first and look for Adam second, but finding his shoe and being this close to where he went missing, means that all previous plans are out of the window.

Phil frowns. "Come on, dude, that's not even a question. We need to head into that jungle and see if we can find him. Like you said, it's gotta' be his, so let's lock and load and get going." Phil reaches into his pocket and pulls out his cigarettes before lighting one. "It's basically what Aiken told us to do anyway."

Ricky looks pissed that Phil has stepped in, and I use that to ground myself, balancing my anger out with some smugness of my own.

"No, it's not. We have to protect Haven's people first, and strangers second," Ricky bites out.

"Well I'm going in and looking for him, with or without you. I'll help with the barn takeout afterwards," I say, giving Ricky a steady look.

"We're NEO, we stick together," he retorts.

"Well, if you're a true NEO then you better come with us," I reply, hoping like hell that O'Donnell and Phil both back me on this, or I'm going to look like an idiot. "Because I'm going into that field to find Adam, and these guys are going in with me, right?" I look at Phil first, and he nods without hesitation. Saving

Fluffy bought me that card. When I look over at O'Donnell she looks a little warier, glancing toward the field and then across in the direction of the barn before taking a deep breath and nodding.

"Sure, I'm in," she says, but I can tell she's not so certain that this is the right call at all, so I try to save the moment, for both of our sakes.

"Look, we can take some of the homemade bombs from the truck, we'll plant them around the back of the barn and head back to the truck. Set off the bombs, and go in and shoot whatever and whoever is left. I'm just asking for an hour to look for Adam before we start blowing shit up. They'll never even see us coming. We'll go in there, blow the shit out of them all, take their supplies, and head home with Adam and a truck full of weapons and probably food. We'll go home to a hero's welcome."

"Easy, tiger," O'Donnell says, but I can tell she's much more at ease with this suggestion, and I know it's because she doesn't want to go against Aiken's wishes

Even Ricky can't disagree with my plan, though I can tell he wants to. "Fine," he finally says.

"Great, let's do this," I say, turning to look at the field. The plants are tall and thick, weeds and branches twisted together to create what seems like an almost impenetrable net. But if Adam went in there, then that's where I need to go too.

O'Donnell heads over to the truck and loads up the homemade bombs in to a backpack. When she comes back she only looks mildly concerned that she's wearing a backpack full of explosives, which is a shit load less concerned than I would be.

"You good with that?" I ask. "I can wear it if you want." I do not want to wear it, but since this was my plan, I will. I'm thankful when she shakes her head.

"Nah, I've got these babies."

"You made them?" I ask, and she nods.

"Alright, let's get going. I'll take shotgun," Phil says.

"You can't have shotgun if there's no shotgun seat," O'Donnell retorts.

"Sure you can," he replies, pulling out a machete. "I'm at the front, with the best view of the house. Therefore I called shotgun."

O'Donnell chuckles. "The best view is always behind me, you know that, Phil."

Phil laughs back and we all head to the truck and load up on as many weapons as we can carry without them being burdensome. Ricky grabs my elbow and pulls me to a stop right before I go after Phil and O'Donnell. I turn back to look at him, taking in his pissed-off serious expression.

"What?" I snap, tired of his bullshit.

"If you fuck this up," he says, his dark eyes boring into mine.

"I won't."

"But if you do." He shakes his head. "Just don't go getting us all killed, or I'll be pissed off and so will Aiken. I haven't survived this long to be killed because of someone like you." He pushes past me, and I want to feel offended by his comment.

Someone like me? What does that even mean? He doesn't know me. He hasn't taken the time to even try to get to know me—the new me *or* the old me. But I don't feel offended, because deep down I know that his comment is justified.

I pull out my hatchet and follow them all, purposefully pushing past Ricky and O'Donnell and walking behind Phil since he's the only one who seems to fully support me—even after the incident with his animals yesterday morning.

I frown as I think about that. And I worry about who let all of those animals out, and why. To make me look bad? To get me killed? Or was it something else? Something worse? Or maybe I'm reading far too much into it and it has nothing to do with anything. Perhaps Phil had left the cover off Lavender's hutch and she'd escaped and knocked over the other containers. She was tired yesterday morning; barely able to give me a quick glance before she'd fallen back to sleep. Was it because she was up all night playing hide-and-seek with her critter friends?

"You're quiet," Phil comments as he hacks away at the brambles. "Something on your mind?"

The way he says it makes me wary, so I shrug. "Not really, just thinking about the kid—Adam–and hoping that he's okay."

Phil grunts a response and continues to hack away. The confines of the field enclose around us. Winding branches and waist-high weeds cling to every part of us, making every step drag and slow us down. Some parts are so high that they tower over us and thrust us into a green-tinted world where all you can smell and see is the rot and decay of dying plants and weeds.

We push through, Phil and I continuing to take the lead with our hatchets and machetes. I stay several steps behind Phil, giving him the space he needs to chop his way through the brambles, sometimes only following him by the sight of his bright blue Hawaiian shirt. I chop the path wider for O'Donnell and Ricky,

189

who both have guns aiming into the foliage around us in case anything tries to run up on us.

It's warm as the sun rises higher in the sky, and the day keeps on growing hotter and hotter until sweat is pouring down our faces and my own shirt is soaked through and sticking to my body.

I can't deny the fact that I'm regretting coming into this field as left becomes right and up becomes down and we get more and more lost. I've never been one to get claustrophobic before, but I can't pretend I'm not feeling it now as the plants and weeds press against me on all sides. Not to mention the extra weight of our backpacks with all of our ammo and extra weapons in them. And then, as if our luck isn't shitty enough already, the sound of deaders can be heard coming from somewhere nearby.

"Keep your voices down," Ricky shout-whispers to us all, throwing his gaze around in all directions as he tries to work out where the deaders are. But the growls seem to be everywhere, echoing back and forth like our own breaths.

We keep our weapons at the ready, barely being able to see beyond the plants in front of us, never mind if there are any deaders close by. Yet still we push onwards. Chopping and hacking at the forest in front of us and hoping we aren't going in circles, and that at some point soon we'll come out the other side of this nightmare. The original plan of coming up behind the barn has pretty much gone to shit now, since we can't even tell what direction we're going in anymore. But at least my plan to look for Adam is on course as we check every inch of the sludgy ground that we walk over.

The ground of the field is covered in a thick kind of gloop made up of rotted plants and sticky mud, making every step we take even harder as it sucks at our feet and tries to keep them planted against it.

190

"As a kid I used to love mazes," I say as Phil stops to catch his breath. Sweat is pouring down his cheeks, and he reaches back and ties his hair away from his face. "My mom used to take me to one every weekend and I'd spend hours working out the quickest and most logical way to escape."

Phil wipes a hand down his face, pushing the hair back from his neck. "Anytime you want to put that logic to use now would be great, dude."

"Ain't no logic in this shit," I say, rolling my shoulders as Phil begins to cut away at the nonexistent path in front of him. "This is insane."

"Then why'd you bring it up?"

I shrug. "Just making small talk."

Phil barks out a laugh. "Small talk."

Ricky quickly hushes him, and I catch Phil's eye as we smirk at one another. Ricky really is a serious bastard, and under normal situations I'd have great fun winding him up. But this isn't a normal situation, and it isn't just my life on the line.

"Sorry," I mumble, grabbing hold of a face-high branch and slashing my machete across it. I throw the branch down to my feet and take a step forward. It's only when I feel something grab for my foot that I know we've stumbled upon deaders.

I look down, seeing skeletal hands reaching through the undergrowth to get to me, and I kick out. Of course a kick doesn't do shit to these monsters who don't feel any pain, and it keeps on pulling itself along the muddy ground toward me, its painfully bony fingers digging into my ankle as it uses my own body as leverage to pull itself free of the brambles.

I'm stuck in the thick of some gnarled branches, the overgrowth scraping against my face and making it almost impossible to try and step away from this thing. I swing down at it, managing to slash across the back of its head and slice its skull right open, but it isn't enough to put it down and all I end up doing is splashing myself with black gore. I swing again, but my shirt snags on a gnarled branch behind me and I have to reach back with my other hand to try and loosen the branch's grip on me. I panic for a second as I feel the deader's mouth trying to close around my booted foot, and I kick out and continue fumbling to free my arm, but I don't want to drop my hatchet and lose my only weapon. Ricky presses his heavy-booted foot onto the deader's back so that it can't move any farther forward, and then he aims his gun downwards and fires a single shot into the back of the deader's skull.

The shot rings out loudly, and the growls of deaders intensify around us.

"Thanks," I mumble, sweat trailing down my face and over my lips, realizing how close he just came to blowing my toes clean off.

"NEO," he replies darkly. And I know he's telling me that he didn't do it for me, but for the group. Because this is the New Earth Order way of life, and if it wasn't, there was no way he'd be risking his life and sweating his balls off in this field with me.

The low moan of deaders can still be heard, and we all try to pick up our pace and get the hell out of the mess that we're currently in, but with the weeds and brambles tightening with every step we take, it's not looking good.

"There's zeds trapped in here, and not enough room to fight them," O'Donnell says urgently. "We need to turn back."

"I agree," Ricky replies.

Phil turns to look at me. His glasses are steamed up with condensation, but he still has on a smile. A cigarette dangles from between his lips, smoke curling up in front of his face, but he pulls it out to speak. "I think we're almost at the other side of the field. We just need to press on, guys. Turning back will be worse than keeping going."

"We didn't want to get to the other side. We wanted to find Adam and then go around the back of the barn!" O'Donnell says, her voice sounding panicked and desperate. I have a feeling that she's suffering from claustrophobia, and I wish she would have warned us in advance.

I drag a hand down my face. "Look, I want to get out of this sweat box as much as anyone, but I think we should press on regardless. If we're nearly at the other side, then we can still make it around the back of the barn. But it needs to be a group decision." I add that last part on to try and gain some sway with O'Donnell, if not Ricky as well. But by the looks of his sour expression, he isn't having any of it.

"No way. We could be walking for miles yet. You can't tell that we're nearly out. We need to turn back!" Ricky snaps.

"O'Donnell, come on girl," Phil says, ignoring Ricky—or at least choosing not to argue with him.

O'Donnell looks uncertain, and her uncertainty seems to grow as the growls of the dead begin to echo around us. Her gaze darts back and forth, and she wipes the sweat away from her face.

"I just want to get the hell out of here in one piece," she eventually says, sounding breathless. "Whichever way is the quickest."

193

"Then let's keep going. Whatever is on the other side can't be as bad as what's in here," Phil replies. He doesn't wait for Ricky to argue, or O'Donnell to agree further. Instead, he turns around and continues moving through the thick undergrowth once more, his sharp blade hacking at the branches, and trampling as much of the foliage back as he can with his feet. I stay behind him, helping to press back the larger branches and clear a better path for O'Donnell and Ricky, who are carrying the firepower.

I look into the thick of the branches, seeing something white flash there quickly—so quick I wonder if I imagined it. I keep on hacking at the branches, my eyes darting left and right as I think I see it again.

My steps slow as I squint into the green mass to the left of me. I strain so hard my eyes blur, but I still see nothing.

"Hurry the fuck up," Ricky snaps behind me.

"I could have sworn I saw something," I say, moving forward again, but my gaze still to the left. Phil has managed to get quite far ahead by now, and I'm grateful to see that the field is beginning to thin out enough for us to walk without being grabbed by branches every step.

"Yeah, you saw a bunch of zeds tracking us through this mess, now let's get out of here," O'Donnell calls from behind. She sounds anxious, and I can't blame her. Her skill is in long-range shooting, and though she can fight hand to hand, it isn't her forte, and of course these aren't the ideal circumstances.

"No, like...I don't know, something else." I squint into the leaves again. "You know what they say about getting a feeling like this."

"I do, so hurry up and let's get out of here," O'Donnell says.

194

I pick up my pace to catch up with Phil, who has disappeared around a bend, but he's at least easily trackable in this field. I see the flash of his Hawaiian shirt just up ahead and jog to catch up, watching as something dives out of the undergrowth and lands on top of him.

"Shit," I call out. I pick up speed, tripping on a thick root sticking up through the mud and almost falling flat on my face. I expect to see a rotten deader on top of Phil, its grasping hands clawing for his face, its teeth snapping to sink into his flesh—you know, the usual stuff. But when I get close, the thing on top of Phil turns to look at me, and I realize that it's not a deader at all.

It's human, whoever it is.

They're wearing a white plastic mask to cover their face, giving them an emotionless expression. They raise a small knife, ready to stab Phil in the shoulder while simultaneously pressing a hand over his mouth and nose. It takes me a second to register exactly what I'm seeing, and another second to jump into action as they let go of Phil's mouth and use both hands to try and stab him. I see another flash of white to the right of me, and I duck just in time as a spear flies past my face, close enough to make my hair move.

"Shit," I call out for the second time. "A little help here!" I yell to Ricky and O'Donnell.

A shot rings out, and I hope to God it's O'Donnell and not whoever was in the barn, because if it is we're already halfway to hell. Deaders, masked killers, and then the barn maniacs. Jesus, can our luck get any worse? All we need now is a couple of wild dogs to finish off the shit paella we've clearly been baking since coming back here.

"Mikey, let's move," Phil calls out. Whoever was on top of him is now lying on their side. Their mask is still on and I have the urge to pull it off and see who's underneath it, but there's no time. Like Phil said, we need to move, and quick.

I drop to a crouch and edge toward Phil. "You good?" I ask.

He raises an eyebrow. "No, I'm not good. The little fucker stole my cigarettes!" he says, his face red in anger as he feels in his top pocket for where he keeps his cigarettes.

"Could have been worse," I say. Another spear lands at my feet, missing my foot by barely an inch and I pluck it out of the ground. "I'm keeping that," I shout angrily.

I grab hold of Phil and start to drag him to standing and then I take point and begin to lead us all out of here, hacking and chopping at the foliage to clear a path.

"What the hell was that?" Ricky calls from somewhere behind me, shortly before he yells and another shot rings out.

More shouts sound out, ringing loudly in my ears, but thankfully none seem to be aimed toward me, and I take solace in the fact. Ricky and O'Donnell catch up, looking flustered, and then we all press forward, all of us hacking and chopping and pushing to get out of this damned nightmare before anything else attacks us.

Whoever those masked people are, they are still here somewhere. Every now and then I see a flash of mask, but no one attacks us. We travel like this for another five or ten minutes more, with flashes of white-masked faces in the brambles and the growls of deaders, and a shot firing out every once in a while as one or both get to close. But they seem like the longest minutes of my life, as the air becomes so compact and thick that I can barely breathe, and the sound of pissed-off and frustrated deaders continues to follow us.

My heart is heaving in my chest and my shoulders are burning from the constant slashing with my hatchet, but I'm definitely inspired to get the fuck out of here.

Eventually the foliage begins to thin out, and the air becomes a little sweeter and a little easier to breathe. Phil glances over his shoulder at me and smiles.

"Almost there, I think I can see daylight," I call, my feet almost tripping over one another in a bid to get out of here quicker.

Almost fifty steps later we all come stumbling out of the nightmare cornfield that's now more or less just brambles and weeds. O'Donnell collapses to her knees, her blade stabbing into the soft earth near her as she gasps for breath. She holds her gun steady and aims it at the field, ready to shoot anything that comes out of it. Her face is pale, her eyes skittish, and I note the blood splattered down her shirt.

"I hate stab wounds," Phil says, pressing his hand to a slash mark across his arm. "They are the least fun injury to get."

I raise an eyebrow. "You're really going to say that to the man who got chewed up by a dog."

"All right, the second-worst injury," Phil replies.

Chapter Twenty

"What the fuck were they?" O'Donnell says, looking thoroughly freaked out, though her breathing has returned to normal.

"Or who?" I reply, my gaze still on the green foliage that's swaying under the light breeze. I feel like we're being watched. "We should keep moving," I pant, happy to have fresh, clean air in my lungs again but not so happy to be so out in the open with nothing for cover.

Phil, O'Donnell and Ricky stand up and follow me, walking backwards and never once turning their backs on the field in case those little mini-demons come out with their spears drawn and their masks firmly in place.

When I figure we're far enough away, we sit back down, with Phil resting against the trunk of a tree. His hand is still pressed to the wound on his arm and blood is dribbling from in between his fingers. Ricky drops to his knees next to Phil and pulls out some medical supplies from one of the pockets in his cargo pants.

"Let me look," he says to Phil before prying his hands away and pulling his shirt to one side. He pokes and prods the wound, ignoring Phil's gasps of pain, and then he grabs a medicated wipe and tears the packet open before pressing it upon the wound.

"Well?" O'Donnell asks Ricky. "What's the deal?"

Ricky looks up at her. "It should be fine. It's clean, nothing important sliced through."

"You say that but it's not your arm that's had a mini-icepick slashed through it," Phil says between gritted teeth.

"Is that what it was?" I ask.

He nods. "That's what it looked like when he was trying to stab me in the eye with it, yeah." He shudders at the memory. "I thought it was a blade, like a pocket knife or something, but it was sharper and pointier than that. Then again, I was fighting for it not to be stuck in the center of my forehead at the time, so maybe I'm wrong."

"Damn," Ricky says, his tone anxious. He wraps the wound with gauze and a bandage and then closes Phil's shirt back up. "You'll be fine, but we should probably get a move on."

"Where to?" Phil asks, his voice pained.

Ricky looks at me briefly before looking away. "We stick to the plan. We didn't find the kid in the field, so now we need to head to the barn. Let's just hope we've come out where we wanted."

I want to argue with him, but know it would be futile. We all just risked out lives going through that field to find Adam, only we didn't find him. Instead we found...so much more.

"Has anyone seen anything like them before?" I ask, recalling their masked faces and their blinking, dark eyes hidden beneath.

"Hell no," O'Donnell says, her breath returning to normal. "I would remember meeting those little freaks. Do you think they had anything to do with the people in the barn?"

"It seems logical that they would," I say.

"You and your logic," Phil says, forcing out a pained laugh.

I grin. "Well, you know, I am the smartest of us all."

He grins back. "Well, that makes me the attractive one then I guess."

"All right, all right, if you two can stop sucking each other's dicks for a minute so that we can figure out what to do next," Ricky grumbles, standing up. He looks around us, heading toward a tree with a wooden sign hanging from one nail. He lifts it, reads the words, and then drops it like it's a dirty diaper.

I frown and walk over to see what it is that has him so freaked out, my own eyes widening when I read the sign. "Guys," I call out. "You're going to want to see this."

Sweat is glistening off of Ricky's forehead. "Do you think this is real?"

I shrug, because yeah, it looks pretty real. "Not afraid, are you?"

"Fuck no," he snaps back.

Phil and O'Donnell finally make it over, and Phil begins to laugh before stopping to have a coughing fit as he lights up a cigarette.

I frown and he grins.

"I always bring two packs," he says. "So what is it that's got Ricky looking ready to piss his pants?"

"Fuck you," Ricky snaps.

"Circus Extraordinaire?" O'Donnell says as she reads the sign aloud. "There better not be any clowns."

"Scared?" Phil jokes, his coughing finally over.

O'Donnell sneers. "Fuck no. I mean, if I can stay away from the weird and the wacky, then I'm gonna', ya know. But it's not a fear, it's just common sense," she says with a shake of her head, though I suspect she's lying. She pulls out her gun, a .35

revolver, and eyes me. "So let's get going." She walks away, and I know she's fronting but I decide not to be an asshole and call her out. I'm saving those nuggets of humiliation for Ricky.

I turn to go after her, but Ricky slams a hand down on my shoulder. "Whoa there, I'm really not sure about this."

"What's not to be sure of?" I ask.

His gaze flits from me to Phil and back again. "Because I can't see any reason why the kid would have gone in there, that's why!"

Phil laughs again. "Sure he would have. It's a circus—kids love the circus. Come on, dude. And the poster says there's animals!"

"We're supposed to be heading to the barn," Ricky says, looking warily around us—but from where we are, there's nothing to see but the overgrown field and tall trees. We need to get to higher ground to be able to get a sense of direction.

"We will," Phil replies. "Right after we check out the circus."

We all turn and head through the path between the trees, leaving Ricky to trail after us, Phil still laughing despite his wound. Considering we all just about suffocated in the undergrowth of an old cornfield and were attacked by little masked murderers, I'm surprised that we're all still in particularly high spirits.

But then, that's what this life does to you: you recover from a near-death experience—or a disaster or whatever—as quick as it happens. There's no time to sit around and analyze a situation. Or work out how you feel about almost dying—again. You just get up, wipe yourself down, and pray like hell you don't run into the same demons twice.

Welcome to the apocalypse, party people. It's a freaking ride, I'm telling you.

I can't work out exactly where we are in relation to the barn, so we keep on walking, following the path in the hopes that it will open up soon and we'll be able to work out where we are exactly. After being in the field and all its many obstacles, I don't hold out much hope of finding Adam alive anymore—if, in fact, any. We barely made it through; what hope would a little kid have? And with that in mind, I decide I need to focus on my own survival now: finding the barn, taking out whoever is inside, and getting back to Haven in time for dinner.

The path finally opens up on a large flattened area with several circus tents of various sizes spotted about. Some collapsed long ago, and the tattered remains of them lie in heaps; others are still standing good and strong, like the day they were put up. Well, almost anyway. There are tear holes down the plastic and dried blood and gore is splattered up the sides. Pretty sure that wasn't around when the circus came to town.

We walk around the place, some of us in awe, others in horror, but none of us denying the fact that this place is creepy as fuck. Even me who isn't normally bothered by clowns and things like that. Because whether clowns chill your soul or not, an empty circus with only bloody skeletal remains being picked apart by crows is enough to creep even the hardest of people out.

"This place is awesome!" Phil calls out as he slips the curtain back on one of the tents, his bloody fingers leaving smears on the material.

Well, maybe not everyone is freaked out.

We hesitantly follow Phil into the tent, the dry scent of death hanging in the air like a thick cloud. This place used to house the animals, and we walk around each of the large cages and crates, taking in the sight of starved tigers and lions, a group of monkeys all huddled together, and even a bear, the skin and muscle

202

withered and pulled back from its jaws. I don't think it had even been legal to keep animals like this for at least the past twenty years, but then again we're in the back streets of beyond, so I guess it didn't really matter to these people.

I stare in at the remains of the bear. Its picked-empty eye sockets stare into the space in front of it like dark holes, and I can't decide what would have been better—for it to have starved to death in its cage, or to have been set free and possibly eaten alive by the undead. Neither death is a good one, I guess.

Phil is more forlorn now, his expression grim as we move around each cage. He shakes his head and taps on the bars with his knuckles, is if hoping that one of the animals might wake up. But of course they don't. They're all long dead.

"I didn't think there were circuses like this anymore. I mean, most of these animals are protected, aren't they?" I ask Phil.

He shrugs. "I suspect in little backwards towns like this, none of it's important. They do what they want. And besides, this was probably a traveling circus. No one to tell them what they can and can't do when they move every other week."

O'Donnell pats Phil on the shoulder and whispers something to him. He nods and looks away. I, on the other hand, stand back from him, giving him the space that a man needs. I side-eye Ricky, who shrugs nonchalantly, and we both turn away and keep on looking around.

I walk past the rows of knocked-over chairs looking for…for something, but I'm not exactly sure what. Adam's jacket perhaps, or some small handprints in the dust? An *Adam was here* sign scratched onto the tent walls? I'm not really thinking I'll find any of these things, but I also don't want to shout out his name and bring half of the undead circus to us, because the quiet moans that are hanging in the air lead me to believe that somewhere around here, there are deaders. And I have a feeling that I won't like it when I find them. But I hold out hope that Adam is safe somewhere. He's a born survivor, and he survived many years without any help. I have no doubt that he could do the same again.

Hope does that to you: it clings on long after you want it to let go, daring you to wish for more.

"It's just so sad," Phil says as O'Donnell leads him out of the tent.

"I know, I know," she replies, and she even sounds sincere about it.

Phil takes a seat on one of the small benches near an old popcorn cart. The cart is on its side, the popcorn long since gone. He pulls out a small tin from his pocket and rolls up a joint before lighting it and taking a long drag.

"I'm gonna' need a minute, guys," he says. He pulls his glasses off his face and rubs at his eyes, and I can't decide if he's crying or if it's just sweat rolling into his eyes. Either way I decide that this is another one of those private moments a man needs.

"I'm going to keep looking around," I say.

"I'll come with you," Ricky mutters, and follows me while O'Donnell takes a seat next to Phil.

We walk in silence as we move past different tents, both of us ignoring the elephant in the room, so to speak. We don't like each other. But we have to make this work, so we get on with doing our job. There's a deader crawling along the ground, its face mostly caved in as if something rolled over it, but not quite hard enough to kill the brain. Its dried-up eyes are bugging out of its head and its hands claw at the earth to pull itself along since its legs are nothing more than crumbled and crushed bone.

"I've got it," I say and I close the small distance between us and the deader.

It sees me, or senses me, or however they work, and it begins to go wild, growling for me and clawing at the ground harder. If it had a tail I'm almost certain it would be wagging it right now like an overexcited puppy.

I stand above it, letting its fingers claw at my boot, and then I raise my hatchet and slam it into the back of its skull. It stops moving instantly, the aged, soft skull no match for my hatchet. I pull my weapon out and wipe the blade across the deader's back and then turn to look at Ricky.

"When Phil first arrived," Ricky says, "he was all cut up about someone. Kept on rambling about some blonde and how she didn't make it and how it was all his fault. So we thought, logically, it was his wife, or girlfriend, maybe even a kid, you know?"

I nod in understanding, though really I'm only half listening to what Ricky has to say because I'm more in shock that he's talking to me at all. It's probably the first civilized conversation we've had since I arrived. We continue to walk, heading over to a larger tent with an ominous stench coming from inside it, and I grip my hatchet tighter.

"We fed him up, rehydrated him, and he perked right back up, but he was still banging on about the blonde," Ricky continues, and looks toward the plastic flap of the tent entrance as it shifts and moves in the lazy breeze. "We eventually worked out that the Blond he was referring to wasn't his girlfriend or wife—not even a next-door neighbor. No, it was one of his ferrets." He shakes his head. "A fucking ferret named Blond, man."

I laugh and look over to Phil and O'Donnell sharing the joint. He has his head back, his eyes closed as he talks to her, and she nods like she understands what he's going through, but I have a feeling that no one knows what he's going through. Some people are just made that way. They're just more in tune with animals than they are with humans. Phil had said it himself: his animals are his family, and he puts them above everyone.

"He loves those critters," I say.

"Probably too much. Have you seen his woman—Aimee? She's hot, too hot for him. They can't live together though because he won't get rid of those animals."

"He sees them as family," I shrug. "It's weird, but it's all he's ever known."

"I guess so, I still think it's weird though," Ricky says, nodding his head to a stripy red-and-white tent. "Let's try this one."

It's larger than most of the others, and I wonder if it's the main circus tent. If I was a kid, I'd probably head to this one, with its bright colors.

"Sure," I say, and I start to walk in but Ricky continues talking.

"I need to give you a chance," he says, and I turn around to look at him properly. "I know that." He looks me dead in the eye before continuing. "We've had people try to screw us over before, and honestly, everything in me tells me that you're trouble and not worth all of this."

"Thanks for the vote of confidence," I say bitterly and start to walk away again.

He grabs hold of my arm and I turn back and glare at him.

"What?" I snap, feeling an overinflated sense of anger at him. Or maybe it's not just him. Maybe it's everything. Maybe it's my guilt for not finding Adam, or for letting him get away in the first place. Survivor or not, this world is no place for a kid on his own. Or maybe it's just the fact that this world is shit and I'm sick to death of it—of the losses and the small wins, and the crazy people.

"The last time we trusted someone, I lost my wife and my kid, not to mention a lot of other NEO's." He lets that hang in the air for a moment so that I understand why he has an issue with me. "I don't trust easily, and I can smell trouble a mile away. And you stink of trouble."

"I hear you," I finally reply because I know he's right.

"Do you?" he says calmly. "Do you know what it's like to lose your entire family, but still manage to hold onto your wife? To survive this long, together, only to have her taken away because we trusted the wrong person?"

"I've lost plenty of people too. I just lost someone right before getting picked up by Aiken, so yeah, I get it," I say, the words clogging my airways.

Ricky shakes his head. "Nah, we've all lost someone during the apocalypse. That's different. What makes that so different than every other sob story we've heard?" He turns away from me.

The anger I felt moments ago is nothing compared to what I feel now. The fire of grief and hurt lick up the sides of me until I'm clenching my hands together.

"She was all I had left," I say. "She was everything to me. And now she's gone. Sacrificed herself because of me...for me. And

Adam." My anger is red hot, but my grief is suddenly drowning. "That's why I have to find him—I can't let her down again."

Ricky turns back to me, the small crease of a frown between his eyes.

I shake out my fists, refusing to lose it with this guy. "I'm not here to hurt anyone," I say instead. I feel guilty for saying that, because I've already warned Aiken of the shit cloud that seems to follow me around everywhere.

"I hope not, because it never ends well for the people that try to screw me or our group over, if you get what I'm saying." And with that, Ricky walks away toward the tent with his head low. Though his demeanor is still ballsy as hell, I feel like we've actually come to an understanding of sorts, and I decide to try and get along with the guy. That is if he lets me.

I look over at Phil and O'Donnell and see that they're on their way to us. Phil seems happier now, if not lightly buzzed, which should probably worry me yet doesn't. I have a feeling that he works better buzzed anyway.

They catch up and we walk as a trio over to the tent, pushing the flap aside and stepping into the shade of it. Inside a stagnant scent hangs in the air like rotting meat—a smell that only means death was here quite recently. I catch Phil's eye and we share a look of *yeah, that's not good.*

This tent isn't like the other one. It opens up on a short corridor filled with wacky mirrors—you know, the sort that bend and distort your body image so much that you look like a skinny leprechaun or an obese strong man. The results are never very good, and my image in these mirrors, splashed with blood and bones at my feet, is even less appealing.

"What is that smell?" O'Donnell asks, looking around us, her mouth turned down in disgust. "That's not zeds, that's something else."

Ricky is ahead of us and he looks back briefly before he pushes a flap out of the way and steps deeper into the tent.

I walk past the mirrors, forcing myself to not look at my reflection and instead focus on the posters lining the wall at the far end of the small corridor where another stripy red-and-white flap hides what lies inside.

"Freak unique spectacular," I say, reading the sign, my voice louder than I expected it to be within the small confines.

"Fuck. That." O'Donnell comes to stand beside me. "The kid won't have gone in there," she says, nodding at her own statement as if to convince herself of the fact.

"We don't know that," I reply, not wanting to go inside either, but knowing that I have to.

"Well he's a little asshole if he did," she splutters out.

"That's probably true," I smirk, and I can tell she's already resigning herself to going inside.

"Come on, O'Donnell, I know you're made of stronger stuff than that," Phil laughs, slapping her on the shoulder. He pushes the loose strands of hair back from his face and then he rolls his shoulders as if gearing himself up.

"It's the weed, dude," she replies, her gaze skitting around the room and then back to Phil.

"I know, I know, paranoia extraordinary. I told you that you shouldn't have had any—you know how you get," Phil laughs. "We've gotta' do it though."

O'Donnell grumbles something under her breath and makes a disgusted noise. "Fine," she snarls, and pushes the flap aside before walking in.

We all follow her inside, the smell making us gag and stare around the room warily. I note Ricky standing still, his head cocked to one side as he listens intently for any movement. It takes a moment for my eyes to adjust in the dark, but eventually I begin to make out the shelves and stands around the room, and I make my way over to them, peering at the jars and cages on each shelf and stand. I can't work out what they are at first, my eyes not quite understanding what I'm seeing.

"Jesus," Ricky mumbles from across the room.

I read the small cards that are in front of the jars and cages, feeling grossed out as I put the item with the name.

Two-headed snake.

Four-eyed turtle.

Largest deformed rat.

Albino spider.

Each item is weirder than the last. Or they would be if they weren't almost decayed beyond recognition. But I can imagine what they looked like originally—a neck stretched wide enough to accommodate two hissing heads, four blinking eyes staring up at me; a rat with half of its face missing yet still walking around and trying to live. I was never a fan of these sorts of places. Staring at oddities, curiosities, a bearded lady or a man with gills was never my idea of a fun time. And at the end of the world, it's the last thing I want to see.

"This is amazing," Phil says from next to me. He's picked up a jar from a shelf and is staring into it in awe. "Can you imagine how cool this thing was when it was alive?"

The jar he's holding has the skeletal remains of a bat inside. It's larger than any bat I've seen before, and I can see the long fangs that hang down from its mouth. The label says *vampire bat*, and I'm guessing this is the literal sense of the word by the looks of those teeth.

"Oh yeah, very cool, right up until it sunk its teeth into my neck and sucked me dry," I reply.

"Nah, it's just a baby. Bet it wouldn't even have been able to get a quarter of a pint off you," he laughs.

I do not see the funny side of it. There are enough things trying to bite me in this life. So as far as I'm concerned, I'm glad it's dead and gone.

"Well, it's a quarter too much," I reply irritably. I drag a hand through my beard and walk away from Phil and his skeletal vampire bat remains. My footsteps seem loud in the enclosed space, and I move across the room toward where O'Donnell is hunched over something on the ground.

She stands up when I get close, her eyes finding me in the darkness. "I'm just as freaked out as I am awed," she says, pointing at the shape on the ground.

I frown, not making out what it is, so I do as she had been doing and crouch down to get a closer look, wishing I hadn't.

It's a deader—a dead deader. A newly dead deader. Oh, the irony of it.

But it isn't normal, and as I stare closer, I realize why.

"Jesus," I gasp almost falling onto my ass when I finally work out what I'm looking at. It's hard, between the decomposing of the deader and the deformity it had been, to make out the bulbous forehead and stretched skin across the bubbled cheeks. "I'm glad it's dead," I say, my voice a whisper as I stand up, not wanting to look at it any longer.

"Me too," she replies, her tone haunted. "It needed to be out of this misery."

I stare at her in shock. I meant that I could imagine nothing more horrifying than this mutated deader chasing after me while it tried to munch on my brains, but O'Donnell is feeling some sort of sympathy. I play along with it.

"Oh yeah, exactly," I reply, still trying to shake the image of this thing coming at me and how much I would have pissed my pants. I look across at Ricky, and for a brief second I kind of wish this thing were alive to scare the shit out of him.

A noise from behind another curtain makes us all stop what we're doing and look over, the familiar shuffle and growl of the undead drawing our attention even further. I hold my hatchet tightly, turning my back on the shelves and the deformed deader, and we watch the shadows move from beneath the flap as the footsteps come closer.

Chapter Twenty-One

The flap of material posing as a doorway moves as the deader pushes against it, and it's a long, drawn-out moment as we wait and watch until the flap falls free and every one of us gasps. Not just me. Definitely not just me.

"Whaaattt?" O'Donnell breathes out from next to me, the word dying on her lips, and I wonder if we're on the same wavelength now or if she's still feeling sympathy for these things.

The deader comes farther into the room, and at first it doesn't spot us. It casts a shadow across the bloodied sand of the circus tent floor and takes another stumbling step forward, its two heads swiveling both ways as it looks around. Its nose lifts to the air as it finally realizes that it's not alone and it lets out a long, drawn-out growl that reminds me of a wolf.

I stare at the conjoined twin deaders and take a small step backwards, feeling a slight repulsion toward the thing in front of me. I get that none of this is its fault, and at one time it was just a normal human like everyone else. Well, it was hardly ever normal, of course. The deaders are joined at the hips, giving it four arms and four legs and two heads. It's a walking nightmare as it lurches forward in the direction of Phil, its teeth bared and all four hands reaching for him. A long, heavy chain is locked around one of its ankles, keeping it in this tent for all these years.

It was an inhumane act, and I wonder why they let themselves be treated like that for so long. They aren't animals—at least they hadn't been—so why had they been chained up?

"Guys," Phil says, his machete raised high, "I might need a little help here."

I wait for someone else to step forward and offer to help, but when neither O'Donnell nor Ricky does, I grip my hatchet tightly and move toward Phil. The deader is smacking its lips as if Phil is a Grade-A prime T-bone steak. It's a surprisingly human gesture that freaks me out all the more. But I still wonder, other than the freak factor, why he can't handle this kill himself.

As I get closer, I realize what Phil's problem is: two heads means two brains, meaning he'll need to take out both skulls to put this thing down. Probably. This is all just speculation until we do it, of course. It isn't like this sort of thing happens to us every day.

I'm behind the deader, and its attention is fixed on Phil so it doesn't even notice me as I come up and slam my hatchet into the side of the head on the right. It continues to reach forward with all of its arms, but then the right side of the deader starts to sag as if it's had a stroke and can't control that side of its body. The weight of the dead right body is pulling the left body down with it, until they're both on the floor, one motionless and the other still hungry and angry. The deader on the left continues to try and drag itself toward Phil, seeming to get more and more frustrated by the extra weight holding it back.

It fights to get back up onto its feet, finally doing so as the loud sound of tearing comes from under the bloodied dress it's wearing. Dark black blood splatters across the floor, and then a gush drops from beneath the tattered remnants of the skirt as the skin between the two conjoined bodies splits open and the dead deader (try saying that when you're drunk) tumbles to the ground in a heap. The other deader pauses momentarily, blood and gore still tumbling from the side and underneath of her, and she looks down at her fallen comrade, a look of sorrow crossing her

214

features, as if remembering what they've been to each other for all of these years.

We should take that moment to crush the other skull in, but I think Phil and I are both in shock at what just happened. Then, before we can even contemplate it, the deader looks back up, fixing her hungry gaze on Phil, and opens her mouth before letting out a hungry, distressed screech. From behind me I hear Ricky cursing something indecipherable as Phil uses his machete to stab into the left-hand deader. The skull, for some reason, isn't as soft as on the one I killed, and he has to yank the blade back out. His second attempt at killing her fails as his blow goes wide and instead of the skull he slashes into her shoulder. This time it's lodged in deep, and with my hatchet still buried in her sister's skull we're both weaponless, barring our handguns, which we do not want to use in case it draws more attention to us.

Phil backs up another step, but then there's nowhere to go as his back hits one of the display shelves. I pull out my pistol and stare at it for a split second before slamming the butt of the gun into the side of her head. Blood splatters out of the wound and she begins to turn toward me, so I hit her again. Phil pulls out his gun, and as she turns toward me he smashes his gun into her head, opening the wound up farther. Blood splatters across his face, smearing his glasses, but he doesn't relent as I grapple with her, keeping her at arm's length as he continues to beat her skull until it finally cracks open and he's able to smash her brain into mush.

She drops to the ground suddenly, her whole body sounding like mincemeat as it lands in a heap. Fluids drain from her destroyed head and the side of her body where he twin had once been, and the most putrid smell escapes, as if she's been holding in a fart for the past five years.

215

Phil is gasping for breath, and he pulls his glasses off and wipes them over with the corner of his shirt before putting them back on. The puddle at our feet has grown, and we both step back so we don't stand in it.

"That was messed up," Ricky says from behind us.

I turn to glare. "You could say that."

"I did," he replies without skipping a beat.

"You know you can help whenever you like."

A small smile rises to his face. "I know."

I glance at O'Donnell, who's grimacing at the smell, and I wonder why I'm not angry at her, yet I am with Ricky. Either of them could have stepped in and helped, yet neither of them did.

Phil sucks in a breath and reaches down to retrieve his machete, putting his foot on the shoulder of the deader to help free it. I feel shaky and a little sick at the killing of these two deaders, but I don't really understand why. Though I know it was necessary, and probably the best thing we could have done for them, it still feels…wrong somehow. Perhaps it was the sound of their tearing flesh as they were torn apart after all these years trapped together, both alive and dead. I'm not sure, but I know the image of them will stay with me for a long time, haunting me in the dark lonely nights. That is, of course, if I make it back to Haven at all.

"Shame we don't have a camera. Moo would have loved these two," Phil says, still sounding shocked and freaked out at the same time. He sheaths his machete and then reaches down and pulls my hatchet free of the other deader's head before handing it to me. I take it with a "thanks," and I feel the small tremor running through him. I'm glad I'm not the only one affected by these two.

"You're disgusting," O'Donnell says, turning around to continue with her search of the tent.

"It's not me, it's for Moo," Phil replies indignantly.

O'Donnell makes a throaty sound. "She's just a kid. *You* should know better."

"What, so keeping the heads as souvenirs and spiked around your bedroom isn't disgusting?" Phil trails after her.

She moves to the back wall. "Of course it's disgusting, but—" she begins, pulling aside another curtain and then jumping back with a scream. "I'm okay, I'm okay," she says as we all rush forward. She drops the curtain back in place to hide whatever is underneath. "Whatever you do, don't go in there."

The curtain twitches and moves as something presses through whatever bars are holding it where it is, and O'Donnell shudders as she watches with a grimace.

"I have no intention of it," I reply.

And I honestly don't. I don't care what it is, because whatever it is would only be as bad as or worse than what I've seen so far, and it's all too much for me to take. I need to get out of here and grab some fresh air.

"I'm heading back outside, this place is giving me the creeps," I say. I've seen enough of this place to know that I want nothing more to do with it. Christ, if Adam came here to hide, then he's dumber than I thought because this may be a circus, but it isn't fun or funny in any way; it's where dreams go to die.

"Me too," Ricky says, following me outside.

He continues to search the circus site while I sit down on one of the benches by the billboards and gratefully suck in gulps of the hot afternoon air. I close my eyes while I try to get rid of the image of those deformed deaders—and their forlorn gaze as they were ripped apart from each other—from my mind. They looked like beasts—chained up, graying flesh—and they were treated like them.

I open up my eyes, wishing I smoked so I could give my hands something to do. The sun is sitting high in the sky now and I look up, seeing it burning down on us, the bright yellowy-orange blob blinding me. I look across at the billboard next to me, squinting as I read it. It has more information on the conjoined twins, and I find myself reading it in fascination, once again appalled that these people had to put their whole lives on display for the entertainment of others.

The Songbird Emma Twins.

Emma Keating and Emma Walker's mother was a French hooker back in the eighties. A talented fire-eater, their mother joined the circus when it passed through her hometown. She subsequently started two affairs with married men as the circus traveled around the world, and when she fell pregnant she didn't know who the father was. With both men not wanting anything to do with her or her unborn child, she took her own form of revenge—and thus when the baby was born and it was found to be conjoined twins, she subsequently named the child after both fathers. One Emma for each father.

The trio stayed with the circus for many years, until the children were teenagers, and the twins were found to have a talent for singing and juggling. Thus their act grew in its notoriety, far outliving their mother's.

One night a note was found. Their mother had left, and wished her daughters a long and happy life. She was never seen again, and both Emma Keating and Emma Walker agreed to stay with the traveling circus, their new family.

"That's so sad," O'Donnell says from next to me, making me jump. She laughs. "You startle easy."

I force a smile. "Yeah, it's this place. It's giving me the heebie-jeebies."

"I didn't think this sort of thing was done anymore. Most of these types of places were shut down in the fifties," O'Donnell says.

"Like Phil said earlier, little backwards towns and constantly moving probably kept them under the radar." I shudder at the mental image of the freak deaders we just saw.

Ricky comes over, his expression grim. "I don't think we're going to find the kid here, but I did find something else."

Phil comes out from the freak show tent, a bag hanging from his hand, looking heavy and burdensome. We all see the bag, but none of us question it. We all have an idea what's in there, and sometimes it's best not to talk about these things, no matter how disgusting they are.

We all follow Ricky as he rounds on the tent we were just in, and the barn comes into view. There's a slight incline, and we follow Ricky's lead and lie down on our stomachs so that only our heads look out over the top.

The barn should be a welcome sight—and it is, after all the other thing we just saw. However, between the barn and this circus there appears to be a swamp of some kind, and I realize how damn lucky we actually were earlier not to walk straight into it.

The field backs up around the side and the back of the barn, just like we had hoped it would. But a small river must run from somewhere around here, and at some point it overflowed. Between the rotting vegetation and the water, it's now like the bog of eternal stench.

But that isn't even the worst of it.

Trapped within the sludgy field of ruined dreams and the morbid realization that we can't get to the barn from this way around, are deaders. Only, just like everything else we've run into today, they aren't just any normal deaders. Trapped within the thick gunk, sludge, and decay are clown deaders.

Bloated and comically horrific clown deaders. And trust me when I say that there is nothing funny about these clowns.

Their faces are stretched and torn from bird attacks and the elements. Some still have their wigs on, though of course they're matted and covered in filth now. For some, just a head pokes up out of the gunk, the mud slowly sucking them down, and their swollen, bugged-out eyes stare at us from across the swamp. For others they're stuck only by their ankles, their bodies toppled over as they lie on top of the sludge, forever reaching for a freedom that won't come.

"Fucking clowns," O'Donnell mutters in disgust. "It had to be fucking clowns, didn't it?"

I'm still in shock at the sight of them, though again, I shouldn't be—not after some of the other things I've seen in this place. Yet I can't contain the small, manic laugh that ripples up my throat at O'Donnell's words. She turns to glare at me and I laugh even more.

"Fucking clowns." I smirk. "Now *that* would be disgusting. Shit, O'Donnell, why does your mind always go to the gutter?"

Phil laughs and even Ricky smirks, but O'Donnell looks less than impressed by my comment. It doesn't stop me from laughing, though. I feel better as I laugh, the horrors of the conjoined twins slipping into the back of my mind.

"I'm going to be having nightmares for weeks," she says. One of her hands is resting on the gun at her waist, and the other is gripping onto her rifle. "I want to take them all out while I can." She raises up her gun. "Say goodbye to your little friends," she says, mimicking Al Pacino in *Scarface*.

"No can do. Not unless you want everyone in a five-mile radius knowing where we are—and that would include whoever is in that barn and the freaks in the masks," Ricky says, pointing across the field toward the barn. "We are massively outnumbered."

It all looks quiet, with no movement at first glance, but as I look closer, staring intently at the trees next to the barn, I see people moving around in the branches and climbing inside the barn through a window at the top. From the looks of it, most of the people going in and out of the barn have white plastic masks covering their faces, and we all recognize at the same time that the masked killers in the field and the shooters from yesterday are one and the same.

"This is all a crock of shit," O'Donnell says, not happy at all. "We're stuck over here with this freak show and a damned swamp with clowns in it between us. Aiken said to take out the barn. Now what the hell are we going to do?"

Phil's eyes grow large as he points over the top of O'Donnell's shoulder. "Well if you thought that was bad, then you're really not going to like this," he says to her as we all turn to look.

Chapter Twenty-Two

O'Donnell turns back around to face the way we had just come, and the sound of her stomach hitting the ground is audible to us all—at least the pretense of it dropping out is. She begins to make a small keening sound when the deader clowns pin her in their sights and snap their jaws at her. Their groaning ups a notch as the thought of fresh meat pokes at their most basic instinct.

Three clowns lurch toward us in their own unique way, their steps slow and broken. One is on its hands and knees, and the other two are limping toward us, their footsteps clumsy in their oversized clown shoes. Their once-funny outfits, designed to delight children and parents alike, are now every person's horror story. Blood and gore are splattered across the front of them, as if they've all been to an all-you-can-eat lobster buffet and forgot to wear their plastic aprons to protect their clothing.

These clowns, must have at some point, gotten themselves unstuck from the swamp, because their bottom halves are covered in the stinky swamp mud, and now that they're out of it they've begun to speed up their decaying process. I guess they'd been wandering around their old tents and had heard us all talking.

The clown on its hands and knees is surprisingly quick and agile as it uses all four limbs to move toward us like a dog hunting its prey. O'Donnell shrieks and steps back as it moves closer. She kicks out with a heavy boot but misses and has to jump around so it won't bite her feet and grab at her legs. I take her place, swinging down with my hatchet in the hopes of hacking its head clean off, but it moves at the last second and the sharp blade lodges between its shoulder blades.

I let go of the hatchet and jump out of the way as it reaches for me with bony, raw fingers, noting that Ricky and Phil are attempting to take care of the other deaders, who have now been joined by some more of the circus's current residents. And I'm at least glad that they're joining in this time instead of standing there holding their dicks and watching. Some of the deaders joining the fray must have been guests to the circus, and some were performers—going off their tattered yet glitzy clothing.

I pull out my knife from its sheath at my waist and kick out as the dog-clown swipes at me again, its hand almost getting a good grip on me. I kick it away, my foot hitting its side and sinking into the side membranes of its waist, releasing a foul-smelling odor that soaks into my boots as its insides tumble out in an explosion of rot and gore. The dog-clown is on its side, and I drop to one knee with my knife high, slamming it down into the side of its temple before it can get back up onto all fours.

Its undead life blinks out immediately and I stand back up before any more of the gore can get on me. I look over at Phil and Ricky, seeing that now that we're creating a noise, more and more deaders are coming out of their tents like they've been awakened by noisy neighbors and are ready to complain.

"Fuck," I whisper under my breath, hearing the chanting groan of the dead.

I scan behind us, seeing our way of escape rapidly closing as child deaders, moms, dads, and even what appears to be a ringmaster deader still wearing his smart sparkly waistcoat are shambling toward us, groaning and grunting in hunger and anger.

223

"We need to get out of here," I call to the others, the moment growing more and more urgent with every passing second.

"I second that," O'Donnell says, taking aim with her gun and firing at one of the deaders that was getting too close.

Ricky turns and glares.

"What?" she snaps, taking another shot.

"You planning on letting everyone in on our location?" he yells, as more groans join in the already loud chorus. "Because it sure as shit seems like you're inviting everyone to the party and there ain't enough beer to go around."

She takes another shot and glares back at Ricky defiantly, and I note that she's aiming for any of the deaders that even vaguely resemble clowns, and forgoing the rest. Her personal vendetta against clown deaders has reached a new high.

"He's right—those shots will be heard for miles, and I reckon those little masked killers will know of a way to get across to us quicker than we can take these deaders out," I say, yanking my knife out of a deader's skull before plunging it into the head of another deader almost immediately. "I think now would be a good time to get out of here." I slam my blade right through the eye of the deader, and green and black pus oozes out of the hole, splattering my shirt when I pull my knife back out.

Phil comes running back over. "I agree, this circus sucks monkey balls—big fucking monkey balls! Let's go."

I note that he still has the bag in his hand, and he grins as I look down at it. Ricky joins us and we stand back to back looking around for a clear escape out of this hell. A gap between the main tent and a fallen one seems the most feasible, and I point to it.

"That way, quickly." I have to yell since there are so many deaders coming out of the woodwork now and it's getting too loud to think. Wait, maybe not woodwork, but tentwork. Is that even a word? Anyway...

We all set off running, heading for the small gap and taking out the deaders that get too close to us—kicking them backwards and into the ones behind, or taking shots as we run. Mostly we pray that there isn't another mini-horde behind the tent, because if there is, we're well and truly screwed. And not in a good way. I'm talking end-of-the-night, last-woman-at-the-disco, beer-goggles screwed.

As we trample over the fallen tent, I feel the bodies underneath the thick plastic sheets moving and hands searching to grab ahold of us. O'Donnell screams and I'm almost certain that Phil does too, dropping his bag in his rush to get off of the fallen tent and away from the deaders underneath it.

We head around the tent and begin running full pelt toward some vehicles which are haphazardly parked. Some are crashed, their owners' haste to leave this place causing them to stay here forever, but one car seems out of place amongst them all and I run toward that, trying the handle and finding it open. I throw open the door and sit in the seat, seeing the keys still swinging from the ignition.

The horde has followed us, and more deaders are making their way toward us from between the parked vehicles. I look up at O'Donnell's panicked face and turn the key, the same look crossing our faces as the engine starts first time.

I'm glad, but also wary. We're smack dab in the middle of rock-bottom nowhere, with dusty fields and empty highways for as far as the eye can see. Yet this car is here, the engine sounding good, the keys in the ignition, ready and waiting...for us?

225

Everyone piles in, and the doors aren't even shut as I start to drive us the hell out of here and away from the surging undead bodies that are beginning to swarm like flies on shit. O'Donnell pulls the backpack full of bombs off and puts it in the foot space, and I grimace and say a silent prayer because through all of that fighting, I'd forgotten about the damned bombs she was carrying.

The dusty field the cars are parked in spews up dust behind us as I drive recklessly, swerving out of the way of deaders and other vehicles, praying to find an end to this madness at some point soon. It's like a maze of cars and bodies, and though I try to avoid it I clip a couple of deaders as we pass them, their gore splattering up onto the windows and making it harder to see.

Eventually the tires hit a gravel road and I speed up, the engine revving as I peel the car down the open stretch of dusty road and away from the circus of horrors forever. I watch in my rearview mirror as the undead show continues to shamble after us, their gazes fixed on their runaway lunch. I pity whoever stumbles across this horde, feeling apologetic to these people who I'll likely never meet, because this is definitely one group of deaders that will haunt my dreams, and I willingly walked into this nightmare. I can't imagine the true horror of randomly stumbling across this crazy bunch of nightmares.

Phil climbs over the armrest and comes to sit in the passenger seat next to me, giving O'Donnell and Ricky some more space. Phil is sweaty and covered in gore, and he opens the glove compartment of the car, searching through the useless crap that's inside until he finds an open pack of tissues. Then he pulls one out, takes off his glasses, and begins to clean the blood off them.

I glance at him as he breathes on the glass, bringing it to a glossy finish, and he looks at me as he slides them back on. Blood is splattered up the side of his face and into his beard, and his eyes are still wide with anxiousness as he catches his breath, the adrenaline of the situation still fueling him. I wonder if I have the same frozen horrified expression as he does.

"Hey," Ricky says from the back, and I look at him in the mirror.

Phil turns and looks over his shoulder, and Ricky hands him the plastic bag Phil had dropped.

"Dude!" Phil laughs.

"Saw you drop it," Ricky replies with a shrug as though it's no big deal, but I see the small smile on his face. He sees my stare and shrugs again. "NEO, right?"

I think about this for a moment, deciding that maybe he isn't as big a dick as I first thought, and I nod. Sure, I think taking whatever is in that bag back to Haven is fucked up and wrong on so many levels, but who am I to judge? In fact, who are any of us to judge anymore? None of us are the people we once were, and I highly doubt that any of us are the people we hoped to be.

We're all just trying to make it whatever way we can.

"Yeah, NEO," I reply, and turn my attention back to the road in front of us, letting my thoughts wander on the new problem we had.

Where does this road lead? How do we get back to our truck and take out the barn like Aiken asked us to do? And what do I do about Adam now?

Chapter Twenty-Three

We drive for miles down the same dirt road, and see nothing on either side of us barring the odd stray deader. The sun is beginning to fall and the day is finally cooling, but of course that brings a new set of problems for us—the main one being, of course, that we're still miles from Haven. I need to stretch my legs and the car has been making some strange ticking noises for the past couple of miles, so I pull it to the side of the road and shut off the engine.

Ricky leans forward between the two seats. "Everything okay?"

"I need to check the engine out, it's been ticking for the past couple of miles." I open my door, wincing as it gives a loud creaking sound. I groan as I straighten my legs and stretch my arms above my head.

"I'll take over driving when we get back on the road," O'Donnell says as she rolls her shoulders and steps around to the front of the car so she can pop the hood.

I watch her in fascination and she grins. "My dad showed me a thing or two about cars. You don't need to worry about me breaking a nail." She rolls her shoulders again and I hear the loud crunching sounds coming from them.

Steam is coming from the engine of the car. Not a lot, but enough to make me worry. But unlike O'Donnell, I don't know a lot about car engines—only that smoke is never a good thing.

"Let's let it cool off. I can't touch anything until then anyway," she says before moving around to the back of the car. "So do you want me to drive on the way back?"

"The way back to where?" I ask, looking around us at the empty landscape. "Where in the hell are we, even?"

Phil sits at the edge of the road and I watch him open up the plastic carrier bag before pulling out something gross and bloody. I look away, not wanting to see whatever it is or whatever he's going to do with it.

"We're in fuckbutt nowhere, Mikey, but there's always a way back," Ricky answers with a laugh. I stare at him, and he shrugs and stops laughing. "What? I can be fun too."

"No, you can't. You're the grumpy asshole, *I'm* the fun one," Phil barks up from his place on the ground. "And the most attractive, remember?"

"Wait, well what does that make me if I'm not the fun one?" O'Donnell asks, sounding genuinely concerned. She walks to the front of the car and pulls the keys from the ignition before coming back around and unlocking the trunk.

"You're the survivor. Because you know out of all of us you're the one that will survive," Phil says, looking up at her sincerely.

She rolls her eyes but smirks. "You bet your sweet ass I will."

She presses the trunk button and lifts the lid, and all three of us jump backwards as a deader reaches for us.

"*Zed!*" O'Donnell calls, already grabbing at her waist for her knife. But Ricky is on hand with his first and he slams his blade through the deader's temple.

Phil has jumped up and is standing with us now, his hands covered in black gore and his eyes wide. "Trunk zed," he says, though it's more to himself than us. "I hate trunk zeds."

229

Ricky and I grab the deader and drag it out of the trunk before moving its body to the side of the road. When we return, O'Donnell is rummaging through the contents of the trunk.

"Anything?" I ask, wiping my hands down my pants.

"Of course not, but it's always worth a shot," she replies before slamming the trunk back down. "I wonder how the zed got stuck in there." She leans back against the trunk and crosses her arms over her chest as she stares back the way we came.

Phil has gone back to whatever it is he was doing previously, and Ricky has begun searching the floor of the car and between the seats. It's a smart move. You'd be surprised what people lost between their seats. I've found a lot of things: twenty dollars, an old Bic pen, photos, and old potato chips. Of course none of that shit is useful now, though, but back in the day a spare twenty dollars was always useful.

"Well first off it wasn't stuck, it was trapped—and on purpose, no doubt. And secondly," I turn to look at her, "are you sure that we're okay?"

I seem to have this knack for getting myself into trouble, especially where women are concerned, and even after all the shit I've been through, that part of me hasn't changed.

O'Donnell looks down at her feet and I watch her chew on the inside of her cheek for a moment before answering me.

"We're all searching for someone, Mikey. Whether it's a friend or more," she glances at me before looking away just as quickly, "people need to connect. It's in our nature. It's what makes us human, and is exactly what separates us from the monsters." She gives a small laugh and shakes her head.

"What's so funny?" I ask.

"It wasn't so long ago that I would have said that differently." She looks at me again, and now I see the pain vibrant on her features. "That it's what separates us from the animals. But now it's monsters." She looks away again. "Zeds."

"Deaders," I reply, and I watch her mouth quirk into a bitter smile.

"I fucking hate them. Whatever we decide to call them." Her forehead creases as she looks down the road. Her gaze is faraway, her thoughts close behind. "They took everything."

I swallow, unsure of what to say. I'm not good at this sort of thing, but worse still, I'm not used to O'Donnell acting so...emotional. From what I've seen of her the past couple of days, she's hard and methodical. She's a survivor, at any costs. She thinks logically, at least for the most part, and she isn't swayed from her decisions. But today I've seen her fears, and now I'm seeing her sadness.

"Yeah, yeah, they took everything from everyone," Ricky says, coming from around the side of the car. "We all know how it goes down. We've all been there, lived it, and breathed it. You're better than this, O'Donnell, get a grip."

I stand up straight and glare at him, and I open my mouth to give him a piece of my mind. She just wants a little comforting, that's all. We all do sometimes. But before I can say anything, she's pushing him in the shoulder and laughing off his comment.

"Sorry." She smiles.

"Don't let it happen again," he laughs back, dragging her into a hug. His gaze flits to me for a split second before they separate, and I wonder if that was all for my benefit. I've finally come to the conclusion that Ricky has a thing for O'Donnell, despite the death of his wife, but it's obvious that the feeling isn't mutual and she sees him as nothing but a friend.

"Aww, look at you two." I smile. "You're like a brother and sister squabbling."

O'Donnell laughs, but Ricky's face falls and I'm glad I touched a nerve. Even if we've come to a middle ground and are trying to get along, I like the idea of keeping him on his toes. I'm good at reading people—I needed it to survive before the world went to hell—and I can read him like a book written for a five-year-old.

"What's that?" O'Donnell asks before Ricky can respond. She points to his hand, and I look and see that he's clutching a piece of paper.

"Map," he says, visibly shaking off his annoyance at my words. "At least part of one. Gives me an idea of whereabouts we are, if nothing else."

"And?" I ask.

O'Donnell makes her way back around to the front of the truck and Ricky and I follow her.

"Uncharted territory," he replies, looking down at the old map page.

I shrug. "Okay, so how do we get home?"

"We don't—at least not tonight," Ricky replies, his statement sounding ominous.

I shrug again. "Okay, so we need to find somewhere to hunker down for the night. No big deal."

And it isn't—at least not for me. This is the way I live, moving from one safe place to another. I've been in several "safe camps" over the years, and moving base is second nature to me. Because nowhere is safe forever. Not the Forgotten camp, not our home in the trees, and not the army barracks. As long as I have a weapon and fuel in the tank, I'm good to go, but as I look at Ricky and O'Donnell—and Phil too as he finally comes back over, his hands covered in black gore and a semi-clean skull in his hands like he's Hamlet or some shit—I realize that they don't live like this. Sure, they're survivalists, and they're skilled too, but each night they go back home and sleep in their own beds, with their own things surrounding them, knowing that someone is on guard, watching their backs while they sleep.

What must that be like, I wonder, to feel that safe and comfortable that being out in the open at night is worrying?

I take the bull by the horns and decide to control the situation, because the anxious looks on their faces are beginning to freak me out.

"Okay, O'Donnell, you check out the engine, and Ricky, work out where the next town is. I'll drive us there, and then we can find somewhere safe for the night. Two of us keep watch and we'll swap out halfway so that we all get some sleep. We may even find some food and supplies along the way. It's surprising the things you find out on the road." I look over at them all, watching them exchange glances between themselves. "Come on, let's get to it, we're losing daylight."

O'Donnell and Ricky set about their tasks, leaving me and Phil to wait for them. He's still holding the now-empty skull and grinning.

I shake my head. "Why, man?"

"It's for Moo. She collects them," he replies innocently. "She has a collection, of skulls." He's speaking slowly, as if I'm stupid.

"Phil, I know what a collection is. I just don't get it. You're covered in that stuff now, and all for what? So you can take a skull home to Moo? Plus that thing already stinks, and it's going to smell even worse soon enough." I grimace.

His smile falls. "You know, for a girl her age there's not much she can collect anymore. Dolls, books, friendship bracelets—that crap is all gone."

"I know that," I huff out impatiently.

"When you strip everything back and pull away all of the presence, she's just a kid, Mikey. She wants to do kid things, and kids have hobbies and collect weird crap." It's his turn to shrug now as he looks away from me and back down to his handiwork.

"I think collecting skulls is taking the 'collection of weird crap' thing to a whole new level."

He laughs. "Probably, but it is what it is. We all have our coping mechanisms, and this is hers."

O'Donnell slams the hood down. "All right, it should get us a little further." She looks at Ricky. "At least until the next town. There's virtually no water or oil in the engine, so keep the revs down, take it easy, and we just might make it there in one piece before the damned thing blows."

Chapter Twenty-Four

We don't make it there before it blows, but it's damned close. The engine gives up on the last mile or so, meaning that a) it creates a lot of noise, and b) we have to run and fight the rest of the way to the town.

The sun is setting as we make it to the town, and somehow we've managed to stay ahead of the horde that's following us. But we're tired and sweaty now, our arms aching from fighting, our legs aching from running, and of course we're running on empty—no water or food in almost a full day.

There seems little point in heading down to the main street, as that's normally where the bigger hordes end up, so we dive in between the buildings and head for the back streets in the hopes of finding somewhere to stop, if not for the night then at least for a moment so we can catch our breath.

But there's no such luck, as every street we pass down is filled with deaders that all turn to follow us as they catch a whiff of our pungent-yet-no-doubt-delightful scent.

I hack across another deader's head, my arm almost too tired to pull my hatchet back out until I kick at it and free my weapon.

I look down the alleyway we turned into, grateful to see only a handful of deaders since we can't go back the way we just came. The light is dying and the streets are filling with shadows as I cut another deader down.

"Mikey, this way," O'Donnell gasps breathlessly. Her hands are gripping holding of the straps of the bomb backpack to try and stop it from jiggling around so much, and I once again pray that she's done a good job of making them.

The deader I just hit is on the ground, and I put my foot on its face and pull with both hands to free my hatchet, feeling the deader's nose and cheekbones crushing beneath my boot.

I'm tiring, but adrenaline and instincts are still keeping me pushing onwards. I almost fall backwards as my hatchet comes free, and I immediately turn and follow O'Donnell, Ricky, and Phil, turning a corner and realizing that if deaders could think then they'd have just ambushed us.

The horde is even bigger back here, and we all take several steps backwards as the horde turns to stare, their hungry gazes fixing on us. I head back down the alley, but the other end is already filling up with deaders so we're blocked in from both sides.

I look up at the high walls of the buildings, which have us trapped, looking for any way to get out of here. There are fire exit stairs to the left, but they don't reach all the way down and there's no way I can reach them on my own.

I turn to Phil. "Gimme a boost," I say, pointing up toward the stairs.

He nods and bends down to one knee, and I climb onto his shoulders. He grunts as he stands up and I reach up, my fingertips brushing against the metal of the stairs.

"Still can't reach," I yell down to him.

"Mikey, they're getting close," O'Donnell calls back.

"Gonna' have to stand on your shoulders, Phil. Can you hold steady?" I don't hear his response, but when I glance down, Ricky's standing by Phil and has a hold of my ankles as he helps boost me upwards. My hands grip onto the metal railing. "Got it," I call, holding on tightly and pulling down hard.

The ladders are stuck through years of rust, but I pull again and finally feel them moving. The hordes are almost upon us, and I pull with the last remaining strength I have, finally feeling the ladder free itself and come loose. Phil steps away and I hold on as the ladder drops down, and then I climb up the steps as quickly as I can, hearing the rest of them following me. O'Donnell is the last up, and as she crawls onto the first floor landing, I help her pull the ladder back up.

A deader is still clinging to the bars, and O'Donnell grips her long-range rifle and swings it down, hitting the deader in the face and then in the hands until it lets go and falls on the ground with an unsavory splat.

"Stupid ass," she calls down after it before turning to face us. She's covered in sweat and gore, her eyes are wide with fear and adrenaline, and by God she looks wild and alive.

"Okay, we need to head up again," I say, turning to head up the next set of ladders.

O'Donnell lets out a scream as a deader from inside the apartment we're standing outside of smashes its face against the glass. Dark blood splatters across the glass and its teeth mash and snap relentlessly. It throws itself angrily against the window again, this time finally breaking through, and splinters of glass shower us all. It lunges for O'Donnell, who swings out with her rifle to hit it while instinctively taking a step away from it, the backs of her legs hitting the low railing and sending her tumbling over into the abyss behind her.

"O'Donnell!" I call, watching the whole thing play out from my spot on the stairs.

She screams all the way down, her eyes wide in shock and horror, arms and legs reaching upwards as if she could cling onto the air around her and stop herself from falling. But of course she can't.

"O'Donnell!" Ricky yells after her as he lunges toward the edge, but Phil grabs the back of his shirt and begins dragging him away and up the next set of stairs as more deaders begin to come out of the apartment, climbing their way over the broken glass and gutting themselves.

We climb the next set, and I drag those steps up and immediately turn to head up the next, until we're finally on the roof of the apartment building. I clamber over the side, falling to my knees. I'd like a minute to process what the fuck just happened, or to at least catch my breath, but instead I grab my hatchet as I survey the scene of deaders before us.

There aren't many, maybe five or six, but we are exhausted. The deaders begin their shamble toward us, the loud gasps of hunger echoing out into the now-dark night air. I stay near the edge, waiting for them to lunge for me, and then grab them and throw them off the edge. Two of them meet their maker this way before Phil and Ricky take care of the rest and we can finally stop and stare at each other breathlessly.

Ricky falls to his knees and begins sobbing, and I look over the edge at the deaders surrounding the building. I can't see much—it's too dark now, the sun finally setting—but I can hear them down there. I look back and watch Phil go over to Ricky and kneel down. He whispers something to him, and Ricky shrugs him off but quits crying.

I'm breathless and exhausted, and now there's crushing guilt about the loss of O'Donnell. I had begun to care for her, at least in that way that survivors do, and now she's gone. And though I know logically that her death wasn't my fault, the guilt still festers inside of me.

"We need to lock this roof up for the night," Phil says, and I nod.

We leave Ricky to his demons as we scour the rest of the roof, finding the sole entrance to it and locking it up as quietly and securely as possible. There's no moon tonight, and I can barely make out Phil's expression as he stops walking.

"I can't believe O'Donnell's gone." He speaks quietly, his words a whisper. "Aiken's gonna' be pissed, she was one of our best shooters. And Ricky..." His words trail off and we both turn to look at Ricky, who's still hunched on the floor. "This is all fucked up," Phil finally says, and then begins walking back toward Ricky.

I can't disagree with him.

I follow him over so that we're all together, and then I sit down. We stay in silence for a long time, none of us having anything left to say, or maybe too afraid to speak in case of what might come out. If I feel guilty, then Ricky will no doubt be blaming me. That's how we work. One of us has to be the bad guy in all of this, and since it was my idea to get to this town, I'll be the one to take the blame. I'm okay with that; I'll take his blame if I have to.

I think of our night together and feel even worse. She had just wanted someone to connect with, and after all these years on her own, and she had chosen me. And what did I do? I turned her down flat.

She had wanted one night to forget the world, to find some hope in a hopeless situation, and I had been too broken up about Nina to do it. I had finally cried, letting O'Donnell hold me until my well of sadness and grief had been empty, at least for the time being. And she hadn't said a thing. She understood; women always do.

I don't regret not sleeping with O'Donnell, but I do feel bad for it. Because, like she said, it's human nature to want to connect with another person. And that was all she had wanted.

I stay on first watch as Phil and Ricky fall asleep, and I watch the horizon for the small flickers of light that show any form of humanity that might still be living. I see none, and all I hear as the night draws in are the incessant groans of the dead below us.

Chapter Twenty-Five

Phil and I swap shifts somewhere between night and day, but I wake feeling just as rotten as I did when I went to sleep. Ricky is still sleeping, and when we wake him he looks like a Chucky doll, with his angry expression. He sits up and glares around us, his eyes red-rimmed from sadness and exhaustion, even though he slept through the night. My stomach grumbles loudly, as does Phil's, and my throat is drier than sandpaper, but I lick my lips out of habit all the same.

The day is already starting to warm up, and we need to move before it gets too hot or we get too weak to fight our way down from here. I stand up and head over to the ledge to look down. There are a couple of shamblers down there, but most of them have moved on. There's a large stain of blood on the ground that I can see even from this height. I feel dizzy as I think of O'Donnell, and I silently pray that she died upon impact and didn't feel a thing as the horde pounced on her still-warm body.

"How's it looking?" Phil asks as he comes to stand next to me. He looks down and then quickly away. "Like that, huh?"

"Yeah," I agree, knowing that he's talking about the bloodstain, "like that."

We turn our backs on the ledge and look around us. The building we're on isn't particularly tall, but we can see sufficiently around the small town. There are a couple of other buildings with deaders on their roofs, but they all seem to be standing still— just the odd tremor running through their rotting bodies.

"So, you thinking down and out?" Phil asks, seeing my gaze move over to the door we secured last night.

"I'm not sure. We don't know what's inside."

"Or how many."

"Or how many," I agree. "And once we get down, then what? We're still stuck with the problem of getting a working vehicle and getting back to Haven. And I'm thirsty—we need water ASAP." I look up at the sun, seeing it rising, a bright orange burning fire in the sky, promising yet another scorcher.

"One thing at a time, buddy," Phil says. He looks around, going over to the other side of the building, and I follow him, stepping over the air conditioning pipes and around the electric boxes and such. He stops at the edge and looks down and I do the same, surprised to see that this way is clear.

Phil steps back and then looks across to the other building. There's another ledge and another ladder, and more windows, but the roof is clear. There's a set of ladders reaching across from that building to ours, though how stable it is is anyone's guess. Not just that, but surrounding that building is a barricade, and it still looks sturdy, meaning the only thing to worry about is what's locked inside it. With the ladder the way it is, perhaps there are people alive? Perhaps not. But either way, we need to get off this roof.

"What are you thinking?" I ask, trying to work out his plan. I watch him slowly nod and rub a hand over his beard before turning to me with a serious look. I have a feeling he has a great plan and is going to blow my mind right now with it.

"I honestly have no idea. I'm not good at making plans," he finally confesses.

Normally I would laugh, but I'm not much in the mood for laughing right now so I shake my head and take over in his thinking.

"So we get inside this building, get to the—" I count the floors on the other building, "—third floor, jump across to the other building, and check out if over there is any clearer? If it's not, we make it to the roof and grab a quick breather before moving on to the next building along. One of these is sure to give us a decent escape route."

Phil nods and looks back over his shoulder. "You're going to need to watch your back with him."

I turn and look at Ricky, who's standing up and looking over the ledge to the ground, his shoulders slumped.

"Ya think?" I ask, worry bubbling in my gut—because I've been thinking the same thing, but hearing someone else voice that exact same opinion makes it seem more real.

"Yeah, dude. He's going to blame you for her death—"

"But it wasn't—" I cut in.

"I know, dude, I know. It wasn't your fault. It wasn't anyone's but the goddamn zeds. You don't need to tell me that, but Ricky," Phil looks at me, "he's always had a thing for that chick, and everyone saw the spark in her eye when she looked at you. She would have followed you anywhere. Even here. Plus, we went against Aiken's orders; we looked for the kid instead of taking out the barn. We're both gonna'' catch shit for that."

I think about that for a minute, letting the silence of the still day descend over us. There's no point in arguing with any of what Phil's said. He's right. I had known how O'Donnell felt about me, but I'd shut down that road with her as soon as I could. As

243

for following me—fuck, there had been nowhere else to go *but* here! I figure we can discuss it all with Aiken once we get back home though. If we make it home. And as for the consequences to my decision, I'll take whatever punishment he sees fit.

"She really cared about you, Mikey," Phil says, lighting up a cigarette.

"She was a good friend, for the little time I knew her anyway," I say sadly.

Phil cocks his head to one side. "It was more than that though, right? I mean, you two hooked up."

"Nope, we never did," I reply.

"Well damn, that's not what Ricky thinks. He was mouthing off about you coming in here and stealing his chance with her. They've both been single since the last attack, everyone thought they'd hook up at some point—and then you showed up." Phil goes quiet as if thinking about everything, and then he shakes his head again. "Damn, dude, what a revelation."

I shake my head, not sure what to say. "Whatever, there's more important things to think about right now," I say, and begin walking over to where Ricky stands.

He turns around as we approach, his eyes full of sorrow.

"We've got a plan—at least a semi-plan," I say.

"Hopefully it's better than your last one," Ricky replies flatly.

I force myself to not rise to the bait. It isn't worth it. "We need to get inside this building. I think we can get across the next building along if we get to the third floor. There's a ladder reaching across. I think if we can get to that one and get inside we stand a better chance."

244

Ricky pulls out his knife and I flinch. His eyes spark at my obvious anxiety. "All right, let's go then."

I look to Phil, who's watching Ricky warily. "I'll go in first, Ricky, you flank the rear, okay?"

They both nod and we fall into line as we make our way to the door. We pull away the barricade that we put up last night, and then I pull the door open and look inside. It's dark and quiet, not a groan or a growl to be heard. I take that as a positive sign and head inside with Phil and Ricky following me.

We take the concrete stairs slowly, ignoring the obvious stench of decay coming from somewhere. It might be deaders, or it might be a genuinely dead body for all we know. I hope for the latter.

The staircase gets darker the lower we go, until we're practically in complete blackness. Ricky pulls out a small flashlight and passes it forward to me, and I shine it in front of us. It's almost dead, the light barely penetrating the ground in front of me, but I'm not complaining as any light is better than none.

We hit the first landing and I shine the light on the wall to see which number we're at, seeing that we're only on number five.

"Two more to go," I whisper, and continue downwards into the black abyss.

On the next landing we're met with the cause of the stench, which has grown exponentially the lower we've gone: bodies— lots of them. They were deaders at one time, but now they're nothing more than rotting mush. I step over the first one, keeping my hatchet tight in my grip in case any of them aren't quite dead-dead, but thankfully none of them move.

Phil is less graceful than me and kicks the bodies out of the way, much to our own disgust. With every body moved, more stench is unleashed until we're practically choking on the rot smell. I gag and keep on going downwards, knowing that it should be the third floor and the one we'll have to enter. I hurry down those last few steps, eager to get away from the smell and back out into some fresh air.

As we hit the third floor landing, stepping over a deader's body halfway up the stairs, its head smashed in, we hear the first groaning we've heard in a while. I don't bother to look back at Ricky and Phil, but instead choose to let the sound spur us all on since it's coming from farther down the building.

The door to the third floor has a small window in it, and I shine my shitty flashlight through the glass to try and see what's beyond. From what I can make out, it's quiet, so I lower the flashlight and pull on the handle before stepping inside.

The air smells stale and humid, a small amount of light penetrating the musty interior from the window at the end of the hallway, and we head toward that to give ourselves a better reference on where we are.

The window is smeared in blood and is one of those that doesn't open. But we can see out of it, and we work out that the ladder we need to use to cross to the other building is at either the third or fourth apartment on the left.

Apartment A68 or A69.

"I say we go with sixty-nine first," Phil whispers next to me.

"I wonder why," Ricky whispers back.

"What can I say? It's a lucky number," Phil replies, his tone serious.

I look back out the window to the ladder, but genuinely can't work out which apartment it is.

"It's as good a guess as any," I finally say as we backtrack to the door. I wipe a hand across my forehead before I try the handle. The door opens inwards, and I slowly push it all the way open to reveal the interior of the apartment.

It's humid inside, the air filled with the familiar scent of the day, which is drifting in through the broken windows. We move to the center of the apartment as a collective group, but find it to be empty—at least so far.

Phil heads off to the kitchen to check out the cupboards, but I've already guessed that they'll be empty of anything. With the windows out and the door unlocked, it's obvious that someone has already been in here and cleared it out.

I head over to the broken window, looking out carefully in case any deaders are on the fire escape landing. It's clear, but to my dismay I do see that we're in the wrong apartment after all. The ladder is in the next apartment across—A68.

I head back over to Phil, who's still searching the cupboards even though it's obvious there's nothing in them. His stomach lets out a long groan and Ricky comes out of the bedroom next door with his knife held high and his gaze darting around the room. It finally falls on Phil as he realizes that it was the groan of hunger coming from Phil's stomach and not from a deader, and he lowers his weapon.

"All clear," Ricky says, closing the door behind him.

"Here too," Phil says, though since it was an open-plan apartment there had never been any worry of a deader being in the kitchen.

"We need to be next door," I say. "Wrong apartment after all."

"Sixty-nine ain't so lucky after all," Ricky replies, glaring at Phil.

Phil shrugs. "Guess not."

We head back to the doorway, but as I put my hand on the handle I hear something moving out in the hallway and I stop.

The slow shuffle of something just outside the door stops, and the telltale sound of growling can be heard. I slowly let go of the handle and turn to Phil and Ricky with a finger to my lips, telling them to shush.

We step away from the door, lest our delicious human scent penetrate underneath to the deader hankering after our meat. And then we wait, watching and listening as the deader beyond tries to get inside. I've seen this before one or twice; some deaders retain some knowledge of things from their past lives—where they lived and how things worked—and as the handle begins to turn I quickly reach out and flick the lock on the door, preventing the deader from opening it.

We take another step backwards and I glance warily at Ricky and Phil, who look just as worried as I no doubt do.

"Did it just try the handle?" Phil whispers as quietly as he can, sounding as horrified as I'm feeling at the thought.

Ricky's expression remains unchanged, though I'm not sure if it's because he just doesn't give a damn or because he's seen this phenomenon before. It isn't the first time I've seen this though— a deader acting with human mannerisms. It doesn't really matter, not in the grand scheme of things. They're still just sacks of dead rot infused with just enough life to hunger and thirst for human flesh. And they still need to be put down.

I look toward the bedroom that Ricky came out of earlier and I point toward it. Ricky nods and turns around, and then we all head toward the bedroom, with Ricky going in first.

The room is small, with another door leading into another room, and I presume it's the bathroom. I don't notice at first, and neither does Phil as he perches his ass on the edge of the bed and the deader that's tied to it makes a throaty groan and arches her back in an attempt to get up.

Phil dives up, tripping over his own feet as he falls to the ground, the flash of his blue Hawaiian shirt bright in the dim light.

"Fuckkkkk!" he calls out, and both Ricky and I loudly hush him.

The deader is dressed in what was once sexy underwear. Small torn panties and a lacy pink bra cover most of her modesty, but not all. And her once-blond hair is now crusted and lank as it sticks to the side of her face.

Phil stands up, his eyes on the bed with the deader on it. She snaps her jaws, her gaze moving across all of us hungrily, and I do a full-body shudder. Phil moves around the side of the bed, almost falling over again as he stumbles over another body on the floor. Whoever it was had been up to some kinky shit with this chick. They're wearing a full-body black latex gimp suit, but I'm guessing the hammer still embedded in their forehead isn't part of the outfit. The body is bloated and swollen, probably due to the heat of being stuck in that suit for so long—not that I even consider helping them out of it, of course.

Phil nudges the body with his foot. The sound of swishing and then the stench of rot leaking out of the body are noticeable to all of us. When it doesn't move he heads to the sex kitten on the bed and uses his machete to quickly put an end to her misery by stabbing her through the forehead.

The room falls back into silence and I head to the window to look out, seeing that we're right next to the ladder and can probably climb across to the other window and then across the ladder.

I turn and look at Ricky and Phil. "We could be waiting all day for that thing to leave, but if we climb over the railing we can get to the apartment next door," I suggest.

Phil and Ricky come over to look. "Doesn't seem safe," Phil says, looking unimpressed with our only option.

"It's not, but neither is climbing across that ladder between two buildings, yet we're still intending to do that," I reply.

Phil looks over his shoulder at the deader on the bed. "I wonder why they didn't kill her."

"What?" Ricky asks as both he and I turn around to look. Not that I want to. This chick is fifty shades of fucked up, from her breast implants (made all the more obvious by her emaciated body) right down to the shit-covered underwear she's wearing.

"She was still alive, but he," Phil says, nudging the gimp deader on the floor, "was killed."

We all ponder on that for several moments, all coming to the same conclusion at roughly the same time.

"Oh God, I think I'm going to be sick," Ricky says, turning away. "Let's get out of here." He reaches for the window latch and opens it, and we all climb out the window and onto the ledge beyond.

Three floors didn't seem so high last night, yet now as I look down at the ground below us I realize how high it actually is. I think about O'Donnell falling. She had only been on the first floor; it was enough to kill anyone, no doubt. Three floors and you'd be pulverized, surely.

I grab at the ladder, noticing that it's secured on the other side by some rope, but not on this side. I stand up straight and look around us, my gaze falling on all the windows and buildings surrounding us. This ladder was put here for a reason. What if that reason is to lure people to their deaths? Surely this is too simple a getaway.

"What are you waiting for?" Ricky asks, looking back inside the building.

I look down again, but there are still no deaders below. The apartment on the other side looks clear too—at least from what I can see. Now is the perfect time to get going. I glance at Ricky, my mistrust evident on my face, and he does nothing to dissuade me from that thought as I watch a small smile quirk his features.

"This was your plan, you can go first," he says, sweat glistening on head. He normally shaves all his hair off, but I guess he's not had chance the last couple of days and it's now growing back. There's even a thin layer of bristles across his jaw as well.

Never one to back down from a challenge, I nod and tuck my hatchet through the belt loop of my pants. "Sure thing, buddy." I turn to Phil. "Keep hold of this end while I go across."

And then I climb up onto the railing and get down on all fours and begin making my way across the ladder. Do I really think that Ricky would try and tip me off the ladder in revenge for O'Donnell getting killed? Not really.

But if there's one thing that I've learned in this life, it's that you can't trust anyone or anything. Especially where revenge or jealousy is concerned.

251

Chapter Twenty-Six

The air is hot and unmoving. Each slow crawl forward feels like moving through molasses as my muscles protest and begin to seize up. I want to glance back and make sure that Phil is still holding the ladder, but I can't. I need to focus on moving forward—not looking behind me or down, or at any of the many windows where someone could be watching and waiting.

It's like life, really. You can't look back or change your plan once you're set on a path; you just have to keep moving forward, determined to get to the other side and make it out of the current situation without dying. There's always going to be another drama, another nightmare on the other side. But you have to live with the knowledge that you're on the right path and you won't be swayed from it, no matter what, or you'll most certainly plummet to your death.

I make it to the other side, sagging with relief and almost sliding off the ladder to the fire escape ledge like melted butter. When I regain my composure, made all the harder by the fact that I held my breath all the way across, I standup, seeing that Ricky is already on his way over. He looks just as shit-scared as I was, which is good to know.

He gets off with more grace than I did, and then Phil is left to come across on his own, in the knowledge that no one is holding the other end of the ladder for him. The thought must cross his mind about halfway across, because his look of nervousness turns into absolute horror when he reaches up to push his glasses up his nose and the ladder wobbles.

As he tries to get off, his leg slips off the edge and both Ricky and I grab for him before he can fall. He looks like he's going to puke as we drag him over the edge and onto the relative safety of the fire escape ledge.

We take a moment to reacquaint ourselves with not being suspended three flights up, with nothing to stop us falling to our bloody deaths, before heading through the apartment window as quietly as we can.

The place has been cleared of everything, though. Furniture is missing, and crockery, and as we check around we find that even clothes are gone. The only thing remaining in this apartment is the large flat-screen television. Not much use for it since there's no electricity, I guess.

"I don't like this place," Ricky whispers once we've checked that the place is clear of deaders.

"Me neither," I agree. "Let's get out of here then."

"Which way are we going, though? Up or down?" Phil asks, pushing his glasses up his nose.

I'm not sure, if I'm being honest. The streets look pretty empty from every window I've looked out of, and there are vehicles dotted around. Whether any of them work or not is another matter, though. The building is definitely secure from further deaders getting in, though, as the barrier looks intact all the way around, meaning the only thing we have to contend with is whatever is inside. Yet I have a feeling that it's going to be empty. If someone took the time to clear out all the furniture from this apartment, then they would have made sure to clear most, if not all, of the apartment building. Surely. Right?

"Down," I finally answer. "We need to get out of here and get back to Haven."

Phil and Ricky don't argue. Instead they follow me as I head toward the door. I lean my ear against it, listening for any signs of movement on the other side, but it's silent beyond. Finally satisfied, I roll my shoulders, pull my hatchet out of the loop of my pants, and open the door.

It's dark beyond, but not the pitch black of the other side. This building is modern on the inside, and there's a window at either end of the hallway, letting in more light. I look both ways, seeing that it's clear, and then we step out into the hallway and go in search of the stairs.

We reach the empty elevator shaft first, seeing that the doors are pulled wide open. I stick my head inside the black hole, using Ricky's shitty flashlight to look down below, but the light doesn't penetrate far enough. The sound from below, however, does.

The unmistakable noise of deaders is coming from in there, and I pull my head back out before looking to Phil and Ricky with a pained expression. We move on, finding the doorway to the stairs near the end of the hallway, and we push through into it with me using the flashlight once again. The stairs have plenty of deaders on them, but the bodies have all been dragged out of the way, like someone cleared a path.

Everything feels intentional right now—the ladder, the cleared apartment, the elevator shaft, even right down to the path being clear of bodies—yet we're unable to do anything but head the way we're being herded. So far all of it has kept us safe, so if we're being herded, surely that's a good thing?

I head down the stairs, flashlight in one hand, hatchet in the other, with Phil and Ricky close behind until we hit the ground floor. The air is thick and dry, almost as if you can chew it, and I know that beyond this door it'll probably be worse. It has to be reaching midday, and that's the hottest part. Traveling on foot, whether running from deaders or walking home, is going to be hellish, especially since we still have no food or water. I can only hope we find a well-stocked vehicle that works, so the journey isn't all on foot.

I press on the handle of the emergency exit, and am half-blinded by the bright sunshine outside. I don't quite realize how used to the dark my eyes have gotten until they have to readjust to the light.

When they do, I see that we're standing in an empty alleyway with nothing more than years-old trash for company. It's the best damn sight I've seen in a long time.

We all step out and let the door shut quietly behind us before heading around to the front of the building and out into the main town center. There was a war here—a real war—and buildings and cars are merely shells of their former selves. Skeletal bodies are scattered the ground, both deader and human alike. The whole scene—the town, the bodies—reminds me of my own humble beginnings, and brings me back to when it all first happened, when the dead first rose and hell broke loose.

We had no clue what we were doing, or what we were really fighting. We were just trying to survive, in any way we could. And if it meant killing other humans—other non-infected—along the way, so be it.

That's how I survived.

In a town, just like this. I killed anything and everything that got in my path.

I swallow, a chill trailing down my spine. I notice Phil staring at me, his eyebrows tugging into a frown. He takes the lead, probably partly to do with the haunted expression on my face, and I fall back, taking the rear as my memories fight with my mind. I don't want to remember, but it's hard not to when confronted with a mirror. And this place is just that.

I didn't see it last night—we had been running for our lives, deaders at every turn and death imminent—but today, now, I can see it. This town is like every other small idealist town in America, and that's why it reminds me of home.

We run down the center of the road, ducking behind cars and vans that are haphazardly crashed as we hope to evade any further contact with the deaders. There are too many here for us to fight; we discovered that last night. We just need to get out of here.

I look up, seeing that we're standing beside an emergency response vehicle, and I peer through the window to see if there are any weapons inside. It's unlikely, but you never know. A hand slams up against the inside of the glass as whoever's inside is awakened by me.

I jump back, causing Ricky and Phil to do the same, and I'm about to walk away when I realize with horror that the person inside isn't dead. They aren't a deader, they're human, and they're alive. At least just barely.

"Guys?" I say as Phil and Ricky start to walk away.

They come back to my side and look in the car.

"Shit," Ricky says.

"Dog shit," Phil agrees.

"What do we do?" I ask. Of course the humane thing would be to get them out of there and take them with us. But since we're already half-starved, dehydrating, and miles from home, the thought of bringing along another person makes me curse myself for ever looking through that window.

The person stares back at me—a man, I realize—his eyes gray and ringed in darkness as if he's seen too much horror already. His cheeks are pointy and prominent on his starved face. He opens his mouth to say something, but his words are barely a whisper so they're inaudible to us.

"What's he saying?" Phil asks.

I shake my head without even looking at him.

"Open the door, we need to get him out of there."

I shake my head again.

"We can't," Ricky says, voicing exactly what I'm thinking. "We can't," he repeats.

"Guys, we have to. He'll die if we leave him there," Phil says, grabbing me by the shoulders to look at him.

"We'll die trying to save him. The best thing we can do for him now is to put him out of his misery," I reply, shrugging off Phil's grip.

"We can't just kill him!" Phil's voice rises, and it's my turn to turn and glare at him until he lowers it again. "That's murder, we can't do that. He's done nothing."

"He'll get us all killed if we bring him with us. He's too weak, and we're starving ourselves. We have nothing to offer him but a long, long walk back to Haven. He'll die on the journey—if the zeds don't kill him, that is." Ricky steps forward as he speaks, his stare intent on the person inside, who's still trying to say something to us.

Remorse and shame are running through my veins like wildfire, but Ricky is right: the humane thing to do is to put him out of his misery. But I know I can't do it. I've done too much bad in my life, and though this would be a sacrifice for the better, I know I won't be able to do it.

"I'll do it," Ricky says, stepping forward, his hand on the handle of the door.

The person inside has stopped talking and is watching him, and I try to work out if it's fear or gratefulness on his face.

"You can't," Phil says, but neither of us tries to stop Ricky as he opens the door, his hands catching the man as he almost falls out.

He pushes him back inside, laying him across the back seat, and we all see the filthy bandages wrapped around the guy's middle with blood staining them. The smell of rot coming from the wound, or whatever it is, is unmistakable too.

"Ricky," Phil says weakly. He grips my elbow, but I don't stop Ricky either. If anything, I'm grateful that he's doing what I can't.

The man is trying to say something again, but I turn away when Ricky places his knife against the man's temple. I don't want to watch what he does; knowing about it is bad enough.

The sound of the knife penetrating his skull is loud, louder than the heavy beating of my heart against my ribs, and when I look back, Ricky is wiping his blade off on the side of the man's jeans. He turns back around to face us, raising his chin when he sees the look of disgust on Phil's face.

"It was for the best," I say, though I'm not a hundred percent certain of that. Regardless, it's done now and we need to keep on moving. I decide that I'm not going to look in vehicles anymore, for fear of who or what I might find.

We begin moving again, with Phil flanking the rear and Ricky taking the lead. The street is long, but after half a mile or so it looks like it's coming to an end. The sound of deaders' groans is ringing loudly in the air, though from exactly where, I'm not sure.

Sweat trails down between my shoulder blades, and we keep low behind some cars as we come to a junction. Between the rows of stores is a herd of deaders. They're moving forward, slowly, and facing the opposite way, but it won't take much for them to notice us. We need to keep moving, but moving forward isn't an option while they're still there, so we back up a step or two until we're out of sight of them. And vice versa.

"Which way now?" Ricky asks breathlessly.

I shake my head and look around while still keeping down as low as I can. There are a couple of deaders on the road behind us now, so going back isn't an option either.

I look at the store we're standing in front of, seeing that it's all boarded up, with a huge padlock on the main door, but it gives me an idea. It's a candy store, the sort my gran and gramps would have loved to visit before all their teeth fell out and they could only suck on candy for fear of it getting stuck in their dentures. Ricky looks over as if reading my mind.

"We can't go backwards," he says.

"And we can't go forwards," I reply.

"So we have to go inside?" Phil adds on, and I nod. "That reminds me of a book I once read as a kid," he says.

I shrug, having no clue what he's talking about.

I use the corner of my hatchet on one of the padlocks on the door, and am about to pry the lock open when I realize that the padlock is a fake. Though it's on the door, it isn't being used. I try the handle and it presses down without even giving a little squeak of resistance, and then opens inwards. Looks like our luck is about to change for the better. It's about time.

"No shit," Ricky whispers in amazement.

"No shit all right," I agree.

So far we've gone from too much shit to no shit. I'm well aware of the irony of that, and am ready for whatever danger lies inside this building.

The deaders are getting louder, and I have a feeling that we've been well and truly sniffed out. It probably doesn't help that the temperature of the day is rising and we're all beginning to sweat profusely. What? It's a tense situation and it's hot as hell—don't judge me.

I crick my neck and step inside, deciding that it's now or never. I don't like walking into a situation like this without knowing what's really going on. Clearly there are people inside. Why else would there be a fake lock? But whether they're going to be friend or foe is a different matter, especially since we're gatecrashing their hideout.

We all step inside, and Phil shuts the door behind us, clicking it back into place. Inside it's quiet. Deathly so. Dark shadows cling to every corner, and cobwebs hang from the shelving. The windows have been boarded up on the outside, and covered on the inside with paper that's aged and yellowed, giving the room a surreal yellow glow. We move around the store, stepping over broken shelving and around old candy signs. It's a little kid's nightmare, seeing everything gone to ruin.

The deaders have arrived, and their shadows pass in front of the front window. The sounds of their strange, garbled growls echo to us from outside. Phil clicked the door shut, so there's no way they're getting inside unless they learn to use handles. I turn away from the window and then my eyes go wide and I dive for the door, slapping the latch in place. The noise is loud—too loud—and a couple of the deaders are attracted to it and begin banging on the boarded-up front. I step backwards, praying that they'll get bored and wander off. All right, all right, maybe not get bored, because they don't ever do that. But if they get distracted, they'll forget about the noise they heard.

We make our way to the back of the store as quietly as we can, avoiding the broken glass and metal shelves. The deaders are still outside, but they aren't in a frenzy, which is a good sign. They've likely forgotten what they're even banging on the window for, and will continue to do it until they get sidetracked on to something else.

"Did you leave the car door open?" Ricky whispers to me, his gaze still focused intently on the front of the store and the shadows moving beyond.

"Car?" I ask.

"The guy I put out of his misery, did you leave the door open?" he emphasizes.

"Oh, yeah," I reply, thinking about that poor bastard once more. "You think he'll grab their attention?"

"His smell will soon enough," Ricky says. "Fresh meat, right?"

We back up another step, and I choose not to answer him. It doesn't feel right to. Yeah, the guy is dead now, and I sincerely hope that the deaders will be attracted to the smell of his dead body. It'd definitely get us out of this current jam. But saying it out loud—agreeing that the mutilation and devouring of that guy's body would be the best thing for us—feels dirty.

Phil taps me on the shoulder and I turn to look at him. "What?"

"Door," he whispers.

I nod, seeing the door too. But what's more important than the door is the light shining from underneath it. I nudge Ricky, who scowls at me until I jerk my head toward the door behind us and he sees the light too.

We head to the door, pulling out our handguns so we're fully armed for whatever is going to greet us on the other side of it. Humans—shoot them in the face. Deaders—stab them in the face. It's a pretty simple tactic, you just have to choose your weapon effectively. And it's always good to be fully prepared for any outcome in unknown territory.

I flex my shoulders as Phil grips the handle of the door, and I say a silent prayer that we aren't walking into an even more hostile environment. This really does seem to be the town that keeps on giving, I think sarcastically.

Phil pulls the door open and I swing my gun around, aiming it at everything and nothing. Because there's nothing and no one in there, except for a dusty old sofa and an old kerosene lamp. We head through the room, me taking the lead and Ricky flanking me, and Phil somewhere in between, looking jittery as hell. Something has spooked him, but I'm not sure what—other than the town overrun with deaders, our now-dead friend, the emaciated dude that we just put out of his misery, and the fact that this old candy store is creepy as shit. Other than that, I have no clue why he's so jittery.

At the other side of this room is another door, but unlike all the others, it isn't closed. It's wide open, and when we peer around the doorframe we see a woman sitting in a wheelchair and watching an old black-and-white movie on a small television set.

"Tim? Is that you?" she calls out, her voice soft. She turns her face away from the television set, her gaze finally landing on us. Her smile falls as she takes us all in, but it rises back up just as quickly. "Well hello there, friends."

Chapter Twenty-Seven

"Hi!" Phil calls cheerfully.

It's overly cheerful if the truth be known, but I decide that it isn't because he's a total idiot and just that he's so damned relieved that we've met a woman in a wheelchair and not some crazy psychopath or a room full of deaders for a change.

She spins the chair around so she can see us without craning her neck. The banging outside has gotten louder, but she doesn't seem too concerned by it.

"Sounds like you made it inside just in time." She smiles wider, the corners of her eyes crinkling as she does. She grabs a small remote control from her lap and pauses the movie she was watching before looking back at us. "I just love this part," she sighs. "So what brings you fine men to this neck of the woods? Can't be my famous candy—not had that for a long time. And as you can see from outside, we're pretty cut off from everything here."

She taps a finger against her chin thoughtfully, her gaze moving slowly from Ricky to me and then to Phil.

"Just trying to stay alive, lady," Ricky finally says.

Her gaze moves back to him. "Aren't we all?"

Silence falls between us again, and this time it's me who feels the fluttering of something in my stomach, the feeling that something just isn't right. Perhaps it's the calm manner in which she's talking to us—three big-assed dudes that just turned up in her home—or the fact that she doesn't seem concerned by the banging deaders at her front door, but something is amiss.

"Who's Tim?" Ricky asks, his voice full of hard steel.

"Tim's my husband," she says, her expression friendly. "He went out to scavenge some supplies." She goes silent, a small smile on her lips before she adds, "We don't have much, but we're happy to share whatever we do have."

"And why would you do that?" Ricky asks through gritted teeth. He'd be better snarling at her for extra effect, the way he's going at it.

The woman looks confused, but her smile stays in place. "Because you're human, and so am I. And there aren't many of us left."

She makes a good case, and I relax my grip on my gun, lowering it slowly.

"Not everyone is good out here," I say. "Sometimes humans can be worse than the deaders."

She frowns. But her smile stays. "Deaders?"

"Those walking sacks of rot outside your front door," I clarify.

She gives a little laugh. "Oh, those, yes. And you're right, sometimes humans can be just as bad as them, but other times they're good. I like to believe in the good." She looks away shyly. "Call me naïve, but there's not enough good in the world, and once we go around thinking that everyone is bad or evil, well, that just about kills the rest of the good. At least for me." She looks back up to us. "Tell me something: are you good?"

I swallow, not knowing how to answer that question. Am I good? I have no idea anymore. I've done bad things. Really bad things.

I've gotten so many people killed, and I've killed so many people. I can't deny that some of them deserved it, but I also can't hide behind the lie that all of them did. Some of those kills were just for me, for my survival. So am I good? What is good anymore? Is there really any purity left in this world? Any innocence? I highly doubt it.

"Are you?" Ricky intervenes. "Are you good?" He still has his gun raised, his aim still on her.

"I like to think so," she replies calmly, either not noticing or choosing to ignore Ricky's hostility. "I never turn away people, and I help when and where I can. I'm just a woman in a wheelchair at the end of the world," she coos.

She rests her hands on her lap, her thumb stroking over the soft blanket that covers her legs. I recognize the logo on the blanket and I can't stop the smile from my face. She notices and looks down at the blanket.

"Never could resist the idea of Jax Teller draped across my knee," she laughs. "Did you watch the show?"

I shake my head no. "My girlfriend did," I reply.

"I always loved *Sons of Anarchy*. What I'd give for one ride on his bike. My name's Clare." She holds out her hand for me to shake, even though we're across the room from her.

I look across at Ricky, who has finally lowering his gun, and then I step forward and take her hand in mine. Her hands are cold, her fingers like ice, and I resist the urge to pull away. "I'm Mikey. This is Ricky and Phil. You can trust us. We're not here to hurt you, I promise."

"Well, I'm very glad to hear that. My husband Tim will be back real soon. He and our dogs went to get a few supplies. You're lucky he didn't leave one of them with me like he usually does. Candy is a vicious little thing and would have gone for the jugular the moment you stepped inside." Clare laughs like this is the funniest shit she's ever heard.

I let go of her hand and step away.

"Should we—" *run* is what I want to say, but of course I don't. But I also don't want to be savaged by another dog.

"Just take a seat. They'll find it less threatening when they come in," she replies, as if reading my mind. Clare points to another small sofa on the right, and all three of us make our way over to it and sit down.

The banging from outside has died down to almost nothing, so either they've discovered that dead dude's body or something else has distracted them. I don't care which option at this point, I'm just glad they've quit banging. The last thing I want is for them to break in here and kill this poor woman in her chair. That would be another death because of me, more blood on my hands, and I already have too much of that on them.

So we sit, and we wait. Clare turns her film back on, and we all sit in silence and watch it with her. And truth be told, it's the most relaxing twenty minutes I've had in a long time. For this twenty minutes I'm lost in a movie, swallowed up by a make-believe world where deaders don't roam and people don't kill for sport. The film is an old black-and-white romance, with actors that had been dead way before the apocalypse. It's comforting somehow, knowing that they're trapped in this movie, in their time forever untouched by the dead and the horrors of this world.

The door finally goes, but not the front door, but one from somewhere else in the building. Clare turns to look at us and smiles.

"That'll be Tim now." She sees Ricky gripping his gun and shakes her head. "I wouldn't advise that unless you want both Candy and Cane to attack you. Stay calm, keep your hands in your lap, and stay seated until I've introduced you and they are settled. You'll be fine, you can trust me."

And I believe her. There's something very calming and soothing about this woman. She's soft-spoken, her features kind, and really how threatening can a woman in a wheelchair be to three grown men? We could also shoot both of her dogs before they even had a chance to attack us, but what would be the point? She hasn't threatened us; she wants to help. And right now, we need all the help we can get.

A man walks into the room, flanked by what look like two wolves, and I feel both Ricky and Phil tense up next to me. The man's gaze falls on us and the dogs stalk toward us, their teeth bared and their ears back.

"It's okay, Tim." She holds up her hands. "Candy, Cane, heel. Be good girls." Clare lowers her hands, showing the dogs her palms, and the two dogs go to stand by her side.

"Sir?" I stand up and Candy and Cane snarl and snap their jaws so I sit back down abruptly. "Easy, easy, sorry. Sir, we're not here to harm you or your wife. We didn't know anyone was in here, we were just hiding out from the deaders."

"Ain't that just the cutest name, Tim? Deaders!" Clare claps her hands together and the two dogs startle and bark. "Oh hush now, girls." She taps them on their noses and both dogs turn to her and rest their heads on her lap.

"I'm pleased to hear that," Tim says, looking at me. "I'd hate for anything to happen to Clare. She has a pure heart and has never hurt a fly."

He's a big guy—tall, thin, but broad-shouldered and with intensely dark eyes. In his hand is a hammer, and even from my place on the sofa I can see the dark stains on it.

"Deaders," Tim says, looking at Clare.

She laughs. "I know, right?" She turns her gaze back to me. "We just call them the *things*. I don't like naming my nightmares. Who wants to know the name of the thing that frightens you? It doesn't make it any easier, but harder somehow—but I could be persuaded."

"I call them zeds," Phil pipes up. It's the first he's spoken since coming into the room. I think it's the dogs that are putting him at ease. He always seems so much more calm when there are animals around. "Can I pet them?" he asks, pointing to the dogs.

"Of course!" Clare says, pushing the dogs' faces from her lap. "Go on, girls, go get some loving from the happy hippy. He's a friendly one."

I choke on my laugh, but she doesn't seem to notice. The two dogs come forward, warily at first, sniffing me and Ricky as they pass. They seem happier once Phil begins stroking them behind the ears.

"Did you find any lunch?" Clare asks Tim, her face hopeful.

He nods and smiles. "I did. Found a couple of possums for meat. We're set for a while, baby, don't you worry 'bout nothing." Tim turns to look at us. "Take it you boys will be staying for dinner?"

"We should probably get going," I say, looking from Tim to Ricky.

"Yeah, we need to get on the road, but if we could trouble you for some water, that would be great," Ricky replies.

"Nonsense, you need to eat. I can hear your stomach growling from over here, and the streets are filled with those things so you won't be getting far on foot. I'm guessing you've done something to disturb them. One of you boys hurt yourself? Or did you lose someone? Fresh blood always brings them out."

"We lost a good friend of ours last night," Ricky says.

"Yeah, that'll do it," Tim says, stroking his chin. "What happened, if I may ask?"

"She slipped off the roof while we were trying to escape," I say and look down at my feet.

"Well shit, I'm truly sorry." Tim moves further into the room.

"We also found someone in a car not far from here," I add, watching as Tim's expression hardens.

"Where are they?" he asks, his gaze moving over to Clare.

"They were close to death already. We put them out of their misery."

Tim nods thoughtfully. "I'm not going to lie, we don't get many visitors around these parts. This town is often overlooked, so the thought of so many new people makes me nervous. But look, once you've eaten and they've moved on, we'll stock you up with some provisions and you can be on your way. I even know of some vehicles that still work around here. You can take one of those." Tim is still holding onto his hammer, but his grip is relaxed. "You keep the wife company while I cook us up some meat. I bet it's been a long time since you had any real meat, right?" He smiles and rubs a hand down his dirty T-shirt and bloated stomach.

"That sounds great, as long as we're not imposing," Ricky finally replies.

Though I feel like we aren't being given much of a choice either way, I can't see the harm in staying for an hour or so. If Tim and Clare do everything they say they will, we'll be set to get the hell out of here in no time, with food in our bellies, and provisions, and a vehicle to get us home. The only thing we'll have really lost other than a day's travel will be O'Donnell, and there will no doubt be consequences to that once we get back home. But right now this seems like the best shot we have of actually getting home.

"Yeah, that would be great, thank you," I say to Tim, and then I turn to Clare. "You're right, there aren't enough good people left in the world. It's good to know that there are some still left."

And it is good to know. Because I can't deny that I had begun believing that there weren't any good people left. They seem so few and far between. The NEOs seem like a good group, but everyone has skeletons in their closets, and I have no doubt that they have theirs too. And I of course have mine. The image that we choose to show people is always very different from the image we have to see in the mirror every day. It's distorted, and normally blurred beyond recognition. Can we change, though? Really? Can we ever make that blurred image our reality? I'm not sure, but it's always a hopeful thing to know that some people are trying.

These people, they seem genuine. They want to help. And people wanting to help is never a bad thing. It only proves that life is still worth it. That we're still fighting for something in this world. Whether it be one person we help, or fifty, everyone is worth a damn. And shit, if everyone did half of what these people are doing, then we'd be halfway to surviving a life worth having.

I wonder about giving them the address of Haven when we leave, in case they ever want to get away from this place. Aiken says he wants good people there, and these people seem as good as any.

After a horrific twenty-four hours of masked killers, freak deaders, and losing O'Donnell, it finally feels like we're getting a little overdue luck.

Chapter Twenty-Eight

Tim brings in a plate full of meat. It's burnt beyond normal recognition, but I figure that's due to the fact that it's possum, or snake, or squirrel, and none of those are exactly desirable things to eat. But food is food and meat is meat, and so we devour everything that's given to us and I suck on the tiny bones of whatever animal it is until my stomach begs me to give it a damn break.

Phil reaches for another slice of meat. I can see from his expression that he feels the guiltiest out of us all. He is, after all, the animal lover. It must be hard for him to chow down on something that he loves so much. But we've been starving, and we're the top of the food chain. We need to eat, to drink, and to rest before we set back out on the road.

Tim shows me around their home, an old candy store that they ran before the fall of mankind. I can imagine it had been quaint at one time, and the kids had come around every day after school to buy their candy before heading home. It makes me smile at the thought, and reaffirms my belief that they're good people.

We learn that Clare has a long history of different illnesses, hence her wheelchair, the shelves stocked with meds, and the fact that they're still here in this town instead of trying to find somewhere less overrun with the dead.

Tim directs me to one of the main rooms upstairs which he's set up as a base of operations. He's scavenged the entire town and has a ton of supplies. It all goes back to the whole "skeleton in the closet" thing, because some of the things Tim has found are damn scary for the everyday man to be hiding under his bed.

273

He's set up a telescope at one of the windows, and I take a look through, watching the horde of deaders at the end of the road. They've stopped walking, as if going into some sort of stasis.

"They do that sometimes," he says, his tone thoughtful. "Then something will alert them—something falls, or collapses, or a wanderer comes on by—and they wake up and go in search of the food again."

"Food?" I say with distaste, pulling my face away from the eyepiece of the scope.

He shrugs. "Sorry, there's only Clare and I here and we're not shy of saying it how it is." He moves around the room, checking out the guns on one of the shelves.

I think on what he just said and wonder if I'm turning into a pussy. I don't think I'm shy about saying things how they are, but perhaps I am, because his statement bothered me.

"If you look at where they are, there's a Humvee. It doesn't work, but just behind that there's an old army truck. It's beat up pretty bad, but it still works," Tim says, coming to stand by my side.

I look back through the scope, moving it so I can look at what he's talking about. Sure enough, there's a big, beautiful, beat-up Humvee haphazardly parked. (Try saying that twenty times as fast as you can!) It looks like it's been through hell and back. Behind that there are several more vehicles, one of them being the old army truck he spoke of. It looks even worse off than the Humvee, and I can't imagine it starting.

"You sure it works?" I move the scope over the deaders, watching them for several moments as they sway side to side like they're listening to some relaxing music.

"For sure," Tim replies. "I start it once a week, let it idle for a couple of minutes to keep the battery charged, and then I turn it off. I leave it where it is, because well, I don't like the thought of people poking around too close to my home and wife."

I turn to look at him in confusion and he smiles.

"The Humvee is our backup plan, should things head south. I worry people will see that thing and want to take it, and if they poke around too much they may find us here. Like Clare says, not everyone left is good. But you gotta' have a backup plan, right?"

I nod in agreement. "Yeah, man. I've been caught out too many times by people without backup plans. But look, if that's your backup plan, I'll understand you not wanting to share it. We'll find some other way out of deader central. You gotta' put Clare first, I get that."

I do get that. If it were Nina, I wouldn't be sharing my backup plan with anyone. But I hope to God that he won't change his mind, because if that's our only way out of here, then we'll have to do whatever we can to take that opportunity. And even if I don't think in that mindset, Ricky sure as hell does. No doubt.

"Cards on the table?" Tim asks, and I nod, feeling anxious. "You said you had a group, right? The NEOs?"

"That's right."

"Well, I'm a useful man, I think I could be of some service to them," he says.

And there it is: his cards on the table. It's lucky that I've already thought the same thing for him and Clare.

"In return for him taking you and Clare in?" I say.

He nods. "And Candy and Cane, of course."

275

I smile. "Of course." I think about Fluffy and Achillies and can't see two more dogs being a problem for Aiken, especially two as ferocious as these. If anything, they'll be an asset. At least that's how I'll sell it to him. Clare might be an issue, what with her health problems, but I have no doubt in my mind that she's resourceful and will be plenty able to help out around Haven. Hell, we found a job for Joan, didn't we?

We head back down the stairs and into the back room. Ricky looks up as he throws another bone onto his plate. Clare is sitting in the corner watching us all, her eyes unfocused. I frown as I watch her, her gaze cold and blank. I begin to worry that her illnesses are more serious than Tim had suggested, because she seems to be in a world of her own.

"Headphones," Tim says from next to me. "She's listening to music. That woman loves her music. Hates the silence more than anything else. She says that she can hear how dead the world is when there's no noise."

I focus in on the thin trail of wire leading to hear earbuds and I feel more at ease. Tim slaps me on the shoulder and laughs before heading over to his wife. He pulls the earbuds out and kisses her on the forehead before whispering something to her. She looks up at me and smiles.

I head farther into the room and go sit with Ricky and Phil. Candy—or Cane, I'm not sure which—has her head in Phil's lap, her nose twitching at the scent of the bones he's still picking at.

My stomach grumbles at the sight of more food, but it's out of greed and not genuine hunger anymore. Ricky leans back on the sofa, his expression dark, and I figure he's thinking about O'Donnell again. I want to apologize, but know there's no point and in fact would make everything ten times worse, for him and for me.

He leans his head back and closes his eyes. "Mikey? You got this?" he asks, his words slurring through tiredness.

"Yeah, man, I've got this," I reply quietly. I look over at Phil, who's looking just as tired. We barely slept last night. The nightmare of the day, the exhaustion and hunger, and of course the fact that we slept out in the open on a roof wasn't ideal.

"You men want a bed?" Tim asks, sitting down opposite us.

"Nah, we're good here thanks," Phil says. "Don't want to put you out."

"It's no bother," Tim replies. "Plenty of room upstairs. Clare sleeps down here now, it's too difficult getting up and down the stairs all the time." Neither Phil nor Ricky replies, so he continues. "In fact, without being rude, that's her bed that you're all sitting on right now."

I look across as Ricky cracks an eye open, his features slack with exhaustion. Sure enough, it's a pullout bed that we're sitting on, and we all stand up apologetically.

"It's okay, don't worry about it, boys," Clare says, wheeling herself over to us. "Tim will put you up in one of the spare rooms upstairs."

Ricky and Phil follow Tim out, and I stay standing up, looking around me and feeling uncomfortable. I promised Ricky I'd keep watch, and though I'm feeling tired I don't want to let him down. But I can't stay down here if Clare's going to sleep.

"My illnesses mean I always have to take an afternoon nap. Pain keeps me up most of the night," she explains.

I'm impressed by her strength and resilience, her determination to keep positive and focused despite everything that's against her survival.

"I'll head upstairs and keep watch with Tim," I say, heading back out of the room. Candy and Cane follow me to the doorway before sitting down by the door as if keeping guard.

"Oh, Tim likes to have a little afternoon siesta with me too, but you could keep guard for all of us, here," she says, grabbing another plate of meat and rolling over to me.

I take it from her even though I'm not hungry. "Thanks, Clare."

Tim comes back down the stairs and Candy and Cane trot over to him. He strokes their heads and they snuffle against his hand. "Your men are asleep in the back room," he says, eyeing the plate of food in my hand. "You should stock up," he says, gesturing to the meat. "Never know when you could be starving again."

"True," I reply. "I'll keep watch upstairs." I head out of the room.

"Thanks, Mikey, it's appreciated," Tim calls after me.

"No problem," I reply, and head back up the stairs.

I take my time, feeling my own exhaustion leeching into my muscles. I roll my shoulders, and drag my free hand through my rough beard and yawn. On my way up the stairs I look at the photographs hanging up on the walls. They're mainly of Clare, Tim, and their dogs—wedding photos, holidays, barbecues with friends. They depict a happy and full life, and for the first time ever it makes me feel jealous.

I never had that. My life, from the day I was pushed into this world kicking and screaming, has been bloody and turbulent.

And at thirty-odd years old, nothing much has changed. I'm still alone, lonely, broken, and still fighting for my survival. Fighting for the scraps of life I can get.

I reach the top of the stairs and go check on Phil and Ricky. They're already flat out, their snores loud before I even open the door. I chuckle to myself, knowing that I'm going to give them both shit when they wake up later, because they're almost spooning. I shut the door and head to the lookout room, first checking through the scope on where the deaders are and seeing that they haven't moved yet. A couple are still crowded outside the front of the candy store, preventing us from leaving that way, and I already know from the back exit that we can get out that way, but it only leads to the front of the store, thus putting us back to square one.

I sigh and move away from the scope, sitting in one of the chairs in the corner. I check my weapons—my blades, my hatchet, and my handgun—and feel confident that they're okay, and then I set them aside. I pick up the plate of meat and grab one of the burnt offerings on it, giving it a sniff as I pick away at the crispy burnt skin on it. It tastes like chicken, but of course it can't be. Tim cooked a mixture of squirrel, possum, and snake, since there were so many of us, and I helped him season the meat with the small amount of things he had.

I take a bite of the meat, my stomach grumbling in resistance, but then I think about what Tim said about needing to stock up while I can and I force the meat down. Because he was right, and who knows what'll happen after we leave here? I don't want to be trapped on another roof, starving to death and wishing I had eaten just one more squirrel leg.

I eat through the entire contents of the plate, throwing the bones into a small pile, and then I check out the window once more before sitting back in the chair. I feel sleepy now that I've eaten so much—sluggish and weary from the past couple of days traveling.

I close my eyes, the image of O'Donnell's face and her tortured expression as she fell backwards off the fire exit flashing behind my closed lids.

And then I'm sinking.

Drowning in exhaustion and sadness and grief.

And feeling relief that at least in my dreams I can still be with Nina.

Chapter Twenty-Nine

"Wha...what?" I swallow, my throat feeling on fire as it scratches against my groggy words.

I blink into the darkness, my muscles aching and heavy. I'm on the floor, the scent of wood and dust and something indescribable reaching into my body and making me gag.

My head feels too heavy on my shoulders, like my neck muscles aren't strong enough, and I lean my head back as I look around the room and try to work out what the hell is going on.

I'm no longer in the lookout room, but a room I didn't see before. It's barren of furniture, barring a mattress on the floor and a single wooden chair in the corner. Yet I'm sitting on neither, favoring the hard floor instead.

My hands and feet tingle, and I stretch my fingers out and try to grip something, anything, but realize that my wrists are tied together and so are my and ankles. I lick my dry tongue across my even drier lips and press the heels of my hands against my eyes to try and wake myself up. My heart is thumping slowly in my chest, but panic is coiling through me like a serpent.

"Hello?" I call out, the single word painful as it wrenches out of my throat. "Ricky?" Phil?" I force out more words but my voice is quiet, even to my own ears. I roll onto my front so I'm on my hands and knees, and then I take a couple of slow, ragged breaths as nausea rolls through me. When I feel it's under control, I crawl toward the only door in the room.

I pull myself up to kneeling, the action incredibly difficult because of my wrists being tied. I lean my forehead against the wood of the door. "Ricky? Phil?" I say again, my voice and body growing stronger with each passing minute.

I put my ear to the door, at first hearing nothing, but slowly sounds come to me: grunts and groans, the slap of hands on flesh, and the thumping of something. I recoil, at first thinking I'm listening to the sound of Tim and Clare fucking, but then I put my ear back to the wood and listen again.

The same noises are there, and I frown as I try to work out what they are. Grunting and groaning, whispers, and something else I can't make out.

"Hello? Is anyone there?" I fumble for the door handle, but there's an empty space where it should be. I press my eye to the small hole where the handle normally is. At first there's just blackness, but then my eyes grow accustomed to the dark beyond and I see the small amount of light coming from somewhere beyond this room.

I bang on the door with my fist, my movements still sluggish and my beatings weak. The noises stop, and then as I stare through the doorknob hole I see a door opened across the hallway. I flinch against the brightness, eventually taking in the shape of Tim standing in the doorway. I can't make out his expression, but he's watching my door, and I thump on it again.

"Tim? What's going on?" My throat spasms and I cough so hard I think I'm going to vomit. I fall to my side, my vision blurring as I continue to cough. When I eventually get it under control, I kneel back up and put my eye to the hole again.

A couple of seconds pass and Tim pushes his door wider open, and I struggle to understand what I'm seeing, my mind not conceiving the possibility until it's too obvious too ignore.

Tim walks toward Phil, whose body is hanging from the ceiling by his feet. He's hanging over a bath, his arms hanging limping by his head. He turns to look at Tim, and I see his battered face. I'm so focused on his disfigured and battered face and trying to understand what the hell is going on that I almost miss Tim picking up his hammer.

Phil's face is swollen and purple, as if he's been being beaten for hours. He's unrecognizable but I'd know his Hawaiian shirt anywhere. I blink to clear my blurry vision, my stomach clenching in knots. Tim glances across at me, holding Phil's swinging body steady and forcing him to look toward my door.

"Say hello to your friend," he says to Phil. And then he swings his hammer into Phil's face. It smashes into his nose, sending an explosion of blood and cartilage spraying outwards like a firework.

Phil calls out, a groan and howl of pain, and then nothing but muffled grunts of agony as Tim swings again, this time catching him in the eye socket and making the bone shatter and his eyeball explode. I call out, my fingernails digging into the wood of the door as I grip the doorframe to stop myself from falling over. Tim swings again and again, blood splattering up his clothing. I gag and call out, my fists hitting against the door as my eyes widen.

Tim turns to look at my door once more, knowing that I'm watching him. And this time I don't miss his smile. He pulls a long knife from his belt loop and reaches across Phil before dragging it across his throat. Blood gushes out of the slice across his neck and into the bathtub below him, covering his already mutilated, bloody face.

I gag and back away from my door, scooting back as quickly as I can until my back hits the wall behind me. I drag a hand across my face, wanting to wake myself up from this nightmare. When that doesn't do the trick I pinch myself so hard I break the skin, but I'm still here, in this living nightmare. I slap myself across the face, once, twice, three times, until my eyes sting and my hand aches. But I'm still here, and this is still happening.

"You okay in there, Mikey?" Tim calls to me, amusement alight in his voice.

I don't answer. I can't answer. The horror of this situation is fully hitting me. The memories of eating the meat and feeling tired. Of seasoning the meat with Tim, and no doubt poisoning us unbeknownst to me. I feel sick and tired and scared. How could I not be? I just watched someone be beaten to death with a hammer—his face smashed in before his throat was slit and the blood drained from his body.

Scared? No, I'm fucking petrified.

More so because what he just did to Phil was for amusement only. He slit his throat *after* he'd butchered him. When he could have easily ended things quickly for Phil, he chose not to. The world is spinning and the sound of my blood is rushing in my ears.

"Ricky?" I call loudly. "Rickkyyy!" I roar out his name, praying to anything and everything that he'll say something—a murmur, a groan, I'd even take a grunt of pain right now—but his voice never comes.

I hear footsteps, the sound getting louder as they come toward my door, and then Tim's laughter. He taps on the door, his mouth close to the wood when he speaks so that his words are muffled but still understandable. "You enjoy your rest?" He laughs again. "You ready for something to eat and drink?" Another laugh.

"Stop playing with your food, Tim," Clare scolds.

284

Tim laughs again. "Don't worry, we don't kill all of our food right away. Sometimes, when we luck out like we've done with your group, we keep you for a while. Fatten you up for when our supplies run low again."

He laughs again and a tremor runs through my body as the full situation becomes so blatant that I can't dismiss it anymore. I can't pretend that this is a dream that I'll wake up from, or a misunderstanding that Tim or Clare will be able to explain away.

I twist my wrists back and forth, testing how tight the ties are around them, and then I scoot back toward the door and look through the handle hole again.

Phil is still hanging from the ceiling, the blood flow a slow drip from his neck now. It's too late for him, and probably too late for Ricky too. But I'm still alive, and from what Tim just said, I will be for a while yet while they...fatten me up. How will they do that, I wonder. When food is so scarce already, why would they waste their valuable rations on me?

Tim puts his hand on Phil's back, dragging the shirt off his body. His T-shirt comes next, and everything is thrown into the corner of the room. I watch in horror and fascination as Tim takes his blade and slices down Phil's side, from hip to armpit, until he has one long thin strip of flesh dangling from his fingertips. Fresh blood dribbles from the wound and trails down Phil's dead body, and I gag and look away.

Sweat is trailing down the sides of my face, dripping into my eyes and blurring my vision, and I rub it away with the side of my arm. I take a deep, shaky breath, chewing on the inside of my cheek to try and calm myself down. My head is becoming clearer and my muscles stronger with each passing minute, but something is still keeping me tethered to the drowsy world in which I awoke. My wrists are stinging from the zip ties around them, my ankles too, but they're the least of my worries.

I look back through the hole, seeing that Tim has stopped slicing away at Phil, but the odor of burning can be smelled from somewhere. I've always been afraid of fire, and the thought of burning to death is my biggest fear. It stems from my own mother almost burning our home down when I was a little kid— her haste to save herself meaning that she left me behind. Luckily firemen arrived in time and got me out, but the fear has stayed with me ever since. Yet right now I'd welcome dying by fire rather than having what just happened to Phil happen to me. It isn't just the thought of becoming someone's meal, their sustenance, that scares me, but watching Phil's head being beaten to a pulp while he was still alive.

Death is never a happy occasion—at least not in this life. There's no easy or good way to go. Death by deader, death by gun, death by knife attack, or even fire. They're all shitty options, but Phil's death is the one I fear, and after all the groups I've been with, it seems the most fitting for me.

Perhaps that's why I fear it so much.

Because it's always been inevitable.

Clare's wheelchair suddenly comes from around the corner and begins rolling toward me. On her lap is her *Sons of Anarchy* blanket and Jax Teller's face grinning back at me. I scoot away from the door as Tim follows her and they get closer to the door. I listen as latches and bolts are slid back, and then the door slowly opens inwards. Tim stands behind Clare, a rifle held high and Candy and Cane both at his side. Clare smiles as I cower in the corner almost pissing myself.

She doesn't say anything for a long time, instead choosing to watch me carefully, her thin smile held steady on her face. Eventually she speaks, and as she speaks, I notice the plate on her lap with the freshly cooked meat on it.

"Thought you might be hungry. It's been a long day for you, I'm sure. I know I get hungry when I worry." Her voice is soft—kind, almost—but there's something maniacal in the undertones. She lifts the plate on her lap and holds it toward me. Both dogs sniff the air, their tails wagging in their eagerness for the food.

I frown but stay where I am. I'm vastly outnumbered, my hands are still tied, and my muscles are still too weak. In the background I can still see Phil's lifeless body swinging over the bathtub, the blood dripping from him. Clare glances up at Tim and he reaches down and takes the plate from her before lowering the gun.

"Girls, ready," he says, and both Candy and Cane come forward. Tim places the plate on the floor and slides it across to me.

I look down once and then back up as the two dogs stalk slowly toward me, their teeth bared at me.

"Best eat that before it gets cold," Clare says. "We don't like to waste food around here, and Candy and Cane are hungry girls. If you don't eat it—" she starts, but I cut her off.

"Fuck you!" I snap. "I'm not eating a damn thing." I laugh loudly, ignoring the dogs' growls growing louder. "You really think I'm going to let you fatten me up like a turkey for Thanksgiving? Fuck. You." I spit at the floor in front of her. "Let the dogs eat whatever that is."

Tim barks out a laugh and both dogs snap their teeth at me. "You misunderstand, Mikey. If you don't eat it, they'll eat you."

At first I think I've misunderstood, but as I watch Candy and Cane stalking slowly toward me, their gazes on me and not on the plate of food, I know he's right. This is what they've been trained to do. This is how they survived. Death by dog seems just as bad as the death Phil just received. I've had a dog bite before, I know how painful it is. How could I stand being eaten to death? Would it be quick? Probably not.

Besides, in the back of my mind there's still hope that I can escape this situation. There's still a chance of getting out of here alive. They don't want me dead yet, and I can free my hands once I get my strength back. The drugs they poisoned me with are wearing off, and my senses are coming back. There's still a chance, and while there's still a chance I still have to try.

I reach over and pick up the plate, my hands shaking so hard that I nearly drop it again. My eyes are trying to work out what's on it. It's dark, and the only light spilling into the room is the light from the end of the hallway, behind Tim and Clare, so it takes me a while to work it out. Eventually I realize it's meat. I pick up the thin slice of meat by my fingertips, noticing that my hands are still shaking with both anger and fear.

It's warm, just cooked, and I frown down at it, feeling like Hansel being fattened up for the witch. Candy and Cane bark and snap their teeth at me and I put it to my lips and take a small bite. I look up, watching as Clare's smile grows larger. Behind her Phil's body swings lightly back and forth, the strip of flesh missing from his side almost like an alarm bell ringing inside my head.

My hand freezes and nausea bubbles up my throat. I drop the flesh and the plate all at the same time. The plate smashes and the dogs bark again. I gag and cough, wanting to be sick, but everything in my stomach stubbornly refuses to leave me, my own body betraying me.

I try to stand up, but my ankles are tied together and my legs are too weak so I fall back to the ground, ending up on my knees. Tim is laughing, his loud boom of a laugh echoing in my head. The dogs are snarling and barking, but I can't get up. I'm frozen on my hands and knees, my head low to my chest as I continue to gag and heave.

I think of the meat we ate earlier, the burnt offerings of what we thought was squirrel and snake and possum, and I call out, my stomach retching at the idea of what I'd already eaten.

Humans. People. Men, women, children? Who the fuck knows.

"You're sick!" I scream, all dignity gone out the window. "You're fucking sick!"

Tim continues to laugh and Candy comes forward, her hot breath at the back of my neck. I cry out and flinch, pulling away from her, but then Cane is at my waist, her face reaching under me to nuzzle and nip at my stomach. I cry out again, trying to get away from them as they bark and push at me, their teeth catching on my clothing and tearing at it.

I scream and roll away, kicking out with everything I have until my foot makes contact with one of the dogs and they cry out.

"All right all right, that's enough, Tim." Clare's stern voice comes from somewhere.

Candy and Cane are pulled off me, and I kneel up and fall almost instantly to the ground before shuffling my body into a tight ball in the corner.

"You don't have a choice about this," Clare says, her tone calm. "You can either try to enjoy these last precious days on this earth, or you can go out now, painfully."

I look around to her, watching her as she watches me. "Fuck you," I whisper back to her.

Tim is holding onto the two dogs by their collars, and at the sound of my voice they both bark and try to attack, but Tim keeps a firm grip on them. Clare looks up at Tim, her expression displeased.

"That man you found and killed, he was Candy and Cane's dinner. We keep one person just for them," Tim smiles. "Gotta' keep the dogs fed somehow." He smiles.

The sound of deaders banging on the doors downstairs draws her attention away from me. The dogs stop reaching for me, their ears perked up as they quit jumping and wait for their master to tell them what to do.

"We'll be back," Clare says. And then she turns her wheelchair around and rolls away.

Tim glares in at me one last time before turning around and dragging the dogs away with him. He must let go of the two dogs because I hear their nails clicking on the wooden floorboards as they run down the corridor, and then the door to my room is slammed shut and the locks put back in place.

I stay in the corner, listening to the deaders and the dogs fighting outside for some time. Listening to the soft murmur of Clare and Tim talking as the rest of the night air fills with silence.

I stare into the blackness, my heart still racing as my thoughts whirl in a hundred different directions at once. Is this it? Is this how I'll go? After everything I've been through. The people I'd helped, the people I hadn't. The deaths I caused, and the ones I prevented.

Is this it?

I squeeze my eyes closed as I think about Phil, and O'Donnell. She at least avoided this death. I'm glad of that for her. And Ricky, where is Ricky? Is he dead also? Or is he locked in a similar room like me, waiting for death while he's force-fed his own friend? The possibilities are endless.

And then I think of Nina. Of the promise I made to her. Of the sacrifice she made for me, for Adam and Joan and for all of the other people that the Forgotten would kill in the future.

I won't give up. I can't.

I look down at my bound wrists and flex my fingers, bringing life back into them, slowly. I press one thumb against the other, pressing harder and harder until the pain is blinding and I feel the pop of my thumb dislocating.

I'm not going to sit here and wait to die. No, sir. I'm going to get out of this room. And then I'm going to kill Tim, and Clare, and those two monstrous fucking dogs.

Or I'll die trying.

Chapter Thirty

Nina

My gun is heavy in my hand as I charge back down the corridor, and I realize the full extent of my stupidity. I am one woman. I can't stop this man—Fallon. What chance do I really have of ending this feud once and for all? Of killing Fallon, and then preventing the rest of his men from killing me and everyone else?

None, that's what chance I have. None at all.

Yet still I run toward my own annihilation. I think of Mikey, of the pain in his eyes when I said goodbye. Of the situation I put him in. The choice I forced him to make. He'll hate me forever. Whether I'm dead or not, he won't forgive me for making him choose between my life and an innocent child's. I know this because I wouldn't forgive him either.

My feet pound the floor, my steps echoing through the darkness. Up ahead I smell blood, Nova's blood, and the unmistakable scent of gunfire in the air. I charge at the door, gripping hold of the handle, and I unleash my fury on the world.

Or at least I try to, but as I squeeze the trigger on my gun, twenty more shoot in my direction and I yelp and jump backwards, the door slamming closed behind me. I stagger into the darkness, swatting myself all over as I check for gunshot wounds. I back up farther into the dark hallway.

"Fuck!" I yell out in anger, annoyed that I can't even get this one thing right. That I can't even go down in a blaze of glory after killing Fallon and ending Mikey and everyone's misery by eliminating his black heart. I sink farther away into the darkness as I try to formulate a new plan.

And then I hear it, through the raging of my own heart and pounding of my blood: I hear yelling and gunfire, screaming and shouting coming from behind the door. My footsteps hesitate for a split second as the door opens and light flashes into my darkness. The door closes and I know that someone is here with me. I can hear them, and they can hear me.

A gun goes off, and there's a flash of light and an explosion to my right as a bullet ricochets off the wall next to me. I scream and move, both ducking and running all in one move. I aim in the darkness, but I don't know where or what I'm aiming at. I shoot—once, twice. I hear a grunt of pain and they return fire, but it's nowhere near me and then I trip on them.

They groan in pain and they lose their gun. And then I am looking down at their body, and though it's dark, up close I can see them more clearly. Their face is turned away from me as I aim my gun down at them and they turn to look at me, their hands held up in surrender. It's a woman. Her dark hair is covering some of her face, but her dark, fearful eyes are unmistakable.

"Please," she begs. "Please don't. I didn't want to do this. It wasn't supposed to be like this!" She covers her face with her hands as if they'll be able to stop the bullet when it leaves my gun. As if her hands of mere bone and flesh will be able to prevent my bullet from sinking into her brain and punishing her for siding with Fallon.

My heart is raging in my chest, trying to escape through the center. I'm breathless, gasping for air as I keep my aim on her and ponder my own life and choices. The things I have done, been witness to. The things I have allowed to happen for my own

293

survival. This woman, Shantell, we're not that dissimilar—not really. We've both made bad calls, chosen the wrong paths at times. We've both done what we needed to to live.

And this is murder. All my kills before this have been haphazard, and spur of the moment, but this isn't. This is a choice, and she's pleading for her life.

"Please," she sobs. "My name's Shantell. I have kids—two little girls, Niamh and Betul. They need their mom…please, I'm just trying to survive…" she pleads, tears escaping her eyes.

Tears fill my own eyes as I realize how similar we are. One small change, and perhaps I would be her and she would be me. And there it is, there's the truth of the matter. There's nothing I can do for this woman. She made her choice, her bed, she chose her side, and now she has to live with it and die with it. She chose wrong. Because she would kill me without a second thought. She would have to, to protect her kids.

So if I let her live, then I'm dead. It's not a choice—not really. I've come too far to die like this, here in this dark corridor, while my friends die on the other side of that door and Mikey drives Adam and Joan to safety. Because it will all have been for nothing if I die—losing Mikey, him hating me. There will be no point in it, because Fallon will still be hunting him. He'll still be in danger and so will my friends. It's not a choice at all.

"So am I," I say, my voice thick and broken with anger and sadness and guilt. And then I squeeze the trigger. "I'm sorry," I whisper. But I'm not, not really. I wouldn't change the outcome, because that change would mean my death, and I don't want to die. Just like she didn't.

I stagger backwards, my hands shaking, a cold chill running through my soul. Whatever happens next will be my decision to live or to die with. This woman's death isn't like the others, and I deserve whatever comes with that.

I step farther away from her, heading toward the doorway. I can see it now: the light is shining from underneath, and the gunshots and screaming are still going on from behind it. I stand in front of the door, and I make peace with whatever God might still be up there. I don't pray to live, and I don't pray to die. I just pray for forgiveness. Because at the end, surely that's all we can ask for—forgiveness. We don't deserve any more than that. Humans are monsters, and we live and die by the gun. That's our cross to bear, and bear it we will.

I slowly push the door open for the second time, seeing the fighting and death going on behind it. Everyone is too busy fighting for their own survival to even notice me—or perhaps they thought Shantell would take me out, so they weren't worried.

I see Fallon hidden behind a bench near an overturned ice-cream stand. He lifts his head and shoots across at Mattie, but misses, and then he ducks out of the way as Mattie returns fire. I take a deep breath and then I run toward him, with bullets firing all around me. I raise my arm, my aim steady and true, and I shoot round after round after round at him.

He sees me too late, his eyes narrowing and widening all at once, and then his expression is pained as my bullets hit him and his body jerks backwards and he grunts in pain.

I dive to the ground as I reach him, and then I drag myself behind the bench, crawling over to him with my gun still clenched in my hand, ready to shoot him again if I have to. He stares up at me with unblinking eyes, blood bubbling out of the wounds in his chest, a small trickle of blood escaping from his mouth as the last breath of air leaves him.

I sob as he dies—a single sound that leaves me unexpectedly. It's not sorrow I feel, but gratefulness. It's over; he's over. Whatever comes now, surely I've given Mikey a better chance.

Fallon was filled with so much rage and fury, but you wouldn't think it to look at him now. His face is calm, smoothed of the angry lines that normally cursed it.

He looks at peace, I decide.

In the end, his death wasn't dramatic. It wasn't anything but a bitter man being shot and killed, and it seems perfect for him. Fitting, almost. We all want to die knowing that we did something great, but he did nothing. Yet he could have, and that was the real tragedy of the situation. He could have done so much good—something that his family would have been proud of. But he chose wrong, like so many others. Regardless of everything did and everyone he killed, I find myself still hoping that in death he sees his wife and children again. At least just once. Because it was the pain of losing them that drove him to his insanity. He must be made accountable for the things he did, but I wish this small act of peace on him, if no other.

I look up as a shadow passes over me and I fire upwards at whoever it is, but my gun is empty so it clicks uselessly. I glare up into the face of a woman who looks so similar to Shantell— the woman I just killed in the hallway—that I gasp in horror. This new woman stares down at me, her mouth pinched in anger as she looks between me and Fallon.

She aims her gun at me and I wince as I wait for the death that I so truly deserve. But it's not me that she shoots, it's Fallon. Her bullet finds its way through his head, embedding itself in his brain and stopping him from returning. I look from Fallon's body back up to this new woman, wondering whose side she's on and thinking that it's possibly mine. Could she have been like

296

Shantell—just another pawn in his game? Someone that he controlled and made to do his bidding? She shot him instead of letting him return and attack me. That must count for something, right? Surely that means she's a good guy—girl, whatever. Surely that means that if she was on his side, she's not now.

Hope swells in my chest. It's not too late to catch up to Mikey. If I get up now, I can go get to him. We can be together, we can leave together, and head for Ben's parents' cabin like we planned. We can still do this.

And then she swings her gun down at my temple and knocks me sideways. I blink as the blackness encroaches on my vision and I feel myself being moved. Blinking doesn't clear the fog, or stop the ringing in my ears, so I give in to the ache and I close my eyes.

Well, at least I know whose side she's on.

Bitch.

Chapter Thirty-One

“God, that hurt,” I cry out, one hand clutched to my temple, the other slapping away at the hands that are grabbing at me.

This other woman is still dragging me into the circle that's been formed. It parts as I get close and then she's sliding me across the smooth marble floor of the mall, through blood and spent bullets and into the group I call my friends. I crash into Melanie's side with an *oomph* and she and Mattie help me to sit upright.

The room spins, the circle of people surrounding us bleeding into one another as I try to focus, but blood has fallen from the cut that Miss Bitchy Pants just made above my eye. It's dripped into my eye and is now stinging and making it even harder to focus. I use my sleeve to wipe it away, and then I press the palm of my hand against the cut to try and stem the blood flow.

A growl of deader sounds out from somewhere and the woman who just dragged me away from Fallon's dead body turns to the man next to her.

“Take care of that, Steve,” she says, her gaze still on my little group.

He nods and leaves the circle, the gap closing almost instantly.

“Do you have any idea who you just killed?” she finally says after several tense moments of glaring at us. I open my mouth to answer but Melanie gets there first.

"A cocksucking asshole," she says and spits on the ground at her feet. She snorts out a laugh, and since she's playing the hard-ass bitch card, I decide to join her and I laugh too.

What? If I'm going to die now, at least I'll go out laughing.

"Wrong answer," the woman replies.

The group parts and Steve comes back to her side. He leans over and whispers something in her ear which makes her look even angrier.

"Santa Claus?" Melanie calls out sarcastically. She turns and looks at me. "Nina, did you just kill Santa Claus?"

I'm in so much shock that Melanie is even making a joke with me, and the tenseness of the situation that is almost palpable, that I laugh again.

"No, I did not kill Santa Claus," I snort out. I wince as my head throbs when I move it. "Damn, that really fucking hurt, lady."

The woman doesn't look impressed by me or Melanie, and she takes a step forward. She crouches down so that we're all eye level, and I notice that her gun is in her hand, my blood still on the barrel.

"It was supposed to," she says, looking directly at me. "You just killed Fallon, my partner, *our* leader. Now you're going to tell me where Mikey is so I can kill him."

"Like hell I am!" I grind out.

She smiles. "And then, when I've got him and I've killed him in the most wondrous way in front of you, then I'm going to kill all of your friends here. And then, and only then, will I kill you. Slowly."

She doesn't even flinch as she speaks, as if killing all of these people means nothing to her. At least with Fallon he had a rage hidden in his depths that drove him forward. Her drive is just insanity. Revenge, cruelty? I'm beginning to regret my decision to kill Fallon, and in my nervousness I spout the first bullshit that comes into my mouth.

"These guys aren't even my friends," I chuckle darkly.

"Really?" she replies.

"Really. Especially her." I point to Melanie. "She's a total bitch. And she has terrible taste in shoes. I mean, look at those things, they're not even real Doc Martens." I roll my eyes exaggeratedly.

"You are as useful as tits on a bull, Nina!" Melanie screeches.

The woman stands up, ignoring both Melanie and me. "You will tell me. Fallon and I had a plan, and I'm going to fulfill it for him."

"I won't tell you shit," I say with a smirk. "Who do you think you are, anyway? So what that you're Fallon's crazy girlfriend? Why does that mean you have to be as big an asshole as he was? Can't you be your own woman? And make your own plans?" I shake my head, my gaze skipping over everything around us as I desperately try to think of a way out of this situation.

"My name's Ashley, and you should be very careful what you say to me. And for the record, I liked his plan," she says.

"Well then you are as big an asshole as he was," Mattie says from the other side of me. "Because he was a murdering son of a bitch!"

"Word!" Melanie agrees, fist bumping him.

"Fine," Ashley says, "I'll kill your little pregnant friend over here."

I laugh. "Like I give a shit what you do to her." I glare at Jessica, who looks heartbroken by my cruelty.

Ashley shakes her head and turns to look at her people. "Can you believe this shit?"

I glance sideways at Melanie, seeing through her façade. She's just as scared as I am, and just like me, she's being a mouthy bitch to help get her through it.

"These people just killed our leader. They killed your friends," Ashley continues, walking in a circle around us all, her gaze on her people. "They let Mikey get away, again. But look, I'm a forgiving person, and despite what they say, I'm not as crazy as Fallon was. Because yes, I think we all know that things got a little out of hand with him." She's stopped in front of me again, her back toward me while she speaks, but the fact that she's not aiming that gun at my head doesn't make me feel any better.

"We should kill them all," Good ol' Steve says. And I want to smack him around the head and tell him to shut up. "Make them pay for killing Fallon."

Ashley turns to look down at us again, her gaze still cold and hard. "I agree." She aims her gun at me and I freeze, my heart pausing in my chest.

Melanie rises up to her knees. "You're such a total ass-fucker, lady! You think you're as badass as Fallon was? That you can gain the respect that he got from these assholes? You're not even fucking scary! My shit is scarier than you, you fuck-nugget!"

301

Melanie is yelling, and honest to God I want to tell her to pipe the fuck down and let it go, because I'd rather it be over like this than any other hellish way, but I can't find my voice.

My words are stuck in my parched throat, my tongue flaccid in my mouth. The more I think of words, the more they evade me. All I can see is the barrel of the gun, aimed at me. *Will it hurt?* I wonder. *Will I feel my life end? Or will it be gone before I can even register?*

"Hey, Ashley, did you ever go to a rodeo when you were a kid? Because there's so much bullshit coming from your mouth that I'm wondering if you might have caught some weird form of mad bull disease!" Melanie is still going on, still raging and yelling and throwing such insults at this woman that I shouldn't be surprised when Ashley pulls the trigger and it's not me that ends up with a bullet through her brain, but Melanie.

But it is a surprise and I can't stop myself from calling out for her. "Melanie!" I turn to her, grabbing for her before she hits the ground.

By the sounds of it, I'm not the only one reaching for her. Michael is behind me, and he has turned around and is helping me lay her down. Our eyes meet, pain flashing between us. Zee is there also. He looks a mess—a legless mess, if you will. I recognize some of the other faces too, but I don't have time to ponder over them.

"All right, all right, everyone, eyes on me!" Ashley calls out with a loud whistle to get our attention back to her. "Let's make this perfectly clear to you all: you should be scared of me. Have I made that obvious to you yet? Or do I need to give you another example of my cruelty? I'm okay with killing every one of you." Her gaze skips to me. "Except you, of course. I have something special in mind for you."

302

None of us say anything, and I think that's what she's been waiting for. There's no more cockiness, and no more outbursts from any of us. Though there's no big surprise there, if I'm being honest.

"So I tell you what I'm going to do. I'm going to lock you up and leave you all to discuss my offer between yourselves. Got it?" She smiles now, a cold smile that is worse than any sneer that Fallon ever had. "In fact, I think you four would make a great team, so how about you discuss business while I take my anger out on these good people of yours here." She turns to Steve. "Take them away."

"Mike," Steve yells to another man wearing a Washington Redskins hoody. "Grab the other guy," he says. "Shane, you get the pregnant one."

All three men come forwards and grab each of us before dragging us away. None of us fight them, because well, what's the point? We've just seen what happens when you fight back. And Ashley just said that she wasn't going to kill us just yet; she needs us. Or at least me. So for now we're relatively safe. As I'm dragged away, I look at Melanie's body and feel even more guilt than previously. I shouldn't have encouraged her to mouth off. I should have calmed her down, but instead I made it all worse.

Steve and his merry men throw us into a storeroom. The room's actually quite big, and I'm glad because I can't even bear the thought of looking at Jessica right now, never mind having to sit near her. She and that demon spawn in her belly are what got me into this mess. It's what got Nova killed. This is her fault, at least partly. And right now I need someone to blame.

Jessica slides herself down the wall until she's sitting with her legs out in front of her. She's sobbing and using her sleeve as a tissue. Mattie goes over to comfort her, and I'm glad he does because I'm fit for screaming at her. I turn and look at Michael, who's still watching the doorway where Steve and the other Forgotten members just went.

"Hey," I say, not really knowing how to open up any sort of dialogue with him. His sister had come with me, and now she's dead. There's no fancy way of dressing that up that isn't going to come out lame and still make him angry. It's two for two now. When I first met him he'd had two sisters, and now he has none. He's going to hate my guts.

"Hey," he finally replies.

"How've you been?" I ask, deciding almost immediately that it was probably the worst way of opening up a conversation with him. "I uhh, I mean, this is shit, right?"

He turns and glares at me. "Yeah, very shit. So, Nova..." He swallows as if bracing himself. "I saw her." He jerks his head toward the door. "I saw her get shot."

Is it bad that I feel some wave of relief? Probably, but I feel it all the same. It means that he knows it isn't my fault that she died.

"Yeah, I'm sorry. There was nothing I could do," I say quietly.

He nods. "I figured. It's how she would have wanted to go out...fighting."

"It was," I agree. "I'm still sorry."

He nods again but doesn't say anything, his gaze falling to the ground at our feet.

I decide to ask the million-dollar question, since no one's being particularly forthcoming with the information and I'm desperate to know how the hell the Forgotten even found them. I turn and look at our ragtag group, just Michael, Mattie, Jessica and her demon spawn, and me. But there had been many more of them. And they'd had a shit ton of weapons too. How did it all crumble and fall? How did it come to this?

"What happened?" I ask, looking back at him.

"They must have been watching the base, and they followed when they saw us all leaving. I noticed them when we were about halfway here, but they kept back, never getting too close. We tried to shake them loose, but they'd blocked the road ahead. I was driving, took our truck off road, made a nice little chase out of it, and prayed that I didn't hit a ditch. Made it here a couple of hours ago, but they'd followed us." Michael cracks his knuckles, his forehead creased in frustration. "We didn't stand a chance. There was too many of them."

"I'm sorry," I reply, trying not to imagine how it all went down—the death he witnessed as his friends had been killed in cold blood. And now his sister is dead too.

"So you keep saying, Nina," he replies. "So where is he?" Michael looks at me, his scowl deep.

We're at a stalemate, because I'm not going to tell anyone where Mikey is—no matter who gets killed. It isn't that Mikey's life is worth more than everyone else's. It's that every death up to this point will have been for nothing if I give him up.

"I have no idea," I reply, holding Michael's gaze.

If he believes me or not, he doesn't let on. Instead he lets out a dry laugh and turns away from me. He paces the floor in front of the door, and I sit down after a quick search of the room, discovering nothing of help to any of us. I sit opposite Jessica and her large, swollen belly, and I know what's inside her. She looks at me several times, the question on her lips, but she never has the guts to ask me and I'm not going to give it up to her for free. My anger at her has increased beyond what's normal, and there's no going back from it now. I hate her for what I lost, who I lost. Not just Mikey, but Nova. Once again, I lost a friend. Someone I trusted. How many more times am I going to have to go through this, I wonder?

I lean my head back and close my eyes. The cut above my eye has long stopped bleeding, but it's throbbing in my temples and giving me a migraine. I picture Mikey, on the road with Adam and Joan. He'll be sad, heartbroken, and full of anger at me. But at least he'll be alive, I tell myself. If he had come in with me, he'd be dead. Or perhaps we all would be and the Forgotten would be taking him to do their dirty deed.

I hope he knows that I don't regret a damn thing. And that at least for once in his life, he knows that someone sacrificed everything because they knew he was worth it. And I would do it all again if I had to. I smile sadly because I know I did the right thing.

At least for him.

Chapter Thirty-Two

The lock on the door rattles and the door swings open. Michael, Mattie, and I jump to our feet, though for what reason I don't know. Steve and Mike look around at us all. I'm not sure what they're looking for, but whatever it is they find it in Mattie, and they walk toward him as another guard stands in the doorway with his gun raised and aimed at Jessica.

The two members grab Mattie and walk him out of the room, and Mattie looks over his shoulder at us as they take him away. And then the Forgotten member closes and locks the door behind him, and we're alone and in silence once again.

Jessica has started sobbing once more, and my head is still pounding from earlier.

"Do you think he'll be okay?" I ask Michael as we stand next to one another by the door, listening intently for any sound.

"No," he replies simply and boldly.

"You don't know that," I say in return and walk away from him. But of course there's not really anywhere to go to, so in ten seconds I'm back by the doorway and feeling even more restless. "This is bullshit," I mutter.

Michael doesn't bother to reply, because, well, there's nothing to say. It *is* bullshit. All of it.

"I'm getting pains," Jessica sobs from behind us.

I don't even give her the respect of an eye roll. Instead I leave Michael to look after her. He heads over and gets down on his knees, and I hear them whispering together. I wonder, briefly,

307

about telling him what's going to happen to her. About the dead thing growing inside her stomach and how it will soon eat its way out of her, whether outwards or downwards, and that either way it's sure to play a delightful role in our nightmares for the next few years.

I turn and look over at them. She's clutching her stomach with one hand, and strangely, he's smiling as he holds her other hand. He looks up and catches me looking.

"Probably just Braxton hicks," he says with a small shrug. "False labor, nothing to worry about. I learned all about this from my mom."

I want to laugh. And then I want to choke on my laugh, and then vomit on the floor and then laugh and then choke some more. And *then* I want to describe the horror of what I found when I saw Hilary. But instead I turn away from them both, because it's all too real and all too painful. And I need to get out of this damn room before it happens.

And then I realize why I can't tell her what's happening, and I want to cry.

She has hope. And I don't.

I'm jealous of her, even though I know what's going to happen to her. She has no clue of the horrors she is about to endure. In fact, because I haven't said anything to her, she probably thinks that it's all going to be okay and that at the end of this, if the Forgotten don't kill her, she's going to get a little baby to cuddle and to have and to hold. And she's not. She's going to have a monster, and then she's going to die, and Michael and I will be left to kill the beast that she births.

I turn back around, the words on the tip of my tongue, but before I can say anything the door opens again and Steve is there.

308

"Perfect," he says with a big shit-eating grin. "Just who I was hoping for." His right hand reaches out and grabs for me. His grip is too tight and I immediately try to pull away from him, but of course he's stronger. "Don't fucking fight it, just get your ass out here."

I kick out and pull to get away from him, and then Michael is by my side and he shoves me out of the way, sending me stumbling into the wall, and then he punches Steve in the face. His nose explodes in a burst of blood, like someone just threw a blood-filled water bomb at his face, and he curses loudly.

"You're going to regret that," he says, though his words are muffled as he covers his nose with his sleeve to try and stem the blood flow.

"You really don't know me well enough if you think that." Michael raises his chin and takes a step forward, his hard glare burning into Steve's.

Steve grins, the expression maniacal on his bloody face. He pulls the gun from his waist and aims it at Michael's head. "Well then let's get acquainted."

"No!" I scream, pushing between them both. "No, don't, please, I'll come with you," I say, because God, I can't be left with just Jessica, I just can't. If Michael gets shot, I'll have no one left. And I can't look after her. I'd rather put her out of her damn misery sooner rather than later. "Please, please, just ignore him, he's just an asshole," I implore Steve. "In fact, I think he might have a couple of mental issues. Maybe his mom dropped him on his head or something when he was a baby. I'm pretty certain he has a false eye and a gimpy leg too."

Despite himself and his bloody nose, Steve snorts out a laugh when Michael taps me on the shoulder and cusses at me. I turn to Michael.

"It's okay," I say to him, my head tipped up as I grab for his face and pull his gaze down to meet mine. "I'll go with him, it's okay, please. You look after Jessica."

He stares at me and I try and put across everything that I want to say to him in those few precious seconds. It's not enough, it's too long, it's all of the above. "You have to look after her—she's going to need it," I say.

His gaze flits to Jessica and his eyes narrow, and I get the feeling he knows exactly what it means for me to say that. But of course he doesn't reply.

I turn back to Steve, making sure that the muzzle of his gun is pressed right up against my chest. "Please, he's sorry, I'll come with you. You don't need to kill him."

Steve looks pissed, but he puts his gun away and grips my shoulder before dragging me out of the room. He looks back in at Michael. "We'll be having some fun later." And then he slams the door shut and drags me away.

I don't say anything as he leads me away. Instead my thoughts are a whirl as I think about what I'm going to do and say when I stand before Ashley again. She said I had to tell her where Mikey was the next time I saw her, but I'm not going to do that. However, the guilt of knowing that I'm sacrificing everyone for Mikey is huge.

It isn't their responsibility, yet I'm making it theirs. And I should feel shame for that, but I don't. I can't allow myself to think like that.

Steve is pulling me so hard that I'm tripping over my own feet, and if it weren't for the fact that he's holding onto the back of my jacket, I would have fallen onto my face and busted up my own nose.

"Will you quit pulling me!" I yell at him, but he ignores me and continues to pull me along regardless until we're back out in the main foyer—as I now fondly think of it, gunslingers' alley. There are blood smears still across the floor, but the bodies have been removed and I'm grateful for that fact.

In the center, right below the glass globe roof of the mall, Ashley is waiting. A desk and some chairs have been pulled into the middle as what I assume is now her command center. Ashley is standing up and leaning against the desk behind her. She's talking to Mike—the guy in the Redskins hoody, but they both stop as Steve pulls me along like a goat to slaughter. Her gaze is unflinching as he throws me to the ground in front of her and my knees crash painfully to the cold marble.

I cry out and turn to say something to Steve, but I come face to face with the muzzle of his gun and I decide to bite my tongue for the moment. I'll cuss him out later.

"So," Ashley begins, drawing my attention back to her. She's a beautiful young woman with dark hair, olive skin, and a full mouth. Even as a woman I can see what Fallon saw in her. But her eyes are cruel and cold, the downturn of her mouth giving away that she's seen too much in her short time. "I'm hoping that you've come to your senses."

"Hmmm, well, I thought about it," I tap my chin thoughtfully, "and honestly, as good an offer as it is, I decided that the best course of action would be for you to go fuck yourself." I smirk when her eyes widen and she huffs out her annoyance at me. "I mean, obviously Fallon can't fuck you anymore, you know, because I killed his evil ass, so you'll have to do it yourself. But I'm sure that's no big deal for a woman like you."

Ashley stands up straight and walks toward me, but my big mouth is open now and the words are spewing forth like an atomic bomb of diarrhea.

"I'm not trying to be rude—you seem like a capable woman. If anything, it's a compliment, a commendation to your leadership, if you will. So yeah, go fuck yourself!" I nod and smile, not having chance to dodge out of the way of Ashley's fist as she punches me square in the face, making my head whip to the left so hard I worry about tendons snapping. "God-fucking-dammit!" I cry out and I grab my jaw, tasting blood in my mouth. I slowly move my head back to face her again, definitely missing the second punch that gets me in the cheek and probably cracks my cheekbone.

There's no time to call out in pain, or even curl into a ball as Ashley grips my head and then knees me in the face, and I'm choking on my own blood as I slide backwards across the floor. I stare up through the glass ceiling into the blue sky beyond, watching the tiny shadow of a bird fly past. Ashley's booted foot kicks me in the side and I groan and curl up into a ball, squeezing my eyes closed and waiting for the rain of bullets to pepper my skin and put me out of my misery. Why she'd want to beat the crap out of me makes no sense. Sure I gave her shit, but that's my thing. I can't control how I work.

The sound of footsteps coming toward me has every muscle in my body flinching in expectance, but the bullets don't come and neither do any more kicks or punches. I slowly lift my face away from its hiding place and look upwards. Ashley is leering over me, a small smirk on her face as she tucks a loose strand of hair behind her ear.

"Now see, that was the wrong answer," she says.

I take my time sitting up, my tongue stroking around my teeth to make sure that they're all in the right places before spitting out a mouthful of blood onto the floor in front of us. Ashley watches me with indifference.

"Tell me something," I say and she quirks an eyebrow at me.

"Sure," she replies.

I spit more blood onto the floor again as I try to get my bearings, because everything is aching right now. I clear my throat before I speak and she waits patiently.

I look her in the eye before finally speaking. "Was it the 'fuck yourself' remark that pushed you over the edge?"

She punches me in the face again and I cry out, shake my head, and then look at her again.

"Or was it the 'I killed your big bad boyfriend' comment?"

She goes to punch me again but I dodge. "Ha! Missed," I cheer and give her the middle finger with as much enthusiasm as I can muster. I spit out the blood that's pooled in my mouth and grin up at her, knowing that I look fucking maniacal because I damn well feel it. Plus, my face is all busted up.

Ashley stands back up, her gaze going over my head to Steve. She cracks her knuckles, wiping away my blood from them. "I don't think she gets it yet," she says before turning and walking away from me. She heads back to her desk and sits down. "Bring her back to me when you think she gets it."

Steve reaches for me, grabbing a handful of hair as he pulls me to my feet, and I scream out in pain. Ashley looks up at me as Steve begins to pull me away by my hair, and I'm forced to hold in my scream of agony because I refuse to let her have any more satisfaction in my pain.

Steve pulls me past some of the other Forgotten members, thankfully none that I remember, yet being with these people brings back all sorts of terrifying memories—memories that I've tried really hard to forget—and I wonder how long it will take before I break. Because no matter how hard and strong I think I am, I know that I can't go through what I went through the last time they had me.

As we draw closer to my little makeshift prison, crying can be heard, and that perks up both me and little Stevie boy. He drags me harder, which is completely unnecessary since I'm trying to get back there to see what's going on as quickly as he is.

"What's going on in there?" Steve asks the two Forgotten members standing outside the door.

They both look anxious and scared. But then again, they both look barely old enough to drink, never mind standing guard over innocent prisoners.

"Open the damn door!" Steve bellows.

One of the guards grabs the keys at his waist and searches for the key while the other's gaze goes from my beaten-up face to Steve's fistful of hair at the top of my head.

"Yeah, I know, he's a real asshole," I say, making the guy blush and look away.

"Shut up," Steve snaps at me, giving my hair a quick tug.

The Forgotten member swings the door open and we all look inside. None of us move. Instead, all of us are watching in horror as Jessica's swollen stomach moves and she screams as she writhes around on the floor.

314

Michael looks up, sweat glistening on his brow. "Well don't just stand there, someone help us, she's gone into labor!"

My cockiness withers and dies on my lips, because I know that there is no helping her. Not anymore.

There was a time for helping, but for her, now it's a time for dying.

Chapter Thirty-Three

"What's all the noise?" Ashley yells as she storms toward us all. She pushes me and the others out of the way and stares into the room. "Jesus, what is it with men and pregnancy?" She turns and glares at me. "You too?" She scoffs and barges into the room. "Someone get me some towels and water."

Michael is holding Jessica's hand as she lies on her back, and his pale, sweat-riddled face turns to Ashley as she drops to her knees in front of Jessica. I watch in morbid horror as Ashley starts to speak to Jessica quietly and calmly, and I see a different side to her than I saw only moments ago. She reaches for Jessica's boots and slips them off her feet before helping Jessica to slide off her pants. The entire time Jessica's belly is rippling with movement, until I can't take it any longer.

I look up at Steve. "She really needs to back away from her."

Steve ignores me, so I try again—louder and less polite this time. But I don't think I'm being totally rude.

"Hey, asshole, you need to tell that bitch to move away from the other bitch, because what's happening is not what she thinks is happening. At all!"

He definitely hears me this time but is choosing to ignore me, but Ashley is moments away from shoving her hand up inside Jessica's cooch, so it's really kind of important that he listens to me.

"Hey! Psycho Sally." I whistle loudly, making Ashley turn to glare at me.

"Can someone shut her the hell up?" she yells.

I smile sardonically and carry on with my usual wit and charm. "There's a zombie baby about to bite your damn fingers off if you do that! At least it'll attempt to, but you know, it's a baby so no teeth. Either way it's fucking gross, right?"

Ashley quickly withdraws her hand from under Jessica's T-shirt and turns to stare at Jessica in morbid horror. Whether she believes me or not is irrelevant. The idea alone is horrific enough. I should know, I've been there and bought a franchise in the T-shirts.

"You need to keep your mouth shut!" Steve pulls on my hair again, making me call out in pain, but I've had enough of all this ridiculous hair-pulling. What are we, five? So with every bit of strength I have, I slam my foot down on top of his and make him yelp in pain and let go of my hair. Thank the Lord for my beautiful boots once again.

I choose that moment to run forward into the room, stopping halfway across as Ashley pulls out her gun and aims it at me. I skid to a halt, my gaze moving between Michael and Jessica, who have both paled dramatically.

"Talk," Ashley grinds out. "Right now."

Steve, who has come after me, stops his momentum. I guess there's no need to tear another chunk of my glossy locks out when I'm about to lose my brains.

"So, looks like I'm the one holding all the cards for a change, huh?" I snark, looking from face to face, but no one seems impressed by me so I decide to cut the shit and get straight to the point. I look at Jessica when I speak. "The woman we found— Hilary—she was dead, and so was the baby."

Ashley looks between me and Jessica, her frown deepening. Jessica swallows nervously, though I can tell from the creases of pain on her face that even though she's listening intently to me, she's still concentrating on the baby trying to get out of her.

"What did she die from?" Jessica asks through clenched teeth. "Infection? Labor?"

I shake my head and snort out a dark laugh. "Wouldn't that have been music to your ears?"

Tears escape her eyes and trail down her face. "Then what?"

"You really don't want to know," I reply darkly.

"Tell me!" Jessica screams, making us all jump. Her stomach is moving more and more, and I know she only has moments left before that thing bursts out of her, *Alien*-style. I don't want to be the vindictive bitch. I want to be caring and compassionate, but I've lost too many people because of this woman. In leaving the army base to go in search of Hilary to find out if she had lived or died, I had left the base susceptible to attack. And in turn I lost Emily.

Everything has been Jessica's fault. Every death. Every drop of blood that's been spilled. It's her fault.

I take a step forward and crouch down so I can look her in the eye properly. "The baby was a deader and it chewed its way out of her." I let that stew for a few moments, watching her pupils dilate in horror. And I enjoy every bit of it before I give the final blow. "When I found Hilary, she was dead, with her dead baby still hanging from her rotten cooch. Her husband, Deacon? You remember Nova talking about him, right? He'd gone insane from the grief and killed a bunch of people, so—"

318

"Stop it, Nina," Michael says quietly, reaching down to grab Jessica's hand, but she shoves him off.

"—that thing inside you," I continue, feeling hateful and cruel but not being able to stop myself, "That thing is dead, and it's going to kill you at any moment." I stand back up, watching as Jessica crumples into a ball, crying from both the pain of what's happening and the pain of knowing.

I turn away from her. I want out of this room. I don't want to see what happens next, because by the sounds of it, it'll be any minute. And as the image of Emily-Rose comes to my mind, I can't help but hope that it's excruciating for Jessica. Emily is gone, and Jessica is still here. The world is a fucked-up, twisted, backwards place.

I hear footsteps, but I don't turn to look until the hard edge of Ashley's gun is digging into my spine.

"I didn't say you could leave," she says.

"I didn't say I was going to stay, yet here we are, right?" I reply.

"Can you help her?" Ashley asks as Jessica's wails of pain rise and echo around the small room. I look over at Steve, who's staring in horror. Some of the other Forgotten members have come into the room too—Mike, Shane, and another face that has haunted my dreams for the past few months, but I look away from them all. Ignoring the screaming of Jessica, and the fear and horror on everyone's faces.

"Can you help her?" Ashley yells louder.

I shake my head but still don't turn around. "No, no one can help her now. She brought this on herself, and now the reaper has come for his payment."

Jessica's screams rise louder and I squeeze my eyes closed, wanting it to stop. All of it.

"There must be something we can do," Ashely says, sounded genuinely concerned.

I turn around to look at her, taking in her ashen face and the look of disgust she's giving me. I shake my head again.

"You can look at me like that all you want. This was her doing, not mine." My gaze falls on Jessica. She's on her side, her arms wrapped around her middle. Michael is talking to her and wiping her hair back from her face as she stares up at him in agony.

"Do something for her!" he yells to Ashley. "She's fucking dying over here."

Blood is pouring from between Jessica's legs and she's holding one hand between them, as if to hold back whatever is coming. I still feel no sympathy. Instead, Mikey's words are ringing in my ears.

She's gone, Nina. Emily is dead.

"The only thing that you can do for her is put her out of her misery," I say, feeling traitorous to Emily.

No one had been able to help Emily, to put her out of her misery as she was eaten alive. As the man she loved devoured her. She had suffered at his hands, and I hadn't been there to protect her. I realize that I hate myself as much as I hate Jessica—blaming both of us, and not just her. Perhaps that's the real reason I sacrificed myself to the Forgotten: I want to die. To take that as my punishment for leaving Emily behind.

Jessica's scream rips through the air and Ashley's gaze is fixed on mine. I watch her make a decision—the grit of her teeth and clench of her jaw before she turns around, takes two steps forward, and shoots Jessica through the head, killing her instantly. Her screams are silenced immediately, but it isn't that simple. Not really.

With her screams abruptly cut off, the tearing of her flesh as the deader baby rips through her, making its way into the big wide world, is more than audible. Michael falls on his ass in his haste to get away from it as it bursts from between her legs in a spurt of blood and gore. Its mewling and gargled growls are loud in the shocked silence it has created of its audience.

It turns its head to look at Michael, its small, deformed arms and legs writhing on its tiny, devilish body. Behind me someone is retching, in front of me Ashley is silent, and inside of me, a small piece has just died.

Ashley raises her hand, but it's shaking so much that the shot she fires misses and bounces off the floor. She fires again, but that one misses too. She takes a step forward, and I silently pray that she won't miss this time, because I'm not sure how much longer I can stand here watching this nightmare. Her finger is on the trigger, but her arm is still shaking.

I think of Hilary, of the injustice of what happened to her. And I think about Emily, her death forever on my conscience. And then I think about life, and how fucking unfair it is for everyone. We shouldn't have to live like this, but we do. I don't want to be the cruel person that I can feel myself becoming. It's not what Emily would have wanted.

I step forward, closer to Ashley. "Let me," I say, my words barely audible, but she hears me all the same. "Let me do this for her."

I still hate Jessica, but somehow I get it now—here as she lies dead, and her monster baby writhing on the bloody ground between her thighs. I get it. For Jessica, the baby had meant hope. Hope of a future. Hope of something better. Hope that gave her something to live for, something to fight for. I don't have that now; not now that Emily is gone. She had been my reason for existing, for pushing forward when everything seemed lost.

I hate Jessica because she made me lose everything, but I also understand why she felt the need to have a baby by any means necessary. Besides, everything happens for a reason. Without Jessica getting knocked up with deader semen, we wouldn't have looked for Hilary and Deacon. We prevented many deaths. We put that entire family out of their misery. There was some justice to all of this. And this story ends now, with Jessica.

"Please, let me do this," I say again.

I hadn't been strong enough to do it for Hilary; Nova had done it. But I'm strong enough, and hard enough, to do it for Jessica. For myself.

Ashley hands me her gun, but pulls out another one from her hip and aims it at me. I can't blame her. It isn't the normal thing to hand a gun to your prisoner to kill a zombie baby.

I take the gun, still warm from her grip, and I step closer to the baby before kneeling down behind it. Michael hasn't taken his gaze off of it until now. And he scoots backwards until his back hits the wall behind him as I aim the gun at the back of its head. My hand isn't shaking, but I'm not at ease with what I'm doing either. It is, however, necessary.

The baby continues to squirm in the gore around it, its deformed arms and legs writhing amongst the mess. It must sense me behind it, because it starts to turn toward me, so I squeeze the trigger before I have to look it in the eye. Its brain explodes in a flurry of pink and gray brain matter that escapes out the front of its head.

I sit back on my haunches, feeling numb and barely registering as Steve takes the gun from my hands. The room is silent, revulsion rolling off all of us.

I'm not sure how long I sit there before I feel someone's hand on my shoulder. When I look up I see that it's Ashley. Her expression is hard again. The soft misery which encapsulated her only a few minutes before is gone, and now she's all business again.

"We need to talk," she says.

"I won't tell you where he is," I reply, my words coming out broken.

"I know," she says in return. Her gaze falls to the bloody mess in front of us. "I know."

Chapter Thirty-Four

"So, what now?" I say, my gaze on my hands in my lap.

We've all retreated away from the baby death room and are back under the glass globe ceiling. Turns out that's where Mattie's been all along. They didn't kill him, but they did beat the crap out of him for information. He looks in pain and seriously pissed off, but his wounds are being tended to by a cute-looking brunette, so I'm certain he'll be all right. My face and body are aching from the beating I took, but it's nothing compared to the heavy heart I have, so I quietly refuse any offer of help. Mike and Steve still have guns at their hips, but they aren't aimed at me and Michael, which is always great.

"What now?" Ashely repeats my question back to me and I look up. She's looking up at the blue sky beyond the glass. "I'm not entirely sure. Things can't go on like this," she says, and I nod in agreement. "That was…the most disturbing thing I've ever seen." She looks back at me and I nod again. "You've seen this before?" she asks, her face pinched in revulsion and confusion.

"Yes. There was a compound that was testing on people. They impregnated a woman there, for whatever fucked-up reason. It ended the same way as this." I swallow, feeling sick as I think of that place. I don't mention that Michael knew anything about it, and when I glance over at him, I see him watching me, his gaze full of gratefulness.

"We need to take that place down," Ashely snarls, anger leaking into her. "We can't let this happen again."

"It's already gone. Everyone was dead by the time I found it." My thoughts coil around the memory of the deader with green sludge leaking from its brain. It's something I had forgotten about until now. What did it mean, I wondered. Is there some type of new deader out there? What capabilities does it have? Is it stronger? Faster? Or was it just coincidence? "But there may be more places like that."

"Okay, so we'll find them," Ashley replies. "We'll find them and end whatever it is that they're doing. Everyone deserves to die for doing that..." Her words trail off into nothingness, but when they come back they're filled with rage. "What is wrong with people?" she yells.

I sit up straight, not having the answers she's looking for.

"Is there not enough death and horror in the world without people doing this to each other?" She pushes her chair back as she stands up, and it flips and falls over. "I just don't get it!" she yells, cracking her knuckles and coming around from the back of the desk.

"You're not much different," I reply, my voice even and steady as I wait for a bullet to enter my brain. "The things the Forgotten have done to others...you're just as bad."

Ashely glares at me, her mouth twisting in anger. "We're nothing li—"

"You're every bit as bad as those scientists, only you know the outcome of the things you do. You shoot someone, you kill them. You torture them, you break them. You tear families apart and you chase people until they have nowhere left to run to. You are every bit as bad," I grit out. And damn it feels good to finally say it. To have someone to say it to. It isn't that Ashley isn't as scary as Fallon was, or that I don't believe she would kill me in a heartbeat; it's that I know I have to say these things now or die with them bottled up inside of me.

Ashely opens her mouth to respond, but then she closes it again and looks around at her fellow Forgotten members as they watch this entire thing unfold. They're followers, just like she had been. And they had followed their leader through hell so they could survive. They had obviously felt that they owed him something for protecting them and keeping them safe. But he's gone now, and maybe they can start again.

"Those people behind the walls, they are not protected. They are tortured, and starved. They are beaten, and raped. And all in the name of survival." I stand up and take a step toward her.

Mike pulls out his gun, his expression determined, but Ashley holds up a hand to tell him to stop, and I take that as my cue to carry on.

"These people are you, and me, and every other survivor out there. They are not your enemy, they're the victims. The true enemies are the undead, and they are winning this war. Things happened at that compound where the experiments were taking place. I saw things, and I don't know the outcome of them yet, but I have a feeling that whatever they created there is worse than what we've seen before." I turn to look at the group of Forgotten members, and to Michael and Mattie. "We're all going to die if we don't stop this," I plead, my voice breaking.

Do I want to die? Yes.

Am I tired of fighting, and of the death that surrounds me at every turn? Yes.

But am I ready to give up on this world, on the few survivors that are left? Do I truly believe that we're all as bad as the rulers from behind the walls? That there's no coming back from it? No changing for the better?

A leopard doesn't change its spots. That's how that old saying goes.

But could mankind?

The Forgotten are whispering between themselves, their gazes moving to Ashley as she thinks over what I just said. And God do I hope I've said enough. I get that she hates me for killing Fallon. And maybe that'll be my exit from this world. I'll take that with my chin held high, as long as it means they stop fighting against the friends I have left. As long as they try to help people instead of killing them.

Because I'm not lying—it doesn't have to be like this. We can help people. We can build something together and protect instead of murder and maim. We can make life worth living once more. And isn't that we all want in the end? To live. To survive. Those are our most basic instincts, and everything else is just irrelevant bullshit.

I turn back to Ashley, seeing her gaze move over the crowd of Forgotten and then to me. I don't wait with bated breath or worry for my own life, because this is it now. It's this or nothing.

"You have to be punished for killing Fallon," she says.

I roll my eyes. "Haven't we all been punished enough? I killed Fallon, and you killed Melanie. We killed one of yours and you killed one of ours. This isn't tit for tat, Ashley, this is life or death. And if you're so easy to dish out the death card, then what gives you the right to have the life card in your hand?"

327

The corner of her mouth tugs. "He used to say that," she says. "That this life was all about tit for tat. And now here you are telling me the exact opposite. It's ironic, isn't it?"

I shake my head. "Not really. It's just basic human nature. We're all made from the same skin and bone, and we all want to survive. And we can. You just have to let it happen. Become more than he was. Be better."

I want to sit down. I'm suddenly so tired of all of this, I would happily welcome a gun to the back of the head so I could sleep forever. I long to go back in time and remember fully what life was like worrying about bills and paychecks. When my main concern was if Ben had fixed the back gate or not. And yet here I am, arguing for her to let us all live. To use her group for good and not bad. It's just too much.

I look down at my feet, my forehead pinched in frustration.

"Okay," she finally says. "You're right."

I look up at her. She isn't smiling, but she's relenting. She looks over at her group, nodding as she thinks over what's going on in her own mind, nodding as she agrees with whatever those thoughts are.

"She's right, though I don't like to admit it. Maybe Fallon was wrong."

The group begins to whisper loudly amongst themselves. Some look happy about where her reasoning is going, and that gives me hope. Others look seriously annoyed by it. And I have my eye on one particular man.

Ashley holds up her hands and hushes everyone. "We started this group because we wanted to survive, because we were the forgotten ones. Left behind to die. And we were angry." She shakes her head. "And we had every reason to be angry for that fact. Well, there are others out there that are in the same situation as we once were. The people behind the walls are just some of them. We looked on them as though they were the enemy, but this isn't the first time that I've heard the exact opposite. What if Fallon lied to us all this time? What if his own jealousy and madness convinced us that these innocent people were the enemy when really the enemy had been living with us all this time?"

Ashley walks around the room, looking at the faces of her people. The Forgotten, always so angry and bloodthirsty, so ready for revenge, now look solemn and confused. I look at Michael and Mattie, who are watching me appreciatively. I give them a small smile.

"Let's do something different. What have we got to lose?" Ashley says, and voices rise from the Forgotten in agreement. "Let's stop the mindless killing and instead try living. I know that I've seen enough death since this all began. Haven't you?"

They all cheer again, and my heart swells at the realization of what this could mean.

No more running.

No more hiding.

We could help those people behind the walls. Save them from the brutal dictatorship.

I just need to find Mikey.

Ashley turns back to me, a small smile on her face. And damn she looks like a huge weight has been lifted off of her shoulders. Like the hardness of her responsibility—of the anger that Fallon had made her live with, had been pulling her down and aging her. "That good enough for you?" she asks.

I look out on the faces of the Forgotten, over the men and women that had stood by Fallon and done as he asked no matter what the consequences. I forgive them. I have to, because if I don't, this will never end.

There's just one thing I have to do before I finally let it all go— the hate and the anger and the rage that have fueled me since they captured and tortured me all those months ago. One thing, that might disrupt this entire plan, yet I can't move on unless I do it.

I look at Ashley, stepping close enough so that we're face to face. I smile, knowing that I still have a thin scar at the corner of my mouth where Fallon had cut me that very first time I met him. Knowing that all of this happened because of him. Ashley smiles wider and holds her hand out to me, and I reach out to shake it, but at the last moment I grab her gun. She jerks back but it's too late, and her eyes go wide.

"It's okay," I say. "I'm not going to kill you. I genuinely meant everything I've said, I really did. But there's one thing that I have to do, no matter what." My gaze moves over her shoulder, to the man that had raped and tortured me. The man that had taken great satisfaction in my pain. The man that had smiled down on me as I had cried and begged and pleaded...

I fire the gun at him, feeling a surge of satisfaction as the bullet enters his stomach and he falls to the ground writhing in pain.

"Dante!" Ashley cries out.

The Forgotten members all pull out their guns too, aiming them at my head. And that's okay. I can happily die right now, knowing that I've gotten my own revenge.

I hold out the gun in my palm to Ashley. "He tortured me…for months," I say. "He was the only one who didn't deserve a second chance at anything but death." My voice is shaky, and I have to swallow so that I don't cry.

Ashley takes the gun from me, her hard gaze burning into me. And then she puts the gun away and holds out her hand again. I take it this time, shaking it in agreement that it's over. I let go of her hand, and she turns to face her people again, ignoring Dante's calls of pain and gesturing for them to lower their weapons and that everything is okay. I smile down at Dante, the same way he had smiled down at me, and I find the sick satisfaction that I want in his agony.

I watch him until he dies. And I enjoy every moment of his death. It's probably the only time death has ever been a joy. The only time I've waited anxiously for someone to wake up as one of the undead so that they can be killed all over again.

Ashley hands me back her gun so I can shoot him in the head, ending it once and for all. And when I do, I feel the blissful relief that I so rightly deserve.

Chapter Thirty-Five

I load up the truck with provisions—you know, the typical stuff that you needed in an apocalypse: guns, knives, warm clothes, some MREs, and of course plenty of ketchup. I'm going to find Mikey. Whether I come back here with him is another question that I'll answer when I find him. But I will find him again. And boy does that man love his ketchup.

"I'm coming with you," Mattie says from behind me.

I turn and smile at him. "You need to stay here, Zee needs your help."

And he does. Zee lost both of his legs back at the army base, and the Forgotten, thankfully, have a great engineer who is going to help build him some new legs eventually. Ashley can't do this on her own—or more that I don't think she should. She needs someone else who isn't as bloodthirsty, but who will be willing to do what it takes to protect people. That's Zee, but since he's so banged up that task now falls to Mattie.

Only a handful of our people are still alive. Not many survived the brutal slaughter at the army base. The deaders overran it, killing nearly everyone that wasn't quick enough to get in a truck and get the hell out of there, or hadn't managed to lock themselves somewhere safe until Mikey got there. Good people had died, and so had bad. But I accept that for what it is. You have to, because if you don't, you end up like Fallon: a bitter, sadistic man who so twisted up inside for revenge that he would take everyone down with him. And I don't want to be that person.

"I hate these people," Mattie confides, stepping forward so he isn't overheard. His eyes dart to the Forgotten members that are killing some of the deaders crowded around the gate like they're ready for their next shopping spree.

"I know, but we all need each other. You need to set your differences aside and move on from it. We can make this work, Mattie," I reply, closing the back of the truck. It's tanked up to the max, with another can full as a spare. "Make this work, for everyone's sakes."

"Will you bring him back here?" he asks, and I know he means Mikey.

I'm going to find him, no matter what it takes, just like when he found me. This world is huge, and there's so much of it that I haven't seen, so many dangers that are out there, yet I have to do this. I have to find him. Because when you've found the person that makes your survival mean something, you hold onto it with both hands.

I don't know if Mikey would be safe here. I want to believe he would be, that Ashley and the rest of the Forgotten would finally put their differences aside—that maybe they really have changed. But revenge is a ticking bomb, and I killed Fallon— there's no mistaking that. And of course I had been willing to risk everyone's survival so I could get my revenge on Dante.

"I don't know," I finally admit.

"Fine, I'll stay." Mattie nods, looking frustrated, but he's a good man. I know he'll do good here. He'll help stop everything from turning to shit again. He'll keep everyone from killing each other, and make sure that everyone stays true to their word.

"Well, you can't stop *me* from coming with you," Michael says, opening the driver's side door on the truck. "You're going to need someone who's a half-decent shot if you're going to survive out there, and we all know that you can't shoot for shit." He grins and slams the door shut before I can disagree with him. Moments later the engine roars to life, drowning out the barrage of swear words I yell. His arm comes out of the truck window, his middle finger sticking up, and I laugh.

"So he can go but I can't?" Mattie says, looking annoyed again.

I place a hand on Mattie's shoulder. "Yeah, he can. I got both of his sisters killed—me and him have some unfinished business." I pat him and step away, turning to Ashley, who has come out to wave me off. I turn to her. "Don't let it all go to shit again, okay?" I say.

She nods. "I'll do my best, but people can be assholes."

I let out a small laugh. "Yeah, they sure can."

I walk around to the passenger side door and open it, and Ashley follows me.

Michael looks over and tells me to hurry the fuck up because night is falling, and I look back at Ashley. She holds out her hand and I take it, shaking it briefly, but before I can let go she pulls me close to her and whispers in my ear.

My eyes go wide as I listen, and then she stops talking, lets me go, and walks away. I climb into the truck, closing the door behind me, and I look across at Michael as he starts to drive. The Forgotten pull the gates open for us, their empty stares looking in at us as we leave. And then we're on the road, heading off to find Mikey, and I know I'm never coming back here again.

I watch Mattie in my rearview mirror until we crest a small hill, and then he's gone from view and a new guilt burrows its way into my stomach.

"Are you okay?" Michael asks without looking away from the road.

"Yeah," I lie. "I'm fine."

But I'm not fine.

Ashley may have called a truce between the Forgotten and Mikey, and he was finally free of them, and she had agreed to try and help the people in the walled cities instead of killing them, but I had still killed Fallon, her partner. And that won't go unpunished. I may not be there for the vengeance that she'll inflict on our friends, but knowing what she's going to do and not being able to stop her—that's all the torture I'll ever need.

Go find Mikey, you two go be free. But if I ever see your face, or his, again, I'll kill the both you and I won't help a single person in those walled cities. As for these fine people that you've left in my care, they're all mine now, and I'll have fun playing with them however I see fit. Perhaps I'll turn them all into killers, perhaps I'll just kill them all. Either way, they're not your business anymore. So go, go find Mikey, because staying isn't an option for you. You stay, you die. You all die. Got it?

I nod. "Got it."

"What did you just say?" Michael asks, turning to look at me.

I shake my head and look out the window. "Nothing."

Perhaps I could have done something more, or said something to change her mind. Maybe if I tell Michael, then maybe we could do something. But it's more likely that I'd get us both killed and the Forgotten would never help the people I had left behind in those cities. The real victims of the apocalypse. The innocent. The lost. The true forgotten.

A single tear slips from my eye as the sun sets, and I pull out the map and look where Mikey and I had circled.

"We're heading here," I say to Michael. "That's where Mikey will be going."

ODIUM V

The Dead Saga

Coming Summer 2017

(I promise!)

Read on for a sneak peek...

ODIUM V The Dead Saga

Chapter One

Mikey

The screams echo through the darkness, catching ahold of me and tearing at my skin. I breathe, slowly, deeply. I refuse to let the fear get a grip on me. I lean back on the door, listening to the crying and the sobbing, and the sounds of tools on flesh and what that means for me.

I rub my sweaty palms down my pants, feeling for the folded piece of paper in my pocket, and then I pull it out. In the darkness, with the cries of pain as my mantra, I stare down at the map in my hand and I whisper my apologies to Nina for not going there.

I had thought I was doing the right thing by searching for Adam, and by keeping Joan safe. I thought I was doing what she would have wanted by finding a new group to belong to. But I was wrong. I should have gone to the cabin, like we had said.

The sound of footsteps coming closer has me shoving the map back in my pocket and scooting backwards across the floor. The door opens and Tim is there with a plate in his hand. He smiles down at me.

"You know, nothing tastes better than fresh food. Wouldn't you agree?" he asks.

"You're sick," I reply.

He leans down and slides the plate across to me. It bumps against my foot but I don't reach for it, even though I'm starving. "I'm just trying to survive. That's all we can ever do these days." He stands back up. "Go on then, it's not like you really have much choice."

I kick the plate back to him, and it bounces off the doorframe, the food sliding off the plate. "I always have a choice," I snarl back.

Tim laughs. "You're not dead yet, Mikey, but you can be, if that's what you want."

I don't bother replying to him. Tim crouches down and picks up the food before putting it back on the plate. He slides it back across to me.

"Your only choice is to eat and stay alive a little bit longer, or I'll kill you right now—gut you like a little piggly-wig." Tim smiles. "Those are your only choices. Don't you see that yet? There is no way out of this. No one is coming to save you. This is the way it has to happen."

I look down at the plate, knowing that this could be human flesh—it could be Phil, for all I know—or it could be squirrel, like he'd said. I pick up the plate, feeling sick but refusing to die like this. Because if there was one thing he did say that made sense, it was this.

I wasn't dead yet.

I bite into whatever meat it is, feeling sick but wanting to stay strong. I won't go down without a fight. That's the only certainty I know right now, and I hold onto it with both hands as I chew and force the food to stay down.

I'll make him pay. Even if it's the last thing I do.

Acknowledgments

Thanks, as always, goes to my wonderful fan base, who continue to read The Dead Saga series and enjoy it so much. Thank you for your constant hounding for the next book, your messages of support, and your all-round awesomeness. I wouldn't be writing these books without you guys.

Another huge thanks goes to my sister from another mister and fellow author Eli Constant. You're always there when I need support, advice, or just a good old moan about the world. Thanks for being so awesome. Love you ooo

And of course not forgetting my awesome Street Team – *Little Red's Deads.* Your pimping, and graphic/meme-making, reviews, funny conversations, and general awesomeness never fail to surprise me.

A special thanks also goes out to: **Safari Phil's Animal Adventures** for all of their help. Without them, you would have never have got to know some of the most memorable characters—Miss Foxxxy Love, Zazz Blammymatazz and Lavender, and of course Phil

https://www.facebook.com/SafariPhilsAnimalAdventures/

And finally a huge thank you to everyone who filled in my 'survival questionnaire.' Some of you made it in to the book, and some of you didn't. Some of you played small parts, others big. And of course, some of you turned out to be total assholes—I'm especially sorry about that! Regardless, all of your answers were useful. Most of you, if I haven't killed you already, will be in book five also, so hurray for that!

Therefore thanks goes to:

Clare Parr, Shantell Weeks Harmon, Betul Er, Niamh Colvin, Steve Emery, Ricky Chambers, Shane Bridges, Boon Mills (Alfie) Ashley Marie, Vicki A. Matticks, Emma Keating, Emma Walker, Gail S. Squirell, Mike Goss, Phil Safari Lines-Rowland, Kelli Fisk McElrath, Danielle Kelly, SJ Warner and her daughter Moo, Stormy Grant, Jessica Austin Gudmundson.

ABOUT THE AUTHOR

Claire C. Riley is a *USA Today* and International bestselling author. She is also a bestselling British horror writer and an Amazon Top 100 bestseller.

Her work is best described as the modernization of classic, old-school horror. She fuses multi-genre elements to develop storylines that pay homage to cult classics while still feeling fresh and cutting edge. She writes characters that are realistic, and kills them without mercy. Claire lives in the United Kingdom with her husband and three daughters.

Author of:

Odium The Dead Saga series

Odium Origins series

Limerence (The Obsession series)

Out of the Dark series

Twisted Magic

Books co-authored with Madeline Sheehan:

Thicker than Blood series

Shut Up & Kiss Me

Contact Links:

www.clairecriley.com

www.facebook.com/ClaireCRileyAuthor

http://amzn.to/1GDpF3I

More books by Claire C. Riley

Out of the Dark #1

We are temporary. Finite.

The choices we've made, the people we have loved. Who we used to be no longer matters.

Because now it is all about the ending. And the ending always comes too soon.

There's fear in the dark. And behind every drop of light, the shadows creep and the darkness comes in the form of clawing, red-eyed monsters. They hunt us—stalk us…they are desperate to destroy us.

But I have a reason to fight the darkness and everything in it. A small glimpse of light that lives within my golden-haired daughter, Lilly. She is my strength. She is my everything.

Every life is an untold story, each scene unfolding until the final act. But our ending has yet to be written, and I will continue to protect us, until I can not.

A post-apocalyptic masterpiece – Goodreads reviewer

Printed in Great Britain
by Amazon